WHAT GOES AROUND

A SECOND CHANCE LOVE STORY

TAMALA C. JONES

Line Five Publishing

Contents

FOREWORD

I fell in love with romance before I truly understood it.

I was nine or ten—too young, probably, to be sneaking books off my big sister's shelf, tiptoeing across the hallway like I was stealing state secrets. Those books were my earliest introductions to grown-up emotion: passion, longing, heartbreak, reconciliation. They made me feel things that I probably didn't need to feel but I was hooked.

I devoured them—from sweeping, lushly written historical sagas to short, snappy contemporary stories and everything in between. Romance became an escape, a quiet thrill—early adventures of messiness and need that always ended in a love painstakingly built. But even as a child, something in me noticed what was missing. The women on those covers didn't look like me—or like the women who raised me, loved me, prayed over me, and taught me the myriad nuances of Black womanhood. The heroes didn't reflect the men I knew, who carried entire worlds on their shoulders with tenderness and grit.

Somewhere in my little-girl heart, I registered that absence.

So I started writing my own stories.

Initial endeavors were clumsy—pages scribbled in notebooks, half-formed characters with big feelings and stilted dialogue, plots I stole shamelessly, trying to retrofit them to the life around me. Even then, I was chasing a reflection that felt true. A love story where the heroine could be a Black girl with history—mistakes and triumphs, aches and joys—and the hero could be a Black man who was allowed to be complex rather than stereotyped and pathologized.

I wrote those stories throughout middle school, high school, and beyond. I wrote them in late night journaling sessions, in the margins of my practical academic life, and in the precious quiet moments when the world wasn't asking anything of me. I wrote beginnings I didn't know how to finish—long, rambling manuscripts I never showed a soul. And every time I set one aside, I would return later, armed with a little more life, to try again.

Along the way—between those attempts, between love and life and career and adulthood—the worlds of romance I wanted to create took shape. Worlds where we live and love boldly and deservedly—as we should; worlds where wealth and culture collided—where our families were layered, complicated—and powerful. Worlds where the fullness of Black identity wasn't muted but celebrated in blinding displays.

When I began outlining what would eventually become the *Love, Legacy & Second Chances* duet, I hadn't set out to write a series. I thought I was writing one book—one couple, one arc, one love story. But from the moment Abe Walker and Cassandra Williams appeared on the page, I realized their world wouldn't be small. It couldn't be. The Walkers are a family built on legacy, and legacy always echoes well beyond the first story told.

I wanted the Walkers to feel like a real family: a real family full of secrets and triumphs, responsibility and ambition born of necessity—loving, flawed, resilient—wrapped in the trappings of wealth, access and privilege. But I wanted their wealth to feel comfortable and worn, not flashy and new. Their relationships, shouldering that legacy, were necessarily complicated. And the love that pierced it all had to be strong enough shift the story, the kind that transforms and renews.

Which brings us to Cassandra—*whew*, Cassandra. I wanted her to be the kind of woman who defies assumptions. A woman who grew up navigating instability, who created artistry in the midst of adversity, and who walked into rooms built to exclude her with her chin high and her heart guarded. I needed Cassandra to represent all the grace and fight Black women exude daily—to reflect that special mix of optimism and practicality that fuels us through hope and doubt, dreams and fears. She is a displaced queen, who exhibits queenliness, regardless.

Her relationship with Abe is about more than desire. It's about what happens when two people who've survived loss in different ways learn to trust joy again. It's about receiving the kind of love that doesn't ask you to shrink or disappear to be worthy of it. It's about seeing and being seen wholly—unafraid, unabashed and undiluted.

What Goes Around became a story about love and possibility—but it was also a story about grief—about how that emotion can shape us, bind us to a past we didn't choose. And about the futures we hope to be brave enough to allow ourselves to claim.

And as that story ended, *Coming Around* rose naturally from its denouement. The second book was not meant to be about

Elizabeth Brookes but she demanded to be heard. She required her redemption arc, one that honored her pain and gave space for her complexity. Warwick Walker, the quiet heart of the family, needed room to step into his own story. And together, they completed the emotional circle the first book began of love born in the shadow of loss.

This edition exists because of all the readers—new and returning—who stepped into this world and felt something. Who saw themselves in these characters. Who loved the friendships, girl circles and guy chats. Who recognized their own families, their own loves, their own scars, their own triumphs.

It exists for the readers who've said they felt seen, got angry, laughed and cheered. For the readers who came for the romance and stayed for the family.

This foreword is my way of welcoming you (or welcoming you back) into a world I cherish. A world where Black love is abundant. Where Black wealth is complicated and textured. Where Black families are powerful. Where Black joy is not an accident—or an afterthought.

Thank you for reading with me.
Thank you for loving these characters.
Thank you for being part of the legacy I'm building—one love story, one happily ever after, one second chance at a time.

Prologue

That Night

He wasn't comfortable with this part at all. Getting rid of the woman? Well, that was the job. But this? This was a one-way ticket to hell that he wasn't trying to cash in. He could feel sweat bead and trickle until the collar of his shirt absorbed it.

He had to decide. And he had to decide now because—*shit...*

As expected, the phone rang in the woman's house at the appointed time.

He answered, "Yes?"

"Is it done?" He looked at the woman on the floor, sprawled and unmoving, still positioned as she had fallen. Her color was rapidly draining, leaving her brown skin ashen. The odd angles of her limbs spoke of broken bones—she had fought more than he'd anticipated—but no broken skin. Her thick hair collected the blood from the seeping wound in the back of her head.

There'd be little cleanup, as they'd demanded. It was to be a simple disappearance—a young single woman and her child...gone. Had they been white, the plan would have never worked. But a black woman and her little mixed baby? There'd be a perfunctory inquiry at best.

"Yes."

"And the other?"

The man's gaze tracked to the playpen in the corner of the well-appointed but small apartment. The child was quiet, almost unnaturally so. And she watched him; she watched him with those odd eyes that had no business in that dark face. It wasn't natural. And it scared him. Eyes like that held power.

So, he lied.

"Done."

"Good." The voice on the other line was satisfied. Smug. Female. "Make sure there's no trace."

"Understood."

"This can't track back to me. Or, to him."

"Understood." He hated taking orders from her. But again, it was the job. This job, at least.

The line went dead.

He got to work moving the woman, dead, and the child, alive, to his truck. He had a long night ahead of him. He'd drive for hours before stopping to bury the woman. He'd drive for hours more before leaving the child somewhere. But he wouldn't kill it. Even his soul couldn't absorb that sin.

Chapter 1
Twenty Years Later

Cassandra.

"Andi! Heads up!"

Hearing my name pierced my daydreams and slammed me back into the hustle and bustle of the catering kitchen, where I was supposed to be collecting another round of appetizers to circulate in the area of the ballroom I'd been assigned.

The ability to dissociate from my surroundings was one that I had developed long ago. It was both a gift and a curse. I could easily tune out almost anything happening around me, which was a great protective mechanism when bullshit was afoot. But it also meant I tended to drift...something that wasn't always handy. Like now, when I was supposed to be carrying a tray of canapes into the grand ballroom so the guests could slake their hunger before the main meal was served.

"Coming!" I hustled to take my place in the line of servers, all wearing identical black pants, white tuxedo shirts, and black vests. We looked like a family of penguins, but the anonymity was comforting. I could move through the dining room without having to worry too much about my interactions. The likelihood that the guests could pick me out from among any of the other servers was slim. My hair, relaxed and bone straight, was sleeked back into a low, nondescript bun, just like most of the other girls working tonight. And I learned long ago that my skin was that particular shade of brown that left people confused about my ethnic makeup. So, I blended.

I'd been called everything under the sun: Mexican, Indian, light-skinned, mixed, Dominican... I'd learned to both accept and reject all the labels because I had no idea which, if any, was correct. I knew what my roots looked like when my re-laxer started to grow out, though, so I had my suspicions. And since most people, when I couldn't give a definitive response, defaulted to some sub-category of Black, I did, too.

"Take this to the far end, by the terraces. After this round, we'll guide everyone in for dining. Once we get the entree rounds on the table, your group can cycle for a twenty-minute break while we prep dessert and they start the program."

The head caterer rattled off the instructions as he settled the serving tray in my hands and, with a gentle but decisive push to the small of my back, sent me onto the floor with my offerings.

I immediately headed toward the terrace area. Past ex-perience had me walking quickly with little eye contact. The tray dipped and swooped as I navigated the crowd, avoiding hems and reaching hands until I reached the appointed area and slowed to allow the guests to sample the appetizers. They went quickly. I'd learned that most people, no matter how much money they had, were greedy as hell. I had barely slowed before the vultures emptied my huge tray. Sighing, I began the trek back to the kitchen.

This time, though, my feet moved far slower as I took in the scene. The wealth in the room was staggering. The women were draped in the best fabrics. Fabrics that were pulled, nipped, and tucked into a range of styles on a range of bodies.

Most of the gowns were gorgeous, some were horrible. My mind was whirling, redesigning, cataloging the changes I would make for this woman or that. Considering how the woman in the peach gown should have chosen something with an empire waist to better flatter her neckline and camouflage her tummy. How the woman in the royal blue floor-length sheath could have carried a far more dramatic piece, tall and confident as she was.

By the time I made it back to the kitchen, helped the crew serve and clear the salad course, and finally got the entrees on the table, I had a laundry list of ideas to add to my final portfolio. I would make the updates on my break. Twenty minutes wasn't long, but I had to get the ideas out of my head before they flitted away.

"Girl. My feet!" Margeaux grumbled as we dipped out of the kitchen and into the little annex that was reserved for members of the catering team and our personal belongings.

A little smile ghosted my lips. "I told you."

"Yeah, I know. And you were right." Margeaux fell into one of the surprisingly plush club chairs in the room. "Never wear new shoes on a job. But hell, they're tennis shoes. Why the fuck wouldn't they be comfortable."

She pulled the offending sneakers off and wiggled her toes. I pulled my backpack from the bottom of a pile of coats and bags and headed toward the exit that led to the gallery's wraparound terrace. I sympathized with her plight but only had twenty minutes to brain dump.

I shrugged. "I don't know. But I'll run you an epsom salt soak when we get home. I'm going outside." I gestured toward the terrace doors.

"Okay, well, I'll be here. I'll come get you when it's time to go back in." Gogo was more than familiar with my tendency to wool-gather. We'd been sisters for a decade. Not by blood, but by choice. When we crossed paths through the same group home three times in twice as many months, we cautiously became friends—and later, sisters. I can't say that having a friend made the hell of child protective services pleasant, but it certainly helped.

"Thanks," I said. "I only have a few notes to make, but I don't want to forget them."

"Don't worry about it. I'm setting an alarm." She set the alarm on her digital watch and settled more deeply into the club chair. "I'm going to take a power nap. I have to pull an all-nighter when we get back. Business law tomorrow." She said, referring to the next exam on her schedule.

We were both seniors at NYU. Both on full scholarship. Both determined to eke out success from our shitty starts in life. I knew without a doubt that if she and I hadn't found each other, we'd be in very different places right now.

When Margeaux's aunt had finally come for her, we had fought to stay together. It had been a little like a fairytale since that aunt was comfortably established and determined to do right by Margeaux for the last years of her childhood. Everything they had taught her, she had told me. Those messages had been sent through slowly delivered snail mail, and late-night whispered phone conversations with me on the shared group home line. I had become an expert at trading fifteen-minute phone privileges so that she and I could have longer snippets of time to plan my great escape. They had ultimately fostered me just as I entered high school, giving me a glimpse of what stability looked like.

We had fought for it and we had almost made it. All that stood between us and the next stage of our dreams was two weeks of final exams.

On the terrace, the air was warm and thick. We were miles outside of the city. The catering company had offered transport vans for the crew, most of whom didn't have cars to get them to the venue, which was nowhere near the transit lines. The venue was particularly exclusive, with part of that exclusivity attributed to its distance from the hustle and bustle. I had been surprised when I first entered the ballroom to find that the majority of the guests and the hosting family were Black.

Those thoughts drifted away once I found a seat on the terrace, pulled my sketchbook out, and flipped to the page of the design I was currently finalizing. I was deep in my thoughts, trying to recreate the vision in my mind using paper and soft lead, when someone stepped into my light, throwing shadows over my work.

"I'm almost there, Gogo. Two more minutes."

"I'm not Gogo." A deep voice poured over me. I was startled at the unexpected response and turned to see who had interrupted my moment of quiet. I was annoyed; only years of experience and a deep-seated desire to *not* have to start over had prevented me from leaving a random streak of gray across my sketch.

Brows twisted in irritation, I looked up and up…and up until my eyes landed in the vicinity of where this person's eyes would be if I could see them clearly.

"I'm sorry. I startled you." The deep, slightly amused rumble sank into my skin and poured over my nerve endings setting them to tingling. I shook myself.

"Well, yeah." I said, belatedly trying to school the irritation out of my voice because my visitor was obviously part of the party and not on the service side. His tall frame was clothed in a conservative black tuxedo that had clearly been made specifically to fit his trim form. Brushed merino wool, and heavy satin combined in the well-made garment. The seams were perfectly aligned, the nap of the fabric flowing in the same direction across all the areas I could see. It was exquisite workmanship that made the simple traditional suit scream money.

"I'm sorry to be in your space," I said, peeved that I had to stop early, but cognizant that a significant part of my job was to remain invisible and unobtrusive. Even though *he* was intruding on me. "I'll head back in." I began to gather my things.

"No, no. Take your two minutes to finish. I didn't mean to disturb you."

That deep baritone eased over me again, and I shivered even in the heavy humid New York summer night. I wasn't sure I believed his words, given that he was standing over my shoulder, staring at me and my work.

I said as much.

He chuckled. That huff of amusement wrapped in the deep, melodic voice had me tilting my head further and shielding my eyes so I could see him better. He was standing almost directly in front of one of the sconces that threw soft, warm light across the terrace. His features were backlit and barely visible.

"Hmm. You're right. And now I'm making you crane your neck to see me." He shifted his position, coming around to settle into the remaining empty chair at the little bistro table I'd commandeered. *Woah.* My heart thumped once. Stopped. And then started a frantic beat.

Deep-set dark brown eyes, heavy eyebrows, peanut butter brown skin, and a close-cut Caesar fade. All set off by a strong, straight nose with flared nostrils and almost too-full lips; the top one sported a light shadow. His ears were slightly pointed at the top and curled at the lobes, making him look like a mischievous warrior elf even though he was clearly trying to exude hot and sexy. And he wasn't missing the mark. The whole package oozed wealth and sex. It was a heady combination, and my stomach clenched in a natural feminine response.

"I'm Abe." He held out a hand. I didn't shake it. Only stared like an idiot. "You're...Andi?"

That shocked me out of my stupor. "Yeah..yes. How...?"

"It's on your nametag."

Oh, yeah.

"Oh, yeah. I'm Andi." *He already knows that.* "I'm working the party. I'm just on a little break. But I can go in." I repeated the offer to vacate his space, reaching to gather my things. "Or did you need something? Wine or..." I trailed off.

"No, nothing. Really. Sit." He waved me back to my seat from the awkward half-crouch I was holding, midway between sitting down and getting up.

"Your lines are excellent."

"What?"

"On the day dress you're sketching. The lines are beautiful. What fabrics are you thinking for it?"

"What?" I repeated because one, he'd said 'day dress' as opposed to just 'dress', and two, what the hell did this beautiful man know about *lines*?

"Are you thinking chambray? It would be a surprising choice, I think."

I looked at my sketch because I had indeed been thinking about combining chambray and linen, which would create a more structured bodice with a beautifully draped skirt. I shared as much.

"Mm. It's a good point. It's really going to be about the colors, right?"

"Right. It's a simple enough design. It's the patterns that will make it pop. But I have to make sure it's not too much."

"What's too much?" He seemed genuinely curious. His heavy eyebrows drew together.

"Well. There's a balance between color and pattern, right? I have trouble walking that line sometimes, I think," I said quietly, remembering the last feedback I'd gotten from my final project supervisor. *Cassandra, your work is lovely, but the colors you choose are sometimes too...aggressive.*

"Mm." He hummed again. A deep rumble that I felt in the most unexpected places. I wasn't much about the dating scene.

I wasn't naive. Naivete was a trait lost early in child services. I knew all about boys and men and what happened between men and women behind closed doors. I wasn't interested in either the distraction they seemed to provide or the deterrence from my goals. But I could appreciate beauty in all its forms. And he was beautiful.

"You're right about making it pop, though. It's such a simple piece. The right combination of color and pattern...something simple but big scale maybe...will keep it from being boring."

"Exactly. But I'm thinking about recreating it as a jumpsuit. Lengthen it here, pull it in here." I made a couple of quick updates to the sketch and tilted my notebook toward him.

"Yes. I can see that. What if you...," he held his hand out for my pencil. I just looked at him, one eye-brow up, because I wasn't interested in having him mess up my work with some ham-handed additions.

"Okay," he laughed. "What if you add darts here," he tapped a finger on the sketch, "and here, but then loosen it up here," another tap, "and here." I considered, and rather than adjust the piece I was working on because I liked where it was going, I quickly drafted a new model on a clean page incorporating the ideas he'd shared but also adding my own because this was mine.

"Like this?"

"Exactly," he nodded twice, considering. "You're really good."

"Thanks," I sent a smile his way, stunned again by how strikingly fine he was...*Jesus, he's dangerous.*

I was confident in my abilities, but validation was something I received little enough of in school, so I appreciated receiving it from what seemed like a knowledgeable source. It was something Destiny had told me I would need to work on my need for. "You are, too. You know a lot about this stuff for a guy."

Another deep chuckle. His smile was wide and open. It made his sleepy brown eyes crinkle at the corners. "What? Guys can't do fashion?"

"I mean, they *can*." I leaned into the word a little bit. "But they usually *don't*."

"Word. I can't front like you're not right. But I'm not most guys." He winked. Another shot of electricity zinged to that hollow right between my legs. I shifted in my seat. Abe's eyes slipped quickly to my lap and back again. An extra light flashed in their depths, faintly amused, definitely interested.

I felt my eyes roll a little. But not too much. He was still a guest.

"Seriously. I'm special."

"Really?" I tilted my head at him.

"Yeah, really." He leaned toward me, and I realized he had scootched closer to me while we collaborated. Odd. Because I was usually hyper-sensitive to men in my space. I didn't have a problem with them, *per se*, but I wasn't wholly comfortable around them. A byproduct, I knew, of living in the home, a man-free zone where girls talked and where self-preservation became an offensive pursuit. But I didn't lean away when he shifted closer. And that's when I learned how good he smelled. And how the smell of a man was a *thing. Wow.*

My eyelids fluttered. I inhaled. Deeply.

"Andi!" And my eyes popped wide. *Damn!* He was right there, gazing at me. Contemplating...what?

"I'm coming!" I called back, certain that I was going to be late getting back to my station. I couldn't afford to lose this gig or to be sent home early. I needed every single cent of the two hundred dollars that had been promised for tonight's six hours of work.

"I have to go." I quickly gathered my items, stuffing the pencils and sketchpad back into my worn backpack. It had seen me through all four years of college. It was a gift from Destiny, a luxury I would not have splurged on.

"Yo, Abe!"

His face broke into another grin, and I found myself frozen by how his face shifted. All the sexy slipped away, and he looked like a little boy caught. Laugh lines deepened around his eyes and mouth. So pronounced for him to be so young. How much laughter did a person have to have in their lives to have laugh lines at what? Twenty-five? Twenty-six?

"Let me get your number. Clearly, you need me to help you finish your little project here."

This time I let the full weight of my eyeroll loose on him.

"*Puh-leez,*" I scoffed. "You wish."

"I do. I do wish." Then he, too, stood from his chair, responding to whoever it was who had called his name.

"Yo!" He called to let them know they'd been heard. He turned back to me, "Lemme get the digits, though. For real."

After another moment's thought, I decided *why not*. I scribbled the number to the phone in my dorm on a scrap of paper from my sketchbook and lay it on the table between us. I don't know why, but putting it directly in his hand seemed too personal, too invested. But he scooped it up and slipped it in the inside breast pocket of his seriously well-made tuxedo jacket. I hadn't touched it, but my fingers itched to smooth over the wool and satin lapels.

One day, I promised myself, *you'll be wearing the same quality fabrics with the same level of ease and comfort.*

But on *this* day, I needed to get back to the kitchen before I lost the last installment on my tuition payment.

"Talk to you soon, Andi." He said and patted his coat pocket where he'd slipped my number.

"We'll see," I replied and dashed inside.

Chapter 2

Moments After

ABE.

"Yo, bruh. Who was that little shorty?" Trey clapped a heavy hand on my shoulder, damn near making me stagger.

"Man, your heavy-handed ass. Chill," I shrugged him off as we wound our way through the crowd of way more folks than Mom and Dad had let on would be here.

"Okay, okay." He chuckled and instead wrapped an arm around my shoulders to pull me closer to him. "But who was she?"

"I don't really know, but she was bad as hell." And that was no lie. I don't know what it was about her sleekly floating through the room, serving drinks and snacks, that caught my attention, but once she'd snagged it, I was done. My gaze had locked on her, and my dick immediately stood at attention. I hadn't gotten that hard that unexpectedly since I'd left high school. I had to know who the fuck she was.

She was low-key one of the finest girls I'd ever seen. Not an in-your-face stunner but a quiet, sneaky beauty. Unadorned. Rich, warm butterscotch skin that looked lit from the inside, even in the low lights of the banquet room. Her hair was dark and sleeked back from a center part into a bun. The style suited tonight's work but, for some reason, didn't feel quite right. I pictured it big and frizzy all over her head, sparking and crackling with energy.

I'd lost sight of her, my attention pulled away by some nonsense falling from my father's lips. But then I'd spied her through the terrace windows. It had taken only a moment to decide to slip out behind her. She'd been ghosting through the banquet hall all night, quick and efficient, but clearly, her mind was somewhere else entirely. And then she was sitting outside, fully focused on whatever she was doing in her notebook, no...I realized as I got closer...her sketchbook.

My mind was still processing the fact that she was sketching designs...really good designs...when she'd spoken and blessed my ears with a distracted, slightly impatient, unexpectedly breathy murmur telling whoever *Go-go* was that she was *almost there*.

It was a one-two that hit me right in the dick. Again. The jump I'd felt there surprising me so much that I'd fucking scared the shit out of her.

Then she'd landed the knockout punch when she'd spun around and pinned me with those eyes. What the fuck?

My senses had hit overload. Her energy was all prickly; she was clearly trying to tamp down her irritation at having been interrupted while not offending me as a guest. Her wild, mismatched eyes were full of annoyance that I was all up in her space, taking up her precious time. There hadn't been a lick of concern that some random dude had followed her onto the terrace. Something I acknowledged was kinda creepy now that I thought about it.

Worth it, though. Hell yeah, worth it. It was the eyes...I'd never seen anything like them. Were they contacts? I didn't think so. They were too fucking bright. My gaze had tracked from her beautiful eyes to settle on full lips, naturally tinted and flushed like her cheeks, where the color had been riding high with her irritation. I'd desperately wanted to kiss her. Still did. And if I had anything to say about it, I'd be doing just that soon enough.

I rubbed my hand over my breast pocket, unconsciously verifying the safety of the scrap of paper that connected us.

I scanned the room for her now, wondering where she had to rush off to.

"Oh, you still tracking her?" Trey joked. "You got the number, I know."

"You know I did." A quick exchange of dap before we reached the head table where Mom and Dad were seated.

I dropped a kiss on my mother's cheek and accepted the little pat she gave me in return.

"Sir." I spoke to my dad, shook his hand, leaned in for..something..it was never quite an embrace. Not the man-to-man back slap. Just a lean-in. Even at home. So, yeah.

"I'm glad Godrick had the presence of mind to find you. I suppose your mother and I have become too accustomed to your absence," my father started in immediately. Over his shoulder, Trey crossed his eyes at me—a juvenile acknowledgment but enough to temper my response.

Father cleared his throat and turned to face me fully. The faint gleam of low expectations darkened his eyes. "I trust the waitstaff meets with your approval."

Man, fuck this.

"Godrick." My mother chastised, the exhaustion evident in her voice. Not for the first time, I wondered why she was still with him. I'd felt guilty for most of my high school years. I'd thought I was the reason she stayed, but I'd been gone for the better part of a decade now. University of Pennsylvania first, then Parson's, rarely coming home during the years in school. And now, all degreed up with nowhere to go, I was traveling. Spending the old man's money and pissing him off more and more with each red cent. It wasn't a bad way to pass the time until I figured out something else. I'd been home for two days.

"Oh, I'm just joking with him. What do I care if he fucks the waitresses? Just make sure you keep it wrapped." He clapped me on the back. "We can't muddy the waters, can we?" He gave another smarmy laugh, but his eyes dared me to contradict him.

I had learned over the years and could now identify this as a trap. If I leapt to defend the moment with Andi that he'd so obviously observed through the terrace windows, it would open the door for him to ridicule me for being too ready to imbue the moment with meaning. Or I could laugh along with him, an invitation for him to take the next vulgar step, testing my will to go along to get along. It was a no-win game; one he'd been forcing me to play for as long as I could remember, for reasons I had long ago stopped trying to decipher.

Before I settled on my choice, Trey stepped into the role he had been playing for just as long: deflector, mediator, interceptor.

"Dad. Come on." Trey guided him into his seat, placing Mom and himself between me and Dad. The two-person buffer was both familiar and welcome.

My eyes scanned the room again, but Storm...Andi...was nowhere to be found. I signaled the server closest to me to bring me a bourbon. I had intended to wait until the little afterparty our cousin Warwick and I had planned for Trey before I took my first drink of the night. But the old man just went down better with a few fingers of dark.

After a couple of swallows, the liquor's heat settling in my stomach, I nudged Trey.

"You ready for this?"

This little shindig with a couple hundred of our closest friends, business associates, and family was to announce the passing of the mantle, or at least the start of the process, to my brother. This good man Godrick Cyrus Walker the third, Trey to me and other close family members, was heir to HeirLoom Textiles founded in 1913 by Great Granddaddy Cyrus who, at seventeen, had managed passage on a ship to Barbados and returned with bolts of rare and beautiful fabrics that it turned out people were willing to pay a fair penny for. He'd flipped those profits into longer and riskier ventures that allowed him to introduce the fabrics that built the reputation for which HeirLoom was famous.

When great-granddaddy died, the company passed to Grandpa G, who was now in his seventies and had happily tapped my dad in not long after I was born. That man was a machine about it. The only acceptable topic of conversation for any exchange with him was The Company. It was past, present, and future. And all members of the family were expected to behave accordingly. If you or your efforts didn't meet his expectations well, just look at me.

He shrugged, "Does it matter? It's time."

"It couldn't be me," I spoke the truth. "But I'm proud of you. You know you're a good role model and big brother and all that shit. Not that I'm trying to be a CEO, following in your footsteps, though, because I am not."

I laughed because that truly wasn't my thing, but Trey being Trey hit me with the consistent big brother affirmations.

"You can do whatever you want to do. You just have to figure out what it is. I like all this shit. I really do,"

I already knew this and said as much. To which he responded, "But I also don't have any choice. I am grateful that I was born for this shit because I wonder what the hell Dad would do if I wasn't with it. You know he's on that manifest destiny shit." I tried to camouflage the explosive laugh with a cough. I was unsuccessful.

"Ow!" I whispered-yelled, rubbing the spot on my thigh where Mom had just twisted the meat off my leg in a vicious pinch.

"Stop talking!" Mom whisper-yelled back.

"It's not me!" I defended and looked at Trey. He, of course, had his attention laser-focused on the emcee who was introducing my father. His lips twitched.

"Traitor."

"Yo, it's a dog-eat-dog world out here, man."

Mom popped his leg, too. He yelped and rubbed the spot, giving her his best offended face. Our twin pouts finally pulled a laugh from her, but she still shushed us one last time before she settled back in her seat for the rest of the program.

***

"Finally," I lifted my glass toward the center of the low-slung table around which Trey's, Warwick's, and my chairs were arranged. We had escaped the banquet as soon as possible after the congratulatory handshakes and pats on the back. Now, we were cranking up the afterparty at *Glori*, a nightclub in the city that boasted three floors with three DJs. We were on the hip hop floor in VIP where we could overlook the crowded dancefloor while still having a little privacy.

We leaned in, the better to hear my impromptu words over the pounding bass of Biggie's 'One More Chance'.

After Dad's rambling introduction that spent way too much time on his portion of ownership in the history of HeirLoom, Trey had taken the mic to accept the new cloak of responsibility. He'd said a few words about upholding tradition while ushering in a new era of vision and innovation that would solidify Heir-Loom's position in the world of textiles for years to come.

I'd been impressed and, as I'd told him before, proud. And now, I told him again, "To the best brother a guy could have. Here's to you taking this shit to the next level." The warm liquid reminded me of the conversation we'd begun at the banquet but had to cut short due to the injuries to my person inflicted by my loving mother.

I'd been asking Trey if he was ready. I considered returning to that conversation because, even having watched his years of preparation, I couldn't quite understand the level of responsibility he was stepping into. I was grateful that it wasn't me. Grateful that as the second son, I might not have the undying adoration bestowed upon the firstborn, but I had my freedoms. And that was more important than anything.

I would talk to him about it again. And I would make sure I was around anytime he needed to talk to me. He was made for this, but the mantle was a heavy one. I would make sure he didn't turn into the old man and become single-minded to the point of tyranny.

Already, he was checking his watch. We hadn't been here an hour, and I could feel him gearing up to leave.

"Yo, Trey! Cut that shit out!" I yelled to make sure my voice cut through the music. "We're not cutting out yet." I wagged my finger between three of us. "We're shutting this shit down tonight!"

"I know, I know. I'm good." His grin caught the blues and reds of the strobe lights as he shifted to the chair nearer mine. "I'm glad I came. Thanks for talking me into it. It's going to be a while before we can do this again, you know."

"Yeah, I know. But not too long. I'm not going to let you turn into the old man." I gave voice to the thoughts that had stuck with me earlier. "You're going to run that shit and stay human all at the same time."

"Fuck, yeah," Warwick chimed in, his baritone barely audible over the noise of the club. As it was, it felt like another beat of the bass.

"Hold me accountable then because I don't want that shit either," Trey spoke between sips of his drink. "And we're doing this shit together, low key. You know once I get in, I'm flipping things around."

"From your lips to God's ears. Man. Dad is never going to switch it up. The formula has been working this long, why change it?"

"If we don't change, we die. HeirLoom is exemplary in what it does. But it's time to do more. It's time to expand beyond just trade. We need to produce. We need to *create* something. And I want us to create it together."

I chuckled but didn't completely shoot it down. I appreciated that my brother consistently wanted to include me, consistently tried to convince me that there was room at HeirLoom for me. He almost made me believe it was possible to, this dream he had of us somehow working together at the helm to take HeirLoom into the future. I couldn't see it, especially with Dad's deep and abiding distaste for change, but apparently, he could.

"I hear you; you don't have to sell me on it. You get your father to buy in, and we'll see what's next. Til then, I gladly leave it all to you." I leaned back and away from the conversation. I didn't want the night tainted by my relationship with my father. This was Godrick's night and as much as the tension between my father and I displeased him, he was excited and happy. And I was happy for him.

Two hours later, after a few sweaty rounds on the dancefloor with a trio of agreeable young women who seemed excited about the celebration we were hosting in VIP, Trey did call it quits.

"Aiight, A. I'm heading back. I got CEO-type shit to do in the morning, and we both know the old man is going to be on one." He whispered a few words in the ear of the girl who had seemed most enthralled by him before leaning in to say his goodbyes to us.

"Aiight, bro." Dap, thump, half hug. The routine. He repeated it with Warwick who was moving much more slowly than I was. Maybe it was time we all took it on home.

"Yo, we'll go, too. We can take the car together."

"Nah, don't worry about it. I'm good."

"You sure? Because..."

"Word. I'm sure." He pulled me close once more. "I love you, bro."

He was always free with the words. I knew it was partially because the old man was such an asshole to me, but I valued and appreciated him. I wasn't too proud to admit that they mattered. A lot.

"You, too, bro. Be careful."

He tossed a final wave, then took his leave.

I patted my jacket breast pocket and felt the slight crinkle of the paper I'd stashed there earlier. Despite some less-than-endearing moments with the old man, it had shaken out to be a good night.

My brother was the shit, and I had met a dope little shorty who I was actually excited about calling.

Tomorrow, I'd learn her last name, and the day after that, her favorite color, and the day after that, well, who knew? But I was looking forward to it.

CHAPTER 3
TEN YEARS AFTER THE GALA

ABE.

Inhale-two-three-four, hold-two-three four, exhale-two-three-four. *Fuck.* The curse skittered through my mind, making a mockery of the moment of meditation I was trying to embrace. *Focus, Abe.*

I repeated the sequence, drawing in breath, holding it, and exhaling slowly. Intentionally.

It wasn't working. My pulse was galloping. My heart was pounding against the confines of my ribcage, a by-product of the photo that had just blown a gaping hole through my carefully curated calm.

It has to be her. Those eyes. Even in the black and white printout, they were striking. I was certain. So much so that I pulled my phone out and googled the name...something I hadn't intended to do before tonight's reception. But my instincts were right. Those oddly colored eyes stared back at me from my phone screen. One, crystal clear cognac with flecks of green. The other, the opposite, a bright clear green with hints of brown.

I rarely dealt in regret anymore. A key takeaway from the meditation and yoga practice I had trained my mind and body into was not dealing in regret. It was about living in the moment, in the now, moving forward at all times with the pace of time. Learning from the past and embracing the future but residing steadily here in the moment. The practice had saved my life. Giving me structure at a time when everything around me was shattered.

As I stared at the photo in front of me, my body was already responding to the memories flitting at the outskirts of my consciousness. I was being sneakily tugged backward toward that time and space that had left me lost, lonely, and terrifyingly untethered. My head was starting to tingle, feeling too small for my brain. My eyes itched, and I blinked them slowly while my mind desperately sought a hold in the swirl of unwelcome memories.

Andi. No, not Andi. Cassandra. Cassandra No-Middle-Name Williams.

She did it. Through all of the mental upheaval this discovery was putting me through, I grasped hold of that thought. It was enough to give my mind something to focus on and put order to my churning thoughts.

Ten years ago, my senses had been captivated by a young woman who loved the same things I did and who, under the anonymity of a black sky blanketed with pinpoint stars, had shared a dream of becoming a great designer, respected and world-renowned. She had achieved much of that goal. Success as executive creative designer of HeirLoom's inaugural fashion line would solidify the rest.

A fashion line for HeirLoom was a plan I'd always had. No, that wasn't right. It hadn't always been fully formed enough to qualify as a plan. It had initially gained life as a simple dream. One shared between brothers. One we should have been realizing together, with him at the helm of the company and me leading the creative process. Instead, I was standing here as CEO, preparing to present Cassandra as creative director.

Ironic. Ironic that the evening I found a woman whose dreams intrigued me as much as her appearance was the same evening I lost the most important person in my life.

My mind drifted toward that night despite my attempts to keep it firmly planted in the now. My body tensed in a knee-jerk, protective impulse, bracing itself for the racking pain. The memories came in bright, disjointed flashes.

The strobing lights and the pounding bass of the club. War wick...Deuce...grinning, dancing off-beat, not giving a fuck. My boy Vince laughing his head off when Deuce flicked him off for calling him Wiz, yet again...Deuce was smart as fuck and hated that shit. Then, my phone ringing...ignored because it was my father, surely looking to kill my fun. Then Deuce's phone ringing. He answered because, well, because he was Deuce.

And then everything ground to an achingly slow pace, every detail painfully clear. Deuce's face told the story. He had answered the call, countenance full and animated, the joy and drinks of the night reflected in his carefree grin. As he listened, his face had morphed. First, confusion as he tilted his head and plugged one ear with a finger, trying to better hear the voice on the other end. His brown eyes tracked and locked with mine, struggling to understand. Then horror. Then, abject pain.

My heart had thumped once hard and stopped because I had known. I had simply known. The numbness that had begun to creep into my soul at that moment had since settled, eventually coating the heart-rending pain. That numbness remained. Integral. Necessary.

I had finally accepted but still didn't understand why it had been Trey and not me. Godrick had been ready to take on the world and put good into it, leading the family and the company into the next millennium. I...was not. I felt myself giving in to the spiral. My mind tried desperately to find some fingerhold that would stop the descent. It came in the form of a soft knock. *Thank God.*

"Are you ready? Your car has arrived." Shanice Young, my executive assistant, tapped lightly on the jamb of my office door and stuck her head around the corner. Her lips twisted in a sly smile when she saw the folder open on my desk, with Cassandra's photo front and center.

"Ha! I knew you would look!" Her chipper, playful chastising was jarring, given the thoughts floating around in my head. But I knew my internal upheaval wasn't reflected on my face. I'd had ten years of dealing with the loss of my brother to create a persona that the world was comfortable receiving. Cold and emotionless, they could handle. The screaming, raging part of me that continually railed against the unfairness of it all, not so much.

I gave her a nod. "Indeed. The blind interview process was successful, and the right choice was made. But I'm not in the mood for surprises tonight."

"I figured." She bustled in, straightened a few things on the desk, then settled primly on the edge of one of the oversized lush office chairs to run through my timeline for the rest of the evening. We had done this before, but she had exceedingly high standards, which is why she was here.

After verifying that I would be where I was supposed to be when I was supposed to be there, she forwarded, again, the content for tonight's speech and introductions to my phone.

"It'll all be on the podium, of course, but I know you like the content to review on the ride over." She scrolled through the digital pad that seemed permanently fused to her hand while her left foot, shod in impractically high heels, bounced where it was crossed in front of the right. "Yep, that should be it. I'll see you there unless you need anything else. I'm on my way over to make sure the setup is as expected."

"Thank you, Shanice." It was an acknowledgment and a dismissal, and she took it as such, bouncing up from the chair and slipping out of the room to go work her behind-the-scenes magic and leaving me alone, again, to brood over my memories.

I gave myself a mental shake. *Move, Abe.* I had ten years of managing this and had a carefully constructed space in my brain for everything associated with the night Trey died. Carved out, separated, buried, and rarely, if ever, accessed. I didn't like being spun into that room unexpectedly. And seeing Andi's photo was doing just that.

I crossed my unnecessarily spacious office, accessing the concealed bar I used when working late. Truthfully, my office was more comfortable than most of the studio apartments young New York professionals paid an arm and a leg for. Hidden behind various floor-to-ceiling pale wood panels that blended perfectly with the decor was a fully stocked kitchenette, the generously appointed bar, a full bathroom and comfortable bedroom, and a small, comparatively speaking, lounge space complete with built-in flat screen and surround sound audio system. I could live comfortably here for weeks, which was appropriate because there were many periods when these four walls were the only ones I saw for days at a time.

Now, with the panels concealing the bar recessed, I poured a stiff two fingers of bourbon and tossed it back. My eyes closed as the smooth liquid eased the pressure that had settled in my chest when I saw the woman in the photo.

And woman, she was. The lovely young girl I had met had been replaced with a strikingly beautiful woman. I tossed back one more half-shot before pouring a far more modest amount to sip before leaving for the gala.

Better prepared now, with far more objectivity, I returned to the photo. The woman staring back at me was confident and, I knew, exceedingly capable. Our conversations during the interview process revealed a combination of drive and creativity that almost immediately placed her head and shoulders above the other candidates.

The pool had been extremely small. HeirLoom would only consider the best of the best for the role, but, at the same time, I didn't want a publically established name for the job. We wanted the line and the artist to be a breakout breath of fresh air. We wanted to catapult both to the forefront of the fashion industry. The face of HeirLoom should be associated only with HeirLoom.

I believed wholeheartedly that we had made the right choice. Now, I just had to figure out how to live with it when just the sight of her on paper sent me reeling.

Chapter 4

Cassandra.

"Okay, girl. You've got this. This is the dream. You are capable. You are prepared. You are worthy."

I repeated the affirmation in the mirror twice before applying my favorite cocoa berry lipstick. It was the perfect shade, and while I wore it frequently, I *always* wore it when I needed a boost of confidence. Like tonight. Tonight when I would be introduced to the fashion world as the creative mind behind HeirLoom Textiles' long-anticipated foray into high fashion.

When the whispers had begun three years ago that the billion-dollar textiles company was expanding into design, most of the folks in the fashion world had dismissed it as idle chatter. Similar rumors had surfaced before, and nothing came of them. After all, HeirLoom, the oldest and most successful Black-owned fabrics company in the world, supplied, in one way or another, over a third of the fashion houses in the world. There was no need for them to expand into this area with their own line. To do so would set them in direct competition with much of their clientele.

But this time, the rumors had proved true. And more, they wanted a relative unknown to lead the charge. Someone whose name wasn't already connected to another house's success. Someone on the cusp of greatness to propel HeirLoom and themselves into this particular spotlight.

When the talk had continued, when no counter-statement was released denouncing the rumors, a little spark of 'that should be me' had flared to life in me. I had fanned it carefully, quietly, patiently.

At the time, three years ago, I was well into my third job after killing the game at both NYU and Parson's. Each role moved me closer to my dream of creating my own line, something I could put my name on and reflect my vision instead of seeking satisfaction in the exceptional execution of someone else's. Talks with HeirLoom promised just that. My work wouldn't be hidden behind the company. I wouldn't be a grunt, working feverishly to design and produce according to someone else's expectations. I would have full final creative approval. I would be prominently included in the marketing and placement. For better or worse, my name would be written in fashion's history books.

I would work closely with the CEO of the company. Apparently, he was a bit eccentric, and this was a pet project. Assuming a million dollar investment in a new arm of a multi-billion-dollar company could be called a pet project.

I paused because, from a percentage standpoint, I guess a milli was a drop in the bucket for HeirLoom. But for me, this was everything. This was the launch of my public career.

I knew my work was excellent. I worked too hard for it to be anything else. My designs had been seen on hundreds of runways, at multiple US and international fashion weeks and on the racks of the most exclusive boutiques in and out of the country. But always under someone else's label, someone else's name. That would change with this position.

This was my opportunity to shine or fail on a spectacularly public stage.

"You are capable. You are prepared. You are worthy." I repeated it because, *woo, the nerves!*

My internal musings were interrupted by the melodic sounds of *Money* by Cardi B. It was my ringtone for Margeaux, best friend, hype-woman extraordinaire, and, coincidentally, owner of not one but two of the most exclusive salons in New York.

I slid my pinky across the phone screen to connect the video call.

"Hey, girl, hey." I grinned because I had known she would call. There was no way she would let me walk into a gala event on such an important night without giving my face and hair the once over.

She had come first thing this morning, well before the sun had peaked over the horizon and, more importantly, before she headed into the salon to start her own business day, to give me a fresh blowout. She'd set the fat barrel curls with long silver pins and ordered me not to sweat. I hadn't left the house for the rest of the day except to grab hairspray, choosing instead to calm my nerves with good music and putting the final touches on the gown I'd created to wear this evening.

Contrary to some other designers, frenemies I'd made in school and in the industry, I had no problem designing for myself and loved doing it. My first designs had been for myself, completed out of necessity when buying the latest middle school trends had not been an option. But a sewing kit, a sharp pair of scissors, and an endless supply of fabric from our local thrift store had provided me the tools I needed for my own attempts at being fashion-forward and creating some sort of identity for myself.

Those first efforts led to some full-on bullying experiences. But that wasn't new territory. *Freak. Mutt.* And, of course, *Witch Bitch*, which was my favorite and hardly an insult.

But the unexpected joy and accomplishment I took from actually making something outweighed all that. By the time I hit high school, the same girls with the hateful words had come to me to make their prom dresses. I charged their asses extra.

"Girl. Prop the camera. I can't see you. Have you taken the pins out?"

"No, ma'am. I still have an hour before I need to leave, and you know my hair won't hold a curl." I followed her instructions, rearranging and securing the phone so she was no longer staring at my bathroom ceiling.

Margeaux's gorgeous face filled the screen as she leaned in, trying to see me better. She was stunning but couldn't see for shit. I was constantly amazed that she didn't send someone out of her salon looking crazy.

"Where are your glasses, Gogo?"

"Somewhere around here. Shit. Hold on." She disappeared for a moment, then came back on screen wearing a cute pair of cat eye frames that perfectly complemented the little pixie cut she sported. My eyes roamed her face. Rich dark skin, sharp cheekbones, huge slanted eyes exaggerated by the tip-tilted glasses. All topped with short blue-tipped black curls. Her full lips were pursed with offense.

"Ma'am, speak for your own paltry hairstyling efforts. When I put curls in, those curls stay." She sucked her teeth before continuing, "Did you pick up the holding spray I told you to get?"

"Yes, mama. I did." I'd wrapped my hair in a huge silk scarf for the quick walk to Duane Reade. I hadn't wanted to expose my curls to the New York humidity before absolutely necessary. I'd felt quite ghetto chic.

"Good," she was in professional assessment mode. "Your makeup looks great. You did that, sis," Margeaux threw compliments around like manhole covers, so I felt good hearing her praise my makeup application skills. Lord knew they were a long time in the making. But it had been Margeaux who, when I had lamented about looking so much younger than my actual age, taught me the fine points of shaping my face, enhancing my features, and essentially creating my mask for the world.

I didn't wear heavy makeup, but I did wear it artfully. I checked the mirror, reviewing my handiwork once again. My skin was smoothed with a light matte foundation. Strategically placed contour gave me more cheekbone than I had, shaped my jawline, and sharpened my chin. My eyes were defined and lightly lashed. The eyeshadow had taken the longest. I'd fussed with it, trying to get the color and contour just right. I didn't want to look raccoonish, but I also wanted the vibe to be appropriate for an evening event.

"I see you got your disguise on," Margeaux quipped, referring to the contacts I sometimes wore when I didn't want to deal with people staring into my mismatched eyes. One was brown, one was green. I understood people's fascination with my heterochromia, but that didn't make it any less jarring when people stared me down like some kind of circus attraction. At least the adults realized that the difference was a natural, if uncommon, hereditary occurrence. As a child, it had been the source of most of the early teasing I'd endured.

I was in college before it occurred to me to get contacts to make them match.

I'd popped them in tonight before beginning my makeup routine to give my eyes time to adjust. I didn't particularly enjoy wearing them, but given the magnitude of the night, the slight annoyance was preferable to the added attention my eyes were sure to garner. So tonight, I had deep brown eyes. The color most other people of my *cafe au lait* coloring sported.

"Because I'm not trying to spend all night with people staring all in my face. I'm nervous enough as it is."

"Nervous about what?"

I paused in spraying my setting spray to look at her like she'd lost her mind.

"Okay, okay," she acquiesced. "I get it. But look, you're fully prepared to knock this out the park. You've been working toward this your whole life."

"Doesn't make it any less stressful," I mumbled. Margeaux was unceasingly optimistic, it was a trait I admired in her but had trouble replicating in myself.

"And tonight," she continued, "isn't about being stressed or worried. Tonight is just about accepting the fact that you've been chosen, ma'am. Give yourself tonight to simply celebrate the victory. As black women, we don't give ourselves enough opportunities to just say 'job well done'. That's what tonight is about. You can worry yourself sick...for no good reason, I might add...about the actual work tomorrow. Tonight, we party!"

"You're right. You're right," I finished my final touches and picked up the phone to relocate it in my bedroom so we could continue the conversation while I slipped into my gown. "You know I get in my head."

"We all do. That's why I'm here. So we can handle that shit for each other. You need me to run down your resume right quick? These mofos are lucky to have you." Margeaux's words were muffled and distant now.

I eyed the phone suspiciously. "Where are you? What are you doing?" The screen had gone dark.

"Hmm? Who me?"

I wasn't at all surprised by the knock at my door. When I checked the peephole and saw her laughing eyes, I threw the door open.

The sight of her immediately calmed me, and the hug she wrapped me in finished the job. This woman had been my backbone and best friend from the very beginning. When neither of us had been sure that we'd find homes, that anyone would want either of us, we'd had each other.

The room was dark. It was well past lights out, and if anyone caught us up, the punishment would be swift and severe. Ms. Isabel didn't play. She scared me.

"We have to make a cut. So there's blood." Gogo's soft lisp was sure. I nodded. Nervous but excited because now I would have a sister. And if I had a sister, then we'd never be alone.

We had already discussed this. Our scheming led us to this moment, in the dark, under the covers with a razor stolen from one of the big girl's makeup bags.

"It might hurt a little bit, Cassandra." Her lisp made my name sound like Cathandra, which I thought was the most beautiful thing. She usually shortened my name, her abbreviation sounding like Thandi, but this was serious.

I nodded again. I was ready.

A careful nick on each of our palms, at the fatty part. It had been harder to accomplish than we'd expected. The sight of Gogo's eyebrows drawn in concentration, her being so very careful as she tried to make a little opening in our skin, made me brave.

Finally, a little swell of blood on both of our hands.

A triumphant grin bloomed on Margeaux's face, and the little gap between her front teeth showed through.

We clasped our hands together, making sure the blood smeared into one.

"Now what?" I whispered, awed by the moment.

"Now, we're sisters. Blood sisters. Forever."

A final squeeze before she let me go, and Margeaux was pouring into my condo, a bottle of wine in one hand, a steam trunk-sized tote that probably cost more than half a month's rent slung over her shoulder, and a dress bag laid across a forearm.

"How did you even get up here with all that? And hold the phone?" I started pulling items from her hands.

"I am a woman of many talents. Now let's get you dressed and get your curls popping for this most momentous occasion. You're about to turn the fashion world on its ear."

I followed her, her gapped grin, and the bottle of wine back to my bedroom.

CHAPTER 5

ABE.

I could feel the scowl crawling across my face as I prowled through the room. There were too many people here. I could feel the push and press of their eyes, and it was pissing me off.

I was out of sorts and I knew it. Shanice had worked hard to make the night perfect, but all I could think about was finding Andi...*Cassandra*...and getting to the bottom of...what? Why she was here? *Because she was the best person for this job.* Why she had applied? *Because she was the best person for this job.* Why my heart was pounding hard enough to break free of the ribs confining it? Well, that was a harder question to answer.

So, I was looking for her. Scanning the room. Avoiding eye contact with all the people I should be schmoozing and glad-handing as I made my way across the room. The arched exit into the foyer of the ballroom was my goal. It was where I had last seen Shanice, complete with earpiece and data pad, greeting guests and handling the things that needed to be handled. She'd know where Andi...fuck, *Cassandra*...*Ms. Williams*...yes, that was even better...Shanice would know where Ms. Williams was.

I skirted the edge of the ballroom, avoiding the large, round, heavily decorated tables clustered in groups in the middle of the space. Objectively, I could appreciate that Shanice had done her fucking thing. Again.

The grand ballroom at The Phoenix was exquisitely appointed in its own right. Gleaming wide planked hardwood floors that had been in place since the twenties anchored the space. Huge, twenty-five-foot tall windows encased in intricately carved wood lined two walls and soared upward, admitting the light needed to keep the place from feeling heavy and dark. The floors and wood trim echoed the elaborately turned wood that bordered the arches and other architectural features of the historied hotel. But those visual touches were where the vintage ended. The most recent remodel of the place had blended perfectly with the soul of the building to create a seamless meld of old and new that whispered of battles won and triumphs ahead. It was a perfect location for tonight's announcement that would move HeirLoom into a new arena, expanding its reach beyond the backroom and into the forefront of high fashion and luxury fabrics.

Where is she? Thoughts of tonight's announcement naturally gave way to Cassandra. My heart thumped as it had been doing since I opened that fucking folder on my desk. I rubbed a fist in the area, circling the space until I caught myself and lowered my hand. *Would I even recognize her?* The photos were definitely her, but different. What would she look like in person? Would I get that same kick in the gut that I had when I'd first seen her slipping in and among the tables at that other banquet? Before that other announcement?

In-two-three-four. Hold. And out-two-three-four. I tried to corral my breathing, harnessing my thoughts before my mind careened, unchecked, down that path that only led to heartache and anger. I was only a few steps from where I hoped to find Shanice.

I was formulating the excuse I would give her for needing Ms. Williams' whereabouts when I heard my name called in a tenor that I, unfortunately, couldn't dismiss without being outright rude. And while rudeness between my father and myself wasn't a foreign concept, we were in public. And beyond all else, proper public appearances must be maintained.

"Abe." I halted. *Inhale, exhale.* I turned, schooling my features into a neutral mask that reflected none of how I felt. There was a time when I tried to shift my face to reflect a respect I didn't feel. But that had obviously looked as fake as it felt. The numerous directives to '*wipe that smirk off your face, boy*' resounded.

"Yes, Father," Godrick Cyrus Walker, II, wasn't a big man heightwise, but he commanded a room. His voice boomed from a barrel chest set atop a thick middle and equally thick arms and legs. He was stocky. I had inherited his broad-chested, thick-muscled build, but it had been tempered by my mother's slim height. So, whereas my father was blocky, with a blue-collar build, I was longer and leaner with a build that had lent itself well to the track I ran in high school and college.

"This is an impressive turnout for your little spinoff project." He shot his cuffs and clasped his hands in front of his slightly protruding belly, encased in the finest brushed wool and silken cotton. "I'll be happy when you've gotten this itch scratched so you can refocus on the real business of the company." He lobbed the veiled insult. I heard it, and it rankled, but I didn't take the bait.

"Understood, sir." There was a time when I would have continued to try to make the man understand that this move was in the best interest of the company. That to stagnate meant death or at least dwindling profit margins, but I'd since come to realize that nothing coming from me would be received with anything other than disdain. Trey was supposed to have led this foray. Trey had provided the input to prevent my father's and my relationship from devolving into what it was now: this harsh, prickly, consumptive thing that constantly sought to seek out and amplify each other's weaknesses and pain points.

The old man raised an eyebrow. "Is that all you have to say? *Understood, sir?* You've always been a little pussy, though." He clasped a hand on my shoulder as if that statement were something to bond over. "No backbone to speak of. Not like Godrick. But a father takes what he gets and does the best he can."

I felt my lip curl. He honed in on it immediately.

"You got something to say?"

"No, sir." Faint disappointment skimmed his features. Under normal circumstances, I might slip down to his level and engage his bullshit, but I didn't have time tonight. Any additional delays would make it impossible to get to Cassandra to warn her.

"'*No, sir*,'" he mocked again. "Where's the woman who's supposed to be leading this fiasco? Or are you still on that blind audition bullshit? You should've put Elizabeth in charge. At least then, we could've managed the message. Better minimized the fallout when the time comes. A man is supposed to tolerate his wife's little projects. This would have been easy to push off as an indulgent husband catering to his beautiful wife."

"This isn't a little project, Father. And Elizabeth isn't my wife. I have no inclination to indulge her or hand the expansion of HeirLoom over to her."

"So, are you planning to fuck that up, too? Godrick understood his responsibility to this family. I expect you to do the same. Make no mistake, I am the one indulging you with this little game you want to play. But don't try me, son. The union of the Walkers and the Brookes has been long planned. You will honor that commitment."

Even I understood that the family line needed an heir. My mother had done her part in providing an heir...my brother...and a spare...myself. Between the two of us, both healthy red-blooded heterosexual cis-gendered males, there was no reason to have thought the longevity of the line was in danger.

But then, we lost Trey. No, we didn't *lose* him. He hadn't been misplaced. He'd been killed. By a drunk driver on a dark road on a night when he should have been home. Would have been home had it not been for my selfishness, my need to pull him closer to me and further from the automaton that our Father would turn him into. Left to his own devices, Trey would have been in his home office that night, pouring over his plans for HeirLoom, preparing himself to walk into those CEO offices the next day, alert, proud, eager.

Instead, he lay in the cold earth. Alone. Because of me.

Thanks for talking me into it.

The very fucking least I could and would do was to see his responsibilities, his dreams, through to their fulfillment. I had no time for or interest in distractions from that goal. First, I would make sure this new launch was successful because regardless of my desire to one-up Father, HeirLoom did need this. Then, I would ensure that what we had built would stay in our family. I'd marry and breed. I'd produce a whole slew of kids so none of them felt pressure to do a damn thing they didn't want to.

"I am perfectly comfortable with my responsibility to this company and this family. You've made my value crystal clear. I'm to identify an appropriate broodmare, mount her regularly, and expand the bloodline with strong, fertile stock. Got it."

The rage that darkened his face brought a smirk of satisfaction to my face. "Watch out, Father. Your annoyance is showing. We wouldn't want anyone to think you're anything but full of pride for your remaining son's new entrepreneurial efforts."

"Fuck you, boy." If my heart twisted at hearing those words, I was happy to attribute it to the twin twist that clenched my gut when I caught sight, over his shoulder, of a slim silhouette floating between the tables, making a beeline for the row of French doors leading to the terraces that edged two sides of the ballroom. *Andi*.

"As much as I would love to stay and apprise you of the myriad reasons that statement is out of line, I have better things to do with my time. I'll see you on the dais. Father." I nodded my head in a mockery of respect because I, too, was a prisoner of perception. The outward face of the family was of utmost importance. Avoiding the airing of our dirty laundry was the only thing on which my father and I agreed.

There was too much to lose.

I turned on my heel and left in pursuit of Ms. Williams.

Chapter 6

CASSANDRA.

The relatively cool air of the wraparound veranda dried the fine sheen of nervous sweat that coated my skin. Inside, the gala was a sparkling, teeming crush of people full of speculative gazes and ready smiles of congratulations, the sincerity of which my personal insecurities made me question.

The super-efficient Shanice had captured me as soon as Margeaux and I entered the venue. Clearly, she had the driver's GPS location since she had been waiting at the top of the wide marble steps for our arrival. In the forty-five minutes since that arrival, she had put faces to the names and voices of the people with whom I'd interviewed over the last several weeks.

Shanice herself looked exactly as I had pictured. Petite, incredibly curvy, scarily well-put-together, and equally organized. Tonight, she wore an off-the-shoulder, daringly low cut, empire-waisted gown of iridescent bottle green silk that allowed plenty of flowing freedom of movement while still being beautifully appropriate for the formal event. The dark changeable color acted almost as camouflage as she moved with unerring precision throughout the hall, tending to this and that.

I had only escaped her and her second-by-second schedule by begging for a moment of quiet in the ladies' lounge. And I had stopped there for a moment. But I quickly realized I wouldn't find any respite in that room full of chatter about the goings on of the other attendees and buckets of money poured into the latest charity or DIY project that these people absolutely were *not* doing themselves.

My head was swirling with new faces. Added to Shanice's were several members of the c-suite: the chief creative officer, the chief marketing officer, the chief operating officer, the chief financial officer. Even with knowing their names, matching the faces was harder than I anticipated. My strengths lie in the creative process, not the business one. The only person I was sure to remember was the CCO, Annabelle Gavin. Her title of chief creative officer had been so at odds with her stark black sheath dress, severe bun, and nondescript jewelry that it had been jarring.

My mind had immediately drifted to redesigning her look, nay, her whole wardrobe, which I had already imagined to be a study in tweeds and practical cotton. I had to focus. I knew there was a curve that allowed for artistic musings, but as the executive creative director, I was about to undertake a lot more than just the fun parts of this effort. I had to hire a whole design team and manage them through the process of giving life to this new line.

I would have to boss up on every level.

It was overwhelming. But every professional step I had made thus far was part of my preparation. I could absolutely do this, and I knew it. But still, it was overwhelming, and I needed a breath of air. Just a moment to collect myself, put my game face back on, and focus.

I wrapped my fingers around the railing; the coolness of the metal helped slow my racing thoughts. It felt good to just let my eyes close for a second.

"Andi." My eyes flew open. Jesus, could I not get a single moment alone?

"Cassandra?" My body jerked. *That voice.* Deep and melodious and confident and enthralling.

"It is you, isn't it, Andi?" My body physically reacted again, a little shiver running through it. I was losing it. Memories too long forgotten bubbled to the surface. '*I'll talk to you soon, Andi.*'

I shook my head to clear that weirdness from my brain. I was clearly more overwhelmed than I'd realized. I had the passing thought that I needed to get more sleep before I pasted a passable smile on my lips, preparing, if not really ready, to meet another new colleague. I turned around and felt the ground shift unsteadily beneath my feet.

Impossible.

I felt a strong hand close around my arm, steadying me.

"Are you okay?" This apparition kept talking, wrecking my mind with the voice that had haunted my dreams ten years ago.

"*Abe?*" I lifted my eyes to take in the fullness of this man who had shaken my twenty-two year old world. I saw confusion and uncertainty dance across his beautiful features before they flattened into a pleasant neutral.

"Yes. It's me," he confirmed, releasing my arm.

I was steady on my feet but I kept one hand resting on my stomach since it felt like the organ might disconnect itself from the rest of my body at any moment. My other hand remained on the rail of the balustrade that edged the terrace. I supposed I looked like I was about to faint. I wasn't. I'd never been rescued from unwanted situations by something as convenient as a swoon before. No reason to think I'd luck out now.

"I wondered if you'd remember me," he stepped back, allowing the cool night air to fill more space between us.

"I remember you," I replied, too flustered to play coy. Oh, I remembered him, alright. No man before or since had so immediately wrecked my equilibrium. He had thrown me off kilter that night years ago and did so again tonight.

I let my eyes roam his face. Youthful, early-twenties-Abe had been something to reckon with, with his easy smiles and sparkling eyes. Grown-ass-man-Abe was something entirely different, equally enthralling but infinitely more dangerous with more shadows than sparkle.

My heart, which had started racing at the first timbre of his voice, settled into a pounding rhythm that took my breath.

"What?" I tried again, "What are you doing here?"

He held out a big hand in my direction, "Abraham Elias Walker, CEO of HeirLoom Textiles."

I extended my hand toward his, "You? You're the..."

"CEO, yes." He took my hand briefly, dropping it almost immediately but not before sparks shot up my arm, swirled in my chest, and streaked down my spine to settle at the cradle of my thighs. I brought my legs together beneath the voluminous fabric of my gown. *Jesus. Still?*

I had convinced myself when he'd never called that our connection, my body's immediate response to him, was a byproduct of my overtired mind. When we'd met, I was stressed from exams and the constant pressure of figuring out tuition and life. I'd been on a 24-hour sleepless work-study binge, and it made perfect sense that I would be ripe for misinterpreting our casual conversation. Plus, I'd been in my early twenties, and he'd been fine as fuck. Of course, my body responded. I had bought into the narrative that all these components had overinflated his impact.

The burning in my palm let me know that that was all a crock of bullshit.

He rubbed his hand down his tie, smoothing it and maybe wiping my touch away. I felt my head tilt slightly, taking it all in.

"I just realized today that you're...you." He waved a hand at me. "The blind interview process and all." He explained briefly. I nodded. Right. The blind interview process.

"I thought you might like to know that I'm...me," he cleared his throat before continuing, "before we're on display together."

"Right. The announcement."

"Exactly. I thought you might want a moment to process."

"Oh, right. Yes. Thank you." I was shaken.

"Not that there's anything to really process. But it was a surprise to me to realize that we'd met before, if only briefly."

"Agreed." My breathing was slowly returning to normal. I would take my cue from him. It had been kind of him to seek me out and give me a moment. But he was right, there was nothing really to process about a five-minute, ten-year-old conversation. I said as much.

"Yes. I appreciate that. It was thoughtful of you to let me know." He nodded. Cool and aloof and not nearly as affected as

I was. "Thoughtful, but unnecessary." One of his brows crawled upward. "As you said, it was only a brief meeting. And it was a long time ago."

"Brief but fairly impactful, I would say." He quipped.

"Would you?" I redirected my attention, which had been firmly and rudely glued to his ridiculously handsome face, cataloging the changes that the last ten years had wrought. That coolness in his eyes hadn't been there before. The smile that I remembered stretching his full lips was nowhere in sight. In fact, it looked like this man hadn't smiled in ages. The deep laugh lines that I had noted at our first meeting seemed to have disappeared or at least stopped expanding. I wondered fleetingly what had happened in this man's life over the last ten years.

If he'd called like he said he would, you might know.

With my gaze dancing everywhere, anywhere to avoid his, I continued. "I don't know that I'd use the word impactful. It was a passing moment years ago." I could hear the faint breathiness in my voice and rolled my eyes at myself. *Get it together.*

"One that you remember, though." He sounded irritated. Why would he be irritated with me? Even if our meeting had been *impactful*, which it wasn't to me at all...*yeah, right*...he was the one who had flaked on the follow-through. He had no right to be irritated.

"I suppose. Vaguely. But again, thank you for being so considerate. I'm looking forward to my time with HeirLoom. I wouldn't want any awkwardness."

I could feel his gaze on me. Hot and searching. I kept my focus on the critically important task of straightening my gown, which didn't need straightening because well-made clothes didn't need to be tugged and pulled on all night.

When he didn't respond, and I couldn't reasonably avoid it any longer without appearing to be a total idiot, I met his gaze. *Fuck.*

Heavy-lidded, sleepy brown eyes held mine; that much hadn't changed. I was older now, though, and had some experience under my belt. The eyes that I had considered dreamy at twentyish now put me in the mind of long hot nights of sweaty, satisfying sex with that low-lidded gaze holding mine while he did *all the things* to my body.

I swallowed. His eyes tracked the movement.

"Nor do I." *Nor does he what? Dammit, Cassandra, stay with the conversation.* "I have no doubt that we've made the right choice with you as executive creative director. I don't expect this to change anything."

"Why would it? Again, five minutes, ten years ago. And I seem to remember you have some modicum of fashion insight that might make this a workable scenario." I accompanied the statement with a little smile. Hoping he would take the little joke for what it was: an effort to relieve some of the fucking tension because otherwise, I might indeed find respite in a faint. I needed to get out of his company. He needed to leave.

He nodded, no smile but maybe a little tick at the corner of his mouth?

"Fair enough. I'll do my best." Another long look during which he still seemed dissatisfied. But he must have resigned himself to whatever it was he saw because he quickly followed up with, "It seems that stealing a few minutes on the balcony is your thing, so I'll leave you to it." He checked his watch. "We'll need to be seated inside in the next five minutes, though. Shanice will come looking for you if you're not around."

"Thank you for the warning. She's a force. I'll be sure to be in place on time."

"She is indeed." And with that, he left me alone on the balcony to gather myself.

I sucked in air, feeling slightly woozy and completely shocked.

"Who was *that*?" For the second time since I'd slipped out of the gala in pursuit of peace and quiet, I jumped out of my skin. I was completely over being scared out of my wits by people sneaking up on me.

"Fuck, Gogo!"

She giggled, "Sorry, sis. I thought you heard me. I should've known better." She smoothed a hand across my bare back. "But again, who was that? He was fine as hell."

"That was Abe. Abraham Elias Walker, CEO of HeirLoom Textiles." I recited the introduction he had offered me earlier.

"*That's* the CEO?" A little hum trilled in her throat. "You lucky, lucky girl."

She turned to look in the direction Abe had taken when he left. My gaze followed hers, but he was nowhere to be seen.

"Not so much. That's Abe." I repeated. Margeaux knew about the mystery meeting on the patio years ago, but she didn't know how very much that night had meant to me. I wasn't keeping secrets from her, I just had not had the words to describe the interaction or the man. Dreamy, sexy, smart, funny...they were all accurate but insufficient to convey the totality of encountering all those things at once in a package that looked like *that*. But now, she'd seen him.

"Abe, who?"

"Abe, from back in the day. From that last catering thing we did together. The one who never called?"

Her eyes widened, and her mouth dropped open in an O. "That's Abe? No wonder you were all fucked up when he didn't call." Oh, maybe she did know.

"I wasn't fucked up," I defended. "I was disappointed."

"Girl, please," she scoffed as only a best friend can. "You were disappointed when Dr. Kevins didn't teach fashion marketing in our last semester." She turned again in the direction of Abe's exit. "When *that* nigga didn't call? Girl, you were fucked up."

I shrugged. "Maybe. But it's neither here nor there now. I'm about to be working with him every day, and whether he called or not ten years ago is a nonissue."

"Is it, though? He's still fine as frog hair." I burst out laughing because every now and then, Margeaux came out of her mouth with some crazy shit. "How do you plan to look at him all day and still get work done?"

"I don't know." I moaned, blatantly honest with Gogo because that's how it was between us.

And there was no use pretending that he wasn't fine as frog hair. But his vibe had been standoffish and prickly, so maybe that would offset what he looked like. People could go from 'fine' to 'fuck you' real quick, depending on how they acted.

"What did he want?"

"To let me know that he was...him, I guess. He said he'd realized we'd met before and wanted to give me a heads up before he introduced me in front of everyone."

"Well, that was cool of him."

"It was," I thought a bit more about our interaction since putting a little distance between Abe and me was allowing my head to clear. "He seemed a little weird. Standoffish."

"Maybe he was worried you were going to trip or something," she offered.

I thought about it. Could that have been it? If so, I was glad I had assured him that I didn't want any weirdness between us.

I sighed, straightened my shoulders, and spoke the truth, "It really doesn't matter one way or the other. I'm grown as hell and have too much to lose. So, what I *won't* do is fuck up this opportunity behind some man. I'll work with him, look at him, talk to him, and get this shit done spectacularly because that's what I have to do. That's what I *want* to do. I'm about to be rich and famous in this bitch. I'm certainly not about to get derailed by another man. Been there, done that." My thoughts flitted briefly to Jeffrey and danced away. There was no way I was about to let thoughts of him ruin this night for me.

"Well, okay, then." Margeaux chimed in with the requisite finger snap and neck roll. "Let's go get these rich bitch coins."

For the rest of the evening, I held my game face in place, accepted my introductions, shared my excitement and vision for HeirLoom's foray into fashion, and generally assured the hundreds of well-heeled people in that room that they could rest easy with me.

But underscoring it all was an incessant awareness of Abraham Elias Walker, CEO of HeirLoom Textiles.

CHAPTER 7

ABE.

"*Thoughtful, but unnecessary.*" I threw my jacket over the bench in my entryway and strode through the expansive space toward my lounge area. "*A passing moment...*" I blew out a breath as that line floated through my consciousness, where it had been tap dancing for the last three hours.

"You good, bruh?" Vince's voice pulled me out of my musings as he grabbed my jacket from where I'd tossed it to take it to...wherever he took things.

"I'm fucking fantastic." I tossed the rest of my shit, Italian leather laptop bag and catchall, silk tie, diamond-encrusted cufflinks, and exclusive line Mandeaux loafers.

"Of course you are." He shadowed my steps, collecting things, then disappeared briefly. Moments later, he reappeared sans my castoffs but with a heavy crystal tumbler, a third full of what I knew to be bourbon over a single large globe of ice. He passed it to me and then wandered back out of my line of vision. I heard the clink of another glass before he returned.

"Good night?" He asked.

I grunted.

"So it was all a disaster?"

I growled but gave him some words as well.

"Good enough. The gala was successful. We introduced *Ms. Williams* to everyone she needed to meet. And then I got the hell out."

"As expected. And how did *Ms. Williams* fare?" Hearing him echo my snarly emphasis on her name made me relax a little. I was definitely tripping.

"She fared just fine. Gave her little speech, hung out with her safety net, and generally charmed the room. So, yeah, she did fine."

"So, what's your problem?" Ah, there it was. Vince didn't give a damn about decorum. He'd been with me professionally for the last eight years or so and several more years before that. We'd met in boarding school in Philadelphia when we were eleven or twelve. We'd spent the next several years running, wrestling, and hooping on the same teams. But more, we'd spent the time building a bond based initially on shitty ass fathers, but that eventually grew to include shared interests and unconditional support.

He was the closest thing I had left to a brother outside of Warwick. And though that man was love and family, Vince knew me in a way that allowed me to be myself freely. There was nothing I hadn't shared with him. Our friendship was far more transparent than that between most men. We'd been accused of being more than friends multiple times by people who couldn't wrap their heads around what it looked like for two Black men to fucking give a shit about one another on a level that extended beyond sports and finding women to fuck.

But that's where we were, so I responded to his inquiry with, "Man. *Ms. Williams* got me fucked up."

"Oh, yeah?" He chuckled and settled onto the long-ass L-shaped sofa that was big as hell but still barely took up any space in the room. I loved that shit. "Tell me more."

"Ms. Williams is Cassandra Williams." I paused and sipped my drink. "Sometimes she goes by Andi."

Vince paused with his drink midway to his mouth. To his credit, his hand didn't wobble, and he didn't choke on his spit.

"Andi of the beautiful eyes, Andi?"

"One and the same. But her eyes were brown tonight. So I don't know what the fuck was up with that. Contacts, I guess."

"And?"

"And, what?"

"Nigga, *and everything*. Did she remember you? Clearly, you're still feeling her since you're all up in your feelings about it."

"Man, whatever," but he was right. "Yeah, she remembered me. Said it was a 'passing moment, years ago' and it shouldn't impact what we're doing now.

"Well. It *was* a passing moment years ago. And it *shouldn't* impact what you're doing now. You said even back then that she was a talented designer with something special. *Her lines, her use of color, her grasp of movement and structure...*"

When I turned my glare his way, his expression didn't change...just some undercurrent of bland amusement skated across. Calmest nigga ever.

"I'm just saying," he spread his hands, then continued, "that was then, this is now. So, what's up? What are you going to do?"

"I'm not going to do anything. She's right. We're going to let sleeping dogs lie, get this line produced, put a new feather in HeirLoom's cap, and keep it moving."

"Yeah, okay, bruh." He paused again, letting a minute or so elapse before he asked, "She still fine?"

"As frog hair."

He sat with that for a minute. "Well. I don't know what to tell you." With that, he slapped his palms on his thighs and rose. "I threw together a beef roast. It's in the oven on warm. Put that shit in the fridge when you're done. And eat some fucking vegetables."

He looked at his watch. "I'm out. I'll see you in the morning."

"Yeah, okay." I was distracted, thinking about fine as frog hair Andi Williams.

"I'll let myself out."

"You do that."

He laughed again. "Aiight. Don't stay up all night dreaming about little miss Andi. Liz wouldn't like that."

"Nigga, please. This ain't got nothing to do with Liz."

"Yeah, you tell Liz that. You know that girl fully expects you to marry her like your brother was going to."

"And I plan to do just that. She's a good girl. Smart, beautiful, understands the life. I could do worse."

"True. True. But how's she gonna feel about her husband being *in love*," he sang the words, making me laugh in spite of myself, "with another woman?"

"Now see, there you go doing the most. Nobody's in love with anyone. I'm a grown-ass man. That was a little boy's crush. I'm fully capable of appreciating a woman without...all that shit."

I waved a hand to encompass 'all that shit.' "I know what my responsibilities are. I have no intention of shirking them."

"Hmm," was all he had to say, but I was used to Vince's various hems and hums. I knew what this one meant.

"Nah, V, for real. She's definitely all that, but she's not for me. I have one job, and that's to move HeirLoom forward like G would have done. It's the only way I have left to honor him."

"Well. You know how I feel about that, but I'll leave you to it." He checked his watch again. "Aiight for real, I'm out. I'm catching up with," he pulled his phone from his pocket, swiped a couple of times, and finished with, "Sundee...that's with two 'e's so I have high hopes for the evening." He turned the screen my way to show a cute, curvy redhead.

"Bet. Be safe out there." And Vince disappeared through the wing that lead to the guest suites. He wasn't a guest, but he stayed on that side for the privacy it offered. He didn't have to live here at all...I paid him more than enough, and he had his own professional shit going on...but I was glad for the company.

I, on the other hand, picked up my drink and wandered in the opposite direction, which would lead to the master suites. At the last minute, I detoured into the gym, where I took another sip of the drink before entering the changing rooms to swap the rest of my suit for running shorts and shoes. I knew it wasn't the best pre-run nourishment, but I swallowed the rest of the bourbon before exiting the exterior gym doors to access the half-track. The track encircled an NCAA regulation-size basketball court and a half-field for other track-related sports. A huge heated swimming pool set cattycorner to the track featured stone loungers and fire pits. It was an indulgence, but I had enough money to indulge.

The cool night air raised goosebumps on my exposed skin. I considered turning back for a tank but figured I'd build up enough heat soon enough to burn away the goosebumps and the itch under my skin that hadn't dissipated since I'd first seen Andi on the hiring documents.

What I'd told Vince was true. I did understand my responsibilities and was committed to them; had been since G died. I just wished there was room for something...or someone...else in my carefully constructed cage.

I half-ass stretched before strolling onto the track. I could already feel the tension falling away as I settled into a light jog. I picked up the pace, going faster as my thoughts started to tumble against each other, bouncing between Andi and Elizabeth, Godrick and my father, and Vince's words...because I did know how he felt about my goal of essentially replacing Godrick, of fulfilling his dreams and giving life to his goals.

He'd made it clear more than once...and my therapist didn't disagree...that it was unhealthy to have absorbed Godrick's dreams as my own. That I needed to figure out the closure so I could live my own life and find my own fulfillment. What they didn't understand was that this was my fulfillment.

And it was the only way I knew to make up for taking him away.

CHAPTER 8

This wasn't at all what I expected. When Margeaux said 'day party' and 'winery' in the same sentence, the images that popped into my head were not these.

The boring ass party, which I was actively trying to formulate an excuse to leave without appearing rude, actually had potential. If only someone would play some decent music and remove the sticks from the asses of the collective attendee group.

The venue was beautiful. The winery occupied acres and acres of the Hudson Valley, right along the river. The views of the vineyards to one side and the expanse of the river to the other were stunning. The weather was perfect, with a light breeze dancing off the water.

The big-ass rich people's picnic shelter was fucking gorgeous. Pale, knotted pine floors and walls housed what were probably five thousand dollar picnic tables. Those tables were decorated within an inch of their lives with wildflowers and greenery native to the area. So it looked like fairies had just picked a bunch of stuff from the river banks and fields and spread them in the space. It was natural and beautiful. Any available space remaining on the tables was occupied with elaborate charcuterie and fruit trays, finger sandwiches featuring salmon, crab, and caviar, and dip trays with fancy breads and crackers. There was not a mosquito nor fly in sight.

Even the music wasn't horrible, but it definitely wasn't *day-party* music. Part of the problem was that there was no DJ. Instead, a whole ass band played quiet covers of 60s and 70s ballads. It was a pretty inclusive mix. I'd definitely heard both Stevie Wonder and Bobby Caldwell, and I wasn't mad at either, but I could easily recreate this vibe at the house where I could also be getting some work done.

"Gogo, this is boring as fuck." I knew I was whining, but I was giving up a precious Saturday afternoon for this bullshit. I had work to do. I'd had a good first week at HeirLoom, but every day still felt like I was drinking information from a firehose, and I had no expectation that the pace was going to slow down.

"Stop whining. I know you want to be working, but you need to get out for just a minute. You've been going sunup to sundown all week."

"Yes, and I have every intention of continuing. And you're not the one to talk Miss Four Hours of Sleep is Plenty." She ignored the last part but commented on the first.

"Of course, you will, but you have to take care of yourself. A few hours unwinding with good wine and good views isn't going to hurt you."

"*A few hours?* The hell, you say. You have two hours, *two maximum*, before I'm gone. I'm not spending my whole day here with these people." I hissed it to her, smiling as a couple passed by us, arm in arm, with globes of wine.

She hissed back, "You'll go when I say you can go. I'm driving, ma'am."

"I knew that was a mistake when I agreed to it."

"Tough titty. Here." She plucked two long-stemmed glasses of white wine from a passing attendant's tray and passed me one. "Plus, I have to be here. When a client invites you to a function like this, you go. Who knows who she'll put me onto? And I'm planning to open another location soon. I need the referrals."

Margeaux was endlessly ambitious. I understood why. She was driven by the same need for security that I was.

We wandered a few more steps taking in the views of people and the landscape.

"How are they managing to balance these glasses?" Margeaux mused, following along as the attendants moved silently among the party, offering wine. I was more surprised at the fact that there were attendants at a *day party*. Yeah, right.

"I mean, I know we did good work in our day, but these stems are like thread," she shook her head. "Glad it's not me. Could you imagine Sherlene's ire if we'd dropped one of those trays?"

I shuddered. "Hell, no. But it wouldn't have been you, it would've been me. Every fucking time."

She giggled and bumped my shoulder, "I really don't know how you didn't break more stuff. I stayed worried about your ass."

"I'm quick on my feet, and my balance is impeccable," I joked. But she was right. I'd had more close calls back then than

I cared to remember. The night I met Abe had been my final gig. The money I made had rounded out my last tuition payment, and I was free to concentrate on exams.

I'd done so well that I secured the top spot in the most sought-after internship in the program. That internship had taken me to Milan and the start of my career. It was almost surreal that I was heading up my own line only ten years later. Just the thought of it had my nerves rising and me thinking again that I needed to get my ass home.

The week had been spent fleshing out the members we'd need for the team that was going to make this line a reality. Next week, the interviews began. I appreciated Abe's lack of micro-managing. He'd made it clear all around that all final decisions about the unit and its output rested with me. Again, wonderfully stress-inducing.

I didn't know what I would do without Shanice. She had been invaluable in getting it all arranged. But I also realized quickly that I would need my own administrative assistant. I added the role to my list of team members just yesterday. Shanice was amazing, but this was more work than even she realized.

"Look." Margeaux nudged my shoulder and nodded behind me. We were currently seated on teak Adirondack chairs angled to give us views of both the river and the vineyard. I had to scooch up and twist around to see where she was pointing...which put my gaze on a collision course with Abe's tight ass.

"Your fine ass boss is here, so surely you can take a minute, too." She nudged me.

"Hmm?" I responded, attention caught by the sight before me.

"Well, I'll be damned. This nigga still got you fucked up," she breathed quietly.

"He does not," I argued weakly because he kinda did.

The whole week had been a study in me not letting my tongue drag the floor every time his good-smelling self came into my purview.

And while he didn't micromanage, he was around...a lot. Not intrusive but very present. And it was driving me insane.

I shook my head. It was hard to put my best foot forward when he was prowling around my workspace, looking good and smelling better.

It had started on my second day, this habit he was developing of popping into my workspace, asking questions, and touching shit.

"So, you're adjusting." His deep voice boomed in the cavernous room, causing me to nearly fumble my laptop from where it was perched... on my lap...while I sketched with my feet propped on the nearest sewing table. I'd come to find some peace and quiet and an hour to unwind.

It was after seven, and I had spent the day in meeting after meeting, doing the circuit, getting the lay of the land. I should go home, but I was still on such a high that I couldn't bring myself to leave. So, I'd come here to start grounding myself in my space. The space where we would create the magic that catapulted my name into the tableside conversations of fashion's high rollers.

"Jesus, Abe." I laid a hand on my pounding heart, glad that I could attribute its racing to the surprise of his appearance

instead of his appearance itself. Because he looked good. Yet another perfectly tailored suit. I'd seen him in four so far if you included tuxedos, and I definitely did. This one was a beautiful, rich aubergine, the warm reddish-purple color was paired with an equally well-fit pale pink shirt and a houndstooth patterned necktie in shades that tied it all together perfectly. All of it, combined with his tobacco brown skin, close fade, barely there beard, and the glitter and aura of a monied man, was just too damn much.

It really was unfair. He seemed so unimpacted by my presence, and here I was, damn near quivering. It made me pissy.

"Why aren't you using your office?" He queried, motioning toward the other end of this huge space that had been designed especially for this project, especially for me. It was the sewing room of my dreams. It was really overkill, but I appreciated it. I'd been in many patterning and sewing rooms that were too congested. It made the work hard and unpleasant.

In addition to being ginormous, there were eight fully stocked sewing tables, each long enough for patterning, cutting, and sewing to all happen with plenty of elbow room. The tables were in the middle of the room. On one end was a brainstorming space complete with glass boards, touch screens, casting, and co-editing capabilities. It was absolutely everything I could have dreamed of.

Along the side were floor-to-ceiling windows that let in the most beautiful light. While the sunshine was lovely, I was more excited that the windows could be shaded to protect the fabrics. At the touch of a button, the glass itself tinted. Along the other side of the room were breakout spaces in case privacy was needed, a comfortable lounge space, and a fully-stocked kitchenette.

Bolt after bolt of beautiful cloth lined all the free wall space. This was, of course, only the tip of the iceberg in terms of fabrics available to me through HeirLoom. There were four or five times this many bolts on the textile floor. There was also a huge glass wall case filled with accessories, many of which were donated from other big names in the industry.

Finally, at the far end were the offices. Two smaller ones and mine, which was set in the corner so that it also sported two walls of windows. The wall adjacent to the sewing room was clear glass that could also be shaded for privacy.

I couldn't be happier with the setup, but no matter what, I still felt most comfortable out in the sewing room. The energy of the creations we would produce was already pouring through me.

"So you're just not going to acknowledge the fact that you keep sneaking up on me?"

He wandered further into the room.

"I'm not sneaking up on you. You're just not very aware of your surroundings." He leaned against the table. "Do you not like the office?"

I tilted my head, still a little annoyed but unable to stay so when I was in designer heaven.

"I do like it. It's beautiful and perfect. Sometimes, I'm just more comfortable out here."

When he said nothing, I filled the silence. "I'm used to the sewing room. Even in my last role as creative director, I spent more time at the tables than in my office. I find everyone works better when their leadership is present and engaged."

He held my eyes for a moment. He seemed to be contemplating saying something but decided against it.

"Hm." He fingered the fabric samples I had spread across the table. He had good hands. Long fingers, neat, short nails with a little buff on the surface. What did you expect, Cassandra? He's fucking rich. Of course, his nails are manicured.

"Are these the fabrics you're thinking about for the line?" He rubbed the silks between his fingers, and God help me, my lashes fluttered. I was pitiful.

"Not really. This is just, I don't know, stress relief?" I could've slapped myself. You don't tell your new boss, in your best breathy voice, that you're stressed in week one. "I mean, not stress really, just getting ideas out of my head, you know?"

Another noncommittal hum. He was making me nervous. And he kept staring at me with those sexy fucking sleepy-ass eyes.

I cleared my throat. Enough was enough. "Is there something I can help you with?" It didn't come out nearly as authoritative as I'd intended.

He chuckled. My lids lowered. "I just wanted to make sure you were settling in comfortably. I spoke with Shanice and realized she has you on a pretty tight schedule."

I wasn't a hundred percent sure how I felt about him checking on my schedule.

"Do you check on all your new people's schedules?"

"Yes. I find that everyone works better when their leadership is present and engaged." His lip twitched.

Asshole. *But it reminded me a little of the slickly funny guy I'd met years ago.*

"But, also, you hold something very important to me in your hands. Get used to me being around."

I felt the same rush of hot nerves now, thinking about that interaction, as I'd felt then when I'd lived it.

"Huh. I guess he's fucked up, too." Margeaux murmured.

"What?" I asked, realizing that I was, again, wool-gathering and *shit* that wouldn't do at all because I'd stared so long that Abe must've felt my gaze on him. He'd turned this way and was staring back. *Shit*, again. I knew I should've stayed my ass at home.

"Fuck. Now he thinks I'm a slackard because I'm out at this fucking party."

"Hush. That's not true, and you know it. It's the weekend. You get to have a life. And you get to help your bestie navigate this party so I, too, can get my coins."

"Girl, you have plenty of coins," I grumbled.

"It's never enough," she quipped, reminding me of an old viral social media clip. But she had a point. I sipped from my glass, less interested in the wine itself than the cooling sensation I desperately needed now that Abe was in my vicinity.

"And I see my client now. Let me go show my face in the place in case she wants to introduce me around." Margeaux gave a little shimmy at the prospect of adding to her client roster. "She wore the lip color I recommended. Mmhmm. I knew it would be perfect." She patted my knee as she rose. "I'll be back in twenty. And if you still want to leave, we'll start in that direction."

"Cool. Go do your thing. I'm fine." *Yes, girl, you are fine. Just fine and dandy.* I swallowed the rest of my wine and plucked another to keep my hands busy. I rose along with Margeaux, intent upon walking casually in whatever direction was most opposite Abe. I wasn't avoiding him. It would be ridiculous to avoid my boss at a social function.

Also, avoiding someone is hard when your eyes constantly stray toward them. So it happened that I was walking in one direction but looking in another and almost plowed down an older gentleman who had the misfortune of being in my path.

He took my elbow to steady me, his grasp unexpectedly strong.

"I can't say I mind when a beautiful woman tries to put me on my back, but our surroundings may be less than ideal."

I wasn't sure whether to be creeped out or amused by his comment. He was markedly older than me. His neatly shaped beard was fully white. I wasn't sure if it complemented or high-lighted the ruddiness of his skin. He had a slim face that was clearly once very handsome. Even now, his sharp cheekbones, strong nose, and full brows over slightly faded green eyes were not hard to look at. He had a full head of heavily salted dark hair. Combined with the beard, the effect was striking.

He chuckled at my silence. "Oh, don't get all *me-too* dramat-ic. One slightly off-color comment shouldn't send you scurry-ing." He had that rich-person lilt to his speech. Not quite an ac-cent, but something that let me know he was part of the reason this party was so wack. He also had that rich, say whatever the fuck I want vibe.

I felt like I should be offended by the whole interlude, but all I could manage was, "I'm sorry?"

"Don't be sorry, dear. I'm quite all right. No harm done." He swept a long-fingered hand across the front of his finely knit cashmere sweater before glancing up. I saw surprise flash on his face. "Your eyes are lovely," he offered.

I supposed he was sincere, but his focus on me was the very reason I often wore my contacts. Having a stranger hold prolonged eye contact was a decidedly creepy sensation. I watched as his eyes went from one of mine to the other and back again. I saw the usual fascination as if the viewer couldn't quite believe their own eyes and wasn't sure which of mine to focus on. But I also noted something else I couldn't put my finger on that made me additionally uncomfortable.

"Thank you." I tugged my arm from where it was still in his light grasp. "My apologies for running into you. I was distracted."

He glanced somewhere behind me. He couldn't possibly know that my flight was fueled by a desire to avoid Abe, could he? And so what if he did?

"Of course. It's not a problem." His gaze hadn't left my face. I felt him cataloging my features as he stared. I wasn't quite sure how to feel. I wasn't catching a lecherous vibe, but his focus had surpassed the normal period when most people realized they were being rude and fell back. He continued to watch me.

"We've not been properly introduced. I'm Benjamin Whyte. And you are?"

"Cassandra Williams." I held my hand out, expecting a light shake and release. Instead, he used the opportunity to tug me forward and tuck my hand into his elbow. He turned away from the direction I'd left Abe and began walking. I had little choice but to go along unless I wanted to appear rude or cause a scene. We were out in the open, surrounded by a number of people and I could see Margeaux. His path was taking me away from Abe, and despite myself, I was a little curious. So, I walked with him as he had obviously assumed I would.

"Cassandra. A beautiful name for a lovely young woman. Are you from the area?"

"Not originally," I hedged. "I just began working at Heir-Loom." It was common knowledge. "How about you?" I asked, politely shifting the conversation away from myself. I had an easy story ready about who I was and where I was from, but it was all around easier not to start conversations on the topic and I just didn't have the energy.

"Oh yes," he patted my hand. "My family has been in this area for generations. We're in textiles as well."

Benjamin Whyte. "As in Whyte's Fabrics?" Next to Heir-Loom, they were one of the most successful and well-known textiles companies in the world. I knew both were based out of New York.

"Ah, you've heard of us?"

"I'd have to live under a rock not to. My role at HeirLoom is the executive creative director of their new fashion line. Of course, I know all about Whyte's Fabrics. Next to HeirLoom, there's none better." A little dig, but loyalty to the home team was ingrained in me.

A chuckle from my escort, "Ah, yes. I heard that HeirLoom was branching out into the fashion business. Risky. I'll be eagerly awaiting their failure."

I shot a look at him and halted. I was all for meeting new people, but I wasn't about to get caught fraternizing with the enemy.

"I'm joking. Somewhat." He started walking again. So did I. "HeirLoom and Whyte's certainly have a healthy respect for each other. We keep each other on our toes, I'll say."

Still prickly, I replied, "Well, if you're waiting on the new line to fail, you'll be waiting a long time. It's my baby, and I plan for it to be a raging success. So, prepare yourself for disappointment."

"Ah, feisty. No less than I would have expected." It was an odd statement...why would he have expectations about me? But he stopped walking, and I realized that we had meandered our way to the edges of the party. We were fairly alone and near the exit into the vineyards.

"I'm unconcerned about your expectations." I wasn't sure why he set me on edge, but my pulse was picking up in a fight or flight kind of way.

"Fair enough." He paused and scanned my face again. Still searching for something. "Where did you say you were from?"

"I didn't." I could feel the homegirl in me rising. Why was he all in my business?

"Come now, there's no need to be rude. I'm just making conversation. I'm sure I can read any of a number of articles about HeirLoom's new protege and learn where you're from."

It was true; he could.

"I was raised in Baltimore."

"I see. Your parents are from Maryland as well?"

"For the most part." I definitely wasn't getting into the whole story with this man. He could read about that, too, if he wanted.

There were at least one or two articles that briefly mentioned my background beyond hometown and education.

"I suppose you inherited your unusual eyes from one of them? Which one, if you don't mind my asking?"

Could he really just be stuck on that? Maybe I needed to relax. This thing with Abe, which actually wasn't a thing and wouldn't be a thing if I could get out of my own head, had me on edge. "I'm not sure, honestly. I don't know who my parents were, so it's a bit of a mystery."

"Hmm. I see." There was something about the tenor of his hum that set me on edge again. I wanted to put a little distance between us. I tried to surreptitiously look around for Margeaux. Maybe I could send her an SOS.

"Cassandra. You should surround yourself with better company." My heart thumped, as it always did when that baritone swept over me. Abe.

"Abraham. It's always a pleasure." Benjamin extended a hand toward Abe.

"Indeed." Abe shook. "Are you harassing my newest partner?"

"Not at all. Just making her aware of her options, in case she realizes that she's affiliated herself with a subpar entity."

Abe turned to me. "Ms. Williams, have you found your time under my care satisfactory?" He made 'under my care' sound like something far more exciting than it had been. Or was that the two glasses of wine wrapping around his words?

"Of course, Mr. Walker. I've been immensely satisfied."

Abe's eyes took on a little sparkle before he turned back to Mr. Whyte.

"Well, there you have it. Your attentions are misplaced and misguided. You can move on and enjoy the rest of your day confident that Ms. Williams is in good hands."

Whyte tipped his wine glass in our direction before nodding. "Fair enough, Abraham. Ms. Williams, if you ever decide you'd like to bring your talents to an operation where they'll be appropriately appreciated and compensated, don't hesitate to reach out."

With that, he took his exit, leaving me standing relatively alone with the very man I'd been trying to avoid.

CHAPTER 9

ABE.

What the fuck are they talking about?

I had arrived fifteen minutes ago at this fucking party that I did not want to attend, escorting two women I did not want to escort.

Well, that wasn't wholly true. I had promised to escort Elizabeth weeks ago. This annual afternoon soiree by Lambert Wines was penciled on all of our calendars. Elizabeth and I had decided to mitigate the boredom by going together. We would be killing two birds by showing our faces and feeding the expectation of our coupledom. So, I was completely prepared this morning when I arrived at the Brooke home to find Elizabeth ready to go.

What I hadn't been prepared for was her mother. Juanita. She had also been ready to go. Apparently, she had decided at the last minute that she also needed to see and be seen this afternoon.

My nerves were already shot. I had worked my body beyond what was customary last night, trying to rid myself of images of a mismatched gaze and riotous curls. It had worked briefly. I had fallen onto the sectional in my rec room, leg muscles on the verge of cramping and chest heaving after too much time on the track, followed by forty-five minutes of supersets in the gym. My mind had been blessedly blank, and I'd slipped into slumber on the comfortable couch.

I woke this morning offended by the smell of myself, eyes gritty and throat parched but still delightfully unbothered by thoughts of Cassandra. Until my morning yoga and meditation, when all I could think about was how I wasn't thinking about Cassandra, and then, boom. There she was again. Front and center. So I hadn't been in the best of moods when I'd arrived on Elizabeth's doorstep some hours later.

It irritated me that I couldn't control the path of my thoughts. And it irritated me that I felt like I needed to. But here we were. And here I was again surrounded by a bunch of people who, for the most part, grated on my nerves.

Elizabeth and her mother had peeled away almost immediately upon arrival to avail themselves of the ladies' rooms. I had enjoyed a full forty seconds of peace before my eyes lit on a familiar shape, a familiar sweep of sleek brown hair that I still, after ten years, imagined in loose, wild curls. *Fuck. Why is she here?*

I needed a fucking break from the incessant pull of her.

I watched as her companion glanced my way, whispered something to Cassandra, and then left her alone. Why the fuck my feet started moving in that direction, I had no idea. But then she got up and started walking...in the *other direction.* Was she running from me? The thought jolted me to a stop. Not running, certainly. But surely moving intentionally away. Huh. How about that? *Maybe you've made enough of a pest of yourself, showing up in her office all the damn time.* Those visits were necessary, I told myself. *Necessary for who?* Each time I wandered into her space, I told myself that seeing her would slake my hunger and let me think about something else. Each time, I was wrong.

But, instead of following her, I made my way to the bar. I saw several familiar faces as I did so. The same people were always at these things. I'd just seen many of the same people at HeirLoom's announcement for Cassandra. I spoke and shook hands. Let folks know that, '*Yes, things are progressing nicely with our new plans, and we're very excited by what's to come*,' and '*No, I can't give you a sneak peek at what we're working on. I could show you, but then I'd have to kill you, ha ha ha.*'

I'd grown to enjoy much of the responsibility I'd taken on with HeirLoom after Godrick died. But this part, the mingling and grinning and pretending to like the company of these people, I'd never grow to enjoy that part. It just felt too insincere, too orchestrated.

I sipped my drink, back against a wooden post, mind whirling with thoughts of how soon I could reasonably leave and get back to the office. Of their own belligerent accord, my eyes sought out Cassandra again, which brings us to this moment and my confusion because,

What the fuck are they talking about?

Cassandra was in the company of Benjamin Whyte, strolling around with him, hand on his forearm as if she didn't have a care in the world. It was like watching an innocent kitten stroll alongside a vicious cobra, unaware that the wide smile being offered was really a lure into the pit of its belly. I set my drink down and began a slow stroll designed to cut them off at the pass.

I interrupted their party of two just in time to hear him quizzing her about her background. Why that pissed me off, I couldn't say, but I didn't know anything about her background beyond what I'd read in her application documents, and I didn't like the idea of this asshole having more personal information about her than I did.

"Cassandra. You should surround yourself with better company." She jumped slightly, and I winced. I was forever sneaking up on this woman. But, when she turned to me, the look in her beautiful eyes was one of relief. She didn't feel comfortable with Benjamin. I felt my chest swell a little bit. I had been right to offer an escape.

I kept it simple with Ben. Let him know that she was in good hands and that he could dismiss himself. It was a hint he chose to take, and I was grateful. Not that I ever minded tangling with Benjamin Whyte, but it wasn't the impression I wanted to leave with Cassandra.

"Are you okay?" I asked, now that he was gone.

"I am." She paused. "But that's an odd question. We were just talking."

I nodded. "Of course. But Benjamin can be...challenging. Did he step out of line?"

Instead of answering directly, she said, "I'm capable of handling men who step out of line. You didn't have to swoop in."

"Did I swoop?"

A light flush rose on her caramel cheeks. Fascinating. "Maybe a little," she said. "Do you two not get along?"

"We get along as much as rivals can, I suppose. Whyte's and HeirLoom have been in a tug of war since we were both founded. We pretty much mind our business, but he spends more time than he needs to trying to buy us out one way or another."

I wasn't sure why I'd shared that. Corporate-level affairs weren't something that I tended to discuss with the people who worked for me. Especially not newly hired people.

"Really? I would think there'd be plenty of business to go around."

"There is. But some folks just don't like healthy competition. Especially when they don't think the competitor should have ever been allowed on the field."

At that, she turned those pretty eyes up to me, confusion and query in their depths. "What do you mean?"

I motioned toward the generously laden tables, and we walked that way.

"Well. HeirLoom and Whyte's came into existence at much the same time in the late teens and early 20s of the 1900s. It wasn't the most inclusive time, even in the northern states. My great-grandfather Cyrus was a rebel, though, and didn't give a fuck." I heard her chuckle at my description of my grandfather. I could feel her eyes on me as we walked, so I continued, giving her the spiel I had heard many times.

"In the early 20s, Cyrus managed to find passage on a boat bound for the Caribbean islands. He'd planned to make his fortune in rum and eventually bring his family to the Caribbean with him. As the story goes, he was gone for four years. His wife, Mozelle had given him up for dead and taken up with another gentleman from the church, but that's another story. When he came back, he returned with bolts of cloth that he'd gotten from several Caribbean Islands, Venezuela, Guyana, Spain, Portugal, and, most important for HeirLoom, Morocco, Algeria, and Senegal. The man had been home to Africa." I paused because that fact always blew me. In 1920, a black man in my family returned to Africa. It had to have been mindblowing.

"Woah. That had to be something else. Can you imagine being, what, 50 or 60 years out of slavery and going to Africa?"

"It's hard to imagine. But my family through that line was never enslaved." At the look of surprise on her face, I expanded. "Yeah. He was a descendant of one of the Cimarron colonies in Virginia. People think every African who they shipped over here ended up in chains. Many did. Most did. But not all. Some fought and escaped right off the boat. There were villages of free Black people all up and down the east coast, especially in the swamp areas because our people knew how to work that land. They got away and just disappeared."

"I had no idea. That's amazing...and why don't we know this?"

"Because knowledge is power, and they don't want that for us. But anyway," I continued the story. "When he returned, he declared all the fabrics he'd acquired as 'fabrics from the homeland'. Mozelle was butter with a needle and thread, and they started HeirLoom. It began as a combination tailor and fabrics shop, but when word got out about the quality of the materials, it became clear that that's where the money was. Mozelle reserved her crafting and sewing for the wealthy Black families in the area, and Godrick set out on another trip to

Africa. They say he went back and forth five times before he got too ill to return. He died of 'the fever.'" I accompanied it with air quotes.

I started building a plate. "Do you like all cheeses?"

She looked at the table skeptically. "I don't know a lot of cheeses. I only recently expanded my palate to include baked brie."

I felt my lip twitch. "Fair enough. I'll make you a little sampler platter of some of the more palatable options. Some of this shit is disgusting." A little giggle burst from her lips. My heart gave me a high five.

She was silent for a bit as we made slow progress along the table. She requested fruit instead of crackers to sample her cheeses with. I made adjustments as I added tastes to her plate.

"That's an amazing story. It must be something to know you're descended from him, from that kind of strength and fortitude," she paused, "but I guess all our ancestors had crazy strength and fortitude. They had to have, just to survive. But to be in the midst of all of it and build something so long-lasting is wild."

"Facts," I agreed.

"How does Whyte's play in?" She asked.

"Well. Around the same time, Benjamin White's family was building its own haberdashery and modiste business. It wasn't the same level of rise and grind, of course, but his grandfather, I guess, was sailing back and forth to Europe, bringing in the fabrics that were popular in good old England. You know, stolen silks from India and such." Another chuckle from Cassandra. I was beginning to formulate one-liners in my mind that might amuse her.

"Right, right. They were out there 'discovering' things," she said wryly.

"Exactly. Well, back home, it seems that some of the white folks that Whyte's was supplying...the irony of that is not lost on me...were getting wind of the 'exotic' fabrics offered by HeirLoom. And they wanted in. Godrick refused to share his contacts with Benjamin and refused to sell. The rivalry was born. They say Mozelle put a bullet in the backside of more than one Whyte who tried to burn them out of business while Godrick was at sea. She wasn't to be fucked with."

"Clearly." She took the plate I had prepared. "Thank you. It's wonderful to have such a rich family history and to actually *know* it. You must be incredibly proud."

"It's a hell of a legacy, certainly. I am proud to be part of it and to have the responsibility and privilege of carrying it. I'm the last of the line, you know. Gotta get married and make some babies soon."

What the hell made me say that? Cassandra choked on the tiny bit of gouda she had scooped and tasted. I took her plate and passed her a cloth napkin.

"I'm sorry. I don't know why I said that."

"Right. I'm fine." She said after she'd regained her composure. "You probably said it because it's true. You need an heir and a spare and all that, right?" She reached for the plate again, and I let her have it.

"Exactly. I was the spare. And look at me now." I tried to make light of the absolute worst part of my existence. Based on the look on Cassandra's face, the faint pity in her eyes, I hadn't done a good job. That pity was more than I could stand, so I changed the subject.

"What about your family? How'd you get so interested in design?" I'd heard the 45-second 'How did you come to apply for this position?' spiel that gave a bit about her background, but it was a highlight reel at best. It certainly hadn't provided real insight into what motivated her initial interest in fashion.

"I don't know anything about my family, honestly. I grew up in the system." She said it quickly, like she was trying to get past the factoid. "I usually tell people I'm adopted. It's less pity-inducing but just enough to make folks move on to another subject." She gave a little self-deprecating laugh.

"And it's not completely untrue. I spent my high school years in a stable foster home, the home that adopted my best friend."

"That sounds like an interesting story."

"Interesting when I tell it, maybe. But it was a lot when I was living it."

I nodded and opened my mouth to encourage her to go on with the telling of it. I wanted to know everything I could about her, a fact that I might unpack later, depending on how I felt about it.

But before I could offer a prompt, Juanita interrupted. Elizabeth stood nearby.

"There you are, Abraham. We've been looking all over for you." Unlikely, since I'd observed her talking with Ben Whyte for several minutes after I liberated Cassandra, a fact that I noted but didn't ask about.

"Luckily, you've found me." I sighed inwardly, resigned to return to business as usual. "Have you had the opportunity to officially meet Ms. Cassandra Williams, our executive creative director at HeirLoom?" I presented Cassandra. "Cassandra, this is Juanita Brookes and her daughter, Elizabeth."

Juanita extended a heavily jeweled hand, angled as if Cassandra were meant to kiss it. Cassandra threw a confused look my way before giving the tips of Juanita's fingers a little shake. Juanita raised an eyebrow and withdrew her hand.

"I haven't yet had the pleasure." Juanita drawled, wiggling her fingers as if to rid them of the contact. "Congratulations on such an exciting job. Everyone expected my Elizabeth to head up HeirLoom's first line, but we all agreed that it wouldn't seem appropriate, given her and Abraham's relationship. We wouldn't want the public to cry foul. Isn't that right?" She asked no one in particular.

Elizabeth, accustomed to her mother's machinations, responded. "Now, Mommy, I'm sure no one would have said a word. But we know that I was never in the running for that position." It was a decidedly noncommittal comment on the whole. She gave Cassandra a little wave. "It's nice to meet you, Cassandra. My mother fancies me a great designer just because we own Heritage. But the fashion bug only nibbled at my fingertips."

"Nonsense, dear, you have the most original concepts. Not everyone is meant for the drudgery of production. We need visionaries in the industry, don't you agree, Cassandra."

"Absolutely," Cassandra responded. She kept her response short, which I respected. She was smart enough to know she'd been caught in some bullshit and chose not to move too much for fear of sinking into it.

"Well, I'm sure Abe will be able to talk you into sharing your gifts with the world once you're married, dear." Juanita took on a decidedly smug look at the sound of Cassandra's quick inhalation. She was clearly surprised. Did she care that I was to be married? *Why do you care if she cares?* I had every intention of meeting those unofficial expectations, so why did I so desperately want to explore Cassandra's reaction? It was too much to think through while Juanita droned on.

She patted Elizabeth's hand and threw another once over at Cassandra. "Perhaps it would make sense for you and my Elizabeth to collaborate on this first line. It would make sense that Abe's wife be included, given her penchant for design."

"Um," Cassandra began, gathering herself and formulating a version of *fuck no* that wasn't overtly disrespectful to a woman more than old enough to be her mother.

"Now, Juanita, I'm sure you don't want to put the cart before the horse. I don't doubt that Elizabeth would like some input on where her affections and talents are applied," I stepped in before Cassandra needed to respond.

"Nonsense. If her mother doesn't know what's best for her, who does? Just as your father has your best interests at heart, Abraham," she paused, a sly look crawling across her face as she noted, "He and I have chatted several times, you know."

"Yes, I'm aware. And at the risk of disrespect, I am a full-grown man. My father plans his life. I plan mine."

An odd sound escaped Elizabeth, and I glanced her way to see panic growing in her eyes, something I didn't want, so I relented. "But, I'm sure we'll figure it all out. In the meantime, let's enjoy the rest of our afternoon." I turned to Cassandra, reluctant to set her free but recognizing that I needed to do so if I wanted to prevent the afternoon from disintegrating into an exercise of Juanita staking her claim all day.

I wanted to pull her away and explain...what, exactly? That I was all but promised to Elizabeth, a woman who I cared for like a friendly but distant cousin, but was madly attracted to Cassandra? What was I about to offer? A situationship before marriage? I wasn't about to risk this move for HeirLoom, and I wasn't a fuckboy.

Plus, Elizabeth wasn't a bad person and I didn't want to upset her. We'd known each other for years, played together as children and pre-teens, and connected socially on rare occasions when I'd come home from boarding school and college. The circle of wealthy black teenagers and young adults in the upstate area was close-knit. She'd been part of that circle since I could remember. She'd been there when Godrick died along with Vince and Warwick. I wouldn't purposefully cause her distress.

"Cassandra. It's been a pleasure chatting outside of the office. I hope you have a restful weekend. We have another busy week ahead of us."

She lifted her hand with the perfectly reasonable expectation of a parting handshake.

I hadn't touched her all afternoon; had held myself in check the entire time we walked, through each pass and return of her cheese plate. *Inhale.* I took her hand in mine.

It was a mistake. Sparks lit, her hand trembled in mine, my dick rose. *Fuck. Exhale, nigga.* I exhaled slowly, willing every part of me to be cool.

It was a discomfort built purely on pleasure, and I knew I'd held on a beat too long when her odd eyes dropped to our clasped hands.

"I'm ready." She breathed the words, and my dick jumped again at the prospect of hearing her whisper those words against my ear when she was slick with need for me.

I walked away from her with my hands in my pockets, an unforgivably rude posture as I was escorting both Elizabeth and Juanita but less rude, I figured, than showing off the chubby I'd grown for another woman.

Chapter 10

ABE.

Strolling around the room with Elizabeth was starkly different than doing the same with Cassandra. Objectively, I couldn't pinpoint the difference. They were both intelligent, beautiful women, and while I would never consider women interchangeable, it galled me that I didn't have the same visceral connection with the woman I should have it with. Though, perhaps that was for the best. Perhaps emotions and visceral responses shouldn't be guiding factors when making long-term plans.

Elizabeth opened our conversation haltingly. "I'm sorry about my mother, as usual."

"You shouldn't worry about it," I responded automatically. "She's just looking after you. She wants the best for you." My eyes were skimming the room, but I was definitely *not* looking for Cassandra.

"She does. And she's decided that's you." I shifted my attention to her in time to glimpse a play of emotions on her face that I couldn't quite interpret.

"Do you disagree?" I was intrigued. She sounded less than enthused about an outcome that was, for the most part, a foregone conclusion.

"I don't...," she said softly, hesitantly.

We had made our way to the area where I'd first seen Cassandra. I handed Elizabeth around so she could settle herself at one of the many bistro tables positioned to enjoy the views. I took a seat facing her. Objectively, she and Cassandra resembled each other. Their warm skin tone was within half a shade of each other; both wore their hair long and straight. Their features were similar, the full lips and wide eyes combining to make both women quite beautiful. Elizabeth had several inches on Cassandra and perhaps five years, as did I, but there was no reason that I could put my finger on that would account for why I was obsessing over Cassandra and unmoved by Elizabeth.

It made no sense, and that irritated me. I had to be responding to the fact that Cassandra was off-limits; otherwise, I could address whatever this pull was and move on. I'd felt strong attractions for women before, and I'd respectfully, discreetly gone about addressing those attractions. The fact that I couldn't do so now was simply grating on my nerves.

"I understand if you want to have a thing with her before...," her words trailed off.

I felt the shock register on my face. "A thing with who? And before what?"

She scoffed, "With Cassandra. Before we," she faltered, "I don't know. Commit. Become official. Whatever."

"Elizabeth," I began.

"No. You don't have to do that. We both know what's expected of us. But...," she trailed off again. She wasn't normally this hesitant. Quiet, yes, but not unsure.

"But, what," I asked, curious now to see what words she would put around our situation. We'd never really talked about it explicitly, both of us content to float along on a sea of expectations. But now, I suspected she was feeling the same change in the currents that I was. Things were on track to come to a head soon. We needed to address the elephant in the room.

"But I don't want you to be forced or to feel trapped. I understand if you want her. She's beautiful. I get it if you need to," she waved a hand, "get her out of your system."

I felt an eyebrow twitch. I forced it into stillness. Get her out of my system? It was too close to what I'd just been thinking, and the double whammy landed in my groin.

"I know you have needs," she continued, "and we've never really talked about it. As long as you're discreet, I mean, as long as we're both discreet, there's no reason we can't have a perfectly workable relationship."

I was intrigued despite myself. What was she saying? I shifted in my chair to face her more fully.

"Are you offering an open marriage, Elizabeth?"

She flinched slightly, and I kicked myself for being so direct. I reached out to cover her hand with mine. "I'm sorry. Continue."

Dark brown eyes, lovely but unremarkable, rose to catch mine. She turned her hand so that rather than covering hers, I was now holding it. It was impossible not to notice the lack of spark, the lack of electricity.

"I'm not completely naive," she began, "though Mother would like to think I am." She shifted in her seat, slid her palm along mine before completely breaking contact, and pushed her hair behind an ear. "I know you don't love me; I don't love you either. But we like each other well enough, I think. I also know we're both bred for responsibility." Her lip twisted.

I'd never seen or heard Elizabeth whisper a word of rebellion, so that little sneer was tantamount to her screaming her frustrations to the world.

There was a lot to unpack in that speech. I'd known her for as long as I could remember. I cared for her, but she was right that there was no love there, nothing akin to romantic love, at least. But she was right that love didn't factor into this decision. This was about responsibility, legacy, and Black aristocracy. We were building generational wealth here. There was no room for personal wants. Maybe my kids could have it, at least some of them. But I didn't. I was all that was left. My decisions would set the course for the future of our entire family line.

But still, I wanted to know, "Are you not on board with this?" I asked, momentarily putting aside the fact that I may not be fully onboard either.

"I am. It's a good move for both families, both companies, and for us personally," she responded. "I just don't want you to feel forced or trapped."

"It's rare that I can be forced into anything." I quipped. I didn't let my mind ponder the second half of her description because feeling trapped was something I could definitely identify with.

"Says the CEO who never planned to be CEO," Elizabeth said.

"Pivoting to meet responsibilities doesn't equate to being forced." It was an automatic response, one that I had crafted to address my own early feelings that were exactly aligned with being forced, trapped, and unable to see my way clear to a different path. It was the only way I could survive the time I spent after Godrick's death plodding through an MBA program, and forcing my brain to reshape itself to process the business ins and outs of our corporation. It was the least I could do as penance for making Godrick come out that night.

Eventually, it had become easier to think of my current path as chosen, one born of responsibility to my family but more to Godrick and doing all I could to preserve his dreams. To preserve him through that which he loved. Now, it was second nature. I almost believed that I was happy.

She chuffed, "Pivoting. I see. Well, it appears that I'm part of that pivot," she gave a wry little laugh.

"Elizabeth. You know this isn't an arranged marriage." This was the first time she and I had spoken so openly, and she flinched slightly. "We don't have to move forward with it," I offered in what I hoped was a comforting tenor.

"Isn't it, though?" She asked head tilted. "I don't know what the messaging is in your home, but in mine, it's very clear." She sipped the glass of wine we had snagged on our way to the tables and turned her attention to the river.

While she gazed at the lazy movement of the water, clearly lost in her thoughts, my musings drifted to her suggestion that I get Cassandra out of my system. Her skating around an open marriage was interesting, but a non-starter. Regardless of whether or not I was blindingly in love with my wife, I would never be with someone else under that covenant. Whatever marriage I cultivated, it wouldn't include giving ourselves to other people.

But before the marriage? Before the engagement even? Discreetly? With Elizabeth's blessing?

The fantasy took hold for a moment before I ruthlessly burst that bubble. Cassandra was still the lynchpin to the success of this line, and I had no room for error there. Between my dad's gleeful anticipation of my failure and my own need to succeed, Ms. Williams remained firmly off-limits.

Chapter 11

ABE.

The conversation with Elizabeth at the winery had been swirling in my head since that event two weeks ago. It was still at the forefront when I walked into this board meeting, which might explain why I felt like I was playing catchup when I finally tuned back into the conversation. I internally kicked myself for having let my attention wander when I realized the discussion had veered to focus on Heritage's new line.

This wasn't out of the ordinary, obviously. The board had been made well aware of the new venture, and the members had signed on, if somewhat reluctantly. Ultimately, the final decision regarding the pursuit of the effort was mine as CEO. However, my role as CEO was ultimately up to the board. I had done my vetting and my schmoozing. I had provided the numbers...the data...to uphold the decision and we had reached an agreement. Which was why I was so *fucking* confused as to why we were discussing this shit again as if we hadn't already gone well down the road. It was too fucking late to turn back now; too much had been invested in terms of both time and money.

"We may have been too hasty with this decision. It's a risky area, and the economy has tightened. Investments in luxury items aren't where they used to be." Corbin Abrams offered this bit of blinding insight.

"We're investing one point five million in this, correct? I stand by the belief that this money could be better deployed to improve our supply chain. Develop new warehousing and transport systems that won't be at the mercy of international whims." Janice Dupree, unsurprisingly, returned to a song she had been singing for months. She wasn't wrong. It was just that investing in warehousing was a one-time investment with a single source of payout. This line, if successful, when successful, would create returns and a new line of revenue that would dwarf anything we could create by following Janice's suggestion.

I listened as Corbin, Janice, and the other members of the board went back and forth, debating a dead subject. I glanced at Gavin Finley, one of the two members of the twelve-person board that I had recruited rather than my father. The other of those two members, Maksym Shea, wasn't here today, which was an annoyance. I would have appreciated his insight as to why everyone was returning to this topic a month after the vote. Gavin caught my eye and shrugged. He was as lost as I was.

I cut through the chatter with a question, "Can someone explain to me why we're talking about this now?" The question itself was innocuous enough. The tone of my voice made it clear that I was fucking pissed.

"Now, Abraham," Horatio James began. Horatio was a long-time friend of my father, a well-known, well-heeled real estate mogul who owned a disgusting amount of residential property in New York and New Jersey. He was ridiculously wealthy, though much of his profit was earned at the sake of his tenants, who did not enjoy nearly the same quality of residence that Mr. James did.

Horatio continued in that shit-eating smarmy ass tone of his. "There's no need to be short. We're just revisiting."

"To what end, Horatio?" I used his first name purposefully. He was one of those old-schoolers who thought that no matter how old I was, I'd never be his peer. Forcing him to respond to what I knew he'd interpret as a faint disrespect was petty, but with my mind stretched out over Cassandra, I was feeling petty. "You do realize that we've hired the executive director, built out the facilities, and begun the marketing? Please help me understand what, exactly, we're revisiting." My voice was soft, my focus unwaveringly on him. No one could call me disrespectful, but there was no mistaking where I landed on the issue.

"Of course. We're not interested in pulling back. But perhaps there are some...guardrails...of sorts that we could put up. We know you're very interested in moving the company in a more diversified direction. We're just eager to see the outcome."

I felt the heat rising with each word that tripped and slipped from his mouth. This was the same shit the board had been doing since I'd been voted in, officially, as CEO five years ago. I'd spent two years on the MBA followed by three years to inundate myself in the company, trying to cram what Godrick had been fed all his life into an appetizer portion of time. When the vote had come around again, after my father had retained his position as CEO five years beyond his expected time, I had been quietly terrified. Terrified that I would be selected and terrified that I wouldn't be.

Being voted in as CEO at my age with my experience had opened the floodgates for criticism. Criticism of my father...surely he had shoved my nomination down the throats of the board members; criticism of me...how dare I even accept the nomination with so little experience. That vote had also come with a revisit of Godrick's death, the media taking the opportunity of my potential election to the coveted CEO seat to drag out all the details of losing Godrick. They'd held him up as a paragon...perfect in all ways, especially for the job of leading Heritage through the next era. I didn't disagree with them at all. He had been perfect for the job.

But they had voted me in. I never knew, and didn't really care, how much my father had to do with it, his desire to keep the company in family hands at all levels constantly warring with his inexplicable desire to see me fail. And since they had voted me in, I wanted them to get off my fucking back and let me do the damn job. Because what they refused to admit, refused to even acknowledge, was that I was good at it.

Three years and I had already put practices in place to increase our bottom line in all our domestic markets with plans to adapt and extend into our international markets. I had enabled our sales teams and expansion teams so they were significantly more productive, putting new business in our portfolio at a pace we hadn't seen in a decade, and still, I had to deal with their shit. The bit of deference they may have been afforded five years ago had been burned to shit when I realized that no matter what I did, I wouldn't catch a break from any of them.

So, as I listened to old-ass, liver-spotted Horatio James talking about guardrails and guarantees, I steeled myself for the shoe that he was about to drop. Because while I might be CEO, I was there by their good graces, and as much as it galled me to admit, I wanted to stay here. I let my eyes close and open in a slow blink.

"I think we would all be more comfortable if we had some timeline around which we could expect some results," he spread his hands and cast his cloudy but still shrewd gaze around the room. "Do you all agree?"

The question was clearly rhetorical. The speed with which the majority of the heads in the room started nodding made it clear that at least several of the members had been having this conversation outside of this meeting space.

"A timeline," I repeated, feeling the setup being put in place but powerless to stop it. "What, exactly, did you have in mind?"

"Well," Corbin spoke up again. I shifted my gaze to him. "We were just thinking about some deadline, maybe a date by when the line will launch, and then we can see how it's performing, whether it's being well-received, and decide whether to keep moving forward or not."

"Yes, Corbin. I am familiar with the concept of a timeline, but thank you for the explanation." That man had the good graces to look chastened. Keeping the sneer off my face by sheer dent of will, I turned my attention back to the board as a whole.

"Again, I ask, what did you have in mind? Since you feel the need to put parameters in place despite excessive evidence of my ability to lead this company to the money, please, enlighten me as to what they are."

"The CEO review and vote is in a year, well, thirteen months." My heart thudded in my chest at Janice's comment. They couldn't possibly...

"That's just after fall/winter New York Fashion Week, isn't it?" *You fucking know it is, Horatio.* "I would think that would be an excellent deadline. You are planning to show there, aren't you?"

Horatio was a savvy businessman, more than savvy...he was fucking brilliant at business even if he was shady as fuck. I knew beyond a shadow of a doubt that he had done enough research, probably over scotch with my father, to know that a year to bring a line from inception to showing in New York's Fashion Week was damn near impossible. Even getting on the roster for the show would be nearly impossible. We had planned to launch with the September show, which would give us an additional five or six months...still a tight timeline. A year, technically eleven and a half months, was a death wish.

"We had our sights on the spring show next September, actually."

"Oh, posh," Juanita Brookes spoke up. Yep, HeirLoom board meetings were yet another opportunity to engage with my monster-in-law-to-be. Getting her and most of my father's lackeys out of the room was on my long-term agenda. Half the reason HeirLoom was stagnating now was because most of them couldn't be bothered to keep up with the times. They were all blindingly accomplished, legends in the community, but change was life, and several of them weren't thriving. They'd put their own businesses in the hands of the next generation and were now spending their golden years keeping HeirLoom in the dark ages.

Juanita droned on. "Pulling a line together for winter is perfectly doable. It'll be a fun challenge for, what was her name...Cassandra."

"I'm not interested in fun challenges, Juanita." Her eyes narrowed. I was enjoying this calling my elders by their first names. And there wasn't shit they could do about it. "I'm interested in taking the fashion world by storm and further solidifying HeirLoom's name in the history books."

"Well, we can do both, can't we? Or are you and your team not up to it."

"Listen, I think we should slow down a little bit," Gavin said, seeking to save the day and put the breaks on what was shaping up to be more of a setup than I could have imagined. "I don't know much about the fashion side of things, but it seems like getting a whole line developed to show in less than a year is more than a little challenge. We don't want to set ourselves up for a less-than-positive outcome, do we?"

"Well, I do know quite a bit about the fashion industry," Juanita snapped. "Heritage has created and launched multiple lines. It can certainly be done in a year. Will it be challenging? Of course," she fluttered her fingers, dismissing that challenge as trivial, "but it should not be beyond their scope." She gave a concise nod. "It is doable."

I looked around the room. *So ain't none of y'all gonna mention the trash-ass reviews Heritage's last lines received?* I rolled my eyes. *Punk asses.*

"Juanita, be that as it may, we're hoping for a certain level of...impact...for this line. It's imperative that it be exceedingly well received if it's to do for HeirLoom what we need it to do," Gavin offered. *My boy.*

"Are you implying that Heritage's work is not well-received?" If Juanita's right eyebrow rose any higher, it would disappear into the melted lace of her hairline.

"Certainly not that. And I'm sure you're right, Juanita." Horatio patted her hand and then turned to encompass the full table. "But I respect your concerns, Abraham. If your team isn't able to meet that deadline, we understand. So be it." He leaned back in his chair. He was a heavy man, and the chair gave a little creak in protest as he swiveled slightly.

"We will hold the CEO deliberations and have the vote based on whatever information is available, as we always do."

Well, that was a veiled threat if ever I heard one.

"Good. I'm glad you all understand." I was ready to adjourn the meeting then and there. I'd spent the last ten years twisting myself into the man I needed to be for this role, but there were times when my store of patience and boardroom professionalism ran low. Now was one of those times. I needed to get the fuck out of here.

Chapter 12

ABE.

The sounds of the city acted as white noise as I made my way on foot from the Drake Hotel, where we'd hosted the board meeting, back to the office. I was still pissed. But I was also crystal clear on the fact that if I wanted to retain my position as CEO of HeirLoom, I could do nothing less than produce a showstopping line by March.

The grain of panic that sprouted to life when I heard *fall-winter fashion week* had taken firm root. I'd needed to walk to keep it from blossoming into something paralyzing and unproductive. To manage it, I was mentally outlining all the steps that we'd need to complete to meet that deadline, from finalizing concepts to sketching, design, and patterning. The time between sampling and production would be mercilessly squeezed if we were going to make this happen.

In-two-three-four...out-two-three-four...

And breathing. I was fucking trying to breathe myself into the *gotdamn* moment. I was holding the anxiety at bay with strategy, order, and breath. Because if I gave this shit just a minute to settle, I'd fucking lose it.

Making the spring show in September had been a comfortable goal, giving us well over a year to settle in, make decisions, and take a leisurely, thoughtful route toward launch.

The winter show in March was ridiculous. Foolish. Damn near impossible.

The walk from the Drake to HeirLoom was unsatisfyingly short, and I arrived in no better mood than I'd been in when I left the meeting. Dare I say I was in an even *worse* mood, which was not improved when I arrived at Cassandra's office to find it empty.

"Mr. Walker," Tamra Melvin, Cassandra's recently hired assistant director, greeted me as I stood outside Cassandra's glass-fronted office, staring as if I could make her appear behind her desk out of thin air. "Is there something I can do for you?"

"Where is Ms. Williams?" Tamra jumped. I could hear the growl in my voice, recognized that it sounded as if I were here to scold Cassandra. It wasn't a good look for her in front of her team. I tried to remove the emotion from my voice. "My apologies, Ms. Melvin...."

"Tamra," she corrected.

I nodded, "Tamra. Do you know where I can find Ms. Williams? I have an urgent matter to discuss with her."

"Oh, um, she went home." I waited. Nothing more was forthcoming.

"Did she say when she'd be back?" And then another thought, "Was she sick?" A new niggle formed in my chest as I waited for Tamra to respond.

"Noooo," she drew the word out, apparently giving my questions serious thought. "She didn't seem sick. Maybe worried.

But I don't know her that well yet, so I can't really say. But if I had to say, I would say worried. Shook. But not sick. At least, I don't think so…"

"Okay," I held up a hand to stop the word vomit. "Thank you, Tamra. If you see her, please let her know I stopped by and would like to speak with her."

"Oh, okay. Of course. Absolutely."

Did she just flutter her lashes at me? I may have to limit my time in the workroom after all.

I turned and left, headed to my office. Instead, I detoured back toward the building exit. I rang Shanice as I walked, "Please send me Ms. Williams' home address."

Chapter 13

CASSANDRA.

"**S**top! Killmonger! Stop!" *Fuck me! How do I get myself into this shit?* "Killmonger, stop!"

I was panting and out of breath, running across the fucking dog park, trying to catch Destiny's little yip-yip dog before one of these *real* dogs ate her ass.

Fuck it. I stopped, wholly out of breath, too old for this shit, hands on my knees, damn near wheezing. And I thought I was in decent fucking shape, but clearly, that was just me stroking my own out-of-touch ego. Cause bay-bee, I was about to die right now.

The dog park was fenced in, so I wasn't worried about Killmonger...the most aspirational name ever...actually getting out. I really was more concerned about her starting some shit she couldn't finish with one of these other actual dogs. I had her in my sights, though. She was fine at the moment. I could take a second to try to catch my fucking breath. And she had clearly worn her own self out with all that bullshit running. She was collapsed on her tummy in the middle of the green space, her four little legs covered in curly chocolate hair sprawled out at all angles. Her little tongue was hanging out, and her belly was doing its thing, trying to draw air.

"Serves you right," I told her as I approached. "All that running and for what?"

Her tail started wagging as I got closer. I stopped.

Don't you dare. I thought it, then whispered it in my most threatening mommie dearest voice because Killmonger was doing that puppy thing. You know, where they crouch and bounce, crouch and bounce, so one minute she was laying there like a rug, and now she was primed to dash if I took another step toward her.

Fuck my whole entire life because I took that step, and she took off again, and so did I. This time, though, she was running straight for the gate, and some asshole idiot was standing there leashing their dog with the gate standing wide open.

"Close the gate!" I tried to yell it, but I was so winded it came out distressingly breathy, like I was trying to seduce the damn gate holder. "Close the fucking gate!" I tried again.

I must have looked like a complete idiot, but Killmonger was on a mission to win this particular game of tag. The asshole at the gate looked up just as Killmonger got to her and tried to swing the gate closed.

"Bitch! What the fuck is wrong with you!" I yelled as I dashed past her in hot pursuit of Destiny's pride and joy. Killmonger jetted down the sidewalk. The gate bitch's *I'm so sorry* was lost behind me as I followed.

Please, God, let her stay on the sidewalk. Please, please, please. I could feel hot tears gathering behind my eyes at the thought of having to tell Destiny that I had lost her baby because now I couldn't even see her. There were so many people. Why the hell were so many people out in the middle of the fucking day? Why was she so damn little?

"Killmonger! Come here!" I called her again.

I was just about to run out of steam when I saw God himself walking toward me.

Well, it wasn't God. But it was Abe Walker carrying a squirming bundle of chocolate brown fur in his arms. So, yeah, maybe not God, but damn sure godlike as far as I was concerned.

"Is this yours?" He asked, standing there like this shit was normal. Looking and smelling good as fuck, *again*, while I looked like this. Out of breath, sweaty, dark spots crawling down my back and under my arms, hem of my pants filthy. And grinning like an idiot because he had the damn dog in his arms.

I pushed my hair out of my face and reached for her. And immediately attached her leash to the hook on her harness. I'd let her off to run free in the dog park. I hadn't realized how big it was until I'd let her off leash and saw her playing next to the big dogs. That may not have been a problem, but then she started running that little yippy mouth of hers. The couple of pitties and their cousins that were there ignored her little ass, but there was another taller, shaggier dog that proved less indulgent. That's when I started making it my business to retrieve her. And then, madness ensued.

I was just happy I'd kept all my items on my person at the park. My little fanny pack had my keys, phone, debit card, doggie snacks, doggie bags, and a handy hook where I'd stashed the leash instead of laying it on the table where I had been enjoying the scant shade while Killmonger romped.

"Yes, thank you so much," the words poured out of me on a grateful breath. "She's really fast to have such short legs."

"You're pretty fast to have such short legs, too," he teased. "You were gaining on her for a little bit, but then she cut the corner on you."

"Wait, you were watching me chase her?"

"Not so much watching as being an observant good Samaritan who saw an opportunity to help."

"Mmhmm." I eyed him while I nuzzled my nose into Killmonger's fur. No, not fur, hair. Because she was hypoallergenic and all that. And soft and snuggly, too.

It suddenly occurred to me that we were nowhere near the office, where I should definitely be right now. "What are you doing out here? You're not looking for me, are you?" I'd been checking my messages and had just seen Tamra's email that Abe had stopped by my office before Killmonger went on her run. But what could possibly be so important that he would come looking for me? That was ridiculous.

I had just opened my mouth to retract the question when he said, "Yes, actually."

My mouth remained open.

"I checked your office first," he offered. He didn't seem particularly eager to say more, so whatever was going on must not be particularly pressing. He was rubbing Killmonger's paws, which were hanging over my arm, which meant every so often, his warm finger brushed my forearm.

"A reasonable move," I nodded. When he didn't say anything more, I prompted him, "So, what's up?"

The puppy in my arms reached up to lick my chin. I stretched away. She was cute as everything, but she still ate shit. "Stop, Killmonger," I cooed, scratching behind her ears, "I'm glad you're okay, silly little girl."

"Wait. The dog's name is Killmonger."

It was a statement, but I felt like he wanted my confirmation. I gave it.

"It's a girl dog?" I nodded, laughing a little at his phrasing. 'Girl dog' coming out of his grown-man mouth in that grown-man voice tickled me.

"Is that a problem for you?" I asked, placing her on the ground after verifying again that her leash was securely attached to her collar.

He grinned, "Not at all." And I was momentarily stunned. I hadn't seen that grin in a decade, I realized. And it had lost none of its impact. In fact, it had aged into something more potent, like fine wine... *or cheese*. I smiled to myself.

"What are Killmonger's pronouns?" He asked, kneeling to chuck her under the chin when she bounced toward him. He glanced up at me, and for just a second, his eyes caught that glint I was beginning to think I had imagined.

I watched, feeling slightly confused, as Abe Walker, CEO of a billion-dollar company, crouched in his eight thousand dollar suit to play...no, scratch that, pick up and snuggle this little, *forgive my internalized misogyny*, girly-ass, dirty-footed dog who was, at this very moment, leaving brown streaks of something on his lavender shirt. But he was straight up whispering sweet nothings in her ear. When he looked at me again, the grin had faded, but a comfortable smile lingered.

I sighed because what else could I do? It was patently unfair, but here we were. This puppy-loving, dimple-smiled, boyishly handsome Abe existed within the overly proper, responsibility-driven, sexy-asshole Abe. *Huh.*

I was happy to see it. I had begun to really doubt my memories.

"Well?"

Well, what? Oh! Pronouns! "Well, we technically don't know, of course," I responded seriously, "so we use 'she' and 'they.'" I shrugged and laughed, "We'll update that if we learn something different."

He still hadn't put Killmonger down. Now, she was settling herself in his arms, looking for all the world like it was the most comfortable place for a nap. I suspected she was right.

"So seriously, why were you looking for me." Best to steer the conversation back to work and all its intricacies instead of focusing on what it might be like to nap in Abe Walker's arms. Nothing good could come of those musings.

I watched, fascinated, as his face transformed from puppy-hugging Abe to work Abe. The smile faded, and the light in his eyes was replaced with a new one, something darker and more intense. Could it be that this version of Abe holding a sleeping puppy was even sexier?

"We have work to do. The board is pushing for the winter New York launch."

I felt my eyes go round. "Winter? What? Why?" The winter show was held in very early spring...February or March...and featured designs for the upcoming winter season.

Similarly, the spring shows were held around September and featured designs for the upcoming warmer weather. Designing for the winter show meant we needed to have it all up and ready to go in a little less than a year. It was already the end of March now. And winter designs were more involved, more complicated...just more.

He started walking back the way I had come, still carrying Killmonger.

"It's an internal issue," he said. "Nothing you need to worry about."

"Nothing I need to worry about? What does that mean? You're pushing my timeline up by five months, almost six, and telling me it's nothing for me to worry about?" I stopped in the middle of the sidewalk and planted my hands on my hips. I could see Mother Madison in my mind's eye, hands on hips, eyes wide and incredulous, begging Margeaux and me to explain why she shouldn't whip our little asses for whatever fill-in-the-blank offense. We learned that she had little to no bite, but ooowee her bark was something else.

Anyway, there I stood, hands akimbo, cramming to understand how he didn't think a thirty percent reduction in time to launch was something I needed to worry about.

"Calm down."

I felt my head whip back and forth because *who could he possibly be talking to?*

"Calm down?" I shook my head. "First, my guy, I'm calm as fuck considering the bomb you just dropped on me. Second, how much calmer can I even be? I'm not hollering. I'm not yelling. I'm not cussing you the fuck out. I'm maintaining my professionalism." He looked at me dubiously. He couldn't deny my words, but the tenor of my voice was at distinct odds.

"You're doing okay, I guess."

I wanted to smack him in the back of the head. "You've got to be kidding me." I shook my head in disbelief. "Can you at least tell me *why* I'm losing this time?"

"No."

"Why not?"

"It's internal."

"I see." I stared at him, incredulous. "And if we don't make the launch in this laughably short amount of time?"

"Well. I cease to be CEO of HeirLoom, the new CEO, whoever that might be, is likely to pull the plug on the project, and you'll lose both your position and the opportunity to launch the line that will make you a household name.

Chapter 14

Cassandra.

He delivered that information on an easy breath, like losing the seat as CEO of his family's company wasn't worth more than that. Like me losing this shot at my whole life's dream wasn't worth more than that.

I looked at him more closely, finally noting the tension in his jawline, the stress around his eyes.

"Abe, what's happened? I don't understand."

"Honestly, neither do I," he exhaled a heavy breath and started walking again. I followed because this man was dealing with some crazy shit. Also, he still had Destiny's dog. I don't even think he realized it.

"This way," I made a left at the block in front of the dog park to head to my apartment. I was thinking about the feasibility of what he was asking.

"Abe, I don't know if we can make that timeline. I mean, I can't imagine getting from where we are now, I mean, we just started seriously brainstorming...through production in what, ten months?" I started counting on my fingers.

"Eleven. We kinda have to," he tossed me a wry look. "I want to keep my company," he said with a shrug.

"Well, come on. We can talk it through at my place. We're only a couple of blocks away. I just came home to take Killmonger for her walk." I didn't know why, but I felt compelled to fill the silence. "She's a puppy, so she still needs that midday walk. I usually just take her around the block, which is clearly what I should have done today." I tossed a reproving glare at Killmonger, who gave zero fucks, lost as she was in Lala Land. "But the weather was so nice I thought I'd give her a minute to run around and stretch her little baby legs."

"How long have you had her?" He hefted her in his arms, content to carry her while she slept.

"Oh, she's not mine. She belongs to my girlfriend, Destiny. She's out of town for the week, and I'm babysitting. She's sweet." I ruffled her hair a bit. "She's also a lot of work."

"Do you think you'll get one?"

"A dog? Mmm. I doubt it. I'm more of a cat person. You know, they're super affectionate when they trust you, but they have firm boundaries that they don't mind enforcing, plus they have an intrinsic appreciation for individuality and independence." I shrugged. "That's dope to me. I like dogs, too; they're just so needy. It's like the choice of having a child or a really great friend. Right now, I'm all about the really great friend."

"I never thought about it like that."

"Like now. If she were a kitten, I would be at work instead of here, walking her. And you'd have found me that much sooner."

"True. But if she were a kitten, I may have never met her, and that would be a shame."

I bumped his arm with my shoulder lightly so I wouldn't disturb his baggage. "Clearly, she agrees. I don't know that I've seen her sleep that soundly outside of her bed."

"Well, I have a relaxing vibe, or so I've been told."

"Oh, you just put the women right to sleep, huh?" *Shit*. That could be construed any number of ways now, couldn't it? Flirting with Abe was not at all on my agenda.

I didn't look his way because I didn't want to know how he chose to interpret that little slip. But I could feel his eyes on me, nonetheless.

"This is me." A moment later, I motioned toward a brownstone walkup. He followed me inside, shifting Killmonger slightly in his arms. He stopped in the foyer of the building, eyeing the detailing of the space.

"This is beautifully renovated."

"Thanks. I wish it were mine, but I'm just renting. I'm on the top two floors." We crossed the foyer to the beautiful staircase nestled against the wall on the left side of the room, leaving the large foyer open, where a couple of comfortable seating areas were clustered.

"How many people live here?" He asked.

"There's one other tenant, but I haven't met them. That door leads to their space," I motioned. "They have this floor and the basement, so they get the ground-level outdoor space, but I have a great rooftop patio." I paused before we climbed the stairs. "That door is a half bathroom, and there's the inside access to the screen porch." I pointed to a set of French doors leading to the porch that spanned the front of the house. "So, yeah, these are the common areas. Or where people wait if you don't want them all up in your space." I laughed and motioned him to follow me.

It occurred to me then that I was bringing Abe into my space willingly. The bomb he had dropped fried my brain so much that leading him here so we could get to work as quickly as possible had been my only thought. Now I was realizing that he'd be in my home...I glanced over my shoulder...yep, still looking and smelling good as hell.

I sighed. Once we got up there, I would just grab a few things, and we could take this party back to the office. There was no reason we needed to stay here.

He followed me up the stairs into another small foyer. Here, I unlocked the door to my part of the house.

"Woah, this is dope as fuck." I grinned at the shock and delight on Abe's face when he walked in.

"It is, isn't it? I love living here."

I left him there, taking it all in. I hadn't been here long. So it was still new enough to me that I knew exactly how the space hit for fresh eyes.

I lived in a beautifully restored brownstone. My main level had floor-to-ceiling windows that let light pour into an open space that combined kitchen, dining, and living areas. The gourmet kitchen was on point, making the tedium of cooking far more enjoyable. There was a small bedroom that I'd set up as an office behind a glass-paned door and a half bath behind another closed door.

What he couldn't see was the upstairs that housed two more bedrooms with en suite baths. It was a dreamy apartment. Even better when I learned that the woman I was renting it from was

Black. It made my heart sing to know that if I had to shell out this amount of money for rent it was going in the pockets of someone who looks like me. *I aint mad. Get your paper, sis.*

We'd talked briefly, and she'd agreed to point me in the right direction of some good investments when I was ready to buy something of my own. I liked the idea of splitting the rent with someone else, and if I could find a spot to renovate like this one into a two-family unit, I'd jump on it.

He finally left his spot by the door and walked further in, still cradling Killmonger. I moved to take her from him, but he shifted and growled at me.

"Okay, okay." I held my hands up in surrender. "She's your dog now. But you'll have to explain it all to Destiny when she gets back. I want no parts of it."

"I don't know this Destiny person. But I will fight for my dog," he declared. Another laugh spilled from me, and one side of his mouth quirked up in response.

"Do you care if I sit on the couch with her? Do you let her on the furniture?"

"Yeah, that's cool. I'm going to run and change real quick. This outfit was not made for dog chasing." I looked down at my silk slacks, high-waisted with a wide belt and wide-legged; they were both stylish and incredibly comfortable. I hoped they'd come clean easily. I was less worried about the halter I'd paired with them. It was also silk, so there was that, but the material was a vibrant print that was more forgiving than the cream slacks.

"Make yourself at home. Um, there's beer in the fridge if you want." With that, I ran upstairs to do as I'd said.

Upstairs, I stripped as quickly as possible, changing into the work-from-home uniform of yoga pants and matching dri-fit tank in a cerulean blue that always made me smile. I pee'd because that was a lot of running and tamed my hair, brushing it back into the ponytail it had been in before Killmonger's amazing race. At the last minute, I switched the traditional yoga pants for a loose-fitting pair of lounge pants. I didn't want my ass on full display.

"Alright, Cass," I addressed myself in the mirror. "This man is not here for you. He is not your man. He is your boss and engaged to another woman. Your job is to do your job. And maybe be his friend." *Because it looked like he was carrying the weight of the world.*

When I got back downstairs, Abe was sitting smack in the middle of the sofa, long legs spread and braced wide in that quintessential male sitting posture. One arm was laid along the back of the sofa; the other was still wrapped around Killmonger, his hand cupping her bottom and securing her against his chest. He was slouched so that she was mostly flat on his chest, and his head lay against the back of the sofa. There was half a beer on a coaster on the coffee table.

"Oh, so you took that to heart, huh?" I laughed as I walked back into the room. He didn't respond, and as I got closer, I realized he had fallen asleep.

Huh. How about that? Right there in his suit, too. I hated sleeping in restrictive clothing. It was one of the reasons that midday naps rarely happened for me. If I was going to sleep, I needed to strip down and get comfortable.

So, now, what?

I stood for a moment, contemplating. Should I wake him? Take the dog so he could sleep more peacefully? Cover them both?

In the end, I decided to snap a picture because they were so fucking cute and leave them both be. I went to the kitchen and began to stir up something quick and simple...a pot of spaghetti. I diced onions and peppers to sautee in the ground beef and put a jar of spaghetti sauce, a can of fire-roasted tomatoes, and the extra spices I preferred in a pot to simmer. I could make sauce from scratch, but I could also doctor the hell out of a jar and make you think I'd been slicing and dicing all day.

While the beef, onions, and spices sauteed, I went to the dining room table, which was my actual, functional office space, and started thinking about the rework of my production plan to meet this new, frankly terrifying, deadline. I'd need to get that admin in place today. I already knew who I was going to hire, I just hadn't pulled the trigger.

I shot an email off to HR, letting them know that we needed to get Adam in as soon as possible. Adam had been the last person to interview. In fact, we'd just had his interview two days ago. I was glad I had waited on this one...none of the other candidates quite hit the mark...but as soon as I met Adam, I'd known he was the one. Over the course of the interview he'd nailed, it became clear that I was absolutely correct. He wasn't necessarily passionate about fashion, but he was passionate about project management, organization, and efficiency, and that's what I needed. And he was funny. I needed that, too.

I also alerted Tamra that we'd need to round out the rest of the team within the week.

Done with that, I added the browned beef, onions, and peppers to the sauce, checked the flavor, punched it up with a little more heat, and left it to bubble. I put on a pot of water to boil so I could drop noodles whenever Abe woke up.

And then I just stood chewing my lip because now, what the hell was I supposed to do? I had this man in my place, knocked out snoring, taking up space and oxygen. But he clearly needed it. Having putzed around him cooking and shooting off email, the shock and awe of having him here was wearing off. He was *snoring* for fuck's sake. Lightly, but still.

What would I normally be doing if he wasn't here? *I'd be working.* Okay, so work. *Fair enough. I damn sure have plenty to do.*

So, I settled at my dining table to consolidate eighteen months of work into less than a year.

Chapter 15

ABE.

It was the wiggling in my lap that woke me—the wiggle, followed by the lapping at my chin. My eyes slid open to see brown curly hair and a busy pink tongue. And a black nose and whiskers. *Killmonger*. I had fallen asleep at Cassandra's. *Fuck*.

I shifted on the sofa, still holding Killmonger, who seemed to have no interest in her feet ever meeting the floor again as she tried to wiggle her way onto my shoulder. That was until she heard the clatter of kibble in her dish. She jumped down, tumbled, rolled, and, after scrabbling to get her little feet under her, shot into the kitchen. I felt too good to get up, but I turned my head on the sofa to follow her path and found Cassandra. Well, Cassandra's ass, at least.

She was bent over, adding water to Killmonger's bowl, whispering quietly to her and ruffling her fur. It only took a second—it was a little bowl for a little dog—but, yep, there was the afternoon wood. With one foot still in the world of sleep, I didn't have the energy or inclination to talk it down or to turn my head. She finished with the water but apparently not with the love because then she dropped into a yogi squat like it was nothing and hung out there with the puppy a little longer. *Yeah.* If she'd been in a yoga class the instructor would have certainly told her to tuck her tailbone to protect her lower back in the squat. But from this perspective, that curve in her lower back set her ass off to perfection.

Get it together, nigga. You can't just sit on her sofa staring at her ass like some perv. What the fuck are you even doing here?

I adjusted both my heads, sat up, and cleared my throat. She turned.

"Oh! Hey, Sleepyhead." She rose, smiling, and walked toward me with an impish grin, mismatched eyes sparkling, and those fucking pants that skimmed and flowed over her curves. *Fuuuuck.* I hustled to sit up and, *dammit,* pinched my dick in the process of trying to hide it from her.

She stopped at the sharp hiss of air I pulled in through my teeth as I tried to make my boy more comfortable without full-on palming and shifting.

"You good?" Her head tilted, and worry bloomed in her eyes. I could feel the grimace on my face because I was definitely *not* good in this position.

"No, yeah. I'm straight. Just..." I paused as her head straightened and her glance dropped to my lap where I had loosely clasped my hands, elbows on knees, trying to keep it cool. When her eyes shot back to mine, the worry was replaced with something much more interesting...a sort of stunned intrigue...which immediately shifted to faint horror.

"Oh, well, um...I made spaghetti." She immediately switched course, heading back to the kitchen area. "The bathroom is, um, over there," she cleared her throat, clearing the telltale breathiness from her already husky voice, "if you need to freshen up after your beauty nap." She waved over her shoulder toward the closed door she'd shown me earlier.

"Oh, you got jokes?" I chuckled at both her reaction and her words. I'd stood up the instant she changed direction, doing the shallow squat, leg shake, and readjust because first her ass, then the squat, then those fucking pants, *and* the clear interest in her gaze combined to give me a full-on hard-on. Not the easiest thing to manage in flat-fronted suit slacks.

"Only a little. I'm glad you got some rest. Clearly, you needed it. Are you hungry?"

Oh, I definitely wanna eat. "I have to get back to the office. This nap was unplanned. I'm sure Shanice is freaking out." I struggled to keep my eyes respectably high. Her bright blue tank was made of thin drytech athletic material that draped over her lightly toned upper body. And those fucking pants. Soft cotton that loosely hugged her butt and thighs and flowed loose at the bottom. She couldn't possibly know how clearly they put every curve...and the soft vee between her thighs...on display. So yeah, I was struggling. I needed to get out of here.

"You sure?" She tilted that pretty head again. "I make excellent spaghetti, and I can show you how I'm thinking about reworking the process."

Hell, I'd forgotten all about the board's bullshit for a glorious...I checked my watch...ninety minutes. I'd definitely needed that respite. And now, maybe I could have the clear head I needed to make this happen.

"You're right. I'll call Shanice and see what she can do."

What was the point of being the CEO if I couldn't adjust my schedule as needed? I headed to the bathroom because that nap was long as hell, and I needed a leak. I wrapped up in there and washed my hands, then called Shanice asking her to adjust my schedule for the rest of the day.

I listened to her sly *mmhmm's* with an eyebrow raised. "Is there something you have to say, Shanice?" I kept my tone curt because what I wasn't about to do was give her any reason to think her perspective was needed beyond the tasks I gave her.

"Oh, no, sir," her self-correction wasn't nearly as contrite as I wanted it to be. "I'll take care of it. You have fun."

I pulled the phone from my ear to look at it, *What the fuck?* "Thank you, Ms. Young, but I rarely categorize the management of a billion-dollar enterprise as fun." I paused for effect. "Please let me know when you've rescheduled today's appointments. I'd like to make a personal follow-up call to Mr. Cartwright."

Her slightly less exuberant *yessir* made me feel some kind of way for a moment, but she'd been getting too damn familiar lately. Sly looks and lingering in the office for no good reason that I could discern. I tried not to toot my own horn, but it was hard as hell to keep someone at that damn desk who didn't have hopes of also being spread out across my desk. I wondered how much longer she had in the role before she did something out of pocket. *Like, show up at your house in the middle of the night in faux fur, knock off red bottoms, and nothing else,* which was the tactic employed by my previous admin. That had not been a fun night. Nor had the fallout when she'd tried to suggest I'd encouraged her behavior. It had been my intention to hire a male assistant after that, but those were few and far between. I'd had no luck and needed to get the position filled.

But we'd see. I hoped Shanice would reel it in because she was damn good at the job, and when she wasn't trying to slide up in my proverbial DMs, she made my life infinitely easier.

Sighing at the thought of having to potentially reopen the hunt for an exec admin, I hung up and moved to the dining table, where it was obvious that Cassandra did most of her real working.

She had a glass whiteboard mounted on one wall. It was hidden from the entry so I hadn't seen it when I walked in. On it, she'd fleshed out a few scenarios that I pondered while she was in the kitchen, making two plates of spaghetti.

It smelled delicious and my stomach growled in appreciation. I saw her cheeks dimple when she smiled in response.

"Can I help you get something? Glasses? Silverware?"

"Um, yeah, sure. The glasses are to the left of the sink, and the silverware is in the drawer underneath. Can you grab me a beer?"

"Yep." Then, there was a too-easy silence as we moved about her kitchen, getting ready for lunch.

I shifted a few of the things on the dining table, careful not to disturb or combine individual piles. I set our places catty-corner to each other facing the board, which put the majority of her notes between us. It seemed most reasonable for collaboration.

"Yo, that smells amazing. So you can cook-cook? Let me find out..." I took the plates from her hands and set them down. I poured both our beers and added bottled water that I'd found in the bottom of the fridge. When she'd settled herself, I sat down and did the same.

"I can cook-cook a few things," she laughed, then raised a finger to put a pin in the conversation. She closed her eyes in a quick prayer, not at all self-conscious about it, then picked the conversation up again. "Spaghetti is one of them."

I looked at her for a moment, then closed my own eyes, blessing my food before I ate. It was something I hadn't done in ages. I couldn't remember the last time, but it felt good. It felt right. Something settled in me.

"Do you cook for yourself often?" I, too, flowed right back into the conversation.

"Mmm, no," she half covered her mouth with her fingertips so she could keep talking. My father would be horrified. "I'm a takeout girl. I mean, I cook sometimes. A few times a month at least. But," she took another bite, chewed, covered, spoke, "there's soooo much good food around here," she swallowed. "And the portions are so generous that I can usually get two or three meals out of an order, so," she shrugged, "I don't really have to cook unless I'm just in the mood. What about you? You have a private chef, I guess?"

"Actually, I do," I laughed. "He's more my boy who looks out for everything, but he does cook."

"Your boy?" She tossed an inquisitive look my way but was still putting in work on her plate. That shit was sexy as hell. It had been a long ass time since I saw a woman take a full hearty bite of food and act like that shit was good to her. Women were always nibbling, trying not to mess up lipstick or cause wrinkles or gain a pound or what the fuck ever.

Also, the spaghetti was good as hell. I was planning on seconds. I hoped she'd counted on that.

"Yeah, we've been boys since middle school."

"You went to school in New York? You grew up here?"

"Yes and no. I was born and raised here until middle school when I went to boarding school in Philly."

"Really?" She leaned back. "I didn't know Black people went to boarding school."

I laughed again. I'd taken my jacket off earlier and now pulled off my already loosened tie, rolled it, and slipped it in the pocket of my jacket that was hanging on the back of my chair. I opened the second button on my shirt. Much more comfortable, I picked my fork up again to eat.

"Oh yeah. Mine was all Black."

"Really?" Her eyes got bigger. I still hadn't asked her about them. I knew now though that she sometimes wore contacts. She'd had them in at a few interactions including the gala and the more informal cocktail hour we'd held with friends of the company.

"Who was there? I know Obama's kids didn't go there."

I almost spit out my beer. "No, they didn't. Well," I thought about the kids I'd met in boarding school. "There were some ballers' kids. Some music people kids. Jack and Jill kids. You know the guy who plays in all the Marvel movies?" She nodded. "His kids were there."

"Huh. Well, okay."

"Oh, a lot of international Black kids, too, so that was cool. It felt like an HBCU, just middle school."

"Was it dope? Did you like it?"

"Yeah, it was cool. I didn't really want to be there, though." Why was I telling her this? "I would have much rather been home with my brother, but my dad said it was necessary." I shrugged. Trying and failing to shut the fuck up. "Said I needed it."

"Needed it for what?" Her fork had paused.

"Fuck if I know." I could feel the bitterness rising. "But it didn't work because he's still not satisfied."

"Abe," she reached a hand toward mine, paused, and must have realized that holding her boss's hand was inappropriate because she pulled it back. "I'm sorry."

"Oh, it's nothing. I'm not that rich kid who's all 'I'd trade it all for the love of my parents,'" I tried to joke because *would I?* "My dad has worked his ass off to keep building this legacy for us. I'm grateful. And privileged and all that."

"What about your mom? And your brother?"

"My mom is great. My brother," I inhaled because, after ten years, the sentence had not gotten any easier to utter. "My brother is dead."

"Oh, Abe," her genuine distress, as opposed to being heavy and sorrow-inducing, lightened me. It wasn't pity. It was pure empathy for what I might be feeling. And it was something only my mother and Vince had provided so far.

I refused to repay her honesty with lies, so I avoided my usual response of, 'It's okay,' in favor of a more heartfelt, "Yeah. It sucks. It's been ten years, but yeah." Ten soul-grinding years.

"Do you want to talk about it?" she asked. "You hinted that day at the winery."

"Maybe. At some point," I said, because I kind of did want to talk to her about him. Tell her about him. I thought, for some reason, that she'd get a kick out of him. And he'd been so fucking happy that I was so happy after meeting her.

This time, when the memory of that night twisted my chest, it wasn't quite as tight.

CHAPTER 16

CASSANDRA.

My heart was breaking for him. He'd lost his brother. I didn't have one, but I couldn't begin to imagine the gaping hole that would take me over if I lost Margeaux. It had to be infinitely worse.

"Do you want to talk about it?" I had to ask.

"Maybe. At some point," he said. His voice was hollow, and I could kick myself for having pulled a cloud over what had, so far, been a wholly unexpected but fun experience.

"Okay. I'd love to hear about him if you ever want to share." *Jesus*, the look on his face. He nodded.

"What about you? I'm dying to hear the story of how you ended up being fostered by the family who adopted your best friend."

"Um," it was the natural progression of the conversation, obviously. "Well. My earliest memories are living in the group home. I was maybe five or six, I guess, when I realized that it wasn't normal to live like I did. That's when I realized I was missing the whole mommy and daddy thing. It was," I hadn't revisited this in a long time, "a lot for a little girl to process."

He nodded, but didn't interrupt.

"Anyway, I was pretty stable at the group home. I never got bounced around, really. I got fostered a couple of times, but they didn't stick. I don't know why." I shrugged remembering Mama Porter, who I had really thought was my mama for a while. She'd been one of the first women I'd ever seen my skin color with big bushy hair like mine. When I'd been picked up from her house and returned to the group home, it had been the single worst day in my young life. I'd cried for days.

It was how Margeaux and I originally met. She'd comforted me when I'd had none from anyone else. Even the house mother had apparently tired of my tears because when Margeaux had slipped into my room, the room I shared with five other girls in three sets of bunks, I had been as much angry as sad. Angry at what the house mother had said. Angry and confused because I didn't understand what she'd meant when she'd said someone who looked like me would be just fine. That I should be glad I wasn't Fatima. I didn't know what that meant. But I was old enough to understand that it was mean and that the venom in her voice was directed at me.

So, when Margeaux appeared, she was an angel. She'd wiped my tears even though she wasn't much older than me. From that night on, we slipped into each other's rooms as much as possible, shared our meager belongings, traded lunches, and generally built an unbreakable bond.

"But it let me meet Margeaux, my best friend."

"Not Destiny, whose dog I'm about to steal?"

I giggled, and pushed my empty plate away. "No, Destiny actually used to be my social worker."

His eyebrows shot up. "Okay. Another interesting story. We'll circle back." He motioned with his fork, "Carry on."

I laughed for the thousandth time since he'd caught Killmonger for me. "Right. Well. So, I met Margeaux at the group home. She's only a year older than me, but she was so fucking wise." I shook my head, remembering. "When we met, I was seven, she was eight. And by that time, this was her third trip. Her parents were in and out. Eventually, her aunt came and got her." I shrugged. "I assumed that would be the last I saw of her, but we talked and fought to stay in touch. She eventually convinced her aunt to foster me, too. I was fourteen."

"Wow. How was that?" I appreciated that he didn't automatically start talking about how dope Gogo's aunt must be. I mean, she was because who would take in a whole nother kid because the kid you already took in wants you to? But it definitely hadn't been all flowers and rainbows.

I picked at the crumbs of garlic bread on my plate. "She was strict as hell. Like, she assumed that since we'd been in the system we were, at our core, trash. It felt like she was always just waiting for us to mess up."

He hummed in his throat.

"But, hell. I sound crazy complaining. She took me in, provided food and shelter. She was kind enough. And she was so smart and accomplished. She made sure me and Margeaux knew we had options. I just think she was surprised that we took them instead of, I don't know, getting pregnant and running off with the circus."

He laughed. "That's one option, I suppose. I'm glad it's not the one you chose."

"Me, too. I really like what I'm doing now, and I know having her guidance helped put me on the right path. So, ultimately, I'm grateful."

He nodded. "I hear you, and I know what it's like to be grateful, but still wish you'd had a different experience at the same time."

He pushed back from the table, "Now, before we both get too maudlin, can I have another helping?"

He hit me with the puppy dog eyes. I patted his cheek, intending to give him an 'awww, poor baby' but electricity shot through me at the contact. I paused, breath caught in my throat. His eyes darkened.

The place where my hand met his skin was on fire; I half expected to see the connection aglow. The soft scrape of his beard on my hand send my mind reeling to thoughts of how that beard might feel on other, sensitive parts of my body...my neck, my breasts...the inside of my thighs. The heat exploding from our contact point was licking across every inch of my skin, making my nipples peak and my core clench.

Our gazes stayed locked together, the dark desire I saw in the depths of his eyes only fueled the fire; I licked my lips.

The movement drew his gaze from mine. His eyes dropped to focus on my lips, damp from the swipe my tongue, before his head dipped ever so slightly. The movement brought us on a more even plane, caused our breath to align and mingle. I was caught. Completely snared, wholly ready to sample what he seemed on the verge of offering. I wanted it. I wanted him.

Killmonger, who had been happily gnawing on a chew toy in her crate following her own dinner barked, breaking the spell.

I blinked and recovered, pulling my hand away in embarrassment, trying to ignore the trail of sparks that danced along my fingertips.

"Poor baby," I said anyway, trying to return to the playful teasing that had preceded the contact. I was unsuccessful. The words fell flat.

He said nothing, just continued to watch me with that unwavering, unnerving, panty-melting low-lidded stare.

"Abe?"

"Yes?"

"Um," I searched my mind desperately, trying to pick up the threads of our prior conversation. "Help yourself." His eyebrows winged up.

"I think I will, thank you," he leaned; my eyelids fluttered as I followed the movement bringing his lips closer to mine.

Stop! What the fuck are you doing?

"Spaghetti!" I spat the word out. He stopped, blinked. "Help yourself to more spaghetti. I always make too much. There's plenty in there. Have two bowls if you'd like."

Killmonger barked again, hopping up to dance around Abe's legs, lifting up onto her hind legs to put soft paws on his calf.

I rose, heart pounding, still blabbering to scoop her up. "It's Margeaux's recipe and I never cut it. I can freeze whatever you don't want." I pulled Killmonger into my chest creating a barrier between myself and this man, my boss, someone's one's kinda sorta fiance, who I desperately wanted to kiss. And who, it seemed, might want to kiss me.

He blinked again and nodded briskly. Clearly pulling himself together as well. If I wasn't mistaken, he was as shaken as I was at what had almost happened.

He rose as well. "Does she need to go out again? It's been a while."

"I'm sure she does. You eat, and I'll take her around the block again."

"Please, you can't be trusted with my dog," he said, working as hard as I was to get us back on joking friendly ground. "I'll take her around the block." He reached for her.

"You're kidding."

"Not at all."

"We'll go together," I said. The fresh air would do us both some good.

"You don't trust me?"

"Psh," I sucked my teeth, "Bruh, I don't know you like that."

"Umhm. Okay." He picked up Killmonger's leash, sending her into a frenzy until he'd clicked her in place.

He opened the door for me, and as crazy as it sounds, we stepped out to walk the dog. I hoped his love for her extended to scooping her poop.

Chapter 17

ABE.

I skimmed the email again, though I had already read it three times. It was from Cassandra, updating me on the progress of the team.

After the Killmonger Episode, as I had come to consider it, we hadn't spent any significant time together. I was hard-pressed to admit it, but that was probably for the best. The last time we'd been together, I'd almost kissed her. I'd been so close, literally and figuratively.

It wouldn't do.

I clicked through the scarily thorough market research summary she had included. I couldn't fault her methods or her interpretation. I was actually thrilled with the strides she was making. The research they were conducting was thorough and extensive, especially given the timeline. She'd managed to include focus group interviews in the short time, too. It was impressive, to say the least.

I was eager to see the concept sketches the email hinted at. *Eager enough to take your ass to her office?*

I sighed and spun away from the computer screen. It was the end of the workday. Actually, well after the end of the day, if he were going by standard 9 to 5 hours. She was likely gone for the day anyway. And I needed to be not here in my office pining and trying to decide whether to go see my executive creative director.

Stop being ridiculous. Reply to her email, thank her for the hard work, and take your ass home.

That's what I did. I composed an appropriately congratulatory email, hit send and gathered my shit to head home. It was the smart choice.

I was about to walk out when my phone rang. I pulled it from my pocket to check the caller ID. Elizabeth. I sighed and then immediately felt guilty. I should be looking forward to hearing from the woman I was slated to marry, not wishing she were someone else. I hated this shit.

"Hey, Liz. What's up?"

"Hey, Abe. I'm glad I caught you," she sounded funny. Distracted, maybe? Nervous?

"Yep. You caught me. What's going on?"

"Mom is doing her thing again. She's given me her list of places I need to be seen, and I'm hoping you can escort me to a couple of these."

I hesitated.

Why? Shit. I didn't really know. But whereas in the past I had no qualms about coming and going with Liz. I actually enjoyed the hang out because we could come and go without the stress of misunderstandings. Now, though, I felt like things were shifting and I couldn't figure out whether they had shifted enough that I needed to have another conversation with Liz. What was I supposed to say? *I'm going to take you up on that offer to get Cassandra out of my system?*

Compounding the pounding in my chest that had started at Liz's request was the slick of disgust that rolled through my belly at the thought of getting Cassandra *out of my system*. That just felt...wrong in every way.

"You there? I'm going to shoot the list over now," her voice got a little faint. I supposed she'd pulled the phone from her ear to compose her text.

I made a noncommittal sound. "I'm not sure how my calendar is lining up, but I'll have Shanice take a look and see which events align."

"Should I send it directly to her?"

"Yeah, you can do that."

"Okay, thanks. And look, if you can't—or don't want to—it's no problem. I can ask Warwick, maybe."

That would be interesting. She and Warwick were like oil and water. We all hung out together, but they were constantly snipping at each other. It was good-natured...mostly...but I still figured she would have a laundry list of potential escorts before she arrived on Warwick. Liz was stunning. She couldn't be lacking for suitors.

"Warwick? That's wild."

"Well, you know, maybe class him up a little bit. Show him something fancy."

I laughed. Warwick had been to plenty of fancy shit, as she well knew, but there it was, the snipping even when the other wasn't around.

"Oh, you gonna put him on, huh?"

"Somebody needs to."

"Okay, well. I'll have Shanice let you know."

"Thank you, Abe. I really appreciate it." She hesitated. "You know, I've been thinking about what you said at the vineyards. We've never really talked about...everything...between us and, you know, the expectations," she leaned into that word in a way that made my mouth quirk. "Maybe we should grab a drink or something and, you know, explore things a little more seriously."

Fuck me. But maybe she was right. I needed to figure some things out. I just wish I had a better handle on how to do it. And if I was going to have a serious conversation with Liz, I needed to be able to go into it with a clean spirit. She deserved nothing less.

"Yeah, we can do that. Let Shanice know to set something up."

"Abe."

"Yeah?"

"I think if we're going to have drinks, we can make it a little more personal than having our assistants set it up," I could hear the amusement in her voice. "Look, I'm out of the country for the next few weeks, but when I get back, I'll call you."

"Yeah, okay," I knew that response wasn't particularly enthusiastic but she was throwing me for a loop with this. How did this desire to 'explore' align with me getting people out of my system and open marriages? "Be safe."

"I'm going to Italy by the way," she offered.

"Okay. Well, have a great time. Be safe," I repeated.

She sighed. "Okay, Abe. I'll see you when I get back."

I hung up and walked out, not eager to unpack that conversation at all. I wanted to push it all to the back of my mind and just leave it there.

It wasn't until I was standing in the open door of the sewing suite that I realized my feet, rather than my brain, were guiding my steps.

Cassandra was in her office this time. I knew this because almost everything in here was glass, which would make it damn difficult to do the things to her that I wanted to do...like wrap my hands in all that silky hair and kiss her until we were both satisfied; like feel her thighs in my hands as I scooped her up and wrapped her legs around my waist; like press her up against the wall and bury myself as far inside her as I could get.

It was the first time I'd given free reign to the thoughts my body had been having about her since I'd seen her again. Hell, since I'd seen her the first time ten years ago. The stream of consciousness had me swaying on my feet.

Maybe getting her out of my system wasn't such a bad idea. There had to be some component of just *not knowing* that was keeping me off kilter. I still couldn't wrap my head around fucking her. Well, that was a lie, I had both heads firmly wrapped around the idea of fucking her...but my moral compass wasn't having it. But I could spend a little more time with her. Maybe that would be enough. Eventually, she'd say or do something that would burst the bubble. I was, after all, notoriously picky, which is why I was one: single and two: barrelling toward an essentially arranged marriage.

"Oh! Hey, Abe," Cassandra spotted me loitering and thinking impure thoughts. "Did you get my email?" She was bustling, gathering her jacket and purse, clearly about to head out.

"I did. You've been incredibly productive in such a short amount of time."

"Well, yeah. The board isn't leaving us much choice, is it?" She breezed a little past me, laid her stuff on the sewing table closest to the door, then returned to move around the room, shutting things down for the evening. "But I'm just glad we have the team fleshed out and that they're so strong. Tamra is a gem, she almost knows what I'm thinking before I think it. And Adam," she made the chef's kiss motion, "he's exactly what I needed. That guy is a wizard with Slack."

I made some noise of agreement, while I watched her fiddle with the electronic pad that managed the lights and shading in the room. I watched as the glass front of her office clouded over to full opaque privacy. *Huh. Good to know.*

When she finished, she returned to grab her stuff, "Well, I have to go let Killmonger out again."

I felt the smile spread across my face.

"Oh, you wanna come see your boo?" She offered, jokingly. I knew it was a joke but chose to ignore that fact.

"Sure. I'd love to. No telling whether you'll lose her in the streets again."

She twisted her lips and rolled her eyes at me. I don't think I'd ever seen Liz twist her mouth up or roll her eyes. That couldn't be true though, could it?

"Well, come on then. I'm an hour late already and I have to catch this train that leaves in," she checked her watch, "fuck, ten minutes. I hope she hasn't wee'd all over her crate."

She walked out at a rapid clip, pressed the elevator button and stood tapping her toe waiting for the car to arrive.

"I can drive us," I offered, following her onto the elevator when it arrived. "I can have my car pulled around. It'll be waiting by the time we walk out."

"Oh, you fancy, huh? That would be perfect, though. Thank you."

"No problem." I pulled out my phone and sent the request for my car to be pulled forward.

When we stepped off the elevator and crossed the shiny first floor to the giant revolving exit doors, I could see my matte black S-class idling out front. Good.

"This is me," I said, lengthening my stride to get in front of her and open the door. The woman moved fast as hell.

"Oh! Thank you," she slid into the car a little clumsily, she had a bunch of shit in her hands.

"Here, let me take that." I reached for her collection of items.

"No, it's fine. I'll hold it. Or toss it on the back seat," she shifted to look in the back at the spotless interior and continued, "or maybe not."

I laughed and got around to the driver's side as quickly as possible without running. I didn't want to miss a thing.

"What do you mean, 'or maybe not'?"

"I mean, you have it as clean as the Board of Health back there. I won't be me that introduces a speck of dirt," she was laughing but the look on her face was skeptical.

"Man, stop playing and put your shit back there if you want to. You can throw a whole party back there, I don't give a fuck."

She hummed a little in her throat, which I interpreted as, "Okay, nigga, don't trip when your shit ain't clean no more." But she slid all the crap off her lap and twisted to dump it in the backseat. When she did, the slim pencil skirt of the dress she was wearing rode up, showing off smooth, toned caramel thighs.

"Do you work out?" I asked. Which, as soon as it left my lips sounded pervy, because why would I ask if I hadn't been looking at her very fit form? But she didn't seem to mind.

"I do. I have to."

I glanced at her, one eyebrow raised.

"Yeah, I have too many clothes that I love to risk outgrowing them. Also, stress."

"I get that. What do you do?" I checked traffic and pulled away from the curb. Before she answered, I added, "Put your address in," and tapped the screen to pull up the GPS.

"Eh, a little bit of everything really. I hate doing the same thing over and over. I love that y'all provide a gym for the employees. I used it for the first time last week and yesterday, I lifted." She lifted one arm to show off her biceps. "I got guns, you know."

"Do you now?"

"Indeed. You don't wanna fuck with me."

I tossed her another look because *didn't I, though?*

"Not at all, I don't want the trouble." I said instead. "Do you run?"

"Not if I can help it," she answered immediately causing me to chuckle. "I do yoga and pilates, I lift. I kickbox, which is really fun," she ticked her fingers as she listed the forms of physical exercise that made the cut. "Sometimes I'll spend some time on the rowing machine but ugh. Oh, I swim when I can. Love that."

"Bet. We'll have to hit the gym together sometime."

"Uh, no thank you. I'm not interested in working out with my boss. I don't want to be seen as a lightweight in any aspect, thank you very much."

"Seriously? You won't workout with me? What if I need a spotter one day, you just gonna walk away and let me kill myself."

She shot a look my way, and another eyeroll. "Please, I'm sure you toss around much more weight than I can help you with. How about this, if I see you struggling, I'll push the little help button on the wall."

"Give, give, give..."I replied.

"Yep, that's me. An unending font of support and encouragement."

"Speaking of support and encouragement, you've really gone above and beyond with moving things forward. I didn't expect this milestone for another several days."

"Thanks, I appreciate it."

We spent the fifteen minutes it took to get to her place talking about the line and next steps. Hearing her put the information that she'd sent me in writing in her own words made a strong start even better. Knowing that she had a firm handle on all aspects of what needed to happen made me breathe easy.

By the time we pulled up in front of her brownstone, her eyes were sparkling, she'd turned toward me in her seat, one knee bent, shoes off, hands wholly involved in the explaining.

I couldn't deny that I was caught up. Fuck she was stunning.

"Why do you wear contacts sometimes?" The question just jumped out of my mouth before I could stop it.

"What?"

"Contacts. Sometimes your eyes are brown. I noticed it that first night at the gala. I thought, then that maybe the mismatch I'd remembered were contacts but, they're not."

She shook her head, "No, they're not." She stepped out of the car before I could, and I wondered if I'd offended her, but then she threw open the back door, climbing across the seats to gather the papers that had slid during the drive. I walked around to her side to help and was met with her bottom half in the air, wiggling while she stretched to reach a pen that had fallen on the opposite floorboard. Did she not have a briefcase or portfolio or something for all of it?

I went back to the other side and grabbed the pen.

"Oh, thanks," she said, looking up at me from her frankly disturbing position half stretched across the backseat.

"No problem," I muttered, rounding the car again to keep the door from closing on her legs.

"I wear them because it's just easier sometimes. People are weird. They'll get all in my face and just stare. It's awkward." All her stuff gathered, she crawled backwards out of the car, ass towards me.

If it weren't so fucking hilarious, I know I'd be damn near drooling. As it was though, I was sporting a half chub and a grin. I stepped aside to give her room, steadying her by the elbow when she was on solid ground again.

As if she hadn't just fried my brain, she slipped by me to head up the steps to the brownstone. I followed her through the somewhat familiar space to the second floor and her door.

As soon as she started pressing the code into they keypad, I could hear Killmonger kick up a ruckus.

"Hurry up, woman, my dog is waiting."

She giggle, "I'm going as fast as I can." The lock clicked, she swung the door open we went in. The place struck me again. It really was a wonderful renovation. I could see why she was happy here.

I lightly hipchecked her when she went to let Killmonger out of the crate, beating her to the task.

"Well, okay, then. I'm going to change real quick. I'll be right back."

She ran up the spiral staircase and I bent to scoop up the chocolate squirming bundle at my feet–I really was a sucker for her; she was so damn cute, like her auntie. She gave me all the licks and puppy hugs until I put her back down and clicked on her leash.

"She's getting restless, woman, hop to." I could hear her laugh float down the stairs.

"I'm coming, I'm coming!"

While I waited, smile still lingering on my lips because this was shaping up to be a great evening, I wandered over to the kitchen.

"Can I grab a beer?" I called.

"Sure!"

I went to check the utensils drawer for the bottle opener and saw a manila envelope open on the countertop. I wasn't a snooper, but on top of the envelope was an 8x10 glossy of a man. He was handsome, maybe in his late 40s or early 50s, possibly a little older but it was hard to tell. He look mildly familiar. I picked it up, flipped it, saw no identifiers on the other side.

I was holding the photo, trying to place the face when Cassandra came back down.

"You know who that is?" She asked as she approached.

"I feel like I do. He looks familiar. Who is it?" I was still studying the picture because I *knew* I knew the face.

She shrugged. "I don't know. It came in the mail yesterday. I figure it was meant for whoever used to live here. You know how it is with rentals."

"But it's addressed to you," I noted, flipping the manila envelope to check the return address.

"True," she paused. "I don't know." She grabbed the photo and looked at it again.

"It looks like somebody's headshot. Why would they be sending it to me?"

"Good question. You're sure you don't know who it is?"

"I'm sure. And I also don't care," she took the photo and envelope and slid them both in the trash under the sink.

"Let's go." She grabbed two waters from the fridge, passed me one, and opened the door so I could pass in front of her with Killmonger trailing on the leash.

CHAPTER 18

CASSANDRA.

When Abe and I walked out with Killmonger, we immediately ran into Destiny, powerwalking the sidewalk, bearing down on us with all her energy.

"Hey, girl, hey!" she immediately hugged me and then dropped to her haunches to hug and kiss Killmonger.

"How's my baby? There's my girl. Have you been a sweet baby?" Whispering baby talk, and love words, she scooped Killmonger up and squeezed lightly.

"She hasn't peed yet, be careful," I warned.

"Oh, mommy's baby wouldn't peepee on mommy, would you? Would you, baby?" More baby talk and snuggles before she set her back down and finally acknowledged that at the other end of Killmonger's leash was fine-ass Abe Walker.

She made that acknowledgment with one eyebrow up and her hip cocked.

"You're Cassie's boss?" She asked, knowing full well that he was.

"I am," he answered. His voice, laced with laughter for most of our time together, took on that aloof, stilted quality. It was such a contrast that I turned to look at him. He returned my confused glance with that patented, low-lidded gaze that could mean any number of things. I narrowed eyes at him slightly, contemplating. He returned my stare, letting one eyebrow float up ever so slightly.

"What are you doing here?" Destiny asked.

I felt my head jerk, horrified. "Destiny!"

"What?" She widened her eyes at me, completely unde-terred. "I'm just asking," she shot him a side-eye. "My boss doesn't come see me at the crib."

"Fair enough. I took it upon myself to ensure Killmonger's welfare after," I looked at him with panic in my eyes and a slight shake of my head. He gave me a slow blink, and continued, "after Ms. Williams lost control of her some weeks ago, and I rescued her from certain demise."

The fuck?! Was he serious right now?

I stared at him in shock. *How dare he?* Then I saw the light dancing in his eyes and realized he was struggling not to laugh, though little of that struggle showed beyond a clenched jawline. He was teasing me. *Fascinating.*

"So you can consider it a home visit," he coughed into his hand to cover the threatening laughter.

He had been wholly enjoying the entire interaction. And in this moment, with his eyes twinkling at me, I was beginning to enjoy it, too. Even though Destiny was going to rip me a new one...all over again. I had, of course, told her about the incident and took my verbal lashing like a big girl.

I started giggling, "It wasn't that bad."

"You did lose her, though. Anything could have happened to my sweet baby." She had forgiven me but hadn't forgotten. I was prepared to hear about it for years to come, which was fair. I still felt like shit and was eternally grateful that Abe had come along when he had.

"Now that she's safe with her mother, I'll head out. It was a pleasure to meet you," he addressed Destiny. "Ms. Williams," he nodded my way.

Then he looked at Killmonger, clearly wanting to give her a loving goodbye. Instead, he nodded at her, too, "Killmonger. Be well." She barked and hopped, then started tugging at her leash because she still hadn't pee'd.

Abe slipped into the beautiful car that smelled just like him, and Destiny and I started down the block to let Killmonger find her relief.

"Girl, what the fuck is he doing here? *Again?*" Destiny wasted zero time.

I laughed, "He came to see Killmonger. You saw how he was with her. I showed you the picture."

"Right. Uh huh. That man can buy his own dog if he wants one. No need for him to pencil my dog into his schedule."

"He didn't pencil her in, silly," I bumped lightly as we walked. Killmonger had taken her immediate relief and was now weaving from grassy patch to grassy patch, investigating the dogs who had come before her, I guess.

"We hit a nice milestone today, and he came to my office to congratulate me, but I was heading out to walk her. He tagged along."

"Mmhmm. Sounds like a setup to me."

"Girl, how can it be a setup? He didn't know I was leaving when he arrived. And, really, you should be thanking him. I was running late, and he gave me a ride. I was able to get to her a solid twenty minutes faster."

She shot me a side-eye, "So you leaving my baby to suffer all day?"

"Whatever. She was just fine. And very excited to see Abe, if you must know."

"Clearly she wasn't the only one."

"Destiny! He's my boss. I see him almost every day. I'm becoming immune." That was a flat-out lie.

"Immune, huh?"

"Yes, immune. I barely notice him anymore. It's just like having Tamra or Shanice or Adam around. We get work done; we're professional."

"Have you often found yourself looking at Tamra's lips, contemplating how she kisses?"

"Well, she is a beautiful woman," I teased. "Okay, no. He's not like Tamra or Shanice or Adam. But cut me some slack. I'm trying to manage this shit."

"Having him at your house doesn't seem like the best approach. Especially since he has a whole-ass fiancee."

"I know that, Destiny. Nothing is happening with us. And if my boss is kind and wants to help me get to my house twenty minutes faster when I actually need that to happen, what do I look like turning him down?"

"You look like a woman who's about the business of maintaining appropriate work boundaries and protecting her heart."

"Protecting my heart? That's a little heavy-handed, don't you think? My heart is not at risk. But I do hear you about appropriate work boundaries. But HeirLoom isn't like that. People hang out."

"With the CEO?"

She had a point. I'd heard plenty of conversations between coworkers in the halls at HeirLoom, and in my own workspace, about catching up for drinks or hitting up a party or social event after hours. It was true, though, that none of those conversations mentioned Abe.

At HeirLoom, he was visible and available, he checked on his employees, and I often saw him walking the halls, popping his head into this office or that. But I didn't see him engaged in what felt like casual, friendly conversations. The general consensus was that he was kind and fair, but didn't give off an air of 'let's be buddies outside of work'.

So maybe this was more unusual than I was allowing. But what did that mean?

"Look, I just don't want you hurt. I know you met him a long time ago and all, but he's not the same man he was then."

That was true. He'd lost his brother and inherited a company. I'd be willing to be there were a thousand other things that had changed. And, I could admit to myself, at least, that I wanted to know what they were.

"None of us are. And he seems so, I don't know, sad all the time," I said. "I just want him to not be so sad."

"That's not your job, boo, to make him not sad. That's his fiancee's job. Let her have it."

"But we can be friends," I tried. It felt critical to me to make it clear that I wanted...needed...to be his friend.

"Dangerous ground, baby girl. You don't have a friendship history. You have a 'damn he's fine and I wanna fuck' history. Nothing came of it, true, but that's where it started and I suspect, if you're not careful, that's where it'll end. With you fucked and him married to someone else."

"But I don't want to marry him. I just want, I don't know. I just feel like he needs a friend. He feels so lonely."

She sighed. "You have got to be the biggest-hearted person I know. I don't know how you do it." This time she bumped my shoulder, "Again, that's his girl's job. But you go ahead and be his friend and feed your spirit if you need to. I'll be right here, ready to fuck him up if I think he deserves it. That'll feed *my* spirit."

I laughed a little because everything she was saying was right. Maybe I did need to put some boundaries in place. We walked a bit longer before turning to make our way back to my brownstone.

"Don't stress it, Cassie. You're just being who you are. If he takes advantage of it, that makes him the ass. And me and Gogo will deal with it for you." She accompanied that last part with a look that honestly frightened me a little. I was always glad itty bitty Destiny was on my side.

CHAPTER 19

The tiny scary woman named Destiny was right. Why *was* I there? I could have easily driven her to her place and dropped her off. I could have easily just let her take the subway like she'd planned. Killmonger wasn't my damn dog, why did I care if she got let out on time?

Fuck. I eased the Benz through Manhattan traffic until I reached The Haven, a dope, contemporary hotel with one of the best craft cocktail bars in the city. It also happened to be owned by Warwick. I entered my code into the parking keypad and slipped into the underground garage when the gates rose.

The quick elevator ride opened into a small lobby beyond which sprawled the exclusive bar. I stepped out into the cool, lightly scented air. The Haven was a newer brand. Where the Phoenix was steeped in history, the Haven was a nod toward the future, toward the spirit of black innovation. The vibe was new money with clean lines.

I could hear the thump of the bass coming from the bar and followed it. I texted Warwick as I walked in, just in case he was around. I just wanted a drink to clear my fucking head and maybe gain a little perspective. I eased onto one of the black and chrome barstools.

"Yo, bruh," Warwick announced his presence moments before his hand landed on my shoulder in welcome. I turned and dapped him up.

"Yo, what's up."

Warwick slid onto the barstool next to mine and tossed a nod to the bartender, who got to work setting us up with a couple of generous pours of scotch.

"What brings you out? I'm not used to seeing your face in the place."

"Got shit on my mind, man, needed a drink and figured your little dive bar would be as good as any place."

He laughed, "Yeah, you funny. But I got you." The bartender slid our drinks to us in heavy squared crystal tumblers etched with a simple block H.

We toasted and sat with the burn for a minute before Warwick got to business. "So, what's up? What do you need?"

Since I'd lost Godrick, Warwick had stepped into the big brother role as much as I would allow him to. Our relationship meant as much to me as mine with Vince, but it was different. Somehow, talking to Warwick always brought it home that I *wasn't* talking to Godrick. But still, I valued his advice and insight.

"Have you heard that the timeline on the line got moved up to September?"

He sputtered, "September? Is that even possible?"

"Fuck no. But we're making it happen."

"You and Cassandra?"

"Yeah, who else? She's been great. Already sent me finalized market research and concept visioning. If she keeps this pace, we can hit it."

"Mmhmm. Why the short deadline?"

"Seems the board is getting cold feet all of a sudden. And instead of giving me the fucking time to make it great, they want results by the next board election."

Warwick swirled the dark liquid in his glass, wheels turning. "Are they trying to get rid of you? Is that something your dad would allow?"

"Actually allow? Nah. I don't think so. But he would love to have me think he would, and to have me scrambling to prove myself."

"It's a dick move."

"It is. Especially since he's risking a lot. If he's pushing for this...agenda...or even endorsing it by not shutting it down, he's got to know he could lose control of it. Regardless of his long-term plan, the board *could* vote me out if this line doesn't hit the way we expect it to."

"You think the board would go against his wishes?"

"I don't know. I think the board is mostly old and ready to get out with fat pockets. I think the loyalty he expects is built on the past. It's a messy situation."

"So what are you going to do? Are there ways you can solidify your position?"

"You'd know that better than me. You've been dealing with this CEO bullshit for far longer. So, you tell me."

"Well. You'd have to be able to prove that the board members were making decisions in their own best interests as opposed to the best interests of the company."

I nodded. That made sense.

"Or, you'd have to prove that your father was behind stirring up a takeover and that *that* wasn't in the best interest of the company."

"That sounds like almost calling him incompetent."

Warwick was silent.

"Nah. I can't do that. I'd walk away from it before I did that."

"That's on you, bruh."

"Man, yeah, I ain't about to launch that kind of scandal."

"I hear you. No worse than losing the company to hands that aren't in the family, but you're right. That's burn-down-the-house shit. Your better bet is to set Vince on the board members. See if you find information that can explain why they switched up on you. And if that doesn't work out, shit. Do what you gotta do. I got your back."

"I'll look into all of it, Wiz."

"Man, fuck that," he grunted at my use of Vince's favorite jab. "Now back to the other bit. It sounds like Cassandra is killing the game."

"She is. She is. No complaints on that front."

"Yeah? That's good. Tell me about the work she's doing."

So, I spent the next few minutes listing Cassandra's accomplishments, gushing over the work she was doing, and getting excited about the next steps, which would mean concept designs and samples.

"So, yeah, we'll be getting into the sketching and design next now that we know the route we're taking."

"So, as executive creative director, she's in charge of all of it, yeah?"

"Yeah," I looked at him skeptically because he knew this.

"She seems fully capable, more than capable, and mad talented. Creative and visionary and all that?"

"Absolutely."

"So, why are you micromanaging her?"

"I'm not micromanaging her." Was I?

"Oh, so you're just trying to be in her space?"

"Bruh, what are you talking about?"

"Nothing, man, I'm just saying she's fully capable of executing greatness without you in her face all the time."

"Yo. You know this fashion thing is my baby. I want to be involved."

"I know you do." He paused. Then, "You talked to Elizabeth lately? She hit me up about some events or some shit. Are you not taking her to this shit?"

I hung my head. "Man, I don't know. The deadline is crazy, so I'm not trying to commit to a bunch of travel."

"Uh-huh."

"Listen, man. You and your grunts and uh huh's and shit bout to piss me off." I tossed my drink back. "You got something to get off your chest?"

"Oh, you mad now?" He started laughing. "Man, chill; nobody's trying to piss you off. I'm just wondering if Cassandra has your nose open. If she does, better to admit it so you can manage it instead of lying to yourself about it."

"She doesn't. I'm fine."

"Vince said you knew her from way back. That she's that girl you met the night we lost Godrick."

"We didn't lose him." It was my biggest pet peeve. "A drunk driver killed him. And Vince has a big fucking mouth."

"So listen, maybe you need to let yourself see what it is. I mean, she had your little baby nose open back then; and clearly, she has it open now. What's the problem?"

"Can you hear yourself? She works for me. I'm not about to push up and then something go wrong. The whole line is fucked up. I lose my damn company, and everything Godrick wanted just, poof, disappears. Now why would I go down that road?"

"Because what if it doesn't go wrong?"

"Nah. It's not worth it. Plus, there's this thing with Liz."

He shifted. "Yeah, that shit is crazy. But it's never stopped you, or her for that matter, before."

He was right about that. I knew Liz had dated and kicked it with other guys. She probably had one on standby right now because, again, she was a stunner by anybody's standards.

"Plus y'all aren't really taking that shit seriously, are you? Because I'm not sold. Y'all don't even really kick it like that.

I shrugged. "Does it matter? We're cool. We get along. She's got her head on straight, and she'd make a great wife and mother. What's there to be sold on?"

"Man, you can't build a life like that. You don't want more than that?"

"Like what? What my parents have?" I chuckled. "I'm cool going into it with my eyes open and with a strong partner who knows the game."

He just looked at me. Then his cell rang in his pocket; he pulled it out and shifted his attention. I watched as a strange look crossed his face, then he stood.

"Well, that was fun. I got work to do, my boy. I'll hit you up later."

"Yeah, I'm heading home anyway. Roll through if you get off at a reasonable hour."

"Bet." We exchanged dap and went our separate ways.

I was pulling out of the garage, waiting to merge into traffic, pondering Warwick's words...did I want more than a comfortable understanding with someone who understood the assignment...when I saw the strangest sight. Strange because of the composition, but oddly familiar because I had just seen a similar sight at the winery.

Across the street, in front of what looked like an Italian restaurant, were Benjamin Whyte and Juanita Brookes engaged in passionate conversation. They were caught in the entrance lighting of the restaurant, and I could see their faces fairly clearly. It didn't look like they were arguing, per se, but it was intense. *Interesting.*

Benjamin Whyte didn't care for Black people. Oh, he would collaborate and engage for practical and business purposes. He did not discriminate against the expansion of his bottom line. But if he could finagle, usurp, or downright steal what he wanted, he would do so before having to enter into a relationship of any sort.

So, it was very interesting indeed to see him out and about having intense, intimate conversations with Juanita Brookes. Not once, but twice.

As I watched, Benjamin turned more fully to the light, and something clicked. *Couldn't be.*

I grabbed my phone to call Cassandra.

Her slightly hoarse voice answered, "Hello?"

She sounded mad sexy. It wasn't the first time we'd spoken on the phone, obviously. But this time...on cell phones, at night, yeah...it hit different.

"Cassandra." I cleared my voice, "It's Abe. Can you send me a picture of that photo you received in the mail?"

"What? Why?"

"I think I might know who it is, after all."

"Who?"

"Just send the picture. I want to see if I'm right."

"No. I want to know who you think it is first."

"Damnit, woman," but I was grinning again, "I think it might be Benjamin Whyte. A younger version, of course, but him nonetheless."

"Why would someone be sending me headshots of Benjamin Whyte?"

"I don't know, but I sure wish you'd send me the picture."

I could hear her rolling her eyes. Shuffling in the background. No yipping dog, so Destiny must have taken Killmonger home with her.

"Is Killmonger there?"

"Nope," she verified, "she went with her mama."

"Are you lonely?" Not sure why I asked that or what I was going to do about it if she was.

But she laughed, "No, not really. I mean, it's nice to have life in the house, but again, dogs and kids. She's a lot of work."

"So, what are you doing with all the free time now that she's gone? Just laying around, reveling in your lack of responsibility?"

"Well, I was in bed, binging trash TV in celebration of hitting my personal deadline. But that was interrupted by my overly demanding boss."

"In bed already? My bad," I checked my watch because maybe it was later than I thought. Nope, it was just before ten. "So you're an early-to-bed kind of person."

"Kinda. Hold on," she went silent, then my phone alerted me to a new message. She'd sent the picture. "I just like being in bed. It's the most comfortable place in the house."

"Good to know." *Fuck.* That *was completely inappropriate.*

"Is it now?" *What?* That was also completely inappropriate. But she chuckled. "Sorry, force of flirty habit. I sent the picture; now what? Is it him?"

She had my head swirling. How's she gonna drop that line and then go right back to the previous topic of conversation?

"I don't know yet. I'll keep you posted."

"Mm. Okay. Well, thank you, I guess."

I chuckled. "You're welcome. I guess it's back to bed for you."

"That's the plan."

"You have a good night. Rest well."

"I will. Goodnight." She cut the line.

CHAPTER 20

CASSANDRA.

My nerves were on a hundred. I had a stack of shit I needed to run by Abe, and I was running up to his office, yet again, to see if I could grab him for an impromptu meeting.

Since the launch date had been moved up drastically, Abe and I had essentially thrown out our regular meeting schedule and taken to showing up in each other's offices unannounced to discuss whatever needed discussing. We needed to keep the show moving as quickly as possible, and so far, this approach was working.

He'd gone missing, though. Yesterday, he'd been MIA, and again today, he was nowhere to be found. I'd dashed up to his office as soon as I'd gotten to work, again at lunch and once more during the 3pm slump. Nothing. I'd texted him twice. Still nothing.

It wasn't like him. I knew this because we'd spent the last weeks joined at the professional hip. We worked well together. It had been easy, seamless. We were becoming friends, which was nice. And friends didn't just go AWOL on each other in the middle of a herculean task.

Yesterday, I'd been annoyed and irritated. This morning, maybe a little in my feelings but now, I was starting to worry, which was ridiculous. He was both a grown-ass man and CEO of a billion-dollar company. He didn't report to me. But after connecting every day, multiple times a day. It was strange that he hadn't even returned a text to say he would be out of pocket for a while.

When I reached Abe's office, Shanice was at her post.

"Hey Shanice, how's it going?" She glanced up from her work and to her credit, her face showed none of the annoyance she must have felt at seeing me yet again.

"Hey, Cassandra. He's still not in. He called this morning to have me clear his schedule again. I did let him know in my report yesterday that you'd stopped by." Okay maybe her annoyance wasn't as fully masked as I'd originally thought.

"Thank you, Shanice, you're the best." A little kindness wouldn't hurt. I stood pondering what to do next. I really needed his input so I could put this bit to bed and move on.

"You never heard from him yesterday?" Her inquiry felt genuine, but for some reason, something in my gut told me to keep my cards close to my chest. I didn't let her know that I hadn't heard from Abe.

Instead, I ducked her question. "Oh, we're all good." I looked at the files in my hands again and said, "I was going to leave these, but I think I'll hold on to them." I gave her a quick smile of goodbye and continued down the hall toward the elevators.

What the hell was going on? It was crazy that Abe hadn't connected with me at all, given the work he knew had to be done. And he was cancelling meetings. So this wasn't planned time out of the office. I pulled my phone out to dial him—again—and pushed the call button for the elevator.

This time, the phone was answered, but it wasn't Abe's voice on the other end.

"Hello? Cassandra?" The baritone on the other end was friendly.

I pulled the phone away from my ear to check the screen. Yeah, it said *Abe*. I put it back to my ear.

"Yes. Who is this?"

"It's Vince, Abe's boy. I'm just picking up for him."

"Oh. Well. Ok. It's nice to meet you officially," I'd heard Vince's voice on the other end of several of Abe's calls and even caught a quick glimpse of him once when he and Abe were on a video call. "Is he around?" I stepped onto the elevator, and the doors slid quietly closed. "He's been out of the office the last couple of days, and I have some things I'd like to include him in before we move forward."

There was a pause. "Why don't you bring them by? I'm sure he'd want to see them."

The doors slid open, and I stepped off into the little lobby area of the high-rise office building.

"No, I don't want to impose, if he's dealing with something. I just..." he cut me off.

"No, no. I'm sure he'd want you to. I'll text you the address. When you get here, the last four of your cellphone will open the gate."

The gate? My phone dinged. I looked at it to see an address that would be a forty-minute drive even if I had my own car and there was no traffic on the city streets. As it was, this would amount to well over an hour by train, with a rideshare to top it off. I chewed my lip and checked my watch. No, it would be far too late by the time I got there. I couldn't descend on his doorstep that late. And then the return trip? Nah, I'd pass.

"Oh, no, this…," I stopped and started again. "I don't have a car. It would be far too late by the time I got there. I'll see him tomorrow. It can wait another day." I started to swipe the call to an end.

"Oh, that's not a problem. Hold on." He went silent for a moment. "Okay. Abe's car should be pulling up in a second."

"Abe's car? Isn't Abe's car with Abe?"

"Different car."

"Oh."

I walked to the front of the building where his car had appeared when he drove me home to take Killmonger out.

"Okay, well. What should I look for?"

He chuckled. "I feel like you'll know it when you see it. It should only take another minute or so for it to pull up."

"Good grief," I said when I saw the deep purple Bentley rounding the corner. I rolled my eyes. "Are you serious?" It was beautiful though, sleek and expensive-looking, the deep purple throwing off a shine that was well out of my price range. And I did okay for myself.

"Yeah," he laughed. "He usually drives the Benz. But the Bentley stays there."

"Well, I guess I'll be there soon enough," the driver hopped out and rounded the car to open the door for me. I slid in and settled into the bucket seat in the back. I'd never ridden in a car with buckets in the back, so it took me a second to plug back into what Vince was saying.

"Listen, I'm going to send you something. Take a look at it before you get here, yeah?"

"What is it?"

"It'll explain why Abe hasn't been in for a couple of days," he paused. "And it'll explain why I'm having you come over."

"Look, Vince, I don't know. If Abe has something serious going on…" again, he interrupted.

"Just read it. We'll see you in a little while. And, Cassandra," he continued, "please come." He hung up.

Well, that was weird. I swiped to my messages and found the link Vince had sent. I clicked to open it.

It was a news article about HeirLoom, specifically about Abe's ascension to the role of CEO. It talked about him being the unexpected heir following his brother's death around five years prior to the writing of the article. There was a photo of Abe looking a little younger and much greener. He also looked determined. Resigned. And sad. Definitely sad. This article was linked to another. I clicked.

This one was written five years earlier about Godrick's death. It had happened in June. I checked my watch. Today. *Fuck. Today was the anniversary of his brother's death? No fucking wonder he wasn't answering the phone.* I read the article. It was heartbreaking. Godrick had been hit by a drunk driver the same night he'd been honored by the family as the incoming CEO. They had been devastated, as expected. The article talked about the loss for the industry as well as for the family. Godrick had been something of a prodigy. There had been very high expectations about his impact on the company and on the industry as a whole. His death was an incredible loss for more than just Abe.

Several photos of the family were included. One, in particular, caught my eye. In it, the whole family was dressed in black tie attire. The caption said it was from the night Godrick had been killed, taken at the event celebrating his promotion. In the photo, the family was formally styled; the shots were obviously intended for pubs and promos. I studied the photo of Abe in particular. His parents had been standing together with Godrick to their right. Abe's father had a hand on Godrick's shoulder and looked proud enough to explode. His mother, the same. Abe stood to Godrick's right, on the end. He, too, was grinning from ear to ear. The pride in Godrick clearly the unifying force in the family.

Abe had told me a little more about the tension between him and his father. We'd spent several late nights in the studio, and the conversations had often veered from the strictly professional. Our family situations were fairly regular topics of conversation. I was flattered and honored that he shared so freely with me. And, shame or not, I wanted to know everything. In this picture, though, he looked like himself. Like the happy, flirty guy I'd met at that gala event all those years ago.

Wait a fucking minute. I pulled the picture closer. *It couldn't be.* But it had to be. I rechecked the date. Yes, it was the same semester I graduated; it was early June...which would have been right around exam week. This had to be the same event. *His brother died the night we met.* My heart twisted and shattered for him. I'd been in my feelings about him not calling, and he'd been in the trenches of hell.

I let my head fall back against the lush leather headrest and closed my eyes. *Jesus.* I couldn't imagine what he must be dealing with. What would it be like to have to revisit that every single year? What was I going to do when I got there? What if I was the last person he wanted to see? Would I remind him of that night? Make it worse?

Surely Elizabeth or someone was there with him. Wouldn't he be with his family tonight? Wouldn't they be together?

But if they were, would Vince have told me to come?

The thought of Abe alone with this kind of pain was making me sick to my own stomach, but part of me wanted to call Vince and tell him I wasn't coming. I wasn't good in these kinds of situations. I didn't want to make things worse. I knew part of the anxiousness I felt was fear of saying the wrong thing, saying something stupid and meaningless.

I'd never lost anyone close to me. When Margeaux's grandmother died, I went to the funeral because I was living in her aunt's house. I had been so uncomfortable. Surrounded by people I didn't know, supposedly mourning a woman I had never met. I'd felt like the worst type of intruder but I had been required to attend the services, the interment, and the repast at the fellowship hall. A full, hot day that I spent trying to gather the words to explain who I was to the few people who asked.

But this wasn't that. I knew Abe and I cared about him. Surely something would come to me in the moment. And if Vince, his best friend, thought I should come, then I would go. I wanted to go. I wanted to see him. I wanted to make sure he was okay and look into his eyes. Fuck the repercussions. If someone else was there and I got my feelings hurt, so be it. I'd take my ass home.

The car slowed to a stop. I pulled myself from my thoughts long enough to start taking in what was happening. Even though I'd been staring out the window, the scenery had been no match for my swirling thoughts. We stopped at what I assumed was the entry to Abe's property. I could see tall metal gates, simple and effective, opening for the car; we drove through.

My heart was pounding. I rubbed my hands along my thighs to settle myself and clear the moisture from my hands.

When we finally slid to a stop at the end of the drive, I slipped out the back as soon as the driver opened the door. My mind was focused on Abe, but not so much that I didn't process the sprawling expanse of his home. It was luxurious but not ostentatious. It was clearly built in a mid-century style with flat rooflines and an excess of floor-to-ceiling windows. I took in the mature landscaping, sprawling trees, and lush plantings that adorned the driveway and spilled over the wide cobbled steps that meandered to the front door.

I could see lights on the main level, but the windows on the higher levels were dark. I chewed my lip and started up the long steps toward the door.

It opened as I approached. The man standing in the doorway must be Vince. He verified that once I reached him.

"Cassandra, I'm Vince," he introduced himself and welcomed me in. He wasn't tall, at least an inch under six feet; he wore grey athletic joggers and a dark t-shirt that accentuated his muscled frame. His calm voice settled me. While this man didn't give off an easily-ruffled vibe, I figured he'd be a little more wound up than this if Abe were in a really bad way.

"Hey. Um, it's good to meet you." I looked around, and despite the stunning visual impact of Abe's house...a blend of warm dark wood, rough-cut stone, bright white walls showcasing what I was sure to be million-dollar works of art, and beautifully colored rugs...I was more interested in knowing where he was.

"Where is he?"

Vince gave me an assessing look. "You got the link?"

"I did."

"So, you realize..."

"That today is the anniversary of his brother's death? Yeah." I didn't say anymore. I didn't know if Vince realized Abe and I had a bit of history, and for whatever reason, I thought I'd hold on to the information.

"Yes," a bit of the tension left his shoulders.

"Also. I don't know if you noticed the date. The event in the picture," he hesitated, clearly uncomfortable, but plowed on, "was the night you and Abe first met."

I sighed, "Yes, I realized after a few minutes. And, I really don't know if this is a good idea. I mean, he's mourning, and if I remind him of that night...that can't be a good thing."

Vince opened his mouth to speak but I plowed on, "I think maybe I'll just leave these here," I gestured toward my briefcase. His eyes dropped to it briefly before returning to mine.

"I know this hits hard, and I'm probably out of pocket but he needs something to pull him out and I think seeing you would do that."

"Pull him out? Of what? Has he called his therapist?"

Vince chuckled softly. "Nah, it ain't that serious. You'll see what I mean."

Doubtful, I followed Vince around the sunken den, through an open space that I couldn't figure out a use for other than walking through, and finally to the double doors that opened onto the terrace.

It was dark but the terrace was beautifully, subtly lit so that the whole area was set aglow with faint light. Vince continued passing cozy seating areas and outdoor dining spaces until we came to the pool.

Wow. Bright blue underlit water reflected the lights of the terrace. In one of the lounge chairs at the far end of the pool, was Abe.

As Vince and I approached, I could feel his eyes following me, but he didn't move.

"Hey man, Cassandra's here."

"Yeah. I can see that. My eyes are fully functional."

"Yeah, alright with that. She's got some shit to talk to you about," and he left. I watched him walk away with a little swagger and the deuces chucked.

I turned back to Abe, unsure of what to say. I went with the obvious, "You've been hard to find the last couple of days."

No answer. I hesitated. He was backlit, just like the night I'd met him, his features hidden. But now I knew what was covered by the shadows. Sexy, sleepy eyes, a damn near perfect smile with soft looking lips, warm brown skin.

"Listen," I decided to just rip the bandaid off. I'd leave if he wanted me to. "I know what today is and I'm so sorry, Abe." My voice was just above a whisper. "If you don't want to be alone,

I'm happy to stay. I mean, for a while, if you'd like. We don't have to talk about him. We can talk about whatever. Or nothing. Just, let me know."

He still didn't say anything but he shifted on the wide lounger to make room. Again, I hesitated. And he finally spoke.

"You come to take care of me but you scared to sit down?" His words were carefully formed. "I won't bite."

I set down my case and came to where he was sitting. I perched on the side of his chaise. Closer now, I could see that his usually sleepy eyes were even more low lidded. I could also smell the weed floating off the blunt he held in the hand that hung on the opposite side of the chaise.

He saw my gaze and held his hand up, offering me the blunt with a raised eyebrow. I took it, inhaled, then looked at it in my hand because it was *good*. I took another pull and passed it back to Abe with my own raised brows.

"You good?" I asked.

He let his head move in a slow left to right on the back of the chaise, "No."

We held gazes for a moment before I made a decision. I stood, kicked off my shoes and made a couple of adjustments to my work fit to get more comfortable. Then I sat back down, bumped him over a bit with my hip and lay down beside him.

I held my hand out for the pass, settled more comfortably, and said, "Tell me about him."

I was shaking, terrified that I'd done the wrong thing and made it worse. Then I felt him take a deep breath. And he spoke.

In that deep rolling voice, made rougher by grief, he told me about Godrick...Trey. Eventually, while I learned about their summers with bikes and beaches; about the time Godrick beat up Jimmy Kelly for bullying Abe; about the girls and the late night talks...Godrick became Trey. Finally, he told me about their dreams and how Trey was the one he shared his with.

And at the last, when he'd finished the heavy pour in his tumbler and we'd finished the rollie, he told me how alone he'd felt when his brother died, how miserable it was to be left to weather his father alone, and how he'd do anything to make his Trey's wishes come true. Including stepping into a role that he'd never been cut out for and killing the game.

I didn't know how much time passed but Abe finally drifted off to sleep. We were stretched out on the chaise, legs tangled, his feet almost hanging off. He had snuggled down, his head was on my chest and his arms were around my waist. He was knocked out and peaceful. I didn't want to move and wake him so I just shifted a little and let my own eyes drift shut. I'd get up when he moved to go in for the night.

Chapter 21

ABE.

After a night of drinking and smoking, many people wake up disoriented, trying to remember what happened, slowly putting the pieces of the night before in place.

Not me. I woke up fully alert.

Fully aware that my head was lying on Cassandra's breast. Fully aware of the scent of her. Fully aware of the warmth of her skin under my hand where it had inched under her shirt as we slept.

Fully aware of her leg thrown across mine. Fully aware of the two inches that lay between her thigh and the tip of my dick.

I desperately wanted to flex my fingers. To awaken that tactile sensation in my fingers. To measure the smoothness and softness of her skin. I didn't. I desperately wanted to inhale more deeply and draw in her fragrance. I wanted to turn my head and feel the softness of her breast under my lips, take her nipple in my mouth, and just inhale her. I didn't. I didn't do any of it. Because I didn't want to wake her. I didn't want the day to start. Not yet.

Right now, caught in this in-between time, everything was fine. I didn't have to think about Godrick...*Trey...Jesus...* I hadn't said the name out loud in years. Hadn't talked about him like that since he'd died. My heart thumped hard and heavy, but maybe not so painfully as before. But I didn't have to think about that right now.

Instead, I could think about Cassandra. She'd come. When I'd seen her last night, I'd thought she was a fucking mirage. My first thought was that the weed was off the chain, but then she'd kept walking, solid and real.

She'd been nervous, and I knew my silence made her more so, but I couldn't help it. I'd lost my breath. When she'd settled against me, hit the blunt, and ordered me, in that breathy, smoky voice, to tell her about my brother, something had unraveled inside me. Just loosened and slid away. I felt like I could breathe for the first time since I could remember. I'd told her everything, as many stories as I could think of, chuckling and laughing through many of them. And she had been wonderful, asking questions through her own laughter, forcing me out of the darkness and into a lighter, healthier place where my memories didn't feel like lead blocks dragging me under.

I felt her fingers tighten on my shoulder. *I guess the gig is up.* So I flexed my fingers on her waist. Warm, soft. *Fuck.* She continued to shift, sliding her leg off mine, coming deliciously close to brushing my dick. It was clear that she was moving toward full wakefulness, so I readjusted too, moving underneath her, sliding up so that I could slip my arm along the back of the chaise and have a better view of her as she blinked herself awake.

It was clear that she did *not* come awake with full alertness. I grinned as I watched her process her surroundings and realize that she had spent the night at my house. Outside by the pool, but at my house nonetheless.

She was horrified. I burst out laughing.

"Good morning, beautiful." Her eyes widened. I wanted to kiss her. And that didn't shock me or scare me. It felt right. So, I held her gaze, watching for any sign that she wasn't on board, and leaned in. I supposed I wasn't being completely fair. She was still half asleep, still uncertain about what was happening around her. But, oh well. Life wasn't fair.

I watched her eyelids flutter closed, blanketing those beautiful eyes, until my lips covered hers. *Heaven.* It was the only thought in my pickled little brain. I moved my lips over hers, testing their softness...they were so soft; testing her taste...she was sweet, delicious. I pressed, and she opened, letting my tongue slip inside. She tasted like bourbon and blunts. I smiled against her lips because they were two of my favorite things.

Then she sighed into my mouth and wound her arms around me; she shifted her weight into me and kissed me back, effectively blowing my fucking mind. It was literally blank, my entire being focused on the connection between our lips and the pleasure radiating from that point.

I slipped my hands around her waist and pulled her over me. She fit. Perfectly. Soft against my hardness, pliant where my hands roamed over her back and eased slowly over her bottom. She moaned; impossibly, I got harder. I pulled my lips from hers and laid a trail of kisses down her neck. She was warm and soft from sleep, I wanted to squeeze her, bite her, inhale everything about her.

She shut me down with a whispered, "Elizabeth."

I jerked. "What?"

"Elizabeth," she repeated. "You're engaged. Remember?"

"No, I'm actually not. If I were, I assure you that I would indeed remember. And we wouldn't be doing," I let my eyes roam us, "this."

"But..."

"But, nothing. I'm not engaged to Elizabeth," I felt my lip twist because I wouldn't be a fuckboy and act like there was no reason for her to have concerns. I knew she was remembering Juanita's slick remarks at the winery. So, I explained. "But our parents would love it if we were."

She looked skeptical. I didn't blame her. "Like an arranged marriage," she asked.

I wanted to laugh, but again, I felt my lip curl. I chuffed, "Yeah, they'd love that. But it's not their choice. It's ours." I started to lean in again. Her lips were calling to me, shiny and a little slick from our kiss. I wanted to lick them.

She laid her hand gently against my chest. It might as well have been the hand of an angel the way my chest burned where she touched. "So, what does that mean? Exactly." Her brow was furrowed.

"It means that she and I have no formal arrangement, but," I sighed, "we haven't formally, seriously, dissuaded them of the notion, either."

She lowered her eyes. "Ah. And there it is. I know how you high-dollar families operate," she pushed up so she could look me in the eye. "You want to unite bloodlines and families and shit. If she thinks you're engaged, then you might as well be. You're not going to get me caught up in this and then find my body, drawn and quartered on the side of the road because I interfered with the succession plans. Nope. Not the kid." She began to move away. I chuckled because she was funny as hell, but also, she was really trying to leave. Which was not the move.

I held onto her hand where it lay on the chaise.

"Nah," but she wasn't completely wrong. I really needed to have a serious conversation with Elizabeth. As far as I knew she was still out of the country if she were back, she hadnt seen fit to call...which to me, spoke volumes about the tenor of our non-engagement.

"It's not like that. They're not that," I searched for the right word, "invested." That wasn't true at all. They were seriously invested and intent upon making this union happen. They'd just have to get used to the disappointment. "But I feel you. I'll take care of it."

She reared back. "What do you mean? You'll take care of it?"

"I'll talk to Elizabeth. Make sure she fully understands, but I promise you, she doesn't care," one might also consider that a slight overstatement.

"Wait, what? Abe. What are you talking about?" She sat all the way up. "Make sure she understands what?"

"What are you talking about?" I mocked and grinned at her. She hit my shoulder. "Listen. I don't want Elizabeth. I want you." The look on her face let me know how pompous that sounded. I scrubbed my hand across my face. "That sounded like shit, but it is what it is."

"Yeah, you're right. It sounded like shit," she looked shell-shocked, which wasn't unexpected from her perspective. So I wasn't surprised when she said, "I think you might be doing the most. We kissed and that was, um," she stumbled, "very nice and everything." Her eyes were floating everywhere except across my path.

"But that's no reason for you to blow up your relationship. We're colleagues. And you're mourning," she nodded as if agreeing with herself. "It's no wonder you're acting out of character. Don't worry about it. It's on me. I shouldn't have come last night," she started making moves again to rise off the chaise.

"I'm glad you came last night," I squeezed her hand, tugged it a little bit so she'd fall back against me. "It's been a long time since I've had the chance to just talk about him. You gave me that," I kissed her forehead.

"Abe, I..."

I hushed her and stood, tugging her to her feet. "Don't worry about it. I'll take care of it."

"Yeah, you keep saying that, but there's nothing for you to take care of. This can't...won't...happen again."

"Okay," I said though I had no intention of adhering to that proclamation. As a matter of fact...

I lowered my head to kiss her again. Thank God she didn't pull back; her eyes widened impossibly, but she didn't move away. Then her lids fluttered closed once more and she opened for me. I could already tell that this wasn't a taste I would be able to go long without. Long seconds passed while I made myself wholly familiar with the flavor of her, the wetness inside, the slickness of her teeth, and swipe of her tongue. My senses came to pinpoint focus where our lips melded, the chirping of early morning birds faded away, the faint sound of the water in the pool slipped into nothingness. The warmth of the morning sun on my skin blended with the warmth pouring off Cassandra's body to wrap me in a cocoon of sensation.

I let my hands slip lower to cup the cheeks of her ass. She moaned, and I echoed her because I had been dying to get my hands on her roundness since that day I watched her bend over to water Killmonger. I'd been fascinated to know she was hiding all that under her flowing dresses and A-line skirts. But now I could skate my hands along her narrow waist, rest them on the flare of her hips, cup them under the smile of her bottom cheeks.

She rose onto her tiptoes, and I moved my hands down to catch her behind the thighs, lift her and wrap her legs around my waist. Her arms tightened around my neck, and she tilted her head to deepen our already out-of-control kiss even further.

I lay her back onto the chaise, prepared to stretch out over her and indulge, when I heard Vince's voice, "Aye, Abe."

I knew beyond a shadow of a doubt that Vince was fully aware of what he was interrupting. "What, Vince?" He was approaching, head down, seemingly engrossed in his phone. But I knew this was only to give Cassandra a moment to gather herself.

"Shanice has been blowing me up trying to reach you. You going in today?" Finally, his gaze rose from whatever was so enthralling on his screen...nothing...to meet mine. The mocking amusement in his eyes was clear, as was the faint admonition.

Cassandra hopped to her feet. "Well! I guess I'll be going now because I'm definitely going in." She smoothed her hands over her now very wrinkled outfit. The long flowing skirt topped with a midriff skimming cropped silk blouse had been comfortable enough for sleeping but was now much worse for the wear. She looked beautiful to me.

All bustling energy now that Vince was there, she gathered her shoes and bag and shot me a look that was half frustrated passion and half relief. "I'll see you in the office?"

I nodded because seeing her was all the catalyst I needed to get it together. And, a tentative poke at the grief and misery revealed that it was manageable today. I'd be fine, and I would definitely see her in the office. Preferably spread out all over *my* office.

"Um, could I get a ride back in the batmobile?" She directed her question at Vince, back turned to me completely.

"Absolutely," he told her, holding out an elbow to escort her to the house, "come with me. I'll show you where you can freshen up a bit while you wait for the car to come around."

And just like that, I was watching her walk away. She turned back once. I winked and slipped my hands into the pockets of the sweats I was wearing. Her eyes dropped, widened, and she spun back around to follow Vince to her escape.

She could run. That was fine. But last night, something had shifted and settled. I wanted Cassandra Williams. And I would have her.

CHAPTER 22

CASSANDRA.

"**C**ass!" My attention snapped back to the present, and my fingers started moving again, taming my curls into the mini twists that would hopefully carry me the next three weeks in Europe. I could've rocked my blowout, but something about the air over there and my hair didn't really agree. I wasn't interested in coming back with a broomstick growing out of my head, so here we were, me, Destiny, and Margeaux, in the midst of a twisting session.

Well, Destiny and I were twisting, Margeaux, with her short pixie, was on wine, snack, and TV duty. She'd made it clear when she decided to take her cosmetology business seriously that she'd be rocking a short cut going forward. 'I don't have time to handle all this hair,' she'd said as she cut off whopping chunks of her mid-back length 4c kinky coils, 'and I will *not* be one of those stylists whose own hair looks like shit.' Since then, she'd sported various short styles, the length on top being the only variable. If she really wanted something different, she had no qualms about achieving that look through the use of wigs, weaves, braids, or whatever extension got the job done.

"Girl, if you keep wandering off to la-la land like that, you'll never get done," Destiny was nearly halfway finished with her own shoulder-length hair and she ruffled her hands through the twists fluffing and tossing them.

She wasn't wrong. I had a lot of hair on my head, too. For the thousandth time after starting ninety minutes ago, I was regretting the decision.

"Help me, Margeaux," I begged, tossing puppy dog eyes her way. She'd sworn she wasn't going to help, but that woman's hands weren't happy unless they were making magic in someone else's head.

She huffed and grumbled for show, "Get your ass on the floor, girl."

"Yes!" I hopped up and did a little shimmy before I grabbed a throw pillow from my sofa, tossed it on the floor, and sat down. She settled behind me and picked up where I'd left off. I took two quick sips of my wine, holding the stemware carefully with fingers that were slippery from coconut oil and leave-in conditioner. Then I got back to work on the front...two sets of hands were better than one.

The conversation turned back to the trip I was about to take to Europe. Three weeks. Stops in Paris, London and Milan to immerse ourselves in the fashion week experience in each of those cities. It was the winter show but we could always get a sense of what was percolating in the background for the coming spring shows.

"I can't believe you're about to be traipsing all over Europe with your fine-ass boss." Yes, Abe was going. "That man is too fine for his own damn good."

"He's definitely too fine for Cassie's good. You should've seen the way he was looking at her when I came to pick up Killmonger." At her name, Killmonger's head popped up from where she was lounging on her doggy daybed. When there were no snacks or kisses in follow-up, she lay back down.

"You play too much," I said half-heartedly. "He wasn't looking at me any kind of way."

"Bullshit," they both said at once. I put my hands up, "Okay, y'all. I'm feeling a little aggressed against."

"Well, shit, I'm just saying. Be careful. He's an odd one."

"What do you mean?"

"He's dangerous. He moves like a fuckboy. We know he has a fiancee, but he's all up in your face, grinning all the damn time. I don't like him."

"It's not like that," I offered. Destiny sucked her teeth. I nudged her leg. "It's not. Not that it matters because he is not all up in my face," I added air quotes, "but he doesn't have a fiancee. That's a bunch of legacy shit where his parents and hers are trying to merge the family fortunes or something. But neither of them are really down. And two, again, he's not all in my face. He's just being friendly. We click." The feel of Abe's tongue sliding along mine assaulted my senses. Everything between my legs pulsed. Hard.

I hadn't told them about the kiss. I had already cut back on sharing how much time Abe, and I had been spending together because they really were getting on my nerves talking about how he was out of line. And at that point, Abe hadn't signaled that his interest was anything more than friendly. But now he *had* signaled interest...clearly and definitively. *Fuck.* What was I supposed to do?

"We kissed," I said.

Silence. Heavy, all-eyes-on-me, bitch-what-the-fuck si-lence.

"Biiiiiiitch," Destiny sang it.

I looked at her. Her eyes were big, her mouth hung open. Her hands were frozen, raised to the left side of her head, mid-twist. She looked like Black Weird Barbie.

I turned to look up at Margeaux. Shock warred with an I-told-you-so smirk. Then she blinked and said, "That shit was good as fuck, wasn't it?"

Destiny, still mute, held up a hand for a high five that Margeaux readily gave her.

"And was," I whispered, and we fell out laughing.

When we settled again, I told them about going to Abe's, about him losing his brother, about it being the very night we met. We took a few minutes to exclaim over that fucked up coincidence. And finally I told them about the kiss and the conversation that followed.

"I have never...ever...been kissed like that. It was like he touched my fucking soul y'all. He tastes so good, and his lips are just perfection." I sighed.

That statement was enough to calm the laughter.

"Oh, Andi, you can't fall for this guy. He's with someone. Even if you believe him and he doesn't want to be with this girl, he moves in a different world. If their families expect them to get married, they're going to get married. You're talking about billion-dollar decisions," her voice lowered, and she caught my eyes. Hers held the barest whisper of pity, but it was enough to make my skin shift in annoyance. "You don't need that shit in your life again."

"Believe me, I know," the reminder of Jeffrey was fair, but it still hurt.

I knew Destiny loved me. But her love could be painfully blunt sometimes. It had taken long months of heartache to get through what Jeffrey had done. I'd lost weight, I'd lost hair, I'd nearly lost my job...which is what he had wanted...but I'd stuck it out long enough to let me walk away with my head held high. No thanks to the man I'd thought loved me beyond all measure. I'd learned that he only loved me in the shadows. I was good enough to fuck, good enough to steal ideas and work from, but nowhere near good enough to present to his family.

It had hurt, threatened to destroy me because I had been honest. Jeffrey knew about my past. He'd known I had no pedigree, no silver spoon but he'd claimed to love me. Claimed that I was all he needed. He'd lied.

"He's not Jeffrey," I defended, even while something ugly crawled through my heart. "He's nothing like that." I could hear myself. I sounded like an idiot.

And apparently, I wasn't alone in that assessment based on the expression riding Destiny's face. "Are you serious right now?"

"I am. And I know how it sounds, but..."

"But what, Cass? You think we're going to sit here and watch you go through this bullshit again with some other rich-ass pussy playboy who thinks he's too good for you?"

"Destiny, chill," said Margeaux.

"I'm not trying to chill. I'm trying to understand how you're about to let yourself get caught up in the same shit again. I mean, I'm not mad at fucking him. Do that shit and let me know about that stroke because he moves with exceptional big dick energy." she clapped to emphasize her point. "But this 'he touched my soul' bullshit. Come on, Cass. You're better than this," she huffed in her seat, grabbing another section of hair to twist.

Was she right? The reality was that while Abe and I had continued to work closely since he'd kissed me...we had no choice...but we hadn't spoken about it since. He hadn't changed the way he interacted with me at the office. He was still funny and available, he shared ideas and was prompt with feedback and responses. He still asked about Killmonger and poked fun at me for being a cat person who dog sits. It was almost as if we hadn't kissed at all.

After a week, I had decided that either it had all been a dream fugue or Abe had clearly determined that it had all been a mistake. A conclusion that actually brought me a great deal of relief. Kind of.

In my right mind, the one that made the practical decisions and the one that mattered, I knew that kiss was absolutely a mistake and under no circumstances should it be repeated. He and I both had too much on the line. Whether he was lying to me or himself, or both, about the state of his relationship with Elizabeth, the business end of things was too complicated. I'd worked too hard to risk it by getting wrapped up in family and company dynamics that had nothing to do with me.

On the other hand, now I knew. I knew what his lips felt like. I knew what he tasted like. I knew what his bare skin felt like under my hands. I knew what it felt like to be wrapped in his arms, to be the focus of his passion. To have been on the receiving of all that heat and then, the next day, the next week, nothing? It was torturous.

The only thing that made it semi-okay were the unguarded moments when I could see the memory of that shared kiss all over his face. If I were honest, the reason we hadn't discussed it could very well be because I'd gone out of my way to make sure we were never alone, never in a position in which we could address it.

Things felt safer that way. Which lead me to the reason I was sitting here, trying to do my hair but losing huge chunks of time. I was about to walk into a situation that left no room for that type of avoidance. Abe and I would be together, in close quarters...not alone per se, but still...for three weeks. In Europe. In some of the most beautiful romantic locations I'd ever seen. Doing the thing we both loved most...sucking up fashion.

"Don't worry about it. It was soul-stirring, no doubt. But it was a one-and-done. For real," I added at Destiny's skeptical look. Shit, I was skeptical, too.

"Yeah, I hear you 'one-and-done.' You're about to one-and-done his ass all over fucking Europe," she rolled her eyes at me. "Which, again, is fine. Just don't get your feelings all caught up, Cassandra." She used my full name for emphasis.

"Thank you, mama. But I'm good." I really wasn't good. There was no way I was good. But I was going to make the best out of it. "Seriously. I'm not about to fuck this up. This opportunity is more important than that kiss, than Abe or anything else. I've worked too hard. Y'all know I"m not about to let it slip away."

Destiny and Margeaux both endorsed that approach though I could feel Destiny's eyes still on me, doubting my ability to steer clear. I could also feel Margeaux's more thoughtful gaze. I caught her eye.

"What?"

"Nothing. I trust you. We trust you. We just don't want to see you get hurt."

"I know. And I love you both for it. But I'm not. I mean, in another world maybe. Who knows what might have happened if we'd connected that first time we met. But now? It's too late. He and I both have too much to lose. It's just not worth it."

They both patted my knee because while we all knew that getting involved with Abe was a no-no, we could all agree that not getting in bed with Abe was a serious loss. One not to be taken lightly.

But I would hold strong. I would maintain our distance, keep my lips to myself and my legs closed. I just needed to make it til spring. I could do that.

Chapter 23

ABE.

I was still scratching my head over the crazy-ass conversation I'd had with Elizabeth this morning when I heard my father's voice booming down the hall. That conversation with Liz had left me in a confused, shitty mood. What I certainly didn't need was more shit from the old man's mouth piled on top, but that's what I was in for, I had no doubt.

In a show of pure avoidance, I slipped into the bathroom in my office before he could reach me. The fact that I was avoiding him made my mood even shittier. But the last two weeks had been pure hell. And I needed two fucking minutes before I took on whatever bullshit he threw my way.

In the bathroom, I looked in the oversink mirror and saw the face of a man under duress. And the only escape I could fathom was supposedly off-limits to me. But she didn't feel that way. I scrubbed a hand over my face, but I still looked drug and haggard. Stressed. That stress had several sources. One was the self-imposed deprivation I was dealing with. I couldn't get Cassandra off my fucking mind. And I didn't want to. The constant glow of her mismatched eyes in the back of my mind, the memory of how soft she was beneath my hands, the way her mouth had opened under mine. I could still feel the glide of her tongue, taste her sweetness. I had nasty, dark fantasies about holding her still so I could simply eat her from the inside out.

I felt my dick swell. I'd been walking around with a semi-erection for the last two weeks, and as uncomfortable as it was, I wouldn't trade it because it made me think about her. And that's all I wanted to do.

I knew our kiss...and everything that had come with it...had left Cassandra shaken. When she walked away from me that morning, leaving me rock hard and hungry for her, I knew something would finally have to give. It had been building for weeks and all the efforts I'd made to tell myself that we were just building a friendship, that our relationship was primarily professional were blown out of the water at the first taste of her. Yeah, I was many things but I wasn't a liar, especially not to myself. So she'd been right to throw Elizabeth's name in my face. She'd been right to press me on it.

And because I also wasn't a fuckboy, I made it my mission to get in front of Elizabeth as quickly as possible to quell any lingering thoughts, hopes, or expectations that she and I would ever be more than friends. My plan had gone awry, though, because Liz was traipsing around the Maldives with no planned return date. Warwick thought she was heading straight to London for fashion week.

I certainly could have called her, or even video chatted, but having such a serious discussion via technology felt wrong. So I had waited, planning to see her in Europe if our paths didn't cross domestically.

Luckily, the tides shifted in my favor. Or so I thought when I received a call from Liz this morning saying she was back stateside for a couple of days and looking forward to having that drink we'd discussed. I took her up on the offer.

She suggested Haven. I agreed. It was a nice neutral locale.

I replayed the events in my mind, trying to understand when things went left. I'd arrived at Haven a few moments before she did and secured a two-top. It was early enough in the day that there were only a few members scattered through the area. Most were on laptops, using lounge as workspace.

I'd spotted Liz's entrance immediately. Her golden skin shone with a little more bronze from her time in the sun. She was lovely, and again, I wondered why this woman inspired nothing more than an objective appreciation of her beauty, whereas Cassandra, with all their similarities, made my blood run hot. Just thinking of her now sent another wave of awareness coursing through me.

"What's so urgent, Abe? I hear you've been looking for me." *Liz asked once she reached the table. I had stood to welcome her and she presented first one cheek, then the other, for air kisses. I obliged.*

"We have to talk, Liz," the words sounded more ominous than necessary, and I grimaced.

"Oh, that sounds scary," she'd laughed a little and settled herself in the vacant chair at the table.

I signaled the waiter; he approached immediately, deferentially.

"What would you like? A glass of wine?" I had offered, feeling uncomfortable even though this was not a breakup.

"*Perfect. A pino, perhaps?*"

"*Of course,*" *The waiter took her request and mine and poofed away to make it happen.*

"*I've been thinking about our conversation at the winery,*" *I opened.*

"*Oh! I have, too,*" *she interrupted.* "*I'm glad you want to talk.*"

I nodded, a little taken aback but ready to forge ahead.

"*You said then that I should explore things with Cassandra,*" *I ripped the bandaid off.* "*I would like to do that.*"

"*Okay,*" *she drew it out, looking a little surprised,* "*I'm not sure the word I used was 'explore', but why are you telling me? I told you that I don't care,*" *faint exasperation had colored her voice,* "*but I'm really not interested in* hearing *about it,*" *her lip curled a little. It was an expression I'd not seen on her face before. But I nodded.*

"*Fair enough. But I just want to make sure we're on the same page. We haven't been as clear on this point as I realize we could have been. I don't want to,*" *I shrugged because there was no way to not sound like an asshole,* "*inadvertently hurt you.*"

She'd looked at me more closely at this. Was that anger I sensed? That didn't make sense to me, but something was definitely simmering there.

"*Hurt me? I think we both understand this isn't a love match and was never meant to be,*" *she shrugged one shoulder, bare in the strapless lavender jumpsuit she wore.* "*You're not going to hurt me by doing whatever it is you're doing with her.*"

"Right," I paused as the waiter returned, placed our drinks and disappeared once again. Elizabeth reached for the menu he'd left.

I would have to be more direct. It was clear that Liz thought I was describing a fling with Cassandra, some short-term situationship...an itch-scratch like she'd described at the winery. And while it might turn out to be that, it didn't feel that way. And it's not what you want. *That thought slipped through the barriers quick as fuck. I hadn't been in the position to unpack it, but I'd be a fool not to recognize the truth in it.*

My silence must have clued Liz into the fact that something more was brewing in my mind.

"Abe?" She called my name, pulling my thoughts from where they'd locked again on Cassandra.

"You understand that this is nothing more than a distraction...a dalliance...right? As long as you're discreet, I have no concerns. I know you wouldn't be disrespectful," she reached across the table and laid a hand on mine. I couldn't remember a time when Liz had touched me outside of the most superficial and necessary contact required when I acted as her escort. "But like I said, I don't expect fidelity. Not under these circumstances."

I slid my hand from underneath hers. She let hers stay where I'd left it for a moment before she moved to toy with the delicate stem of her wineglass. When she spoke again, her voice had been much cooler, far less indulgent than before. She'd sounded more like her mother than I'd ever heard.

"But I do expect follow through. I hope you're not talking about walking away from this." Her long tapered fingers gestured between us, "From us."

"Us?" I questioned. "When has there ever been an us?" I leaned back from the table a bit, gaining a little separation because what the hell was going on right now?

She gave a little cynical huff, "There's been an 'us' since Godrick died, and our parents decided you were a close enough substitute." I felt the shock cross my face. "I don't wholly agree, but there you have it." She paused, raking me with a look of resignation laced faintly with contempt.

"This isn't our decision, Abe. It never has been. But I've never given you a reason to think I'm unreasonable, so don't make me be that."

I leveled a steady gaze at her. This felt like a seachange but maybe I had just been obtuse? The nonchalance she'd exuded at the winery, and for all the years prior, had apparently rested on the assumption that the path was set.

"That feels a little threatening, Liz." I chuckled. "I'm sure you didn't mean it that way."

"I meant it any way you want to take it, Abe. But don't fuck this up. Do your thing, play your games. For all I care, let her in on it. But don't expect not to get this done in the end."

"'Get this done?' It's not a business deal, Liz. No matter how much they want us to think it is. It's our lives we're talking about, and I, for one, am not living it according to anyone's plan but my own."

"Says the reluctant CEO standing in for his dead brother," my eyes narrowed at that flippant remark, and I opened my

mouth to let her know she was skating on thin when it came to the remarks about Godrick. But she continued.

"Look, Abe," she sighed heavily. "I'm sorry. That was uncalled for. But I'm just pointing out that neither of us is living life on our own terms. You've done things, taken this role, changed your whole trajectory because Godrick died, and you had to. This is just another responsibility that falls to you. I'm another responsibility that falls to you. And I get it if you're not happy about that, but you're wrong if you think there's another option for me or you."

"Where is this coming from, Liz? This isn't the vibe you were throwing off at the winery a few weeks ago."

"Wasn't it?" She tilted her head as if she were thinking back to that day. "Huh. Well. Maybe you misunderstood. So, let me be clear. My expectations are that we'll be married in the span of two years. Heritage and HeirLoom will join to become a powerhouse of textiles and fashion. You and I will spit out two or three kids, and we'll all live happily, richly, ever after."

I stayed silent, unsure of what else to say. If I closed my eyes, I would have thought she was Juanita.

She drained her glass. "Do what you will, but don't think you're going to fuck up that part of the plan."

This was not at all how I expected this conversation to go.

"Liz, I'm sorry. It's not going to go that way. Again, I don't want to hurt you, but this isn't going to happen." Even if things don't work with Cassandra, I was coming to realize that this part of my life just wasn't up for them to control. The brief glimpse I'd had of...more...made me realize that I'd never be

content with this half relationshiop with Liz. I wanted more for myself.

"Beyond this situation with Cassandra," I ignored Liz's faint eyeroll, "we need to figure out our own paths in this. Our personal lives are not our parents' business. My personal life is none of their business, and it's time they get on board with that. It has nothing to do with you."

"It has everything to do with me, Abe. Are you fucking insane?" Her voice rose slightly, betraying her very real upset. She paused to regulate. "What do you think my life will look like if this doesn't happen? What do you think my life has looked like thus far?" She stared at me, icily beautiful in the strapless jumpsuit that hugged her slim curves, daring me to answer.

I took stock of her, really looked at her. Her hair fell in a sleek golden sheet down her back; the silk press owed her nothing. The color, lighter than when I'd last seen her, was the perfect complement to her warm tan skin. Her makeup, as usual was flawless. But behind it all was fear and worry.

I'd never given consideration to what her life was like.

I had no idea how to answer her question. So I said nothing.

"Right," she huffed. "I've been groomed *first for Godrick and now for you. For this. All I've ever heard is 'when you're a Walker...when Heirloom and Heritage are united'. You think I've been, what, following my dreams? Every bit of my life has been shaped to align with my destiny as a* Walker." *She paused for a moment, "And, with Godrick, that was fine. It was good, actually, and right," she whispered. "I loved him...we loved each other. You know that."*

I nodded because that wasn't something I doubted. Despite the venom she was throwing tonight, I knew what she and Godrick had was real.

She continued, her voice shifting back to that cool matter-of-fact tone, "But now, I belong to you, whether you want me or not. Because if not you, then who?"

I had no answer. During my silence, she rose and slipped the light wrap she carried over her shoulders. Finally, she gave me sad little smile.

"Right. So, have your fun. And I hope it is fun. I like you, Abe and I don't begrudge you this at all. I'll see you at the altar."

What the actual fuck? She'd been groomed *for me? The word left a slimy, sticky feel in my mouth. Was that really how she felt? Really her experience? What did it even mean?*

I'd sat a chewed on that for a while before I tossed a few bills on the table and headed out.

So yeah, that was the shit I was sitting on right now as I hid out in the fucking bathroom, hoping my father would move on to another target.

I wondered how long it would be before this shit settled out. Because right now, I felt like a raging asshole for having never once thought about this situation from Elizabeth's side. Yeah, we had danced around it at the winery, but before that, our references had been superficial and, I'd thought, mutually dismissive.

"Abe?"

Fuck me. What did I do to deserve this shit?

"Abe, I know you're back there. Shanice here assures me of that fact."

Shanice might lose her fucking job.

"I'll be right out." I turned on the water and washed my hands. If I splashed a little cold water on my face to fortify myself, well, hell, sue me. I took another moment to school my face into a mask of indifference and stepped out.

"What the hell is wrong with you, boy?"

Oh, we're getting right to it, huh?

"Beyond having been raised by a self-absorbed, narcissistic psychopath? Nothing, I suppose. Why do you ask?' I was also at the end of my rope and had little patience for his bullshit today.

"Funny. It's just like your soft ass to label hard work and high expectations as narcissism. You should try it sometime. But I'm referring to your latest attempt to run this company and this family into the ground."

He couldn't possibly be talking about my conversation with Liz; it hadn't happened more than a few hours ago.

"Since the mere fact of my existence is an effort to run the company into the ground from your perspective, you'll have to be more specific." I busied myself with paperwork on my desk. The only thing he hated more than backtalk was being dismissed.

He stalked to the desk, standing immediately in front of it, putting his crotch at eye level. Fucking asshole.

"Look at me, boy."

"Fuck you, old man."

Maybe that was too far. He slammed his fist on the desk. Papers fluttered. I leaned back in my chair and raised my gaze to his. I could feel the insolence blazing from my eyes, and I could see the disgust distorting his face. For the gazillionth time in my life, I could feel the whisp of *'why'* float through my consciousness. Why the hell did he hate me so much?

I let the almost unconscious thought melt away while I waited for his next words.

"You think I'm going to let you destroy this family so you can get your dick wet in that mutt you hired?"

I was around the desk and in his face in record time. It was the first time I'd ever seen fear flash in the old man's eyes. It was satisfying. And awful. Who the fuck wanted to be in a position of putting fear in the eyes of their own father.

"Watch your fucking mouth," I damn near growled it.

"Oh, but you knew exactly which mutt I was talking about, eh?" He chuckled deep and ugly. "I don't give a damn if you fuck her from here to Timbuktu. But you will marry Elizabeth. And you will not embarrass this family."

"I will do what the fuck I want to do. And you have no say otherwise. I have no intention of marrying Elizabeth."

"If you want to stay at the helm of this company, you'll do just that. If you want to keep that CEO behind your name, you'll do just that. If you want to live up to your brother's memory, you will do. Just. That. Because if you don't, you *will* be voted out. I will personally see to it." For the second time that day, I felt like I'd been torpedoed. "Don't mistake me, boy. This isn't your decision. Try me, and you'll see how serious I am."

"You'd rather see the company leave family hands than see me happy?"

Another ugly laugh. "Happy? Boy you think I give a damn about you and your happiness? You didn't think shit about mine when you drug your brother out that night. Set him up to get himself killed," he chuckled. "I'll sell it myself before I let you sully it breeding with that mutt. And, you're not the only family, are you? Warwick can have it. At least he understands his duty. Does what his father tells him to."

And then he, too, walked out.

Jesus. I followed him to the door and shut it behind him. Then I pressed the button to frost the glass front of my office. I needed a fucking minute.

Chapter 24

CASSANDRA.

Something was wrong. We'd been in London for two days, and I'd barely seen or heard from Abe. He'd been adamant about joining the trip though I'd tried to assure him, via email, that his presence, while welcome, was not necessary. I'd tried everything to respectfully dissuade him because I needed a reprieve, and two weeks without him in Europe sounded perfect. His silence over the last weeks had been nerve-wracking but not unexpected. It was the heated glances and clear desire that accompanying the silence that were sending me over the edge.

But even those wholly unprofessional gazes had been in short supply the last two days. Something had happened. And despite every cell of my body telling me it was for the best and none of my business, I wanted to know what it was. And why it had Abe so shaken. He looked hopeless.

Which was why I was, against my better judgment and after a full day of running the London streets with my head swimmingly full of the glorious fashions we'd seen on the runways, standing in front of his suite with my hand poised to knock. Regardless of the shit between us, I still felt like I did that day he'd fallen asleep on my sofa...like he needed a fucking friend.

So I knocked. And then immediately turned to go because what was wrong with me? I had absolutely no business standing here thinking I was some sort of savior sent to rescue this man from himself. That wasn't my job, and this wasn't my ministry.

I was a solid twenty paces down the hall when I heard, "Andi?" And my knees damn near buckled. My pussy absolutely clenched. *Fuck.*

"Uh, yeah," I stopped and turned around, took a deep breath, and walked back to the room. "I was just coming to, I don't know, check on you. You've been standoffish, which I get, because of you know, the *kiss*," I whispered it, and one side of his mouth kicked up. "But, the last couple of days, you've also been really...sad, I guess, and I just wanted to make sure you're okay."

He stared at me. Those sleepy eyes, hooded but alert, skimmed my body from top to bottom, setting fire everywhere they touched. He stepped back, opening the door and making space for me to slip in. I took another fortifying breath, perhaps a mistake because I got a lungful of clean, crisp Abe, and stepped inside.

My nervousness was temporarily shocked in to silence when I caught a glimpse of his room. "Oh, this is *niiiice*," I sang it, and he chuckled behind me.

"Yeah, it is," he agreed. "So you came to check on me?"

I wandered into his two-story loft-style room. How did they make two-story rooms in a hotel building? I stared for a minute before answering, "I did. You've been walking around looking like somebody stole your bike or something," I turned to face him, "Are you okay?"

He returned my gaze before giving me a slow blink followed by an exhale. "You know what? I'm not. Come on." Shocked by his honesty, I followed him across the fluffy white carpet that blanketed most of the room, through a nicely appointed sitting area and out onto a wraparound balcony. And I thought my room was something to rave about with its historical touches and old-world charm. Nah. I was mistaken.

"I hadn't really intended to hang out," I said when he motioned to one of the deck chairs while he dropped his big frame into the other.

"Right. Well, you shouldn't have come, then. You wanted to know if I'm okay. I'm not, so now what?" He challenged.

I sat. "Fair enough. I asked, and I meant it. So," I settled myself a little more comfortably but stopped short of reclining into the soft cushions. That didn't seem like a smart choice.

"What's up?" I gave him my full attention.

He looked at me, clearly contemplating how much and what to tell me. I said nothing, curious to see how much he'd choose to confide.

"I told Elizabeth that there was no way we're getting married."

I felt my eyebrows rocket skyward. My heart thumped and stopped. What did that mean?

"What does that mean? Why?"

"Why?" He chuckled darkly. "Because when I look at her, all I see is you. When I think about how my life is going to play out, all I see is you." I'd been staring at his profile as he spoke, but now he turned toward me. I could see his eyes glittering. "When I wake up in the morning, I'm thinking about you, and when I close my eyes at night, you're the last thing on my fucking mind."

It would have been romantic, could have been the speech of a woman's dreams, but he was growling when he said, clearly pissed that I was occupying as much of his day as I was. Not my fault.

My heart was pounding. The butterflies in my tummy were jumping double dutch and cheering. I could only wonder at how well my face was maintaining its calm.

Casually, I shrugged, "I'm sorry?"

He threw another growl my way. "No, you're not."

I tilted my head in question.

"If you were sorry, you'd stop," he said, sounding like a petulant child. And he knew it because he let his lips lift at the corner and blessed me with a little chuckle in that deep baritone.

I laughed a little, too. "I would if I could?" I got another doubtful glare in response to that. "Seriously, though, I don't know what to say, Abe."

"There's nothing for you to say, unless you want to offer a little validation? Give me a little hint that I'm not the only one getting twisted up here."

My thoughts started and stuttered because what could I say? *You could say, yes, that you're also all twisted up.*

"Abe, I..."

He shifted toward me completely. Bringing our knees close. He leaned forward, elbows propped on his knees, big hands dangling too close to my bare legs for my comfort. I should've thought this through. Should've put on more clothes. The stylish silky shorts romper that had allowed me to be comfortably cute all day felt way too revealing all of a sudden.

"I get it," he said. His fingers danced across my knees, causing goosebumps to erupt along my skin. His fingers paused, his eyes lifted to mine. Another little smile ghosted across his lips.

"I get it," he repeated, his fingers resuming their movement, "but I need you to know this. It sounds crazy. I get that, too. But there isn't a lot of calm in my life. For whatever reason, I feel calm when I'm with you. And I want more of that."

I understood. I struggled to put words around how right it felt when we were together. I hadn't had many opportunities in my life to experience calming, trusted companionship. I had been through enough therapy to know that those missed experiences colored my relationships and made me antsy. I also knew that having my heart and self-esteem drug through the mud by Jeffrey didn't help.

My intuition had completely failed me where he was concerned. I never considered myself street-smart, regardless of the way I'd grown up. But I'd always been able to trust my instincts and my powers of observation. I'd learned as a child to watch people to see how their actions and words aligned. It had kept me safe more than once. Stranger-danger was bullshit. It was the people you knew and who knew you that you had to watch. I'd learned that lesson early and well. Jeffrey had completely flown under my radar, though.

His sweet words and professions of love had put stars in my eyes. But it was his proclaimed awe of and respect for my work that had melted my heart and fooled me into letting my guard down. He'd pushed and supported, encouraged, and inspired me. The fact that he was my supervisor during the most intense experience of my young professional life hadn't gone unaddressed. But we'd been so in love, so in tune with each other. I couldn't imagine my life without him. In fact, I spent hours on hours, day after day, imagining my life *with* him. Dazed at how lucky I was, in disbelief that this incredible man, so far out of my league, wanted me, loved me, and needed me.

It was the stuff of fairy tales. Until it wasn't. Until the moment he presented all of my work as his. He'd stolen everything I'd poured myself into. *Everything.* The finished pieces but also the notes, the sketches, everything that I could have pointed to as proof that the work was mine, he'd annexed, rerouted, relabeled, reorganized. And, I had been unknowingly complicit...working in his space, in his office, often using his technology because it was better, newer, more cutting edge. All of it served to time and location stamp my work as his.

The biggest shame of it all was that I'd been willing and ready to forgive him knowing how important his career was to him and how he'd been struggling with creator's block. I was sympathetic to the immense pressure he was under from his family to be successful. I was willing to give it all to him and help him; willing to be the woman who uplifted him and helped him find his muse again. But he hadn't wanted me. At all. It had all been lies.

Now, I sat here looking into the sincere gaze of another man who needed my work to validate his ideas, who stirred things in me that I didn't want to feel, who professed that I was special...and who was way out of my league.

I was scared.

"I still don't know what to say," I whispered it. The words *I'm scared*, hung on the tip of my tongue. I could tell him, but that would be arming him.

"I know. I'll say some more things, then" he took my hands in his. "I've had enough therapy that I'm not scared to talk it out."

I nodded. A man who's been to therapy. That was one significant difference between him and Jeffrey. Jeffrey had been adamant about not seeing anyone. By the time he and I met, I had been under the care of state-appointed counselors for years. Most of the interactions had been perfunctory. But then I'd met Destiny, and she'd given enough of a fuck that I began to see the benefit of having someone to talk to. It was Jeffrey who had all but severed my relationship with her. Therapy was a weakness, an opening for someone to exploit, an admission that you had no control.

"I'm not promising forever. We don't really know each other, although," and his eyes caught mine again, "I feel like we do, which is really strange and irritating," he shook his head lightly. "But I like you," his thumb rubbed circles on the back of my hand, his fingers shifted slightly underneath mine. Every movement sent shocks of awareness coursing through my body. If he didn't stop touching me, I was going to fucking implode. I tugged at my hand, his tightened ever so briefly, then released. But I didn't pull back, which just left my hands resting in his. It was more intense than the petting had been.

"You like me?" I repeated.

"Yes. I do. And I want to have the fucking time and space to see if you like me, too. To fucking *make* you like me if you don't."

I laughed, "You can't make me like you if I don't."

"The hell you say," he growled.

"Well, you don't have to worry about it," I demured. "I like you, too."

He didn't move, he didn't shift a muscle. But his whole body exhaled. The energy in the room immediately shifted. The tension that had been crackling in the air, the tension in him that I had barely registered, simply disappeared, replaced by languid calm.

"You do?"

"I do." His grin was blinding. I was momentarily stunned silent...I'd seen his full smile many times. Especially during our Killmonger walks, often during our brainstorming sessions when we let ourselves get swept away with the fabrics and design, and definitely when we'd binged the most recent season of *Project Runway*. But this smile was different. Dangerous. As if my admission had flipped a switch in him.

"But," I said, regrettably causing his smile to lose a bit of its megawatt power, "I work for you." I held up a hand, and tapped one fingertip, "your family is not at all interested in you liking me," I tapped a second finger, "Elizabeth would be a fool to give you up, regardless of what you say," I tapped a third and, "I'm scared, too. I've been through this already. I'm not interested."

"Been through what? Not interested in what? Me?" He chuckled, "Survey says, that's a lie," he trailed his fingers along my exposed thigh and the goosepimples popped up as expected. The mischief lit his eyes now that I'd admitted that I liked him. It was like he couldn't hear anything else. Cute. *Too fucking cute for my own good.*

"Just because I like you doesn't mean anything can come of it. Seriously, Abe," I smacked his hand where it was creeping, teasing further up my thigh. "Stop," I started laughing because he was truly little-boy-gleeful now. It was a stark contrast to the sadness that had brought me to his room to begin with.

He stopped. "Okay, but why can't anything come of it?"

"Aren't you listening to me? Just because you told Elizabeth," I waved a hand, "whatever you told her, doesn't mean that your family gives a shit. If you're supposed to marry her, then that's what's going to happen. In my experience, your type and my type don't have a great run rate."

"My type? What's my *type*?" He looked half offended, half pissed.

"Rich boy, silver spoon, house in the Hamptons type. The type whose parents arrange their marriages, the type whose marriage is about wealth expansion and acquisition. The type who needs a wife who lunches and dedicates her time to charity. The type who would want to rebel against those expectations by having a fling with a wholly inappropriate woman with no pedigree who grew up in the system. That type." I finished having held his gaze the whole time. He needed see how serious I was and I needed to see his response.

"That's what you think of me? That's what you think I think of you?"

"I don't know what to think, Abe."

"You do, though. You know me better than that. But I understand," he pushed back and I felt immediately bereft. Was he giving up that easily? If he was, then I'd definitely done the right thing by pushing him. If I felt the hot sting of tears. It wasn't disappointment, I told myself, it was budding anger at allowing myself to give his little proclamations even a moment of consideration. I'd almost done it a-fucking-gin. *Stupid.*

"I'll just have to prove it to you." *Wait, what?* "And it's fair, I suppose. I did ghost you all those years ago."

Prove it to me?

"We'll start tonight. With dinner," he continued.

He was up and moving to where his phone lay. My head was spinning. Surely I was misunderstanding.

"Will you have dinner with me?" He paused in his dialing and lobbed the question at me.

"Dinner?"

"Yeah. Like, food. Food that you eat when it's dark outside," he looked at his watch. It was nearing midnight. "Or, maybe supper instead. Let's have supper."

"Supper?"

He held my gaze once the call connected. I listened to him order a car to be brought around and request late-night reservations.

"The car will be here in 30," he grinned and grabbed my hand pulling me to my feet. "You like me."

I couldn't help but laugh, even though the voice in my head and my heart warned me to be careful. "Yes, I like you. And yes, I'll go to supper with you, but Abe…"

His smile faded a bit, and he squeezed my hand, "No buts. Not tonight. Not for the next three weeks. Let's just see what we could be. Let's just see."

So began my first official date with Abraham Walker, CEO.

CHAPTER 25

ABE.

Since Cassandra's late-night visit to my suite, I'd been walking on clouds. She'd agreed, albeit reluctantly, to give us...whatever that meant...a shot for the three weeks we were here in Europe. It was a dangerous game but one I couldn't bring myself to stop playing.

Especially at moments like this. Moments when she was hot and soft in my arms, twisted around me, mouth open under mine, matching my energy kilowatt for kilowatt. I couldn't get enough. My hands, my mind, my very soul, they were all filled with her.

We were currently in her room, having barely made it there after another night full of parties and lights, beautiful people, and free-flowing champagne. We had finished our responsibilities about thirty minutes earlier. Cassandra's team had been running around the city, attending various shows, taking notes, dropping names, and generally getting a feel for the lay of the land. Simultaneously, she and I had been attending business meetings disguised as after-show parties, planting seeds for something big coming from HeirLoom next season.

The energy was high, the buzz of excitement palpable among everyone attached to our project. At the end of it all, the whole team convened in what we'd dubbed the work suite to debrief the day. It was the schedule we'd fallen into over the last few days. Everything moved like chaotic clockwork in the suite that was filled with images, sketches, and fabric samples as we considered and rejected ideas, wanting to make sure that when we finally put the line forth, it was new, fresh, and unlike anything seen on the runways this season or last.

When the frenetic brainstorming began to peter out, the energy in the room finally retreating to normal levels, we wrapped up the session. Some members of the team headed straight for their beds, others returned to the streets eager to see what misadventures the night might hold.

Tamra was the last to leave the suite tonight. When the door closed behind her, the silence dropped, and the hunger that I'd been tamping down all day surged to the surface. I welcomed it, even though I had no expectations of acting on it other than spending another few hours in Cassandra's company, learning about each other, as we'd done the last several nights.

I couldn't...wouldn't...deny that I wanted more than those conversations, but I treasured them. And so, as she padded around the room, stacking papers, sorting piles of samples, filling the silence with chatter about the evening, I poured a couple of fingers of bourbon over ice in two of the heavy crystal tumblers provided by the hotel and contemplated how tonight's hang out might unfold.

When I turned back to bring the drinks to the table, I found her standing stock still, staring at one of the sketches we'd tweaked.

"Andi? What's up?" I moved to stand behind her, still a little stunned that the last several days had brought us close enough that being with her like this, close enough to feel her warmth, was now in our purview.

She leaned back against me, and my arms slipped loosely around her waist. My chin lowered to the top of her head, my nose immediately filled with the scent of her...a little earthy, a little ethereal. My mind temporarily locked up, trying to decide whether or not to lose contact long enough to put the glasses down so I could properly touch her.

I was grateful when she stirred long enough to take her glass, freeing up one hand so I could lay it flat across her belly, holding her close while I peeked over her shoulder at the sketch she held. It was one of many that fit the broad lines of the vision for the show we were creating.

"I don't know. What do you think about this one? I'm on the fence," she sipped.

"Why? What rubs you wrong about it?" I was always curious to hear how her mind worked. The piece she was referring to was one of my favorites, and I knew I'd push to have samples made even if it wasn't included in the final production.

"I don't know. It feels expected, you know? What's making it special?" She tilted the sketch, picked up another that showed the same style from different angles.

"It's subtle. I think the 'special' on this piece will come through the seaming and the combinations of fabrics. What are the fabric notes?"

She flipped the card over to read the notes scribbled on the back and nodded. "You're right, you're right," she added the sketch to the stack she had created. "We talked about this...the tonal color combo in different fabrics...I need to get out of my head. But I'm just so excited!" She whirled in my arms and would've knocked my own glass free had I not lifted it above her head.

"Oops! Sorry," she laughed, mis-matched eyes sparkling. "I'm losing it." She dropped her forehead to my chest.

My free hand slid along her spine, trying to soothe the nerves a little bit.

"Nothing to be sorry about. This is big. And I'd rather you be amped up than nonchalant, yeah?"

I felt her head move against my chest as she nodded.

"A toast?" I wrapped my hand in the skinny twists that waved down her back and tugged gently so she'd raise her eyes to mine. She nodded again and lifted her glass to rest it against mine.

"To dreams fulfilled and happy memories?"

A slow grin crept across her face. "To raging success and all this money."

"Oh, that's how you're feeling?"

"That's how I'm feeling," she laughed and shimmied out of my arms. I missed her immediately, but it was clear that she was still on a high. She needed physical activity...a way to siphon off some of the energy. I definitely had options in mind but wasn't about to press. I suggested the next best thing to hot, sweaty sex: hot sweaty dancing...

"Want to go dancing? Or maybe walk the city? You look like you still have energy to burn."

"Dancing, yes! Give me fifteen minutes to change?"

I'd offered, but my head spun a little at the speed with which she accepted the invite. "Sounds good. I'll meet you at your room?"

"Perfect!" She clapped her hands, tossed her bourbon back, slipped up to me, and rose on her toes to press a kiss against my lips. *Delicious.* "I can't wait," she whispered and skipped out of the room.

Jesus. Down, boy. I cast a rueful glance at my overeager dick and rubbed a hand across my face trying to regain a little control. I felt the stubble on my chin getting a little out of hand and decided to use part of the fifteen minutes to shave. At least it would give me something to focus on other than the prospect of getting hot and sweaty with Cassandra on the dance floor.

Fifteen minutes later, I stood in front of Cassandra's door, lower jaw on the ground, again fighting my body's natural reaction to everything about this woman. Over our weeks of working together and growing closer, I'd been blessed to meet several versions of Cassandra. There was the focused, almost stern version that pulled our debriefs together and ruthlessly edited ideas; the quiet, shy version who whispered her dreams to me as we cuddled on the sofa, listening to music; the self-possessed, practical woman who had not only survived a childhood that was stacked against her but had thrived and the ditzy, head in the clouds artist who could spend hours sketching and looked at me with faraway eyes when she was interrupted.

I had not, however, met intentionally sexy, ready to wear me out on the dancefloor Cassandra. She had changed into skintight low-waisted bell bottom jeans, paired with a tiny crop that barely covered her small breasts. My eyes danced from bare midriff to underboob to sideboob to bare shoulders to sweetly flared hips encased in buttersoft denim. Her twists hung down her back.

If I didn't know her for the highly accomplished thirty-something year old woman she was, I'd have mistaken her for a very off-limits early twenty-something bundle of trouble.

She stepped forward, mischief sparkling in her pretty eyes. Oh yeah, she knew what she was doing. The 'bundle of trouble' part obviously still applied.

"Ready?" Her grin was right there in front of me, so I dropped my head to taste the happiness on her lips. The dip wasn't as far as it usually was. I stepped back to look down. She must've been wearing 5-inch heels, at least. She obliged by kicking her foot out from under the wide leg of her jeans to show me the cute platforms she'd chosen.

"You happy with yourself?" I could hear the rasp in my own voice.

"I am," she gave a slow spin. "Are you happy with me?" A coy little smile over her shoulder, with that beautiful denim-encased ass on display.

So I smacked it. She yelped. I grinned. "Damn skippy, I am."

I grabbed her hand, "Let's go before we don't go."

Then she mumbled something that stopped me in my tracks. "We don't have to go. We could come instead."

My brain stuttered to a stop. "Excuse me?" I couldn't have heard correctly.

"Huh?" Wide eyes met mine. I narrowed my gaze, and dropped my brows.

"Did you say something?" I stepped a little closer and was rewarded by the hitch in her breath.

"Um, kinda?" Her lashes fluttered with rapid blinks.

"Mmm. Would you like to repeat it?"

"I *said*," she emphasized, taking a deep breath, "we don't have to go. We could come instead."

Yep, that was it. Dick on one hundred, just like that. But was she sure? I wasn't about to pressure her into anything she wasn't ready for. I'd waited this long. I'd wait however long it took. And that thought alone was enough to make me pause. Because since when did I wait on women?

While I contemplated my descent into sappiness, she closed the space between us, danced her fingers along the front of the black button-down I'd paired with equally dark jeans. But her eyes were still downcast, and I needed to see certainty there.

I slipped a finger under her chin...corny as fuck...and tilted her head up to see what was written on her face. And damn near got my eyebrows scorched off.

Fuuuuck. I'd like to think I was smooth with it, but I cannot confirm that. What I do know is that I fused my mouth with hers damn near immediately, trying to absorb every part of her that I could.

It wasn't the first time we'd kissed by far. We'd shared some hot ones already, but by unspoken agreement, we hadn't moved further than heavy petting. And I was cool with that; honestly, I'd enjoyed it because how often did grown-ass people take the time to just make out. So yeah, the last few days had been fun.

But this? This was heaven. I felt her hand slide up my back, pulling me closer. I obliged.

I backed her out of the hallway, and back into the room, kicked the door shut, and spun, placing her back against it. My hands drifted down her side, lingering where her breasts swelled against the sides of her crop—enjoying the softness there, skating my thumbs across her nipples. She rewarded me by arching her back, pressing herself into my hands, and deepening our kiss.

I continued my journey, tracing the softness of her exposed skin. I delayed again at the dip of her waist above her hips. My fingers played along the waistband of her low-slung jeans. I dipped a finger behind the clasp, she sucked in air against my lips. I smiled against hers.

I could feel her light undulations against me, rubbing, grinding her softness against my length. I thanked God for the platforms she was wearing. When she lifted one leg to wrap it around my waist, her heat was damn close to where I needed it to be.

I dropped my head to ask, "Are you sure?" I could hear the roughness in my voice. But I couldn't make myself care, my mouth opened against the side of her neck. I sucked. Her standing leg buckled.

I caught her underneath the thighs and lifted her, hoisting her against the door until I was settled between her open legs, pressed against the hot vee in the middle.

She matched my groan and arched against me, grinding in earnest, chasing her pleasure. I leaned back to watch, supported her hips until I caught her rhythm. And then applied rocking counter pressure that sent us both wheeling toward dark satisfaction.

She came apart in my arms, head thrown against the door, back arched, titties forward, with a bright flush climbing from somewhere beneath her top. Stunning.

She went weak; I did not. I was still hard enough to cut diamonds but I needed to make sure she was still with me. If she'd just needed the release, so be it because it had been worth it, even if I was stuck with blue balls yet another night.

I'd been holding her, supporting her weight until she caught her breath. When she shimmied a little in my arms, I figured she was back to herself and let her legs slide down mine until her feet were back on solid ground. I gave her another second to steady herself before relaxing my grip, interested to see what she would say next.

She said nothing. Instead she kicked off her shoes, unfastened the painted-on jeans, and peeled out of them, revealing the sexiest scrap of purple nothingness stretching across her hips that I could imagine. Before my mind could categorize what was happening, she was on her knees, fingers quick and nimble at my buckle and zipper.

And then...dear God...*then*...the hot, slick wetness of her mouth engulfed me. Pulling. Licking. Sucking. My brain simply shorted out. All I could focus on was the wet slurp of her lips, the deep pull of her mouth, the sweet roughness of her tongue, and the sounds...the sounds were everything.

I tried to keep my hips still. I really, truly did. But her hands were at my thighs, pulling me into her; and then I was fucking her mouth against the wall, and my head was exploding in a rainbow tinted kaleidoscope of color. I was dead.

Fuck.

When my vision cleared, and I was able to open my eyes, I peeked down at her ready to apologize for having been so brutal. But I found her staring up at me with bi-colored eyes, licking those sweet lips, with her hand between her legs. Waiting.

Then she smiled, and I was lost.

I pulled her up, picked her up, and took her to bed.

Chapter 26

CASSANDRA.

Never, not once, at no point in my life had I ever felt this way. Never felt so intensely connected to someone, but more importantly, I'd never felt so *safe* in that connection. Which said something because I had been wholeheartedly committed to marrying Jeffrey.

Abe bounced me in his arms slightly, bringing my attention back to the fact that my naked ass was snuggled against his not-naked chest. That by itself was enough to send me directly to heaven. I couldn't remember having ever been picked up. Certainly not by the foster parents of my youth; and then by the time I'd settled with Gogo's family, I'd been too old for such shenanigans. Jeffrey, artistic and nerdy, hadn't been the picking up kind. It wasn't something I'd ever consciously thought about because it hadn't been part of my lived experience. But this was really, really nice. Almost...necessary. Frighteningly so. I'd have to run it by my therapist.

Another bounce accompanied by a squeeze. I lifted my head from where I was enjoying the short ride from the front door to the bedroom of my suite. He was staring down at me with an intoxicating combination of concern and hunger.

"You good?"

I nodded.

"You keep drifting to somewhere else." He was too damn observant for his own good. I decided to be as honest as possible.

"I was thinking that I don't remember having ever been picked up." At his raised eyebrows, I gave a little shrug. We had arrived by the bed and he made no move to put me down. "I like it," I added.

He grinned. "I'm glad. I'll carry you anywhere, anytime you want me to." He shifted, turning to sit on the bed with me still in his lap.

I laughed and spun...awkwardly, but without leaving my comfy spot...to straddle him. "Thank you."

"Of course," his hands had fallen to my ass, where he squeezed and kneaded gently, almost unconsciously.

I rocked forward, bringing my naked center in contact with the rough linen blend of his black shirt. "Maybe you should take this off?"

"Mmmm," he agreed and proceeded to do just that, revealing the sleekly muscled chest I'd seen by the pool at his house. The same chest that my hands had roamed more than one night over the course of the week. During hot, high school make-out sessions that had sent me to bed with my pillow between my thighs. I'd enjoyed the teasing, the flirting, the talking.

But when he'd shown up to my door tonight in black jeans that encased a tight ass and muscled thighs, a perfectly tailored faintly printed black button down, freshly shaved and showered and smelling like everything my tender, horny soul needed, I couldn't help myself. Tonight, I needed more. We both deserved more. I believed him when he said he wanted me; that we could figure something out. And if we couldn't, well, I'd gone into it with my eyes open this time, hadn't I?

So, I would do all the things I wanted to do. I'd let him see every piece of me and I'd require the same.

I lifted slightly as he pulled the shirt off; then he lifted his hips to hook his thumbs in the waistband of the jeans he'd barely pulled up so he could walk us to the bedroom. He raised an eyebrow at me, asking, again, if this was what I wanted.

I rose onto my knees, not leaving my perch but giving him room enough to struggle the pants down and kick them off. Then he slid his also black boxer briefs down to let his hard thick length pop out against me. *Yessss...* the word hissed through my mind as my greedy eyes took in the male beauty of him. He had filled my mouth to overflowing and I could not wait any longer to feel him inside me. I immediately centered myself and sank down on my reward for head well-given.

Our groans of pleasure mingled, loud and ragged. His hands at my waist ground me into him so that he filled me completely, almost but not quite painfully. My clit rested against the rough hair at his base and I rocked to amplify the contact, taking him even deeper inside.

His hands parted, one holding me tight at the hip, the other tangling in my twists to tug my head back. His mouth opened on my throat, tongue rough, lips sucking...I'd have hickeys tomorrow. I didn't care. I *loved* it and he'd picked up on that fact so fucking fast.

His hips began to move under me. I kept my head thrown back, anything to make sure his mouth didn't move. Except it did, trailing across my chest to suck almost my whole breast into his mouth. He was sooo hungry, so ravenous. For me. I felt consumed by him, and it was exactly what I wanted. Exactly what I needed.

His hips and mouth took on the same rhythm so that each stroke was accompanied by a wet, hot suck of one nipple and a firm circling rub of the thumb he'd wet in my mouth at the other.

This. This had to be heaven. The thought flitted through my mind, exploding into butterfly wings as every nerve ending in my body turned its attention to Abe's hands, mouth, dick.

I thought it couldn't get any better. I tried to express my delight with a sexily whispered 'yes, baby.' It came out strangled and broken as I dripped all over him. My wetness and his stroke filled the room with sound; I loved it. Then he shifted again, moving further onto the bed and laying back. He planted my hands on his chest, his pecs acting like handles. And somehow found the leverage to start fully fucking me from beneath. *Dear God.* I held on for the ride, enjoying every minute, being filled over and over again until I felt tears start to gather at the corners of my eyes.

His hands clenched at my waist as I worked him from above. Each pump of his hips, each answering swivel of mine, sent me, my clit and all my insides racing for release. I could hear the short gasps leaving my lips but was powerless to stop them.

The build up had begun in earnest, the faint sporadic clenching had started, I almost wanted to delay, to prolong, but my body refused to obey. I changed tactics, grinding down, but I just couldn't...

"I need..." I whispered.

He flipped us before I could finish the thought. Spread my legs, pressed my knees back, and settled into long, deep strokes that touched every part of me. He used the broad pad of his thumb to match long strokes across my clit. I impossibly opened my legs even further because this man could have *all* of me.

And then conscious thought just skitted away. Sound and sight and smell and taste merged into one swirl of sensation that sent me spiraling and splintering and exploding into the tiniest, brightest pinpoints of light. I screamed. Or shrieked. Or cried. I can't say for sure. I felt him fill me up, hot and streaky inside.

He rolled again, I collapsed on his chest with him still inside me. And I slept.

***

I came awake a while later. I didn't move, didn't open my eyes but took stock of where I was and how I was feeling. The warmth under my ear let me know I was still laying on Abe's chest. It rose and fell steadily. He was either asleep or just calm, chilling.

I was still straddled across him, I was going to be mad sore from holding that stretch. Safe and content, I moved to slide off him and realized he was still *inside* me. I stopped immediately and clenched. *Jesus.* I squeezed again. I couldn't help it. It was involuntary. I didn't want to wake him up but I really wanted to wake him up. Would it be wrong to ride him to another orgasm while he was asleep? I mean, he'd left it there, surely I could use it?

I gave a teeny tiny, infinitesimally small bump and grind. He started to swell inside me. *Oh my god.*

"Good morning," the words rumbled against my chest more than they resonated in my ears. I lifted my head, and seated myself more comfortably.

"Good morning," I ignored the fact that my hips had kept up their steady, barely there bump and grind.

He did not.

"Enjoying yourself?" His normally heavy lidded, wildly sexy eyes, were almost closed but intently focused on me.

"I am. You?"

"Immensely."

"Mm. I'll just keep doing what I'm doing then."

He nodded, "I'd like that."

I grinned. He matched it. And I got on with the business of chopping down his morning wood.

***

Some hours later, after we'd both showered and shared an elaborate breakfast provided by room service, we were back in the debriefing room at the generous dining slash conference table.

A few team members were there as well, having stumbled in after their night of sin and debauchery. We didn't expect the room to be full for another couple of hours. Our schedule was light for the day, and we'd all been going full throttle since our arrival a couple of weeks ago. We had another long week stretching ahead of us before we returned to the States.

Abe and I were doing what I thought was an excellent job of not looking like we'd spent the last several hours becoming intimately familiar with each other. I was studiously not focusing on the taste of his skin in my mouth but the needy little kitty between my thighs was not getting with the program. She was delightedly focused on remembering the precise feeling of being stretched to capacity by Abe. Her feet were kicked up and she was flipping through her book of memories putting post it notes on the pages she wanted to revisit.

My nipples were sore, my thighs were sore, my panties were damp. Life was great.

Abe's phone pinged with a text. Because I couldn't help but watch him, I noticed his expression change from something reflecting languid contentment to confusion, surprise, and shock.

"Who was it?" I asked.

"Vince," he paused. "Remember that photo you got? We thought it was a young version of Benjamin Whyte?"

"Yeah, I remember," mild curiosity tugged; I had completely forgotten about the picture. I was pretty sure I'd thrown it away when I was cleaning up before this trip.

"Well, I sent it to Vince to look into."

"Vince?" I knew he acted as his butler and cook when the mood struck him but I couldn't find a reason for Abe to send him the photo.

"Yeah. He's multitalented. One of those talents is finding shit out."

I nodded, "Okay. What'd he find out?" Abe had my full attention but that was mainly because looking at him was one of my favorite things to do.

He turned his phone toward me so I could see the picture there. It looked like a color version of the photo I'd received. I leaned in. It showed a handsome white man with thick blond hair and a stern, but not mean, expression. The photo felt old but I couldn't put my finger on why. Something about the hair maybe? The choice of clothing?

"Okay. Is that not a young Benjamin Whyte?"

"No. It's his son, Jacob," he turned the phone back to study the photo again.

"Well. Mystery solved I guess. But why did I get the photo? Is he a model or something? Am I renting his old spot?"

"No. But there's something about him."

He handed me the phone again, watching me as I pinched and zoomed on the screen. Nothing jumped out.

"What?"

"I honestly don't know. But something keeps striking me about this picture. I can't put my finger on it," and it was clearly frustrating the hell out of him.

I refocused, zoomed again.

"Well, I don't see it. But you do you," I said, trying to lighten the mood just a little bit, but he didn't bite.

"Mmm." He was being really thoughtful for some reason.

"Abe. What's going on?"

"It just seems weird that you receive a picture of a man affiliated with this community, in this industry, to a place he's never lived," he looked once more, then flicked the screen closed. "I don't believe in coincidences."

"So you think...what, exactly?"

"I think someone wanted you to know about him."

"Why, Abe? That makes no sense. Mail goes to the wrong place all the time."

"Maybe. Maybe," he repeated. "He also sent some screen-shots of new clippings."

"Clippings?"

"Yeah. They're old stories apparently," he was scrolling slowly. I assumed he was skimming through the contents of the news articles he'd received.

"The photo feels old. Is it?"

His response was slow as his eyes moved across the text. "Mmhmm. It's from this article it seems," he paused. "It was written about thirty years ago."

"Huh. What's it say?"

His fingers had stopped scrolling. Some new emotion crept across his face. I was still learning him so I couldn't pinpoint it but his features tensed, shifted into something like determina-tion. He lifted his head and looked around, taking in the handful of team members milling about.

Tamra had joined the room in the last couple of minutes with Adam, and was pouring herself coffee to go with the crois-sant and fruit she'd snagged from the ever-present buffet in the room. She had tossed a slow nod our way upon entry and was now making her equally slow way to where Camran and Ziggy, two junior designers were whispering.

On the other side of the room Marla and Dymin were sorting through fabrics, loosely organizing them according to sketches and ke-keing about the models they'd spent the evening with. It was a slow, lazy morning.

We were relatively private but Abe moved closer to me, sliding his chair next to mine so that the heat from his thigh singed my bare one. I'd chosen a loose baby doll mini today. I'd be lying if I said I hadn't thought about the ease of access it provided when I slipped it over my head, braless with the thinnest scrap of seamless panties underneath. I'd considered going without panties but given how the drip had started with just the thought of Abe peeling the dress back off of me, I'd decided against it. I needed a barrier.

"Hmm? What?" I asked. It took a minute to drag my thoughts back to the photo and article.

Those deep brown eyes dropped to my lips. He licked his. "Focus, Andi. Or I'm going to drag you across this table and stick my tongue as far inside you as I can get it."

I slow-blinked at him. "Um, if that's meant to be a threat, I think you're confused about my concepts of punishment. We should talk."

He growled, actually growled, at me. I grinned. Then, re-membering where we were and that we had a potential audi-ence, I dropped my gaze and turned my attention back to his phone.

"Later," he said.

"Please and thank you," I replied.

He kept me pinned with that smoldering look for a moment longer before he laughed. Because what else could he do right here and right now?

"Look, woman. Read this," he tilted his phone in my direction. "He left Hudson Valley thirty years ago amid 'rumor and speculation.'"

"What kind of rumor and speculation?" We were almost noggin to noggin, looking at his screen. "This doesn't say anything other than he's going to start an international branch of Whyte's. What's so mysterious about that?"

"Vince sent more. A couple of these are from rag magazines. They're saying he was in a relationship and that his parents didn't approve."

"Weird. But also not weird. I mean, no shade, but your family is all up in your business, too" I read a bit further. The article, clearly sensationalized, discussed a secret love affair and hinted at a possible baby but that was unconfirmed.

"What if that's why he left?"

Confusion knit my brows, "You think they made him leave her? You think they ran away together?"

"I don't know. But I'm going to put Vince on finding out. I suspect he's already looking into it. He loves a good mystery." His fingers flew over the keypad of his phone.

"We'll know more soon enough. In the meantime, get to work. You have other things on your plate for later."

"Mmm," I was happy to turn my attention away from the photo and stories of rich boys and forbidden love. "I look forward to being on your plate later."

Chapter 27

ABE.

After our bliss-filled nights in Europe, I hadn't been sure what to expect when we returned to the States. I'd been wholly prepared for Cassandra to pull back. I hoped she wouldn't, but I would have understood. The optics weren't good when it came to sleeping with the boss...even though I considered it more of a partnership...and she had far more to lose on that end than I did. I wasn't so misogynistic that I couldn't recognize the male privilege of it all. So, yeah, if she had pumped the brakes on things once we got back under the watchful eye of HeirLoom, I would have fallen in line with however she wanted to play it.

Thank God she hadn't.

Instead, she had welcomed me into her bed and her body every night since we'd returned. And I planned to be in both again tonight. I shot her a text to confirm and verify that hunan tofu would be a good dinner choice. When she replied with a smiley face, chop sticks and a splash emoji, I laughed and figured I was all good.

Except I hadn't heard her voice today since I'd slipped out of bed this morning before she woke. I'd left her Keurig primed for her. Ignoring the fact that I had literally *just* texted, I tapped the video chat icon...in for a penny, in for a pound...already grinning at the prospect of hearing *and* seeing her, and lifted the phone.

"Hey," I said when her pretty face appeared on screen...flushed?

"Hey, yourself," she replied breathily. Her eyes were slightly out of focus and faintly dazed. This wasn't an unusual occurrence, especially if I interrupted a creative session. When she was on a roll, she completely lost herself in her work, and it could sometimes take a moment for her to plug back into the current reality. In those brief moments, she sometimes wore the most endearing, baffled expression, as if she were unsure how she came to be in this regular world with regular people.

But this was a different sort of dazed...one I thought I recognized, but surely not...

I tilted my head, intrigued. "What are you up to?"

"Oh," she gasped faintly, blinked, "nothing." Another brief pause, "You?"

I remained silent. Listening to her breath catch again, watching her slow blink, followed by a soft sigh. Was she...? Couldn't be. I glanced at my watch. It was 3 in the afternoon. She was in her office.

"Abe?" She called my name when I didn't respond. "What are you doing?"

"Oh, I'm just trying to figure out why you look and sound like you do when you're begging me to fuck you."

She giggled breathlessly, "Do I?"

I squinted and peered at the phone, as if I would somehow gain a broader field of vision. She hummed. My eyes grew wide and I made an abrupt about-face to head, not back to my own offices, but to hers.

"Where are you?" I knew the answer.

"In my office. Where are you?"

"On my way to your office."

"Excellent," she cut the call.

Fuck me. I all but sprinted to her office with visions of her spread across the desk, legs open, fingers in play already wet for me. As I approached, I felt eyes on me, knew my stride was *too* long, *too* purposeful. But I didn't give a shit.

"Hi Mr. Walker," Tamra's voice sang out when I crossed the threshold of the design suite. "Ms. Williams has asked not to be disturbed."

"I'm her boss, Tamra," I tossed over my shoulder without breaking stride.

"Yes, but, she said...," I stopped, and threw my CEO glare at her.

"I don't care what she said. Tamra." She swallowed and nodded. Fingers frantically flying over her keyboard. No doubt sending Cassandra a warning message. My feet landed just outside her office door and I heard the snick of the lock turn.

I turned the knob, met no resistance and slipped in.

My fantasies sucked. Because *this*, this was the stuff of real fantasies.

Warm copper toned skin, hot eyes, sweet lips, soft breathlessness and *need* staring me right in my eyes.

"What the hell have you been doing in here?" I approached her, hands open as she walked in to my arms and slid one of my hands under her dress, between her legs. The other automatically went to her back to hold her steady as her knees softened.

"Thinking about you too damn much," She tiptoed back against her desk, put her hands on my shoulders and applied pressure. I happily dropped to my knees in front of her.

"You've been distracting me all day," she complained as I settled between her open thighs, taking a moment to enjoy the sight of her, wet, glistening, swollen still from the days and nights of our being together. I licked my lips.

"I'm sorry, baby," I hummed against her clit. She gasped and moaned.

"Fix it," she ordered.

"Gladly," I opened my mouth and covered as much of her as I could, sweeping my tongue along her, swiping across her apex and dipping into her opening, gathering and drinking everything she gifted me with.

She was delicious, absolutely, mind-numbingly delicious. I hoisted her further onto the desk and slipped her knees over my shoulders. *Not enough*. I pressed her thighs back and open so she was splayed wide and I could truly fuck her with my tongue. Which I did. Thoroughly. To her vocal delight.

I added two fingers to the mix, letting my tongue play everywhere else I could reach. When she shuddered and came all over my tongue and lips, I licked her clean with long slow strokes, enjoying every last drop like she was fucking Folger's coffee. She lay wrung out on the desk. I watched as her breath slowed from heaving with pleasure to deep relaxed inhalations;

then I held out my hand to help her up, right her skirt, and re-fluff her hair.

"Better?"

"For the moment," she grimaced, and I laughed because she was deadass with it. I was rock hard at the moment for obvious reasons, but my erection hadn't been more than a sneeze away since that night she'd worn the bell bottoms. I felt fucking fifteen.

"What about you?"

I looked down at the obvious tent in my pants, thankful for their dark color. "It'll work itself out. And if not, I'll save it for you later."

"Mm," she hummed, dubious, and began to approach, hand reaching for my zipper. A knock on the door stopped her progress. I let an eyebrow rise, curious to see what she would do next.

She rolled her eyes at me and called out, "Yes, Tamra? I'm still in with Mr. Walker."

"Um, yes, I know, but you're going to be late for your 4 o'clock if you don't leave now."

The look on her face made it clear that she'd completely forgotten about her 4 o'clock. I chuckled, flattered, and pulled her to me. As always, she felt perfect in my arms. I licked my lips again...the taste of her was all over me and I loved that shit.

I dropped a kiss on the top of her head. "I'll see you tonight, baby. And I'll fully address any lingering issues you may have."

She snuggled into me, shy. It delighted me how everyday Cassandra was quiet, a little flighty, and fairly reserved. Professional Cassandra was confident and direct, an advocate for her team. But horny Andi? *Yes, God.* She was demanding, unabashed, downright nasty. This woman was going to be the death of me. I would die happy.

I lingered so we could walk together to the elevators after she'd laughingly given me a makeup wipe to clean my face.

"Where are you headed?" I asked once we were strolling down the hallway and into the waiting elevator.

"I'm meeting Michel," she said, referring to the agent who was handling our model identification. He had photos for final selections. Under normal circumstances, he would have come to our offices, but Cassandra often preferred to get out and walk.

"Are you coming back to the office or heading straight home?" Home referred to her place.

"Not sure yet. Probably back to the office. I don't expect this to take more than a couple hours. We've done a lot of the paring online."

I nodded, gave her another quick peck that she stepped away from as if I were somehow contagious.

"Abe!" She glanced around the elevator as if someone other than we were in there, hiding behind thin air. "Not here."

I grinned and held my hands up, "The doors are closed! There's no one here," I tilted my head in contemplation. "I could do anything I want."

"No, sir. You cannot," her hand was firm on my chest. Cuteness overload. The telltale ding sounded just before the doors slid open.

"See you tonight," she whispered it as she dashed off toward the exits.

I watched her for as long as the elevator doors would allow. When they slid closed again, I directed the car back to the fifteenth floor. I had shit to clear off my plate so I could get out of here at close to the same time Cassandra did.

My mind had clicked over to business mode, efficiently running through tasks that needed completing and calls that needed to be placed. The time in Europe had afforded me the opportunity to connect more informally with a couple of board members who had shown up at the Fashion Weeks. Individually, I'd had dinner and drinks with Elizabeth Holmes, Adrienne Boger and Melvin Chaney. All three had seemed excited about the line and the direction of the company. Granted all three enjoyed the fashion side of the business, as evidenced by their attendance at the shows, so they may have been a bit biased. They had, however, been willing to let me know which of their fellow board members were less than enthusiastic.

Now, as much as I hated it, I needed to lean into campaigning. I wasn't going to get voted out of my role for taking the company in the direction it needed to go. If I walked away, it would be under my volition, not because some old heads who'd spent too much time in the sun golfing away their golden years thought 'making dresses' was a silly way for the company to progress.

I had just pulled my phone from my pocket and was scrolling my board contacts, crafting the phone calls in my head, trying to decide how to best cajole these old dudes into having a couple of drinks with just me...sans my father...when that devil's name popped onto my phone's lock screen.

Just seeing his name was enough to cause the last vestiges of relaxation from my interlude with Cassandra to evaporate. I considered ignoring it but didn't want to risk having to see his ugly mug should he decide to pop into my office in person.

"Can I help you?" I answered after sliding my thumb across the screen to connect the call.

"You certainly fucking can," the usual venom in his voice was running on extra high today. What the fuck was his problem now? "Get the fuck up here. Now." He cut the connection.

Fuck.

There were times when the old man could be ignored. Now did not feel like one of those times. I retraced my steps to the elevator and rode the car another five floors up to the building's apex, where my father kept a suite of offices that put mine to shame. It was a waste of money really. He was rarely here. But appearances were everything according to the Book of Godrick.

I hated the nerves that were creeping along my spine like ants, making me uncomfortable and throwing me back to the other myriad times I'd been summoned to his office like a child. It had always been that way. Even as an actual child, even when Trey and I had been called in together. For the longest time, we always assumed he and I would be equally chastised for whatever mayhem we'd gotten ourselves into. We'd been prepared to stand shoulder to shoulder and accept our punishment. But eventually, we'd learned that no matter the offense, I'd take the brunt of the fallout including responsibility for luring Trey into situations he had no business being in. He'd had enough once I turned twelve. It was when he'd finally separated us...for Godrick's good...and sent me to boarding school. The joke was on the old man though. The distance had secured my and Godrick's relationship. Shifting the sibling bond into something indestructible. It was during those long years, that Trey and I had formulated our plan for when he took over. Of how we'd oust the old man, take over the company, and turn it into something that brought joy to our family instead of casting a pallor of darkness and doom at every turn.

But then Trey had died. Because of me.

Because I'd been selfish. Because I had wanted to rub it into our father's face that Trey chose me, wanted to spend that incredibly special night...the first step in our plans...with his bad influence brother. And we'd paid the ultimate price. The old man had been right after all...I had been the death of my brother, just like he'd predicted.

I grimaced as I approached his lair. The elevator ride had not been nearly long enough, and the doors slid open to dump me into the foyer of his suites. I tried to steady my breathing before entering, tried to recenter my thoughts and turn them away from my brother, away from that gaping hole of loss that was constantly there...except when Cassandra stepped in to fill it.

I hated interacting with him when I wasn't wholly prepared.

Then his gruff voice rang out, shattering my attempts at preparation, "Are you going to fucking stand there doing your yoga shit all damn day, or are you going to come in and tell me what the fuck you were doing traipsing all over Europe dragging this family name through the mud."

Oh, that. That, I could handle. I actually felt a smile ghost across my lips at the anger he must have felt when those photos had hit the stands. Warwick had given me a heads-up.

"What the fuck is this?" As soon as I crossed the threshold, a sheaf of magazines hit the heavy marble table that stood in the center of the large main space that acted as a conference room and lounging space.

As I anticipated, the magazines, ranging from *Us Weekly* to *Inside Design* had caught photos of me in various states behind the scenes at one of the fashion shows. I picked up the one on top. I was naked from the waist up, dressed in a beautifully outlandish androgenous fit featuring close-fitted leather pants covered by an exquisitely constructed asymmetrical skirt fashioned from leather patches that hinted at the shape of Africa and captured the colors of the plains.

I was laughing in the photo. I knew that laughter was in response to some quip Cassandra had made from just outside the camera lens. We had been caught by TJ Adams, an old friend of Cassandra's who was short a model for his upcoming show. His distress, combined with the beauty of his garments and the soft pleading in Cassandra's eyes had made it an easy decision to step in and help out. It wasn't my first time on the runway, much to my father's chagrin.

"Oh, this is a kilt combo designed to mimic and capture the power and beauty of our ancestors. Powerful stuff, don't you agree?" I studied the photo a moment more before dropping the publication on the table with the others.

"Don't fucking play with me, boy," the venom distorted his voice into something even uglier than it usually was. I took a perverse joy in it. Why should he be happy when I was not?

"You're just intent upon embarrassing this family over and over again, aren't you? I'd hoped running this company would make a man out of you, but I see that's a futile dream. You think this is good for us? Huh? You think our investors, our board, hell anyone with good sense, wants to see the CEO strutting around half naked in a fucking skirt?" He was damn near spitting by this point.

"You've been a fucking embarrassment and a fuck up all your goddamn life....playing with dolls," ...*dress mannequins*..."making goddamn dresses,"...*earning a degree in fashion from a world renowned institution...* "like a fucking seamstress. Now you're out here, representing the Walker name in a fucking dress with your goddamn titties out. What the fuck is wrong with you?"

I tilted my head as I took in this new spate of hatred, tried to finally understand why he despised me so.

"Is that why you're traipsing around with this gutter trash," my ire rose, and he clocked it with glee, "yeah, *gutter trash* is what I said. Does she like this frufru shit? Like the idea that her man is a fucking fairy? I bet Elizabeth hasn't even seen this," he gestured wildly toward the stack of publications on his desk. Now he calmed, leaned into fake commiseration, "She'll be heartbroken if she can get past the disgust"

Ahhh. Finally. Here we are. I'd watched as he stormed about the room, grateful that while his ranting was toward me, his attention was not on me. It gave me a moment to process. It had never occurred to me that this was his problem...or part of it at least. In my mind, fashion and fabric went hand-in-hand, inseparable, one necessary for the other. That he was tying my love of it to my sexuality was ridiculous.

"Have *you* lost your mind? Are you so antiquated that you can't separate fashion from sex? You think I like men? What if I do?" I didn't, but my circles included some guys who did, and if it further fueled his anger, let him think I swung both ways. I didn't give a shit. I knew who I was and if he'd ever taken a fucking moment to know me, he'd know, too. So, fuck him.

"What difference could it possibly make to you? I run this company like a fucking legend...numbers are higher than they've ever been when you were at the helm. Maybe that's what you need to focus on."

"You're out here purposefully embarrassing yourself and me for no good fucking reason. Irresponsible," he spat as he stepped from around the desk where his ranting had taken him. "Childish. Self-centered. Egotistical. And dumb."

"You think the board doesn't care about this shit?" He pulled a magazine that showed Cassandra and I walking through the streets of Paris enjoying frozen custard. It had been a wonderful day. Having both been to Paris, we each had our short list of places we wanted to show the other. The day had been a light, airy game of oneupmanship. We'd ended it in bed.

I looked at the photo. "So first you're mad that you think I'm fucking men, and now you're mad because I'm in a photo with a woman?" I hated that he'd spat all over what had been one of the highlights of the trip. I rubbed a thumb over the photo. "All I see is a CEO and his designer having a stroll."

"Well, I see a man grinning in another woman's face when it's common knowledge that he's betrothed to another."

"Would you rather I grin in another man's face?" When he started to sputter, I relented. I didn't want him to have a fucking aneurysm. I should, but I didn't.

"Calm down, old man," I said dismissively. I wasn't relenting completely. "Elizabeth and I haven't agreed to your bullshit plans. In fact, I made it clear to her before I left that that wasn't where this was going."

"And I made it clear that it is. And it's what the board and the public expect. You're embarrassing yourself, Elizabeth, and your precious Cassandra. How is she going to feel when you finally step up and do what you're supposed to do? Or are you going to let your brother's dreams slip through your fingers so you can fuck in the gutter? And make no mistake, she's gutter. A woman like that wants nothing from you but a leg up. You're a stepping stone, son. A means to an end. And you're too damn dumb to realize it."

At that, I stepped into his face, ready to jack his ass up. The doors behind me slid open, and Carter, my father's ever-present bodyguard stepped into the room.

"One finger, *son*," it sounded like the curse it was intended to be. "One finger."

I stepped back. I had no beef with Carter. I could take him...probably...but it would be to no good.

"As long as the title of CEO is behind my name, I'll run this company as I see fit. I will marry, or not marry, as I see fit. I will dress according to my own preferences, and there's not shit you can do about it. Keep her fucking name out of your mouth." I turned to leave, breath lodged in my throat that was tightening in anger, frustration and, if I were honest, the everpresent hurt of having a father who actively hated you.

"Not shit I can do about it? We'll see. Get your shit together, Abe. Or face the consequences," his last words trailed behind me as I stepped around Carter and out into the hallway.

Fuck me. The elevator ride down was not nearly long enough to clear my head before the doors slid open again on my own floor. I headed to my office to try to untangle what had just happened.

I didn't want to take this energy to Cassandra's but also, that was the only place where I could feel clean and whole again. But what if he was right? What if I couldn't walk away, couldn't break the hold the family had on me. I wanted Cassandra, but did I want her more than every dream Trey and I had shared. Was I inadvertently leading her on? It didn't feel like that; it felt like she was my past, present and future all rolled up in one. I could, perhaps, picture not being with her...it was a bleak existence. But what I couldn't picture was being with someone else. That wouldn't happen.

Chapter 28

CASSANDRA.

I let myself into my apartment grateful for the silence after the day I'd had. It had started off so promising, I couldn't understand how we'd ended up here with my head splitting apart from the headache Abe's father had instigated.

My meeting with Michel had gone smoothly as expected. We settled our final model selections, so our pieces could be made with them in mind. I headed back to the office afterward, loosely toying with the idea of inviting Abe back to my office so we could finish what we started. But when I arrived there, I had a visitor. Godrick Walker, Sr.

I'd had no negative interactions with him, so while the nerves jumped at seeing the company founder lounging *inside* my office...I had raised an eyebrow at Tamra, who responded with an apologetic shrug...I wasn't particularly worried about it. I hadn't hesitated to join him though I was secretly glad that I was in one of my more traditionally professional dresses. It was the professional aspect of the dress that had sparked my fantasies about Abe getting under it, thus spurning our afternoon interlude. I had pushed those thoughts to the side when I entered. It wouldn't do to be talking to the CEO while thinking about doing nasty things with his son.

The interaction had started well enough with his simple inquiries into how I was enjoying my time. It had been a fucking setup, though. He'd followed those bland niceties with a hammer. Dropping tabloid after tabloid on my desk showing me with Abe in Europe, at fashion shows, laughing, heads together whispering, and finally, behind the scenes at Armand's show in Italy where Abe, on a whim, had agreed to fill in for a missing model.

"I'm sure you think this is all fun and games, Ms. Williams," he'd begun, and that's when I knew he was about to be on some bullshit, "but my son's future isn't something I like to see trifled with."

I knew I needed to chill, knew this man could make or break me. Blackballing in the industry wasn't unheard of. Jeffrey had done his best to ostracize me from the fashion world after fucking me blind and then stealing all my ideas. Karma had ultimately played her hand; no one would touch any of his subsequent designs with a ten-foot pole. He was a joke in the industry. But still, understandably, I was sensitive. So, I tried to chill.

"Mr. Walker, I'm sure I don't know what you mean." I did know, of course. The papparazzi who had captured the moments between Abe and myself must've been right up on us. I don't know how we could have missed him, but the fucking picture caught my damn molars while my head was thrown back laughing at some silly joke Abe had made.

"Come now, Ms. Williams, let's not play naive. You and I understand what's at stake here. We come from humble beginnings, don't we? Beginnings that have taught us both to under-stand a hustle when we see one."

I felt disbelief crawl across my face. What the fuck did he know about humble beginnings and hustling? And what did he know about me? "Do we?"

"Of course we do. And I understand your desire to elevate your station in life. In fact, I would likely do the same thing if I were a young, attractive woman such as yourself. Abe is handsome, wealthy...talented. He's a great catch."

"He is," I agreed, "but what does that have to do with me?"

"Again, Ms. Williams," his voice was less coddling now, "let's not play coy. It's clear that you're fucking him."

Well, hell. I hadn't expected him to be that direct. I refused to let the surprise register on my face.

"And while that's fine, I suppose," he continued, "I'm simply here to warn you. Abe is not what he appears to be."

"No?" I refused to acknowledge the other because it was none of his business and I wouldn't discuss it with him.

"No. He's flighty and inconsistent. I know he has some mild obsession with you, likely due to your...skill...as a designer. He's always had this...interest," he waved his hand effectively dis-missing my whole livelihood as inconsequential, "and will glom on to anyone who indulges the fantasy, but he's promised to Elizabeth. He likes to pretend he's not, but believe me, he is."

He sounded so certain. "I imagine he's spun some tale for you that he can keep the company and choose his own life path, but in reality,' he spread his hands, "these things are all tangled together. It will be Abe and Elizabeth who merge HeirLoom and Heritage House and take that great collaboration forward."

He paused to judge the impact of his words on me. I stood impassive. "I suppose it's easy enough to see why you'd be drawn to each other," he murmured before continuing. "Please know, Ms. Williams, that this isn't a personal attack against you. These are business decisions. Abe likes to think we have some control over this life we're living, but once one reaches a certain level of success, as HeirLoom has, we become swept along by the needs of the beast. Love and desire have little to do with the choices we have to make. This is out of his hands. You understand?"

I just looked at him. I'd learned how to school my features and stand up to bullies a long time ago. I wouldn't let him smell fear on me. His eyes continued to measure me.

He hummed, slight frustration in the sound. "I see you're a stubborn one, and I respect that. Again, humble beginnings and all. But please make no mistake; you'll be a bump on the highway of this plan. Abe can't thwart it...not without losing HeirLoom. And truthfully, he doesn't want to; he's living out his and his brother's dream. He may buck against it, but he won't allow it to die. And, should you stand in the way of that, he'll ultimately resent you."

I sighed. I had to say something at some point, I supposed.

"I assure you, Mr. Walker, I have no intention of getting between Abe and his dreams. My only goal is to create a line that will put my name and HeirLoom's on the lips of the fashion world. It's what I was hired to do."

"Hmm. Well. That is a delight to hear. I'm glad to know you're reasonable," he rose from where he'd been sitting in one of the bright red stuffed swivel chairs that I'd had brought in. He wandered over to the table where designs were neatly stacked with model photos, fabric choice and patterning details. He glanced through them, rifling the piles and setting my teeth on edge.

"I hope what you're saying is true. It looks like you have a wonderful future ahead of you. I want you to be able to stay focused on that future; not derailed by some misplaced romantic fantasy that Abe is selfish enough to let you believe."

"Thank you, Mr. Walker. You have nothing to worry about on that front. My future is my primary concern and always will be."

"Indeed," he left the table and turned back to me, tugging his suit jacket into place, though it needed no adjustment as exquisitely fitted as it was to his bulky frame. "Well, I'll let you get back to it. I look forward to the opportunity to invest heavily in whatever your next endeavor may be when you leave HeirLoom," he looked my way and raised an eyebrow. "I'm sure seed funding would be appreciated."

"Indeed," I echoed his earlier response.

"I wouldn't be able to make such an investment if I had to worry about Abe's and my company's wellbeing. I'm sure such concerns would severely impact our liquidity."

And with that not-so-cryptic statement, he'd left.

Now I was home and free to unpack all that bullshit, and all I'd unpacked were threats and indications that my initial worries were right on the money. What the hell was I doing, fucking my boss, putting my career and all this shit I'd worked for in jeopardy.

Stupid, stupid, stupid. I muttered as I walked into the living room, glancing automatically at the corner where Killmonger stayed when she was with me. It was habit. I dropped my keys at the doorside table and kicked the four-inch stilettos I'd chosen for the day into the corner. In bare feet, I padded into the kitchen, leaving my work bag and jacket draped across a barstool.

I pulled out a wineglass and filled it near to the brim with a sparkling rose then flopped onto the cushy sofa that took up half the room to drink and ponder. That held me for about two minutes before I popped up again, energy and nerves driving me to pace the room, talking to myself, trying to sort through everything that had been said.

How much of it was true? I knew Abe and his father were at fundamental odds, but that didn't mean his father wasn't right about much of what he'd said. It fell in line with what I already knew, after all. At this tax bracket, the line between personal and business became very blurred. It made perfect sense that Abe might think he had more say in this than he really did. It was a very real possibility that his hands were fully tied when it came to Elizabeth and keeping his role in the company.

And even if he were willing to sacrifice that role for me, would I really want him to? No. No, I wouldn't. I'd been chasing my own dreams long enough that I couldn't bear to be the reason someone else couldn't chase theirs.

I ignored the twist in my chest that was slowly taking up residence. I'd known when I started this...fling...that it had to be only that, a fling. Despite anything Abe might say, I had to protect myself. But was that even still possible at this point?

My musings were interrupted by the doorbell. *Abe*. He'd come over every night since we returned to the States. I was so engulfed in my thoughts of him that I forgot I'd likely see him soon. And here he was.

I took a deep breath. It wouldn't be fair to drop this all on him. I knew him well enough now to know how he would react. He would be furious at his father's visit and ready to go all in on the protector thing. I also knew that if his father warned him away from me that he'd be just as likely to pursue me that much harder out of spite. Not that his affections and interests weren't genuine, I knew they were, but his dad's ire would surely be seen as kindling.

I wouldn't say anything. At least not until I got it all straightened out in my own head. Decided, I crossed the room, and opened the door.

Well, hell. He looked like shit.

"Are you okay?" I stood back, holding the door wider for his entrance.

"I've been better," he offered bluntly, dropping a slow but chaste kiss on my upturned lips before heading further inside.

"You want wine?"

"I'd prefer something much stronger. And food. Are we ordering out, or you want me to throw something together?" It had been a delight this week to learn that Abe could cook. And cook well. We'd been back a little over a week, and he'd cooked for me twice already. It was a rare and delicious treat, both the food and the sight of this big, sexy man moving around in my kitchen like he was home.

"I can't believe you're such a good cook," I shook my head, baffled. "And you actually *like* it. That's crazy."

"Well, I like cooking for you. So that might be it. I hardly ever cook at home. Vince takes care of it." He wandered into the kitchen to look through my cabinets and refrigerator as if something had changed between last night and this night.

"Well, I'll leave it up to you, but as you can see, the grocery fairy did not come."

He laughed, but it was a little subdued, as if his vocal cords couldn't be bothered to produce a full sound.

"You okay?" I asked again, concerned. I wondered if the old man had gone to see him, too. And if he had, what poison had he spread?

"Yeah, just a hell of a day is all," he reached for me then, and I happily slid into his arms. When they banded around me, I lay my head on his chest and just breathed him in. I felt him settle his chin on my head and exhale as he relaxed into the embrace.

Maybe I should tell him about his dad's visit. But what good would it do? No, it was time to start putting a little space between us because as wonderful as the last weeks had been, as much as I was feeling and falling for this man, nothing could come of it. And the sooner one of us put the brakes on, the better. I already knew I was barreling toward heartbreak. I might be able to present a calm facade to his raging father, but in my heart, I knew what I was feeling for Abe was more than an itch to be scratched. I was falling in love with him, and I didn't think there was anything I could do to stop it.

CHAPTER 29

I was on my way to my mama's house. It was a shame I hadn't been in a couple of months, but I was going now. I needed it. I needed the peace. And I needed to see the joy on her face when I gave her what I had to give her. A grin crept across my face as I anticipated her delight.

I also needed the drive. It gave me time to think. To think about the sound of my father's voice swirling in my head. Taunting me. I knew everything he said was designed to hurt me, to throw me off my game, and make me doubt myself. Why, then, was I giving any credence to his words?

Because you're still a fucked up little boy inside who wants to please his daddy. Yeah, I'd been in therapy long enough to recognize the triggers, but it was still damned hard to ignore them. Damned hard not to wonder if what he said was true. Was I playing with Cassandra? Leading her on to some end that couldn't possibly come to be? I did want this dream for myself and Godrick. I did want to stick it to the old man, and I could only do that by succeeding. By making HeirLoom better than he ever could. By proving that my ideas were good ones and in the best interest of the company. How could I make that happen and be with Cassandra? And if I could, did I even want to drag her into this mess? That wasn't what she was signing up for.

The thoughts kept swirling until I turned down the long front drive to my mother's tastefully appointed estate. Her home was a beautifully redone colonial set on a few acres just outside the city. She and my father were legally married but maintained separate estates. My mother, in search of a quieter lifestyle, primarily resided here, while my father preferred the hustle and bustle of the city. Both places were well suited to entertaining extensively and used for such as needed. But on the daily? This is where peace and quiet could be found. Fall in New York could be beautiful, and here was an example. The drive meandered through the trees, leaving a driving path that was littered with fallen oak leaves, the landscape was painted in oranges and browns. I lowered the windows so I could feel and smell the crisp fall air...the stench of the city was nonexistent here...and hear the crunch of the fallen oak leaves under the tires. I felt better already.

The treescape gave way to a wide cleared lawn interrupted by natural seating areas and lovingly untended planting beds. I followed the wraparound drive to the back of the house and stopped on broad bricked area that lead to the garage. I hopped out and, having already spied my mom peeking from the curtains, jogged across the expanse and up the wide to the side entry of the sprawling red brick home. The door swung open to reveal my mom, limbs long and lean, brown skin smooth and unblemished, still strong and beautiful in her sixties. The mostly salt locs she'd finally grown swung loose around her shoulders.

She opened her arms as I entered, and I leaned into my mama's hug. Home. Safe. She looked so young, but she carried the peace of the ages in her hugs. After a moment during which her strong, centering embrace held me tight, I stepped back, grinned and dashed back down the stairs to retrieve the box I'd brought from the back seat of the truck.

"I made you something," I couldn't control the smile on my face as I extended the exquisitely wrapped box to her. She loved surprises like a little kid; anytime I brought her something, I made sure to feed her anticipation with beautiful trappings. "It's purple," I couldn't help but add.

She beamed. Now I could see the spray of tiny lines around her eyes, the deeper smile lines. "Is it now? Well, I'm excited about it," she pulled me into another brief hug and led the way inside. I knew we'd end up in the kitchen, the heart of the house for her.

I slid onto a barstool while she set the box on the table, measuring it with her hands.

"What is it?" She asked. This was part of the game. She absolutely did *not* want me to tell her what was in that box.

"Open it," I enjoyed creating things for her. She hadn't been able to blunt my father's clear opinions of my interests, but she had always shown her full love and support in other ways, in her own way.

She took her time tugging the glittery gold and lavender bow apart. I knew she'd try to peel the tape off slowly. I'd put extra just to make her rip it off; my lips twitched thinking about the pending flash of pique and impatience.

While she picked and peeled, I studied her. She looked happy, her skin was glowing, her locs shiny and full. Her eyes were sparkling with the excitement of my little interruption, and I was glad I could give that to her. I often wondered if she was lonely out here; but she clearly preferred it to my father's company. I wondered idly if she had a lover and wouldn't blame or condemn her if she did. My father had never deserved her and one day, I would learn what had drawn her to him, why she had committed her life to him. Though I suppose he wasn't cruel to her, only suffocating, seeming to require...demand...her love and adoration rather than allowing her to give it freely.

She lifted the lid. "Baby boy...it's beautiful!" She lifted the deep purple cashmere lounge set from the box. It was a blend of silken cashmere and the same fabric in its fluffier more natural state. The blend of finishings made the deep purple appear lavender in some lights as if the fabric were glowing.

"Oh, I love it!" She held up the top. Cut to her exact proportions, it was both oversized and perfectly fit, as were the matching pants that would allow her to lounge in style or run errands as she liked. "You know me so well."

"I think so," I watched as she bent and brushed, twisting and turning to see how the outfit would look on her. Finally, she carefully folded it and lay it back in the box. "It's lovely. Thank you," she said again.

"Of course, mom. I'm glad you like it. I saw the fabrics and knew it would be perfect."

She patted my cheek and rounded into the kitchen, pulling pots from the refrigerator. Despite her polished look, she was every bit the Southern mom, having migrated northward with her parents when she was a preteen. She had been raised in the North but with Southern sensibilities. It was, therefore, rare that she didn't have a full meal within fifteen minutes of preparation at all times. Now she pulled out corningware dishes and distributed them between the oven and the warmer griddle on the gas stovetop. I trailed her, opening the oven and dishes to find roasted chicken thighs, string beans with smoked turkey, and baked sweet potatoes. She'd also set the rice warmer on its base. I couldn't remember a time when there hadn't been a pot of rice available.

"All this food, mama? For who?"

"Oh, it's not so much. You were due for a visit. I knew you'd be by soon enough. And if you hadn't, Janice and Patrice will come over and help me work through it," she said, naming two of her girlfriends. She shrugged the rest of my concerns off.

"I know you're not here to just drop off gifts and grumble about the food you hoped I'd have," she pulled plates and glasses from the cabinets, setting us up to eat at the counter. "Beer?"

"Yes, please," she popped the caps on two, set one in front of me. I loved how free she was. Oh, she could and would zip it all up and be Mrs. Godrick Walker when she needed to, but this version of her was the one I loved. "I also have your gown for the launch." I told her. "It needs pinning and adjusting. Do you feel like trying it on?"

"Absolutely. It's in the car?"

"Yeah, I'll grab it after we eat."

I waited as her eyes did the mama assessment. Scanning me from head to toe, pausing at my eyes to verify that the outward calm reflected inner contentment that I damn sure didn't feel.

I held her gaze, doing my best to project easy peacefulness. I don't think I succeeded, but she didn't quite call me on it.

"You look good, baby boy," she said instead. "How are you?"

"Okay, I suppose. Busy, but good busy. Things are steady at HeirLoom," I hedged. "The line is coming along well," that much was true. We were making exceptional progress. The design team was hard at work finalizing the tweaks we'd decided on in Europe. The final sketches would be finished this week. Then the frenzy of having it all produced would begin. There would be over a hundred pieces made. I couldn't wait.

"Mm. How was Europe? I saw the pictures," she wasn't one to beat around the bush.

"Yeah," I didn't even try to hold my frustration. "Dad's losing his shit." My lip curled at the unwelcome memory of our last conversation.

"I'm sure," she moved from the bar to the stove, lifting lids and stirring pots. The scents began to waft through the kitchen, making my mouth water. I shrugged out of the zip-up hoodie I was wearing, settling in.

"That was the lead designer you were with?" I raised an eyebrow. She would have made it her business to know full well who Cassandra was if she'd seen the pictures. When I didn't respond, she paused in her stirrings to look my way. When she caught my expression, she chuckled. "Okay, that was the lead designer you were with," she repeated the phrase, no longer including the question mark at the end.

"It was," I affirmed.

"She had you cheesing mighty hard," she teased, leaning against the counter after setting her spoon down.

"She did, didn't she," I laughed. It felt good to be in a place where I knew my happiness not only mattered but was precious. I really should come here more often. "I'd met her before, you know. Before I hired her to HeirLoom." It was something only Vince and Warwick knew. Certainly not my dad.

"Really," the word held the lilt of curiosity, and she crossed her arms, settling more comfortably against the counter for the tea. I allowed a half smile, knowing that my next words would bring a pall into the room.

"Yes," I said. "I met her that night. The night Godrick got the company," I paused for the split second it took her to put it together. Gave the sadness a moment to flow and ebb before I continued. "She was there."

"A guest?" She asked, confused, searching her memory for who could it could have possibly been. Then her countenance cleared. "No, the waitress," she smiled. "I remember you being so angry when your father teased you about the waitstaff."

"Was he teasing?" As I remembered it, he was being his usual asshole self.

"Hmm," she murmured, noncommittal. It was a strange thing, my mother and father's relationship. I knew she didn't agree with half the stuff he did, but she rarely went against him, never in public and hardly in front of us kids. "Tell me about her."

So I did. I shared how Cassandra made me feel, relating the story of the first time I was drawn to her and how that interest had immediately resurfaced upon seeing her again. I told her about Killmonger and Destiny. I told her about Cassandra's preferences for cats, love of Thai food, disdain for anything with gravy. I told her how Cassandra creates her own little worlds that she disappears into whenever she's creating and sometimes when she's just chilling. I would give anything to crawl inside her creative mind...it was a fascinating thing, watching Cassandra be Cassandra.

"So you're in love with her," it was a statement; not a question.

I opened my mouth to respond in the negative, but nothing came out. In love with her? Nah, not that. Infatuated, certainly. Intrigued, constantly. But in love? That would be...unwelcome? Certainly unplanned. Majorly Inconvenient.

"It's okay. I didn't mean to make your brain seize up," she pushed away from the counter and patted my shoulder before she returned to the stove to see how things were progressing.

"My brain hasn't seized, Mom."

"It hasn't? Well, you're mighty quiet behind the L word."

"Because it doesn't apply here."

"Okay. If you say so," she let it drop, and a comfortable silence encompassed us both until she decided to fill it. "How's Elizabeth?"

I rolled my eyes, "Seriously?"

"What? I'm just asking. Have you talked to her recently?" She was being coy, lowkey making sure her son wasn't an asshole in these streets.

I was just about to respond to let her know that I'd been forthright with Elizabeth when my phone rang. I glanced down, saw it was Vince, and excused myself to take the call. I was curious whether he'd learned anything more about the Whytes. Cassandra and I hadn't followed up since we'd been back from

Europe. We'd had other, more interesting, more naked things on our minds.

"Yo, what's good?"

He launched into a recap of how he'd been tracking Benjamin Whyte's son in his spare time.

"But I'm still hitting a wall. It's consistent that ole boy had a woman and a kid, but I can't get any further than that. No one knows what happened to either of them or who they were. I'll keep digging, but it might just be a dead end. The Whyte's have enough money to make almost anything disappear."

"Then why are we finding these scraps?"

"I mean, I said 'almost'. Even they can't erase someone's existence. But they can erase whatever might have happened to them. Yo, where are you?"

"At my mom's."

"Well, shit. Hold on," he went silent for a few seconds. "Yeah, that's what I thought. Ask her about it. She was around when it happened. I'm running into a dead end, and the Richie Riches might have closed ranks. Maybe she heard something. They couldn't have squashed all speculation."

"Bet. I'll talk to her. And thanks for the time you've put into it."

"No problem, man. You know I enjoy a good mystery. Let me know what Moms has to say and ask her to send me a plate of whatever goodness she has going on in that kitchen."

"Done and done. Later." I hung up and turned to mom, because Vince was right. Maybe she had clues.

Chapter 30

ABE.

"Mom. Did you know Jacob Whyte? He's Benjamin Whyte's son," I asked without preamble as I returned to the kitchen. I wasn't sure what to expect, but I was wholly unprepared for the way her body froze, if only momentarily, before she resumed her scooping of food.

"Mom?"

She waved a hand to let me know she'd heard me. Which I already knew. She completed the table with silverware and napkins, then returned to the fridge for lemonade, placing two glasses and the pitcher on the table before she finally spoke.

"Why are you asking about Jacob Whyte?"

"What do you know about him?" I met her question with a question.

We were at a stalemate. Her staring at me with the gimpy eye, trying to figure out what I already knew. And me, staring right back, wanting to hear everything she had to say.

"Mom? What's the big deal? What do you know about him?"

She held my gaze a moment longer before she sighed, letting her shoulders drop. A shadow crossed her face before she composed herself.

"I honestly don't know what I know," she said, confusing me far more than I thought possible.

"What does that even mean, Mom?"

"It means I know what I *think,* but I don't *know* anything."

"Well, tell me what you think you know."

"Tell me what you already know and why you're asking," she took a bite of her meal and leaned back in her chair, raising one brow at me while she chewed.

I knew my mom well enough to know that it would only waste time trying to get her to talk before she was ready. So I told her about Cassandra receiving the mailing and how Vince had tracked down the figure in the photo as Jacob Whyte.

"But why would someone send her a picture of him?" She asked the obvious question.

"I don't know, but I want to find out. Will you tell me about him now? Vince keeps hitting a dead end beyond his leaving town abruptly and not returning."

She sighed and then began.

"I haven't thought about Jacob in years. And, I'll say again, what I'm about to share isn't fact. It's just...vibes."

I chuckled despite the situation at my mom talking about vibes.

"Okay. Just vibes. Go on," I urged.

"Jacob was a raging asshole. Just like his daddy. Racist and hateful."

"Okay," I nodded, not really shocked because I'd heard plenty of stories from my father about how the eldest Whyte moved. But I was taken aback by the venom in my mother's voice. I couldn't remember her ever having chimed in during his rants.

She continued, wry bitterness in her voice. "Our paths didn't really cross, but I heard things, knew people who encountered him. They say he set James Cartwright's house on fire because James beat him in basketball in middle school. I don't know if that's true. I do know the Cartwright's house burned down, and they never figured out what happened."

"Okay," that was awful, but it didn't seem to align with her level of upset. "Were you and the Cartwrights close?"

"Not really," I waited. "But there were other stories. Things we heard."

"We? Who's we?"

"Oh, just me and my friends. My girlfriends. We would walk into town, and inevitably there'd be some new story about Jacob. That he'd broken out the window of the ice cream shop, or started a fight with some kid. Usually, it was other white kids, but sometimes, often enough, it was one of us. He was a bully."

"Did he bully you?" I asked, worried and faintly angry.

"Hell no. He was younger. And I've always been a tall, strong girl. I'd've had something for his ass."

The chuckle huffed between my lips, breaking the seriousness momentarily. But I quickly returned to the topic at hand. "So, who then?" I asked. There was that shadow across her face, some memory playing behind her eyes. She was definitely holding on to something.

"When we were growing up, it was the younger kids. The ones closer to his own age or younger. By the time he got older, though, all that quieted down."

I raised an eyebrow. What the fuck did that mean? "He just stopped being an asshole?"

She shrugged and pushed the food around on her plate. "Kind of."

"But why? That doesn't make any sense."

"I don't know exactly." I tilted my head to look at her, to catch her downcast eyes.

"Mom. What does that mean? What do you know?"

"Is that all Vince found? That he just moved away?" She shifted the conversation.

"He said there were rumors about a woman. And maybe a kid." I watched her closely. There it was again.

"Mom. Talk to me."

She pushed her plate away and rose, taking it to the kitchen. She'd barely eaten anything. "Abe. I don't know. It's just gossip."

"Okay. I understand. Just tell me."

"The Whyte's are a powerful family, Abe. You don't need to be poking around them. You know that, right?"

"I'm not doing anything dangerous. I promise. And we're a powerful family, too. Ain't nobody scared of them."

She rolled her eyes. "Little boy. You have no idea. They say that family has done some crazy stuff. Ugly stuff." She turned serious. "If I think you're about to do something stupid, I'm not going to tell you anything."

"I'm not. Seriously. I'm just trying to figure out why someone would send Cassandra, who," I paused, "who I care about, a photo of this man. Does she need to be worried? Do I? I'm beginning to think the answer is yes, and I deserve to know why," I stopped, waited until she'd processed that, and looked up again before asking, "What happened, Mama?"

"The summer Jacob left is the same summer Catherine disappeared."

Who the fuck is Catherine? "Catherine? Who's that?"

"I used to babysit her. She was Harry Brookes' daughter," she gave me no time to process before continuing. "We all figured Jacob had left to build a fortune somewhere. That's what he was always talking about, leaving little ass Hudson and moving to Europe. So that was the story, and no one really talked about it after he left. And honestly, we didn't care one way or the other. Because, good riddance. But," she took a deep breath, "it was the same summer, and that's what we were talking about in our neighborhoods."

That was a lot of information. I combed through it.

Harry Brookes. The name was familiar; I searched my mental files. The only Brookes I knew was...

"Harry Brookes? As in Juanita Brookes?"

"The same," she looked up and must've seen the confusion writ large on my face because she expanded her explanation. "Oh. You wouldn't know all of that, I guess. I forget that you kids were just kids. Harry had a wife and daughter before Juanita. His first wife died before you boys were born. His daughter, Catherine, was really young, maybe 6 or 7. It was just the two of them for a long time, maybe ten or twelve years...it was during that stretch of time that I sometimes watched Catherine. He eventually met Juanita. They got married and had Elizabeth. Catherine disappeared about a year later, maybe eighteen months."

"Disappeared?"

She nodded slowly, as if reminding herself. "Yes, disappeared. She was nineteen? Maybe twenty? She'd graduated high school and was away at school, I know."

"What did the police say?"

She shrugged and wrapped her arms around her waist. She'd eased into the corner of the kitchen; the counter formed a V at her back. "I only know what I heard. I hadn't been to their house to babysit in years, so it wasn't like I was on their shortlist for updates. I never heard anything about it on the news or saw anything in the papers." Her words trailed off into thoughtful quiet as if she were still turning over the why of it all.

I let the silence stretch and after a moment, she picked up where she left off. "At the time, it seemed like no one cared. But I was still young, too. You and Godrick were babies. And I didn't yet understand the politics of it all yet. The Brookes absolutely would have done everything in their power to keep the information out of the news, away from the public. They would have wanted to avoid the scandal, to avoid having anything negative attached to their name. They would have looked privately, tried to handle it privately. I'm sure they put all the resources they had behind trying to find her."

I sat there, watching her. My mind was spinning because there was no way the two disappearances were connected. That would make absolutely no sense. The wealthy white boy and the middle-class black girl. Did their paths even cross?

"But what happened to her? What was the story around her disappearance? There had to be talk."

She nodded in confirmation. "She went missing while she was away at school. They say she went to classes one day and then just wasn't seen again. But she didn't live on campus and didn't have a roommate. I guess that privacy was the perk of having a family who was doing okay for themselves. I know Mr. Brookes spoiled her rotten after her mom died, so I'm sure he'd set her up in her own place somewhere nice, close to campus, you know?" I nodded. "And she would have wanted the privacy. She was a quiet kid, sweet." Mom's voice grew soft, trailed off at the end.

"But, Mom," I asked softly, loathe to pull her from her memories but also needing more. I couldn't connect the events in any way that made sense. When she lifted her eyes to meet mine, I could see the rolling fog of sadness in them. "Do you think her going missing has something to do with Jacob leaving town?

Her hand crept from around her stomach to her neck, and her gaze slipped away from mine for the briefest moment. She gathered herself and shook her head slowly. "I can't imagine how. I really, really can't." She was silent for a moment. I could all but see her also turning the pieces around, trying to make them fit. I could tell it wasn't the first time she'd worked on this particular puzzle. "I think Catherine must have found herself in the wrong place at the wrong time, and God just saw fit to rid us of that devil-eyed asshole at the same time."

In spite of the conversation, I huffed out a laugh. "Devil-eyed? I've heard white folks called blue-eyed devils but not devil-eyed assholes."

"He was both. But he only had one blue eye. The other one was green. So yeah, he was a devil-eyed asshole."

The world spun to a slow halt. The riotous swirl of thoughts in my head came to a screeching halt; all those pieces fell away as her words took center stage. "What did you just say?"

CHAPTER 31

I was still struggling to slot my whirling thoughts into reasonable categories while I maneuvered my truck through the evening rush hour traffic on my return to the office. I was glad I'd driven myself. Having to dedicate a portion of my energy to the snarl of cars provided some structure, a familiar backdrop for the frenzy of unfamiliar shit I was trying to process. I debated going straight to Cassandra's, but I hesitated, feeling like I needed to have a better handle on my own emotions, my own ideas, hell, the fucking truth, before I started spewing all over her.

Because really, what did I know? Jacob Whyte, according to my mother, had heterochromia, the same condition that Cassandra has. It's definitely a genetic thing, but having some amount of the condition isn't hugely uncommon...like different colored rings on the outside of the irises. But complete heterochromia...two wholly different colored eyes...that is fairly uncommon.

Also, according to my mother, a young Black woman, Catherine...potentially Cassandra's mother...disappeared at the same time as Whyte. But that was just a correlation. Mom couldn't say with any certainty whether Catherine had a kid. When I'd pressed her, she'd actually leaned on the side of her not having a child. Her description of Catherine had been that she was fairly shy, quiet, and sheltered. My mother couldn't see her getting caught up with someone and getting pregnant and she was certain that Catherine wasn't married. Of course, that was my mother's take. I was more than familiar with the narrative of the sheltered girl who turns all the way up once she gets out from under her protective parent's watchful eye. Catherine could have gotten to college and turned into the campus freak. Not that I was judging...I was just saying.

She was even more adamantly dismissive of the idea that Jacob would have had any sort of contact, much less a romantic relationship with Catherine. As far as she knew, they didn't move in the same circles. And even if they did, what she knew of Catherine didn't align with her being with a dude like Whyte. And Catherine being away at college made it even less likely that there was some connection between her and Whyte. It just didn't compute.

But that didn't stop the niggling in my mind that said there was something serious here. Instead of running directly to Cassandra with a bunch of loosey-goosey information, throwing her off her game at a critical juncture in our work, it would make more sense to share what I'd learned with Vince first. Let him see what else he could find out with this new information. Verify some theories or maybe disprove them. Then I would talk to Cassandra.

In the meantime, a couple of hours at the office before I headed home made sense. I could come down from this high and figure out how I was going to lay in bed next to Cassandra tonight with this information and not tell her. It didn't feel right, but I wasn't going to hold on to it for very long. Just until I could give her a fuller, more complete picture.

I parked in the deck, entered the elevator, and made my way to my floor on autopilot. I needed to learn more about Catherine. The fact that she was Juanita's stepdaughter was crazy to me. If the impossible scenario tripping through my brain were true, it would mean that Cassandra is Elizabeth's niece. Insanity. I wondered if Elizabeth knew the story.

That thought ran right up against the reality of seeing Elizabeth and Shanice in my office when I stepped off the elevator and down the hallway to my office. What was this all about? I hadn't talked to Elizabeth since my return from Europe. I knew we'd left things in an awkward place, but my position wasn't going to change. I hoped she wasn't here to make things even more uncomfortable. But since she was here, if the opportunity presented itself, I would see if she knew anything about Catherine and her non-baby.

I clocked nerves on Elizabeth's face when she caught sight of me approaching. I slid my gaze to Shanice, who was putzing around the bar area, probably restocking.

I sauntered in, making myself comfortable in my own damn office. "Y'all throwing a party and forgot to let me know?" I said as I crossed the room to drop my cross-body bag on the two-seater. I'd dressed casually for the visit to my mother's and hadn't bothered to change before heading here. Neither my mental state nor the hour warranted the formality.

Speaking of the hour, "It's late, Shanice. Why are you still here?"

"I was just finishing up. I wanted to make sure the bar was stocked before I left for the weekend. You know I'll be working remotely on Monday. I'm taking my mother to the doctor, remember?"

I didn't, but I nodded.

"How are you, Elizabeth? I didn't expect to see you here, but I'm glad you dropped by. I have something I want to talk to you about." I saw no reason not to get straight to the point. After Shanice left, of course.

"Oh?" She was clearly surprised that I wasn't upset at her visit. I might have been had I not wanted to talk to her anyway. But maybe not. I really didn't want her and I to be at odds. I just wanted it clear that we didn't have a future together as a couple. As long as we're on the same page about that, we can all get along.

"Yes. Something I learned of today that I want to run by you," I could feel Shanice's ears perk up, so I continued. "Nothing serious; I just want some insight on Patterson as a vendor. Heritage is also a customer."

She raised an eyebrow. We both knew that while she might have knowledge of the vendors Heritage used, she's not the person I'd be talking to for this type of insight. "I see. I'm happy to help," she played along; I was grateful.

"Well, I'll leave you two to it. Mr. Walker, I'll see you Tuesday," Shanice had finished her work at the bar and stepped away from it to pass a glass with two fingers to me, a lighter pour to Elizabeth, and just a splash in a glass for herself.

"Well, here's the to the freakin weekend," she tapped her tumbler gently against Elizabeth's, then mine, then tossed her light shot back.

I raised an eyebrow. Shanice was getting a little full of herself. We had, on a very rare occasion, shared a toast at the end of a day well-managed. This wasn't such a day, and I wasn't in the mood for celebration.

"Oh, don't be such a stick in the mud. Have a little sip. It's Friday and I have to manage getting my mother ready for the doctor on Monday. She hates doctor's visits. Have a little sip in acknowledgment of my impending struggle."

I sipped. The sooner she moved along, the better. And the bourbon wasn't misplaced at the end of the day I'd had.

"Fair enough, Shanice," Elizabeth stepped in. "A toast to the smooth management of your mother's doctor's visit. Believe me, I can relate. My mother is *not* the easiest woman to manage."

"I heard that," Shanice replied. She tossed me a stink-eyed glance before she exited my office to gather her things and shut down for the weekend.

I continued to sip the bourbon. I supposed I could have been more gracious. The drink was needed and appreciated.

"What brings you here, Elizabeth?" Because while I had my own agenda, I was curious. Our last conversation hadn't ended well.

She sipped the bourbon Shanice had placed in her hands and wandered a little aimlessly around the room, looking at the random crap on my shelves, awards for HeirLoom and knickknacks from my travel. "Well, I wanted to come make some sort of amends. We didn't leave things well, and that sits with me," she finally settled onto the sofa in the office.

I stretched into one of the single chairs across from her. "I appreciate that, Liz. It hasn't set well with me either. I don't want us to be on opposite sides of this," I tested the waters gently but firmly enough to let her know where I still stood.

She had another sip, licked her lips, and glanced up at me from underneath her lashes, "We shouldn't be on opposite sides. I agree. That's not what I want." She slipped her shoes off, stretched her legs, then folded them beneath her in a way that made the already short skirt she wore ride up her thighs.

My eyes narrowed. We weren't this casual with each other. I didn't think I'd ever seen Liz's feet completely bare...nah, that wasn't true. We'd certainly been at Warwick's pool together when we were younger. But I'd follow her lead; maybe loosening up with each other would make this whole conversation easier.

"And because I don't think we should be, I wanted to come talk. Hash things out, I guess. See where your mind is now, after a few weeks."

After a few weeks, my mind and every other part of me are securely wrapped around Cassandra's little finger. But I didn't say that.

"My mind is in the same place it's always been. No change on my end," I swirled the brown liquid in the glass I held, glad for the fidget object. A long swallow distracted me further with a pleasant little burn.

"But why, Abe? I don't understand. Explain it to me, please?"

I opened my mouth to offer an explanation, but what could I possibly say that I hadn't already said? That wouldn't be an exercise in comparison in which she would always fall short? It would be cruel.

"You can't, can you?" She uncurled from the sofa and sauntered on bare feet to the bar to grab the snifter of bourbon. She walked back to where we were sitting, to me, dangling the bottle, letting her hips sway. I wondered briefly if this was her first drink of the night.

She topped off my glass and hers before setting the bottle on the floor.

She snuggled back into her seat again, retucked her long slim legs. The skirt rode up again, and this time, the strap of the dress she wore slipped from her shoulder.

"Is it that I'm not smart enough?"

"Not smart enough?" Liz was incredibly smart. She'd gone to Wharton Business School. And even though I knew she had no passion for it, she'd excelled. Anyone who could graduate summa cum laude from a graduate program they weren't even interested in had to be smart as shit.

"You're plenty smart, Liz. You know it's not that."

"I'm not funny?" she asked, head tilted in inquiry.

I unzipped and hung my hoodie on the back of my chair as I considered. Liz didn't joke around a lot but I knew her to have a dry, snarky kind of humor that actually amused me, but might rub other people wrong.

"I mean, I don't know, Liz. But that's neither here nor there. It's not you. This is about how I feel for someone else."

"Oh, it's feelings now?" She repositioned herself on the seat to sweep her hair up and off her neck, twisting it into a loose knot on top of her head. A few tendrils fell loose and stuck to the long column of her neck. Her blowout was doing its thing tonight; when it was down, it tumbled to the middle of her back in fat loose curls. It seemed a little darker than when we'd last spoken, especially where it curled in the light moisture that had sprung up along her collarbone.

Odd. Perhaps it was a little warmer in the office than it usually was. I rose to look at the thermostat in the room...better than responding to her question. I didn't like the direction her line of inquiry was taking.

"Seriously, Abe. What is it?" she let her arms fall from pinning up her hair. "I've said I don't care if you sleep with her," I glanced back at her...so we were still on that?

"I don't even care if you love her, not really, though it would suck. But why can't we just go on with the plan as-is?"

I turned to her, feeling my blood warm. What the hell was she saying? "You tell me why either of us would want to do that? What kind of sense does that make, Liz? Just live miserable half-lives?"

"I wouldn't be miserable," she whispered. "I'd be content. I'd be okay. I'd be the wife of a good guy, mother to smart, beautiful children. Abe," she unfolded herself slowly and rose from the sofa. Did she sway a bit? My imagination surely.

"Abe," she started her sentence again, "I could and would be content. Don't do this," she laid her hand on my chest. I jerked away because the place she touched tingled to life. *What the hell?*

"Do what, Liz? What am I doing besides trying to give us both the freedom we deserve?" I put space between us, moved back to take a seat, uncomfortable with the hint of response I'd just felt.

She laughed. "Did you hear anything I said when we talked last time? What freedom are you talking about? Do you really think that if you leave me high and dry, I'll be free to just live my life? No, *Abe*," she spat my name like it was something ugly. I didn't like it. *Jesus, it's hot in here.* I began to sweat. I shook my head to clear it and refocus on her words. *Get it together, Abe.*

"Elizabeth, calm down," as the words left my mouth I grimaced. I knew better.

"Calm down?" she sucked her teeth in that universal way of Black women. "I can't calm down. You think I'll just walk away to some life of independent self-exploration? No, not me. That's your fate, oh favored second son. I," she clenched her hand over her chest in a show of melodramatics, "I'll be sold off to the highest bidder."

She pushed to her feet, started pacing the room in long-legged strides. *Beautiful.* It whispered through my brain, stopping the hand holding my tumbler in its ascent to my mouth. That thought was wholly misplaced.

I tossed back the rest of the bourbon and went immediately to the bar for water. I must be more tired than I thought. I cracked the seal on the cold bottle while I listened to Elizabeth. Half shaken by the errant thought and earlier tingle, half horrified by the words coming out of her mouth.

"My mother has one goal for me," she continued, "to expand the coffers. If not you, it'll be someone else. Someone I don't know as well, maybe not at all," she stepped near me again, and I held my ground. Even as her scent, warmed by the heat of her upset, wafted up to me. Even as I responded to it, which made no fucking sense at all.

"Liz. She won't do that. You're not property. Or a child. She can't *sell you off.*"

She scoffed, making me feel hella naive. Could they do that to her? What could they possibly have on her to make her feel that trapped? She was educated and beautiful, wealthy and well-traveled. *What do they have on you? Other than your own pride and promises to a dead man?*

I didn't know her ghosts and secrets, I admitted to myself. Didn't know the dynamics in her household. I couldn't begin to understand her motivations or what the repercussions might be for her if we didn't follow through, but it was clear that she wanted to move forward with our relationship, with marrying me.

"She can, and she will," she sighed, sounding slightly slurry and so defeated that I wanted to offer her comfort somehow. I touched her arm, and she turned to me. I pulled her into me, into a hug. I had no intentions of being with this woman, but I had known her most of my life. I didn't enjoy seeing her hurt, fearful.

"You don't know her. She gets what she wants," she sighed into my chest, her head tucked just underneath my chin so that I had to lift it a bit to make room for her. I held her there. She didn't cry, wasn't really weepy. But she held me tight, with strong arms around my waist. She was taller than Cassandra, curvier in a different kind of way. She would feel different than Cassandra tucked underneath me.

What the actual fuck? My eyes popped open—when had they closed? I gave Elizabeth's upper arms a detached, reassuring stroke and realized that I had been rubbing her back, gently swaying with her. *Christ, Abe. Mixed signals, much?*

I stepped away from her. Shook as hell. What was going on with me tonight? I must be more exhausted than I realized. Between work and this extra bullshit over the last few days, it made sense that I'd be overextended. Stress was a motherfucker for sure, and I hadn't been meditating, hadn't done any yoga to speak of. I had only been centering myself in the mecca that lay between Cassandra's thighs.

I shook my head to clear it, trying to sort through options. I needed to get some fucking sleep tonight. And as soon as I finished pounding Cassandra into the mattress, I was going to be out for the next eight solid. I needed to move this conversation with Liz along before I passed out from exhaustion.

I went with instinct—straight, no chaser. I suspected Liz was about sick and tired of playing games anyway.

"You're right about that. I don't know her. Or you, not beyond the superficial, for that matter." When she opened her mouth to dispute me, I added, "I just learned today that Juanita is Mr. Brooke's second wife, that you have...had...a sister." I watched her closely when I said it, but keeping my eyes open felt like a Herculean task. I returned to my earlier seat and plopped down, relieved to no longer have to support my own weight.

"Oh. Well. Yes. I did, I guess. If you want to think about it like that." She followed and all but sprawled across the sofa across from me, long tan legs stretched out, the skimpy dress leaving very little to the imagination. And my imagination was wrapping those long, toned legs around my hips. *Jesus. This isn't right. Something is wrong with me.*

I scrubbed a hand across my face and sat up, sat forward. Leaning into the conversation, trying to focus.

"How else would one think about it?" I questioned.

"She died when I was little. Maybe three. I don't ever remember even meeting her, so I don't really think about it like that."

"She died? I thought she disappeared."

She tilted her head, thinking. "Maybe," she said slowly. "But I could have sworn I heard Mother refer to her as dead on the phone one time," she shrugged, one shoulder barely lifting. That teasing strap inching down a touch further. "I could be wrong though. Maybe she said 'gone' and I assumed. I don't know. It was a long time ago. And," she shifted her eyes toward me. They weren't as beautiful as Cassandra's, but they were lovely, "it is in no way relevant to the conversation we're having right now." She stretched one long leg toward me, placing her peach-painted toes on the seat of my chair between my legs.

She spun the chair toward her, giving me an unobstructed view up the length of her thighs under the dark shadow of her dress. She cocked her knee to the left, and my eyes stuttered to a stop on all she had to offer, bared to me, plump and beckoning.

I lifted my hand to move her foot; it happened in slow motion, my fingers moving through thick molasses to wrap around her ankle, intending to set her foot on the floor. But I could feel my dick swell at the contact, even more so when she stretched even further, dancing her lovely toes along its length.

I tried to shake my head, but couldn't. The drowsy panic that had begun to build, the lazy confusion, were sliding away under the onslaught of enthralled rapture. I watched, mesmerized and horrified, through lids barely slit open, as Liz slipped off the sofa to her knees and crawled my way.

CHAPTER 32

CASSANDRA.

The cold air on my thighs, the sunlight streaming through my open blinds, and Killmonger's distinct yapping alerted me that my mourning period was coming to an end. I should be grateful that I'd been allowed this much time before Destiny descended on my pity party.

"Get the fuck up." She tossed the covers the rest of the way on the floor and proceeded to start stripping the bed around me. *Not even gonna ease me into it, huh?*

"You stink. And it stinks in here," she raised the windows in the bedroom, letting the cool air in.

"Destiny," I moaned, rolling over and reaching for the naked pillow next to me to cover my eyes. She ripped it from my hands.

"Shower. And then come tell me what's going on. We're not doing this, though."

"I'm not doing anything," I groaned.

"Exactly. You're not going to work. You're not answering your phone. You're not showing up for Margeaux's hair show."

I groaned again. This time in regret because I had completely forgotten that Margeaux was hosting a hair show. Just an intimate affair for some favorite clients. My presence wasn't necessary, but of course I had planned to be there to support her. And I had completely forgotten about it.

"I missed it."

"You missed it," she affirmed. Then, more softly, "Get up, love. Whatever happened, it's going to be okay. But you've been MIA for four days. It's time."

Four days. I lay there, flat on my back. An appropriate position because I'd been knocked flat on my back. My feet swept completely out from underneath me. He'd cheated. He'd lied, and he'd cheated. Or not really. She was, after all, his *fiancée*. He'd actually been cheating on *her* with *me*. How could I have been so fucking stupid?

"No, ma'am," Destiny interrupted my thoughts. "Get up and shower. Start the day," she sat on the bed next to me and wiped the tears I hadn't realized were slipping into my hair. "Put on some clothes, and we'll have some tea. We'll work through it, Cassy."

I shifted to meet her eyes. There was no pity, just acceptance and presence. I sighed, resigned but hearing the truth in her words. I could do this. I'd done it before, hadn't I? After Jeffrey? I'd had my heart ripped out and recovered. *But you hadn't. Not really. Not like this.*

I hadn't truly loved Jeffrey, a fact I'd come to realize in London. What I'd felt for Jeffrey never came close to this. I'd take that level of hurt any day over this heart-rending, full-body assault. With Jeffrey, my pride had been hurt as much as anything else. But this, this was centered in my vital organs. Each one felt punctured and torn, fighting to function. My lungs fought to draw breath, my eyes barely focused. Destiny's voice, which I knew to be firm and strident, was muffled and foggy. Only the most basic need for survival kept my heart beating.

Maybe I couldn't do this after all. I turned my head, ready to curl back into myself.

"Aht, aht," Destiny's hand landed on my shoulder, soft in her touch, but firm with intention. "Come on, love. Let's get you cleaned up," she shifted one hand to my calves, easing them toward the edge of the bed.

I followed her urgings, painfully rearranging my body so that I sat on the edge of the bed. Killmonger immediately attacked my toes with licks that would have normally sent me into peals of laughter. Now, though, nothing. I was numb from the inside out.

"Good girl. That's it. Stay right there," she dashed off, and I heard the shower spray come on.

"Okay, here we go." We stood and shuffled to the bathroom.

Objectively, I could see how ridiculous this was. Me, hunched over as if I had been physically wounded, her helping me along. The rational part of my mind told me to stand the fuck up; my soul, the soul that powered my body, told me to go into hiding so I could heal. Hot tears were building again, making my head and throat thick and hot.

"Destiny, I don't think I can," I whispered.

"You can. We can. Let's go." She stripped us both down. Me to my altogether and her to panties and bra. Then she stepped right into the hot spray with me. She'd had the presence of mind to pull my makeup stool into the shower. I knew I should care about the water soaking the little fabric-covered seat, but

I didn't. I was grateful for it; there was no way I could continue to support my weight on legs that didn't want to work.

"We'll get you a new makeup chair. Sit," she eased me down, positioning me so the hot water hit my upper back, then she turned on the handheld and began rinsing my hair.

This woman, my sister, sat with me under that water, washed my hair, helped me wash my body, and held me until the water streaming from the shower cooled and the tears pouring from my eyes slowed.

She wrapped us both in towels and returned me to the bedroom, where clothes I didn't remember her laying out were neatly arranged on the bed. Comfortable clothes but not slug attire.

Destiny put a bottle of lotion in my hands, "Moisturize," she ordered, and returned to the bathroom. The shower had done me good. It was cathartic. I wasn't, momentarily, debilitated. So, I lotioned and began to dress.

Destiny returned, dry, dressed and pleased with my progress. "Okay, girl. That's what I'm talking about. Let's get your teeth brushed, and we'll do your face routine."

I shrugged. The shower had been a good idea, and I didn't have the strength or inclination to balk when she nudged me back into the bathroom.

I was brushing my teeth when my sense of smell kicked back in. "Is that mac and cheese?" I asked into the ether. A voice responded, "Yes, ma'am, it is."

I looked up to meet Margeaux's eyes in the mirror. Tears sprang back into mine, and I turned into her arms. She held me, rocked me, until the burning of the minty toothpaste in my mouth made me step away to spit. I finished up that process quickly and just looked at her.

"Girl, what's going on? Why wouldn't you call me?"

"I couldn't, Go. I feel so stupid. So fucking stupid."

"Abe?"

I nodded, unable to meet her eyes again.

"Fuck," she said. Capturing the entirety of the situation in that one word. I did see pity in her eyes when I looked at her again. But it was a kindness, a genuine sorrow and disappointment for me. I didn't mind it.

"Okay. Finish up and come eat. I'll do your hair while you tell us."

"Your show, Margeaux..." I began, upset again that I hadn't shown up for her.

"...was a raging success and I'll tell you all about it over mac and cheese."

I nodded again and began my skincare routine never once thinking about not telling them what had happened. I'd had my four days, *four days*, of wallowing. My therapist was effective enough that I knew holding the shit in wouldn't lead to anything positive. And I needed to lean into the trust I have with my girls. To offset the monumental hit my trust reserves had just taken from Abe.

My stomach heaved. *God.* Just the thought of his name was enough to shake my body.

Finished with my short but effective facial, I smoothed night serum over my again smooth skin. It had felt like sandpaper after so long with no attention. I hadn't even washed the makeup off when I stumbled into my apartment that morning, reeling.

"Come on out now!" Destiny, again.

Killmonger bounded into the bathroom, little tail wagging so hard it switched her body from side to side.

"Yeah, yeah," I said, reaching down to pet her soft curls, "I'm coming."

I walked into the living room to find steaming bowls of Margeaux's most excellent mac and cheese, and cornbread spread across the coffee table. Three snuggly blankets were draped across the back of the sofa and I could smell the apple cobbler in the oven. I knew without asking that there would be homemade vanilla ice cream in the freezer from the bodega up the street.

My girls had come through. Again.

There was one comfy chair set to the side. Margeaux's blow dryer, combs, butters and the other tools of her trade were spread on a tray table next to it. That was clearly my seat. So, I sat.

Destiny pulled another tray table in front of me and loaded a plate with a heartbreak portion of steaming mac n cheese and cornbread. I took it and, much like my sense of smell had done earlier, my hunger kicked in on 10.

The first bite of thick cheesy goodness filled my mouth, immediately laying a stone on the side of healing. Margeaux and Destiny got their plates, and we all gave it a few minutes to let the initial magic of the food do its thing.

Finally, Margeaux said, "Let's get started on this head of yours." She shoved one more heaping spoonful into her mouth and then rounded around behind me to assess the damage.

By unspoken agreement, we talked about other things while she blowdried me. Mostly about how well Margeaux's show had gone. The new salon she was planning would not lack for clients. We followed with celebratory stories about good outcomes for one of Destiny's favorite kids and the requisite commentary on how the construction on the BQE was making everyone's lives hell.

Once the noise of the dryer ended and Margeaux had created the initial parts for what I surmised would be a set of braids, the conversation circled back to me.

"Okay, baby girl. Enough of the chitchat. What's up? What happened?"

I wasn't ready. There was no way I could be. But I had to say it out loud. I had to give it life so I could accept it as reality. "Abe slept with Elizabeth."

I saw them look at each other, saw them exchange *that* look. The one that says 'we told you so'.

"Oh, Cass. I'm so sorry," Margeaux said. And I believed her. She'd never want me hurt, but she could be sorry and still think I'm stupid.

"I know. Me, too. Y'all were right," I just cut to the chase. Let them exhale on their rightness, and we could move the conversation forward to the solutions stage. "They never stopped seeing each other."

Another look.

"Tell us exactly what happened. I mean, I know I said to be careful, but I would've bet money that he was truly into you," Margeaux said.

"Same," said Destiny.

I shot her the stink eye because she had been quite vocal about her opinion of Abe.

She held her hands up by her shoulder, palms out, to acknowledge the truth of my stink eye. "Okay, okay. I definitely gave him a hard time, but I didn't really peg him for an asshole of that magnitude."

"Well, he is. I caught him fucking red-handed."

"You *caught* him? Like you caught him fucking?" Margeaux asked, incredulous.

"Not actually fucking, no. But the morning after, I guess. It was obvious."

"Why don't you tell us exactly what happened, Cass?"

"I walked into his office Thursday morning. He hadn't come over the night before. Hadn't called. He'd gone to see his mom, so I thought, I don't know. After the things his dad said. Maybe she felt the same way, and he..."

"What the fuck did his dad say?" Destiny wanted to know.

I waved my hand. "Just stuff. That Abe has to marry Elizabeth. That I'm a distraction. That..."

"That what, babe?" Margeaux asked.

"That I'm not good enough to be part of their family," I could feel the hot tears this time. But they were fueled just as much by anger as despair. Anger at myself that I still let that kind of shit get to me. I'd worked too fucking hard to be feeling this shit again.

"Fuck them, Cassandra. Fuck the whole damn trash ass family."

"Tell us how you really feel, Destiny," I had to smile a little bit because if ride or die was a person it would be Destiny.

"Okay, so you went to see him to see what?" she paused, "Whether his mother had filled his head with more trash?"

I nodded. That was exactly it. I had been so uncertain but hopeful. I knew Abe wanted to be with me. I was confident in that part. Resolute. But I also knew he was tied to his family and that the sense of responsibility ran deep. It was something that made him attractive to me. His commitment to his brother, to his family. It was what his father spoke of even though he made it seem ugly and weak. Either way, I'd never had anything like that, and I wanted it, had begun to feel it. Had let it give my steps confidence. I'd decided to tell him what his father had said as well. We needed to talk through it. It wouldn't work if we built our relationship on lies and half-truths.

"I went to his office. The glass was smoked, which was odd, but I figured he'd been up all night. Maybe he slept at the office. He does that sometimes, just crashes out. He's been waking up and coming over, even if it's late, but he didn't that night."

I paused and reached for my water. My mouth had gone suddenly dry; a hot lump was growing in my throat. The cool water did nothing to help.

"Shanice was there. And she waved me in," I thought about that now. "She just let me walk in. But maybe she didn't know." And if she did, would she have even cared? *She's never liked me*. But I didn't know if that was true or if insecurities were just taking hold.

"Know what?"

I held onto the glass of sparking water with all my might. I wondered how tightly I would have to squeeze to break it. Could it bear my rage and pain?

"That Elizabeth was there. Had been there all night, it seemed."

"What the hell?" from Destiny.

"How do you know?" from Margeaux.

"I don't really, but what the fuck else could it have been? I opened the door, and he's standing there, in sweats, no shirt."

"Just standing there? Doing what?"

He hadn't been doing anything, really. Just standing there looking lost. Honestly, I wondered if my brain was starting to block the whole episode out to protect me. But I told the story as best I could.

He'd looked delicious, standing there, half-naked and completely fine. My feet had started moving toward him immediately, eager to get my hands on all that skin. It didn't occur to me to wonder why he was half-dressed. He should have been suited and booted by now. It had been after nine.

But none of that mattered. I closed the door behind me and drank in all that goodness. It was mine. I had just started to relax into the warmth that was already beginning to spread through my body. We had made love in his office before. And with him standing there in his thot sweats, just asking for it, well, I'd give him what he wanted. My eyes had locked on his dick, my nipples had begun to go hard when he called my name.

"Cassandra." Not Andi. Not Cass. Not even Cassie, which he rarely used. But my full government. My gaze locked on his. Sadness. Horror. Anger. Confusion. Disbelief. Apology. What the fuck?

"Abe?" Oh, hell, no. What the fuck was she doing here?

My eyes shot to the left, following the sound of Elizabeth's voice. She wore his t-shirt and nothing else. She was barefoot, braless, hair all over the place. Sitting on the sofa I'd just ridden Abe to heaven on earlier this week. Wearing the same look I'd worn when I finished that ride.

His shoes were by the coffee table. Her dress was on the floor.

I felt my head tilt. Trying to shift the pieces around so they'd fall into place and make sense.

"Cassandra, it's not what it looks like."

"It looks like you spent the night together."

"Then it's exactly what it looks like," Elizabeth mumbled, dragging a hand through her sex-tousled curls.

"Elizabeth, what the fuck?" From Abe. "Cassandra..."

But I couldn't. I couldn't stay. Couldn't listen to anything he had to say. Couldn't remain in that space with her gloating, his wary tone of voice...none of it made sense...but it all made plenty of sense.

So, I just...left. Before I made a fool of myself in front of them and the whole company. Before my whole soul poured itself out for their judgment and jeering ridicule. Stupid little foster girl thinking billionaire Abe Walker really wanted anything to do with her. Would really risk the whole of his legacy for her. Would walk away from poised, polished Elizabeth for her.

I must've given voice to those last thoughts because my head got a little jerk in Margeaux's tender braiding hands.

"We do not talk shit about ourselves in this collective. There are neverending lists of reasons why Abe should want to be with you, should risk everything for you, and should definitely choose you over Miss Perfection. But that's not the point here."

"It's not?"

"No. It's not."

"Have you talked to him?"

My head whipped around to stare incredulously at her. I turned to see if Destiny shared my outraged confusion. Hell yeah, she did.

"Talk to him? Why the fuck would she talk to him?"

"To see what he has to say? That's usually why you talk to someone."

"What could he possibly have to say, Gogo?" I was genuinely curious.

"I don't know. He said it wasn't what it looked like," she shrugged. "Maybe it wasn't."

"Him half naked. Her in his fucking shirt, hair standing all over the fucking place. Looking satisfied as hell. I know that look. I *wear* that look. Yeah, no. I'm not talking to him."

"Good. And good riddance. *Talk to him*," Destiny huffed and threw Margeaux the most scathing dismissive look imaginable. "You sound crazy as fuck right now."

"Maybe. Right now," Margeaux was never phased by Destiny's antics. "But at some point, you need to hear what he has to say. If for nothing more than closure."

"I don't need closure."

"You will, though. But it's too soon. That's fine. Tonight we talk shit about him and Elizabeth and the whole fucking family."

Cheers to that.

As these things are wont to do, the shit-talking and righteous outrage, fueled by Crown Royal-laced sangria, eventually gave way to more tears, heartache, and regret. But, thankfully

Margeaux and Destiny had begun the whole process early as fuck. So even though we spent the day running the whole gamut of emotions on a runaway rollercoaster, by eight-thirty, I was fully braided and freshly showered, again.

Destiny and Killmonger had left about an hour ago after putting away all the evidence of our emergency breakup session. Now, Margeaux and I were tucked into my sectional, which we had rearranged into sleepover mode. We both had our laptops out, but I wasn't getting much done other than reading a couple of emails. I still had work tomorrow, and I'd more or less blown it off the last four days. I'd sent a vague message about a personal emergency and then went radio silent in the middle of a launch. It wasn't the best look. And I was worried about it now that I had emerged...somewhat...from the darkness.

I told Margeaux.

"It's going to be okay," she promised. "If I know you like I think I do, you had everything planned five steps ahead anyway. Your team is probably glad you've disappeared for a little while so they can get shit done."

I smiled briefly because she wasn't wrong. The schedules and assignments were perfectly laid out. The whole process could probably putz along without me for a full week at this point. We were at an interesting lull in the line's development. All the patterns had been made and fabrics selected. Even the models had been selected. Now we waited while the seamstresses were creating the looks. So it was kind of out of my hands. My team knew the particulars of every single article of clothing designed so they could absolutely answer any questions the seamstresses had.

The preliminary design for the actual show had been approved...the music, the decor, the vibe. We wouldn't be able to do any more there until we choose, from the one hundred twelve produced pieces, the final thirty that we would use in the show. It would be another...I unnecessarily scrolled through the production schedule that I knew by heart for verification...thirty-four days before we reached that stage. Then another two months until the show. We were so close, and still so far. How was I supposed to manage being around this man for another three months?

"Yeah, you do know me. It should be okay," I toyed with the fringe on the edge of the throw blanket that covered us. "But how am I supposed to be okay? Margeaux, why would he do it?" Tears flowed freely, no sobs, no intentional crying. I think my emotions just needed to somehow exit my body and the streams of tears simply provided the most accessible route.

"I don't know, Cass, and I'm so sorry. Has he called?"

"I don't know. My phone has been off." It was one positive of being on your own. I didn't have to worry about family going ballistic if I went off-grid. Destiny and Margeaux would always have access to me...we all had keys to each other places...but I never fretted about turning off my phone.

"You want to turn it on and see what we have? Before tomorrow? Before you might run into him?"

I nodded and uncurled to get my phone from the bedroom side table where Destiny had put it during her cleanup. She'd asked about turning it back on then, but I'd said no. Not at all prepared for either the emotional strain of a deluge of messages from Abe, or the added heartbreak of potentially finding no messages from Abe.

I didn't turn it on until I was safely wrapped up again, my head on Gogo's shoulder and her arms around me.

I pressed the necessary buttons, and the phone powered up. Immediately it began flashing and singing with notifications. I just passed it to Margeaux to vet.

"Okay, let's see what we have," she scrolled while I peeked over her arm. "A thousand from me and Destiny. We can delete these?" she glanced at me for confirmation first, then deleted.

"A few from Tamra, you wanna read them?"

"No, I've looked at her emails. She said she'd sent duplicate texts. Don't delete them, though."

She nodded.

"Well?" I asked. We both knew what I was asking.

"Twenty-two."

"Twenty-two?"

"Yes, eight the first day. Then three or four each day. Four today."

"What do they say?" I whispered.

"Hold on." She skimmed.

"He wants to talk. Says he knows what it looks like. But that he doesn't know what happened, and he needs to explain."

"What does that even mean? What does he mean he doesn't know what happened? Doesn't know how he fucked her? Jesus."

"Girl, I can't call it. How had things been? Do you think he'd been seeing her the whole time?"

"Who knows? Clearly, my judgment is all fucked up."

"I don't think that's true. We all get caught up. And it is not your responsibility to make him honest and truthful. If he lied, if he cheated, those were his choices, not reflections on you. At all. Hear my words, girl. This isn't about you. It's about him."

"It feels about me."

"I know it does. I know it does. The hurt is real."

CHAPTER 33

CASSANDRA.

Walking into HeirLoom Monday morning proved that I could, literally, do anything. It was sheer dint of will that allowed me to place one foot in front of the other, repeatedly, often enough that I eventually ended up in my office. Safe. Behind closed doors.

I really didn't need to be here. There wasn't much at this stage that I couldn't do from home. But after what felt to me like an extended absence, I had to show my face. I'd built up in my head that everyone was looking for me, noticing my absence and commenting on it; and the last thing I needed or wanted was extra attention. So, I'd fought through the fog this morning and drug myself here.

And now, at the bright early hour of nine a.m., I was already exhausted. It was no wonder that I jumped at the knock on the door. Of course, I knew immediately who it was. Had he been waiting for me? Watching to see when I entered the building? I checked my watch. I'd been here no more than fifteen minutes. And, *fuck me*, I didn't have the energy. I

I didn't say come in. But, in he came anyway.

"Cassandra."

I schooled my face into what I hoped was disinterested indifference. "Abe." God, he looked amazing in that fucking suit. It was a favorite of mine. The shirt, too. And the tie. Fuck him. He'd dressed in the Fuck-Me-I'm-the-CEO type of outfit that I loved. I narrowed my eyes at him. He raised an eyebrow back. *Fucker.* He knew exactly what he was doing. I sucked my teeth and turned my attention to the shit on my desk.

"Are you going to let me explain?"

"Explain what?" I flipped through random papers on my desk. I had no idea what they were.

"Cassandra," Abe said with restrained exasperation.

"Oh," I exclaimed as if in the midst of an *ah-ha* moment, "you mean explain why you spent the night fucking another woman? A woman you swore you were not involved with? A woman I expressly told you you should and could be with and to leave me the fuck alone for? Is there an explanation, Abe?"

"I didn't fuck her," he scrubbed a hand along his face. "At least, I don't think I did."

A disbelieving huff burst from between my lips, "Well, it's nice to know you screwed me over for such a memorable experience," I mumbled as I pushed away from the desk to come to standing. I couldn't keep sitting down...it was a position of weakness, and I needed every bit of strength and advantage that I could muster. It's why I was in full corporate dress today...or, at least, my version of it. An at-the-knee fitted pencil skirt, a slim silken shirt that reached my neck and tied with an over-the-top bow, sky-high Louboutins...the only pair I owned. I'd felt sexy and powerful when I left home. Now, I felt uncertain and unsteady.

"No, Andi, seriously. I don't know what happened. I do know I don't want her and would never do that to you. Never."

"What the fuck does that even mean, Abe? *'I don't know what happened?'* Is that the rich boy version of *'It wasn't me?'* And whether you did or not, I don't give two shits. She spent the night? In the room? In your fucking t-shirt, with you? Yeah? Are you sure about that part?"

"She did. But not because I wanted her to, Cassandra. You know better than that."

"I don't know better than shit, Abe. And if you didn't want her to spend the night, why did she? You're bigger than she is, Abe. What'd she do? Overpower you?"

"Just listen, Cassandra."

"Yeah, no. I'll pass on the *just listen*," because I could already feel myself weakening. If I listened, wanting more than anything else to believe him, I'd be even dumber than I was at this moment. No, thank you. "But you know what, don't worry about it. I knew this was temporary," I laughed bitterly. "You almost had me believe that it could be something more than that, but your dad was right."

"What's he have to do with it?" His voice, already strained, took on a brittle quality.

"He came to see me a couple of weeks ago. Not long after we returned from Europe and told me then that I wasn't meant to be part of your life. This whole Walker legacy is planned out. You have a position to play, and I knew that. I knew it coming in. I knew it before your dad told me and I knew it when you tried to convince me otherwise. The problem is that I chose not to listen to my own good gotdamn sense, and here I am, dealing with the fallout."

"Andi, don't put my dad's shit on me." He got in my face. I hated that I loved that face, that he looked so beautiful to me. And I hated that he smelled so good. "You know how I feel about you, and if you don't, let me be clear. It's you. It's always been you. Since the first time we met, you've captivated me. That night, years ago at the damn banquet, went from being the best night of my life... I'd met a girl, a beautiful, funny, NYU smart girl who loved the things I loved...to the worst night of my life. I didn't think I'd ever feel the kind of light and joy I'd felt that night, with you, in just those few moments together, again. After Godrick, I never expected it. But here you are, Andi, bright light and fucking joy and happiness. I want that shit. And when I tell you I don't know what the fuck happened that night, that's the God's honest truth," he stared at me trying to force the honesty behind his words into me. When I didn't give, he sighed, "Fuck, if I didn't know better, I'd think we'd both been drugged."

I rolled my eyes.

"Right. I know. I can fucking hear myself. But Andi, don't do this. Please. Let me at least try to figure it out. I don't want Elizabeth. I want you. I only want you."

My stomach tumbled, my heart leapt. I wanted so badly to believe him. To let those words rinse away the last week. But I couldn't. To do so would be the epitome of dumb girl shit. I mean, what was he really saying? All he was giving me was a moderately eloquent version of 'it wasn't me'.

"You can't have me, Abe. Not anymore. Go figure it out with Elizabeth. I'm not even mad. Like I said, I get it. I wish we could've been honest, but it is what it is."

"It is what it is? You're reducing this to 'it is what it is'?" His voice was all contained fury and frustration, but what right did he have to either? He'd done this. Not me.

I shrugged, dying inside. I couldn't understand why my heart wasn't getting on board with this. Why couldn't it tell that I was doing what was in both of our best interests? "Abe. Just go. We'll finish the launch. It's only a couple of months. And that'll be that."

"That won't be that, Andi. I'm not finding you in this crazy ass way to just let you go again."

"The funny thing is, it's not up to you. You don't get to decide whether I go or not." I met his eyes, saw the blazing possessiveness there. My nipples perked through the soft silk of the blouse I wore. His eyes dropped for an instant and caught mine again.

"Yeah. We'll see." And he did go.

But not without leaving me breathless, horny, exhausted, and devastated.

ABE.

Well, that was a raging clusterfuck. *Fuck!* I stormed through the hallways of HeirLoom, returning to the office I couldn't stand to fucking be in because it was where Andi had seen that fucking bullshit. *Gotdammit!* I swept all the shit on my desk off in a fit of juvenile rage. Even as I heard the clank of metal hitting the floor, I couldn't muster up a single fuck for the work it would take to put it all back right again.

And, I couldn't stay here, so I walked back out, texting Vince on the way.

<Where you at. Can you meet me at the gym?>

Vince: Bet. There in 20.

I hesitated over the next text, but it would be fucked up to let him walk into this level of fuckery without a warning that I was going to be trying to kill him when he stepped in the ring with me.

<It's bad.>

Vince: Ready.

Over an hour later, Vince and I sat on the mats against the wall of the basement gym in my home. After a solid forty-five minutes of pounding each other in the MuyThai ring, we were both sucking air and rehydrating, but I couldn't honestly say I felt any better. The rage at what I couldn't figure out still crawled through me, looking for an outlet. I knew I'd be running or swimming later tonight, maybe both.

"What the fuck, man? You said it was bad, not catastrophic," he touched the lip I'd busted when he dropped his right.

"Yeah, my bad about that. I tried to pull it."

"The fuck you did."

"You right. I didn't. You can take it."

"Facts. No glass jaw here," he flexed it again and returned to downing the Gatorades we'd pulled from the fridge.

"So I ask again. What the fuck? You been walking around here like somebody stole your bike for damn near a week."

"V, some crazy shit is going on. I think someone fucking drugged me and Liz."

"What?"

"Right. That shit sounds crazy as hell, don't it?"

"It does. So why do you think that?"

I told him about Liz's visit. And I told him about waking up wrapped around each other on the sofa at HeirLoom; her in her panties and my t-shirt and me in boxers. I told him how fuzzy we both felt waking up and how off-kilter I'd been the night before, how I'd been attracted to Liz, something that had never happened before outside of the most objective appreciation.

"Man, I woke up like, what the fuck."

"Did y'all fuck?"

"I don't think so, but I can't say for sure, right? My dick didn't feel like we'd been fucking, but if we were drugged, would I know?"

"I don't know, man. What'd she say?"

"Liz? Nothing really. After Cassandra saw her damn near naked ass," to Vince's credit, his face reflected only the slightest widening of the eyes...even that reaction was a testament to how relaxed he was with me...Vince was the calmest nigga I knew. "Yeah, after that, she basically mumbled some wack-ass excuse and bounced. But I can say she was shook."

"Hold up. So Cassandra saw her there?"

"Yeah, Bro. The worst shit. Cassandra struts her fine ass in the office like she owns the place. Which she fucking can because she fucking does as far as I'm concerned. But then," I let my head fall back against the padded walls behind us as the scene played out again. "Fuck me, Vince. Elizabeth was sitting there on the fucking couch, naked as fuck wearing my gotdamn t-shirt. I don't know if we fucked, but she damn sure looked like it."

"Damn, bro. And you think Liz drugged you?"

"I don't know. I mean, what else am I supposed to think? But then she acted as fucking dazed as I was. But she didn't seem mad at it either."

"Why was she even there?"

I rolled my eyes at myself. "She came over initially on some "we need to make it work', shit. Like we've been a couple and agreed on this shit the whole time."

"Sounds like she had motive, means, and opportunity. You said she was there when you got there?

"Yeah."

"Have you talked to her since? What'd she have to say?"

"I haven't. She's not answering and truthfully my bigger concern has been getting in front of Cassandra. I did that today. She's not having it."

"Do you blame her?"

"No. I don't because that was some fuck shit to see. But I would have appreciated the chance to explain."

"Explain what? That you think you were *drugged*? Even if you were, that just sounds like some fuckboy shit."

"It does," I agreed.

"You got tested, yeah?"

"I did. But not right away. Shit, I spent more time than you understand trying to hear Andi's voice railing against the machine. But yeah, I called Dalton."

"And?"

"Nothing. Didn't help that we didn't really know what we were testing for. He checked for the common shit...roofies, molly. But didn't find anything."

"Well, fuck. That doesn't help at all."

"Nah. It doesn't. But I'm going to figure it out. That, and this shit with Jacob Whyte and, get this, Catherine Brookes."

"Who?"

That turned our conversation to the original mystery at hand. I brought Vince up to date with the new information my mother had given me and we eventually left the gym. Me, to go on to the pool to swim a few laps. Vince to see what he could do with the additional details.

My mind was whirling, but the repetitiveness of the swim brought some order to my thoughts. I kept replaying that night in my head. Shanice and Elizabeth being there. The shared toast and conversation. Then the weird attraction. And before that, the warmth in the room. I stopped swimming and started treading water. There hadn't been anything wrong with the thermostat. But she and I had both been hot. She'd been sweating. Maybe the idea of drugging wasn't so far-fetched after all. But to what end? Was this about breaking me and Cassandra up? Or forcing me and Elizabeth together?

CHAPTER 34

ABE.

I genuinely believed that things couldn't get any worse. Like, truly, in my soul felt certain, that this situation...the one in which I'd lost the woman I love because she saw my dumb ass with another woman, specifically the woman I was meant to be engaged to...was as bad as it could get.

Can you blame me? I mean really, when you consider all the components of the situation. Not only had I lost Cassandra, but I may have fucked a woman I have no interest in or memory of fucking. And, oh, I may have been drugged into doing it. By said woman. And, on top of that, if I could ever hope to untangle that mess, I stood to lose my company at my own father's hand. The shit was fucked up.

Granted, it was a first-world kind of fucked up. People were starving and wars were happening and *that shit* was actually on a different level and I acknowledged that. But hell, that's not my story and right now, in my own chapter and verse, shit was going off the fucking rails.

And I naively thought it couldn't get any worse.

The paper I was scanning, the paper that Elizabeth had handed me after fifteen minutes of trying to figure out what was going on, proved me wrong.

Now I understood why she had answered her door with red-rimmed eyes. You know how they say don't ask questions you don't want to know the answer to? Yeah, here I stand.

"You're pregnant?"

She nodded.

"And, you believe it's my baby?" I asked it softly because I wasn't trying to be a dick here and clearly she'd been sitting on this for a minute.

She nodded again.

"Because..." I urged. Because I needed to hear her say that she truly believed we fucked that night and that that singular episode had resulted in her being pregnant. Because it made no sense to me. I mean I understood how science worked and all that, but still.

I'd come here, unannounced to Elizabeth's after she wouldn't answer or return my calls. It had been nearly a month since The Episode. A solid three weeks had passed since Cassandra threw me out of her office and I'd pounded Vince. I'd lost one of those weeks in a funk as Vince called it. Grouching around the office, using any excuse I could to be in Cassandra's space until she'd made it so uncomfortably clear that she didn't want me there, that I'd relented. The work was suffering because of me, I was throwing her off her game and that was trickling down to her team.

The next week, when I'd fought to stay the fuck away from her was even worse. I'd stayed away from the office completely.

Tearing off heads and ripping new assholes via Zoom until even Shanice, who could absorb the sharp edges of my personality with gleeful obtuseness, told me, respectfully, to fuck off.

I'd finally come here to confront and offload on the only other person who could offer any insight into what the fuck was going on. Now I wish I'd stayed my ass at home moping and scheming on how to get Cassandra to listen to me.

That seems like a tiny slice of heaven compared to this.

"Because, there's no other option. I haven't...I don't...," she looked at me from where she was perched on the edge of the cream loveseat. The furniture was delicate; the soft cream upholstery was beautifully complemented by the slender, intricately carved arms and legs of the piece. Elizabeth's space, really just an offshoot of Juanita's home, was hugely traditional, a little stuffy, and ostentatiously feminine.

I was uncomfortable and couldn't help but compare the feeling to the intense peace that always surrounded me the moment I stepped into Cassandra's house.

"Okay. Okay," I scrubbed a hand down my face and pushed up from where I sat across from her in an equally spindly chair. There was no way that piece of furniture could absorb the weight of what I was feeling. I could barely do so. The haze of despair that was hovering like a swarm of noseeums, the constriction in my chest that I was struggling to breathe through, they conspired to send me to my knees.

Long strides took me to the bank of windows, draped with yards and yards of gauzy fabric. The view beyond brought me a measure of calm. My hands, fisted tightly, released, and I stretched my fingers once, opening and closing before tamping down even that physical response.

"Abe, I don't know what to do. I don't know what happened."

I let my eyes close against her words because I didn't know what to do either. And I damn sure didn't know what happened. But if it had happened, and the evidence was clearly pointing that way, my suite of options had just narrowed to one.

I took a deep breath and exhaled...releasing the hopes I'd had that maybe Cassandra and I could figure this out and work our way back to each other, releasing the tenuous thread that allowed me to believe that just maybe, happiness was an option, and releasing Cassandra herself to find what she deserved...someone free to love her as she deserved to be loved.

When I turned to Elizabeth, she was holding the paper in her hands, reading it again, the disbelief obvious on her face.

"I'm not sure what happened either, Elizabeth."

"I'm not making it up, Abe," she whispered, still mesmerized by the results. "I wouldn't do that," she raised teary eyes to me.

"I didn't think you would. I don't think you would." I took the paper from her and scanned it more carefully. It was dated yesterday. She hadn't known long herself.

"You just went yesterday?"

"Yeah. I was late," a blush rose along her neck, "I was due last week."

"Last week? That seems really soon," I probed, trying to be gentle but needing to fucking understand how a fuck I neither instigated nor remembered had resulted in a kid and, let's be honest, everyone, a pending marriage.

"Yes. It does," she continued, her voice flat now, the embarrassment replaced with a faint defensiveness, which I understood. "But I'm extremely regular and always have been. Through stress, sickness, what have you."

"Okay," I nodded and sent her a weak smile, "that seems like a good thing from the complaints I've heard other women make."

"Yes," her shoulders relaxed a little. "It is, actually. It makes vacation planning much easier," she took a little fortifying breath and continued. "I was late," a wry smile skated across her lips as she returned to the intimate subject of her cycle, "I waited an extra two days. Which, for me, is like waiting another week and nothing. It made no sense, but I took a test."

I raised an eyebrow. There was a lot in that statement...what to follow up on first?

"Why didn't it make sense? You were late, and we'd obviously..." I waved my hand, not interested in putting words to whatever may have happened between us.

"Right. Obviously. But, and no offense to you," I acknowledged with a slight nod, "I don't remember what happened," her gaze skated across mine before returning to hands, fingers fidgeting in her lap like she, too, was having a hard time containing her energy. "I thought I'd feel different afterward. I thought I'd be able to tell."

"I felt the same way, Elizabeth," I leaned in because this was big. We hadn't talked about this after she'd left; we hadn't talked about anything, which was insanely frustrating. My life was being turned completely inside out, and no-fucking-body wanted to have a damn conversation. But we were talking now and if she didn't remember either, what could that mean?

"I'd begun to wonder if we'd been drugged." I was desperate enough to just put it out there. Did it matter at this point? If she was pregnant and the baby was mine, then that was that. But still, I dropped that bombshell right onto the coffee table sitting in front of her.

Her eyes shot to mine, rounded, "Drugged?"

"Drugged," I knelt in front of her. "Liz, have you ever not been able to tell the next morning if you'd fucked," she recoiled a little, and I corrected, "had sex? Been intimate? Doesn't your body tell you?"

She looked uncertain, but nodded anyway.

"Mine, too. And I felt none of that," I pushed to my feet again, paced, "I have absolutely no memories of anything sexual happening between us," I spun back to her. "Do you?"

She shook her head. "I don't. But how do you explain this? I'm not lying."

"I know," and I meant it. There was nothing about Liz that made me think she'd lie about something like this. But still, what the fuck.

"The first test was negative." *Wait, what?*

"What?"

"The first test I took. The home test, it was negative. I thought I was crazy for even taking it."

"But..."

"But, my...," another blush, "cycle never started. I waited two more days and made an appointment with my doctor for a blood test. That's what's positive."

"Is that normal? To have negative and then positive tests?"

She shrugged. "They said it could happen. It's very early on. They said the home test should come positive in a few days." After that, she went quiet. I had just opened my mouth to fill the silence when she spoke again.

"Abe. I'll take whatever tests you need me to take to show you're the father. But, I won't do this unmarried. I know there are women who do. And I know that it's horribly anti-feminist of me, but I don't want that. I don't want to be a single mother. Please, Abe," her face was stoic, but tears had begun to leave trails through her makeup. "Please."

I nodded. And I knew. I could feel the oozing claws of responsibility creep around my heart...obscuring the light that Cassandra had rekindled there...caging me, causing the faint image of another, laughter-filled life to retreat. Heart heavy and gray, I tucked it all away. Added it to my little box of things lost when Trey died.

CHAPTER 35

CASSANDRA.

It was too much. It was just too damn much, and if I was going to maintain my sanity and get through this launch, I needed to put Abe and Elizabeth and my broken heart out of my mind. It had been a fling. A delightful, liberating fling. I had stupidly allowed myself to get too attached but that was all. I was not *in love*, I was *in dick,* and that was something I could rectify. As soon as I got this launch handled, I'd go on a few dates, remind myself that Abe wasn't the only fish in the sea.

At least, that's the narrative I was trying desperately to sell to myself.

And it was the batch of questions I was worrying over when I should have been wholly engaged in this immensely important check-in meeting. We were blessedly on track, but I wouldn't dream of jinxing it by relaxing even one iota; couldn't risk dropping the ball by losing focus. This part of my life, the part that I told myself really mattered, was coming along nicely. I wasn't going to fuck it up; and I wasn't going to let this *situation* with me and Abe fuck it up either.

I didn't think he'd want that either, but I also hadn't thought he'd fuck Elizabeth right under my nose after he swore he wasn't interested in her. *But he didn't.* You don't know that. *If he did, it wasn't his fault.* You don't know that either. *We'll never know unless we talk to him, now will we?*

I snarled at the voice in my head.

"Damn, Cassandra. I didn't think you'd hate it that much," Tamra's slightly wounded voice pulled me from my thoughts, thoughts that should have been centered on the music she was playing for me.

The last goal of this meeting was to finalize the music and stage setting for the final show. We'd narrowed the selection to two mockups, but we hadn't made much progress on music. It was a delicate thing. The music set the vibe...they'd hear the music before they saw the clothes.

"I don't hate it. My mind was elsewhere. Run it back for me."

She fiddled with her phone, and the tune began again. I closed my eyes to better immerse myself in the experience we were trying to create. I could see the pieces in my mind blending with the music. I could picture the set, the shifting lights we'd chosen. Yeah, I think this could work.

"I like it," I murmured. The track shifted in tempo and rhythm, the blend perfectly carrying the listener along to the next elevation of the show. Now that I had dragged my attention back to where it needed to be, this mashup was a pretty exact fit for our needs.

"Nice work, Tamra. This is great, go ahead and lock it in." And with that, I adjourned the meeting.

"Heads up," Tamra whispered it as she gathered the materials she'd brought for the day. I glanced up at her absentmindedly, "What?"

"Heads up," she repeated, tossing a quick glance behind me, followed by a meaningful raising of her eyebrow. Shit. I didn't have time to curate my reaction though I had to admit that I was grateful for the split second I had to prepare myself before...

"Cassandra," Abe's voice sounded behind me. I didn't jerk, though the physical impact was jarring even with the warning. My eyes slid closed, granting myself just a moment to allow the smooth silk of him to saturate my senses, coat my tongue with the memory of his taste, fill my lungs with the subtle fragrance that is only him, and ply my ears with the sound of my name on his lips.

I wasn't ready. I would never be ready.

But I could hold my own.

"Abe," I responded to his one-word greeting in kind.

"There are a couple of items we need to discuss."

"Discuss away," I said. I saw Tamra's lips twitch and sighed. I definitely didn't need to be airing our shit, even in the most subtle of ways, in front of the team. So I slid my chair back and rose, heading toward one of the smaller collaboration rooms in the suite. I didn't want him in my office. It was too close, too intimate given some of the memories we'd made there.

Once inside, he closed the door. I wasn't happy with the way my body pulsed at the hint of privacy, but I ignored it. *Jesus, help me.* The air was thick in my ears, I shook my head slightly trying to clear them, but that only made my head swim faintly.

"How can I help you, Abe?" I asked proud of and, honestly, surprised by how steady my voice sounded.

He pulled the low swivel chair from its place tucked under the meeting table and sat. He had a small sheath of papers with him. My curiosity got the better of my nerves and I sat as well.

"Cassandra," he began and paused. He waited so long to speak again that I forced myself to meet his eyes.

There was no way I could disguise my response to what I saw there. A miasma of emotion ranging from pain to hunger, anger to desire, searching hopefulness to resignation, and finally, resolution. I watched it all, giving him nothing more beyond my initial gasp at the force of what he was feeling.

"Cassandra, this," he stopped again, but only briefly this time. "This is a clusterfuck."

"Abe," I couldn't let him even start.

"No. It is. An absolute fucking clusterfuck, and there's nothing I can do about it." To his credit, he didn't hem and haw any further. He just took a deep breath and spit out the sentence that rent my soul from stem to stern, "Elizabeth is pregnant."

Whatever he said in the next moments, I missed. The ringing in my ears made it impossible to do anything more that suck in air and try to remain upright. Try not to dissolve in a puddle of pathetic tears. I drew in a breath and heaved it out.

He reached out a hand and touched my hand where I laid them on the table to steady myself. I drew back as if burned. He nodded.

"Right. I still don't know," he trailed off, eyes taking on a pained expression. "But, yeah, anyway. You were right, I guess," he laughed a sad little laugh. "I couldn't get away from it. Can't get away from it. I wanted to tell you first, so you wouldn't hear it in the streets."

I nodded because I couldn't do anything else. *Pregnant?*

"Pregnant? So you did…"

"I don't know," he paused as if realizing how ridiculous his continued proclamations of having not had sex with her sounded under the circumstances. "I," another pause. "Yea, I guess so. I mean we'll get tested, of course but…"

"Right. But." I stood and started a short pacing in the room. My mind wasn't efficiently processing this at all.

"You didn't need to tell me. I don't need to know this, Abe. We're not together anymore," I huffed. "We were never together. It was just a good time in Europe."

"It wasn't that for me, Cassandra. For me, it was everything. And if you'll let me, I'll still be with you."

"How would that work exactly, Abe?" I tilted my head, both curious as to how he thought it was possible and angry that he would dangle this in front of me, knowing it was impossible. "I'd be your mistress? Your side piece on the weekends while you go home to Lizzy and the bouncing baby, during the week?" My lip curled.

"Never that, Cassandra. Never that. I'd marry you. I'd take care of Elizabeth and the child. We're adults. And adults don't have to get married because there's a baby on the way."

"And how would that track with your family, Abe? No. I don't want that. I don't deserve that life. I deserve a man of my own. All my own," I shook my head, tears threatening to fall because maybe I could share him. "Look, I'm fine. You're fine. We move on."

"I'm not fine. I'm not fine at all. But," he sighed again, "we do move on, I guess. She's pregnant," he said again.

"You don't have to keep repeating it."

"I kind of do because maybe then it'll make some fucking sense."

I stood. "Is that all? You just came to let me know your fiancee is pregnant, and what, you've set a date for the wedding, too? I'm invited? Why are you even here telling me this, Abe? You think I want to hear this shit?"

"No more than I want to say it, but again, I didn't want you to just...hear it elsewhere. I'm not an ass," I snorted before he continued, "current circumstances notwithstanding."

"You're not here to convince me it wasn't you anymore? That you don't know what happened?"

"I want to. With everything in me, Andi, I want to. I want to get on my knees and beg you to believe me when I say I don't remember *ever* touching her. When I say that the only image in my mind, the only taste on my tongue, and the only scent I can remember is yours. It's you, Andi. It always will be."

I let his words drench me, water my soul, fill my pores, but I couldn't respond, wouldn't respond because if I opened my mouth, it would be to accept every word, to plead with him to stay with me, to tell him I believed him, and even if I didn't, I didn't care. He was *mine. Mine,* dammit, and I wanted him. Wanted to just go away somewhere where we could be together in love. But I said nothing. I just looked at him. Willing him to go away before I broke into tears.

He sighed again, "But, I came for another reason, too. Maybe a better reason. Maybe a little bit of a way to make some of this up to you." he opened the folder he'd brought with him and drew out the short stack of papers. "I'm releasing you from your contract and giving you the line. It'll be all yours, no 'HeirLoom' tagline. It'll be released under your name only. It's yours. We'll continue all the funding and support of the release and the manufacturing for the next three years."

What?

"Also," he pulled out another sheaf and spread it before me. "This is a commitment to underwrite your atelier." I slow blinked.

"You would have had access to all of HeirLoom's resources if you stayed. I know you've already talked to HR about leaving, and I understand. I want to, but I wouldn't try to keep you here. But I want you to have everything you would have had," he reached out, and this time I didn't flinch.

His big hand traced the edges of my jawline. Goosebumps erupted. He tucked a stray braid behind my ear. My skin flushed. "I know your dreams, Cassandra. And I know your talent. I won't be the reason that any of that stalls out."

He was giving me everything I could have wanted. The full financial support of HeirLoom but the freedom of being an independent designer. I was stunned.

"Okay. Well. I guess my work here is done," he stood. "Read through everything. Get your lawyer to look at it. It's a good deal, though. It's the most I could do without having the board commit me," he smiled a wan smile.

"I love you, Cassandra. I know I shouldn't say it. Not now. Not with everything. But I need you to know it."

And he left.

CHAPTER 36

CASSANDRA.

The lilting fragrances of lavender and ylang ylang should have relaxed me—same for the firm, but gentle hands that were determinedly kneading the tight, aching muscles in my shoulders. They'd already done a number on my calves and thighs, wrung and squeezed the tension from my arms and lower back, and now the magic was centered in my shoulder blades and traps.

It felt good, I wouldn't lie. But I knew there was no amount of massage, meditation, or pampering that was going to get my feet back under me. Only time could do that. At least I trusted time to take care of it eventually. So far, it was doing a piss-poor job.

We were three weeks away from launch. Or, in the time management system that my brain now defaulted to, we were ten weeks PA, post-Abe. It had been ten weeks since I'd swung his office door open, anticipating dick but finding Elizabeth already on top of that situation; nine weeks since I'd told him in no uncertain terms that I wasn't interested in being his playtoy; eight weeks since he'd stopped following me around the office like a lapdog, making my resolve waver and crumble like the sheerest organza; seven weeks since he'd stopped biting everyone's heads off in virtual meetings. Six weeks since he'd stopped calling, stopped trying to make me listen, stopped trying to plead his case. And five weeks since he'd shared the news of his bouncing bundle of joy...and gifted me my freedom.

Five weeks during which I'd fallen apart and put myself back together innumerable times. Five weeks during which I'd been eternally grateful that this launch was so intricate that I required nearly all of my brain power. I thought I might be healing, but I knew that I wouldn't be sure until I was quiet again. Until life slowed enough for me to peel back the bandages and see if the wounds were still weeping.

But I'd be okay. That was the mantra. Not that I would thrive, not that I would be better off, not that this was a stepping stone to greatness. All I wanted, all I could manifest at this point was just being okay. That's all I wanted.

So, I was here today with Margeaux, at 'Damn Good Stuff,' getting spa'd up because past experience told me that acting okay was the first step to being okay. As long as I stayed honest in the process, doing the things I know I love, even if I didn't love them right now, worked for me.

"Mmmmmm," Gogo's orgasmic moan pulled me from my musings; we were enjoying a couple's day at the spa, so our services were all happening together. There was no rule saying the couple had to be romantic.

"Girl, chill," my giggle was muffled by the towel padding my face.

"Whatever," Gogo mumbled, "this is the most action I've gotten in months."

"What about what's his name," Margeaux was no ho, but she was also not one to spend her time alone. 'What's his name' was my usual tag for whoever she was blessing at the moment.

"What's-His-Name-Who?" she retorted. "You've been in your own little world of recovery, ma'am. I haven't mentioned Kevin in at least a month."

Shit, she was right now that I thought about it.

"Damn, Go. My bad. I suck."

"Nah, sweetie. You've been going through it. And he wasn't worth remembering anyway. Shit," she chuckled, "I damn near forgot about his ass, too."

The massage therapist slightly lifted the sheet covering my nakedness, whispered for me to turn over, and then began to work on my front half.

"Fair enough. I envy you." There was no point in pretending that I wasn't still struggling. Like she said, I'd been going through, and she knew it. "But I'll get there," I said. "Today is helping."

"Good. And the launch will help, too, because you are going to kill that shit."

"I am, you know. It's really good," I sighed because it was *really, really* good. I was proud of what our team, of what *I* had accomplished.

I had channeled all my pent-up frustrations over this mess with Abe into the work. I knew I had pushed my team to their limit, but it was all for the good. The thirty-six pieces we finally settled on were stunning depictions of our vision. They brought together the resilience and beauty of our culture, giving a nod to our heritage from the continent but standing solidly in the distinct gritty eloquence of Black Americanism. We were featuring a variety of body types, male, female, and androgenous; large, small, and extra schmedium; tall, short, and in-between, light, dark, and all the tones, hues, and shades on the continuum.

The colors of the collection were haunting greys, browns, purples, and greens, and the fabrics were rich and sensual. The whole show was hot as fuck, and we'd chosen a playlist with a low throbbing bass line...not overtly tribal, but it called to the rhythm, the vibrancy, and the joy and sorrow to be found in movement. Our set designers had gotten the memo and gone above and beyond, grabbing onto the inspiration as if they'd crawled inside my head and snapped screenshots. I couldn't wait to see it all come together.

"And then, you can bounce."

I could. Thanks to Abe. Which was a weird thing to say. "I can't believe he's giving me the whole line. And my own atelier."

"Yeah, I don't even know what that is, but it sounds dope as shit, and he should give it to you. You deserve it. Not because of the shit he put you through but because you're a damn good designer, and the world needs your shit."

Ah, the pep talks this woman could give.

"Thanks for that and, for the record, I agree." We both met that statement with a smack of the lips and an 'as you should' from Margeaux.

"It's a lot though, Margeaux. I wonder how much trouble he got into with the board. I couldn't have been easy. They've been trying to get rid of him." I didn't want to worry about him. I didn't want to think about how sad and resigned he'd looked when he'd talked about marrying Elizabeth and gifted me so generously. He was doing what he thought was right.

"Boone read the paperwork?" Margeaux asked, referring to the business attorney she used in conjunction with her salons.

"You know he did. And it's all in order. Margeaux, there are no strings. It's free and clear. They make nothing on the line or on anything I create going forward. The physical atelier is in my name and Heirloom is paying the staff for five years. That's two more than he originally mentioned when he gave me the paperwork."

"You've been dreaming about this forever, honey. I hate that it came with a broken heart, but those mend."

I didn't respond to that, just used the excuse of the massage therapist's application of mud to my face to explain my silence.

It was enough to think about that it carried me through the rest of the massage. The Himalayan salt rooms and body whisking didn't allow us many opportunities to return to our conversation. The same could be said for the hydrotherapy, though it was fun as hell and did relax me. It's hard to stay stressed when multiple water jets are beating you up in all the right ways.

But we eventually found ourselves in the steam room. Our next stop would be a return trip to the showers in preparation for the mani-pedis that would end our visit. I was grateful for the day. Maybe I'd journal about it tonight. I'd taken up the habit in the last weeks, trying to lance the pain as much as possible; letting it ooze out onto the pages of my notebook helped. Not much, but some.

"It's thick as shit in here," I whispered to Margeaux, stretching my hand out to touch her fingers on the bench cattycorner to mine. We were laying on the steam room's top bench as usual, backed into the corner, she on one side and me on the other. It put our heads close together so we could whisper in the cloudy steam.

"It is, but that's how I like it. The steam rooms at Reposant are weak. I can't stand being able to see the people in the room with me. Like I don't know you, don't look at me."

I laughed; Margeaux was a trip. "I feel you. I'm trying to feel like this is my personal steamer. None of y'all other plebes exist."

"That part," she laughed. As her chuckle died, the doors to the steam room swung open. We went silent in tacit agreement; I could almost feel her excitement tickling mine. One of our favorite bestie guilty pleasures was eavesdropping, a skill we'd honed and mastered together. It was crazy how much one could learn just by shutting the fuck up and listening.

Ending the day with some random tea that we could laugh about over sushi and wine would be perfect.

"You're worrying too much," a female voice said, slightly acerbic, clearly annoyed.

"Well, you're not worrying enough," the retort was quick and sharp, clipped in irritation and concern.

Margeaux grabbed my hand. This was going to be a good one.

"I could lose my job," the second voice continued.

"Fuck your job. You can work for me when it's done. Or you can stay there. He won't be able to fire you, will he?"

"He will if he figures it out."

"I said don't worry, Shanice. I'll take care of you."

I froze. Shanice? Abe's Shanice? Couldn't be. That would be too much of a coincidence.

"And who's going to take care of you? If they figure it out, you think Liz is going to just be okay with it?"

The fuck? Liz? Come on now. This couldn't be possible. Margeaux was squeezing my hand hard enough to crack the bones; probably to keep me quiet, but she was about to make me scream in pain. I wiggled my fingers, and she loosened her grip.

"She'll have no choice, will she? And what reason to be upset could she have? She'll be rich, cared for. The new first lady of HeirLoom."

That was old news. The internet had already made it clear that the CEO of HeirLoom and Heritage's heiress were in these streets as the new 'it' couple.

"But what about when she realizes she isn't really pregnant."

Isn't really pregnant?? I was glad Margeaux was there because her immediate squeeze was the only thing that kept me from voicing that disbelief out loud.

The first woman...who was she? Who could be talking to Shanice about Elizabeth and clearly, Abe?...made a dismissive noise. "We'll stop the dosage, and her period will start. She'll assume it's a miscarriage. No harm, no foul. He'll fuck her soon enough and put the real thing there."

I couldn't believe what I was hearing. I had to be tripping. There were surely multiple Shanice's in the city. And Liz was about as common a name as there was. There were lots of maybe pregnant Lizes as well...

"He didn't fuck her hopped up on that stuff you gave me. What makes you think he'll do it cold sober."

My head spun. *If I didn't know better, I'd think we'd both been drugged.* That's what Abe had said, and I'd thrown it back in his face.

"Because that's how men are. You fucked up the dosage. That's on you."

"On me? No, that's on you. You gave it to me. I just poured and stirred. You were just too damn scared of getting caught to use enough."

There was a little shuffling noise and then voices again.

"Plus, any woman cold enough to set up her own daughter on some date rape shit...," the woman named Shanice huffed, "you get all the credit for that."

Her daughter? This was Juanita Brookes?

"Watch your fucking tone with me. And stay calm, Shanice. Understand that in the end, *you* drugged the decanter, *you* poured the drinks, and *you* helped arrange them so that they woke up in bed together. All I did was speculate about the possibilities."

"Ms. Brookes..."

"Enough. Let's enjoy the rest of our day, shall we? We have an engagement party to plan, after all."

It was another tortuous ten minutes that felt like an eternity before the steam room door swung open again, and they exited.

Margeaux and I both sat up, and I turned to where her face would be if I could see through the steam.

"What the fuck?"

"Those are some treacherous bitches."

"Treacherous," I agreed. "But what am I supposed to do? He was right. They drugged them. And now they got them thinking there's a baby? Margeaux."

"You have to tell him."

"But, how? I can't just call and be like, I think I overheard your secretary and new mother-in-law, and my bad, you were right. They did drug you and bee-tee-dubs, they're still drugging her; there's no baby."

"*Yes, bitch! Exactly!*" Margeaux returned. I opened my mouth and shut it again. "Well, maybe not quite like that, but kinda?"

"Maybe I could just call the police and report a crime I overheard."

"Yeah, and get caught up in the hows and whys? What do you think will happen when you're like, oh, I couldn't see them through the steam. I just recognized the voices."

"But they called each other by name."

"Your word against theirs."

"You're a witness."

"And also a foster child hairdresser. Who do you think they're going to believe?"

I chewed my lip. She was right. But I didn't want to be the one to tell him. I didn't want to see him. Especially not with this news. Wouldn't it sound like I was just bringing him an excuse for us to be together? And in the end, what would it solve? I was still not of his class, not in his league. If her mother went to these lengths to see them together, what else would she do? And what about his father? I wondered if he was in on it.

"I'll think about it."

"You'll *think* about it? You know for a fact that this man…and this woman, though fuck her, kind of…were drugged. Roofied and mollied. And you're not going to tell him?"

I hedged. "I mean. Does it matter in the end? They were going to end up together anyway. He's not fighting it. Have you seen the pictures? They look happy."

I wasn't looking at Margeaux anymore. I had, in fact exited the steamroom with her hot on my heels and was hanging my towel to step into the shower. She gave me no privacy, instead standing in the opening of the stall glaring at me while I washed off the sweat.

"Can I have some privacy, please?"

"Bitch, no. Because you're talking crazy talk." Then her voice gentled. "I know you're pissed and hurt and confused. But you have to tell him this. Whether you still want him or not," just those words felt like a hot poker in my chest because *God, did I want him*, "he deserves to know."

And with that, she left me to my own devices. I exhaled as I heard her shower turn on. I didn't know if I felt better or worse than I had when I'd arrived. Then, I'd been on the mend, beyond the first shaky steps and making a few solid strides on my healing journey. Now I stood at a crossroads, one path looped back to the beginning…a beginning that was glorious and that I'd love to experience again…but the first time I'd walked that road, it led me here. The second path led to healing, but it would be laced with uncertainty…could we have been together if I'd been braver…and loneliness because while my mind told me I'd be fine, my heart knew that Abe was my person. I could be happy without him, but I wouldn't be whole.

CHAPTER 37

ABE.

"Yo, Abe. You got company," Vince leaned against one of the columns separating the patio from the pool. I'd just drug myself out of the water, and was sucking wind, trying to catch my breath just enough to slide back in. I knew from experience it would take another twenty laps for my body to reach the level of exhaustion it needed for dreamless sleep.

Twenty more laps and a long pull of that ooowee I'd sent Vince out for a couple of weeks ago.

"Not interested. Get rid of them," I contemplated the water, evaluated my breathing, and decided I probably wouldn't drown if I went back in. "You down to roll us up and meet me in about thirty?" I glanced up at him. Caught his nod before pushing off the wall to start my next lap.

"It's Cassandra," he called out.

Well, fuck. I took in water, and sank for a moment before I resurfaced coughing like a kid at his first swim lesson.

I hauled myself out, not at all embarrassed by how fucking eager I was to see her. I didn't care why she'd come, but I asked anyway.

"Why's she here? Did she say?" I caught the smirk on Vince's face as I hopped on one foot, trying to pull my joggers on over wet skin. I didn't want to meet her in my trunks. They would be absolutely no good at hiding how fucking happy I was to see her. The joggers wouldn't do much better, but at least I could tuck my boy under both waistbands. Once I pulled on my tshirt, I should be good.

"Nah, but she looks mighty...resolute," he chuckled.

I raised an eyebrow at his choice of words, Vince was wild sometimes, and blew past him on my way to the living room. I had to stop to catch my breath when I saw her. It hadn't been that long since I'd caught sight of her at work, but I'd made it my business to stay out of her way, out of her space. I knew she was hurting...because of me...and I wouldn't make it worse by being around. So this, having her here in my home again, was like a moment of heaven.

She was nervous. Her back was to me, but she had her finger to her lips. I knew she was chewing one or the other, or both. Her hair was loose and curly. It had grown; the little braids she kept it in had done their job. She was dressed casually, a loose skirt made of brushed fleece hung on her hips and gathered at the bottom like the skirt version of sweatpants. She'd paired it with a slightly fitted t-shirt. I'd seen it often enough to know that it sported an I Heart NY logo on the front. They were comfort clothes. I was happy she'd chosen this approach for whatever she had to tell me. I knew she sometimes went full glam as a form of armor; she'd been full glam at work for the last several weeks. Maybe the fact that she was here in her fuzzy clothes boded well.

What does that even mean, bro? You think she's come to say fuck Liz, let's run away?

Shit, one could only hope. It was something I'd consider if she presented it. I was smart, and she was talented. Fuck HeirLoom. We could walk away from all of it and start our own shit. It was an idea that had been floating in the back of my head but popped forward fully formed when I saw her standing there. Vulnerable. Chewing her nails. Or her lip. Or both.

Would she take me up on it? *Would you actually do it? Could you?* For her, I would. And I could. I shook my head. She had me over here spying on her sounding like fucking Dr. Seuss. But now that the idea had taken serious root, I wondered what it might look like.

I must have made some noise, or the hairs on the back of her neck alerted her to my stalkery behavior.

"Oh, Abe! You scared me," she said with a little breathless laugh that went straight to my dick and made me glad I'd layered on the bottom.

"My bad. I wasn't expecting company."

She grimaced a little, "I know."

"But you're always welcome. You know that, right?" I stood away from her, keeping my distance. The last thing I wanted to do was spook her and send her running. I was trying to drag this interlude out as long as possible.

She didn't answer but rounded the sofa to come perch on the edge of one of the giant arm chairs Vince had selected to accommodate my big frame comfortably.

"Um. I have something to tell you."

Is she pregnant, too? My heart leapt at the sudden vision of Andi, face glowing, round belly sticking out over her sweat skirt, stretching that red New York apple to its limit.

"It's awkward."

It doesn't have to be. My brain was frantically trying to figure out how I could convince her to run away with me. I didn't give two fucks about HeirLoom. But I did care about Liz. And I could support her and her child as well. It wasn't like I was destitute by any means. Whether I stayed with HeirLoom or not, it would take several years and multiple bad decisions before I could cry broke.

I opened my mouth to start to explain how I could take care of her and our baby, to ask her, yet again, to please be with me when she spoke. And the words coming out of her mouth were heaven-sent.

"I believe you."

I won't say the world stopped spinning, but from my perspective, it certainly stuttered.

"What?" I wasn't pretending not to know what she referred to; what she referred to was a continual nagging in the back of my brain. Not only didn't I remember this Night in Question, but the woman I loved didn't believe me. So yeah, when that woman said she *did* believe me, I knew exactly what she meant. I just wasn't sure I'd heard her right.

"I believe you were drugged," she said. "I believe you didn't have sex with Elizabeth."

My knees went weak. I dropped into the closest seat, dropped my head into my hands while whispered prayers of gratitude fell from my lips. I looked up to see tears in her eyes.

At least, I assumed they were in her eyes and not mine. The wetness that dripped on the back of my hand told me I might be wrong.

A quick swipe took care of that moisture, and I fell to my knees in front of her. I didn't give a damn about how I might look; I would prostrate myself before her if she but whispered that she wished it so.

She swiped her thumbs under my eyes, and yes, I could see that she had her own tears.

"You believe me?" I asked because, woah.

She nodded. "I'm sorry that I didn't believe you before," she whispered.

"How could you? Why would you?" I asked her. Yeah, I could get all on my high horse about how if she loved me, she would have trusted me, but bro. I knew niggas in general weren't shit. And a woman had to believe her own eyes to survive sometimes. I didn't blame her. I was just beyond grateful that something had changed.

"I should have."

"Nah, baby. You'd've been crazy to. How the fuck does that shit even sound? I could hear myself when I was saying it."

Could I touch her? Take her hands in mine? Would she draw back? Did this change anything?

I reached out; tapped my forefinger to hers. She curled it around mine, and my heart relaxed into a steady happy rhythm.

"I'm sorry," she said again.

"Stop. You don't need to be. But what happened to change your mind?"

She pulled her hand away and stood up, putting distance between us again. I didn't like that, but I didn't follow her. I slipped back onto the sofa and waited for her to tell me, my heart singing and dancing and putting itself back to rights.

She sighed. "I don't know if it matters, Abe."

"Oh, it matters," I couldn't sit any longer. I rose and tracked her to where she had wandered to the counter and eased onto a high stool. "Whatever brought you here, back to me. It matters."

"Tell me," I eased close to her, probably too close, but I couldn't help it.

She peeked at me from under low lashes. "Go over there," she pointed. "I can't think with you so close."

I nodded. Not letting my joy show on my face. No need to creep her out by jumping her bones and dragging her to the floor underneath me. So, I took my big horny ass and sat it down where she told me to.

"So, a couple of days ago, Margeaux and I went to Damn Good Stuff to get spa'd up," she glanced at me to make sure I knew the place. I nodded. "While we were in the steam room..." and she went on to spin a tale that sounded like it came from an episode of True Crime.

When she finished, she said, "You have to call Elizabeth here. You have to tell her, too."

I nodded absently because she was right, but my primary focus was on tamping down the rage that was boiling in me. How fucking dare they? How dare they fuck with my body, with my future? Try to take away my choice? Purposefully set Cassandra up to be hurt because there was no way I thought this little stunt was just about getting me to marry Elizabeth. Elizabeth. She was going to be devastated. How could her own mother set her up to get...date raped? *Jesus.*

I scrubbed my hand across my face. The heaviness of my beard reminded me that I looked like shit. It was Sunday. I hadn't left the house since I walked in Friday evening after working myself as close to the bone as possible. Another step in my nightly quest for oblivion.

I probably smelled awful, too, like chlorine and funk. A surreptitious sniff confirmed that a shower would not be out of order at all.

"Call her," Cassandra urged.

My mind was racing with the possibilities. The noose that had been circling my neck, getting ever tighter, was loosening. I dialed Elizabeth's number. She answered on the third ring, sounding groggy and something else.

"It's Abe," I said without preamble.

"Yeah. I know."

"Can you come here?"

"What? No. It's late. I'm in bed."

I glanced at my watch. It was 9pm. Not exactly late, but I got it.

"I'll send a car."

"Abe, I'm not coming over there."

"We need to talk, Elizabeth."

"About what, exactly? I've already told you I'm not going to be a single mother, no matter how much you don't want this. We can figure out a divorce or something maybe down the line but..."

"You're not pregnant, Liz." I saw Cassandra's eyes go big, and her head dropped to the side in a 'what the fuck' motion. I shrugged.

"Oh, so now you know what's happening in my body? Are you manifesting a miscarriage, Abe? That's sick."

"No, no," so dropping that nugget wasn't the best approach after all. "That's not what I mean. Listen, you know how that night is blurry for us both. I think I know why. I don't want to discuss it over the phone, though."

"Then you come here. Why would I come there if *you* have something to tell *me*. You're not the gentleman you're cracked up to be, Abe."

"Because you live under your mother's nose, and I don't want to have this conversation there."

A long pause. Then, "What's that supposed to mean."

"Nothing. But you know she's all in on this marriage. I just...we need to talk."

"Abe, you're not weaseling out of this. It was fucked up and an accident, but you're not getting out of it."

"And I'm not trying to. Well, I am. But I think once you hear what I have to say, you'll want out, too."

Silence. Long enough that I thought she'd hung up. When I pulled the phone from my ear to verify that the call was still connected, I heard her voice again.

"Well, I guess that's intriguing enough to pull me away from *Real Housewives*. Send the car. I'll be down in thirty."

"Thank you," the relief in my voice was palpable.

"Mmhmm. This better be worth it."

"Oh, it's worth it all right."

I ended the call and turned to Cassandra.

Could I hug her now? Hold her? Kiss her? Profess my love...again? What were the rules?

She stared back at me. Those beautiful eyes glowing. I tried to decipher what I saw there. All I knew was that the dejection, the hurt, the devastation, and the disappointment were gone. And for that reason, my heart sang. I took a step closer to her, but she held up a hand.

"Not until we've told Elizabeth and put it all to rest, Abe." Damn, was I that obvious? But that 'not until' spurned joy because that meant that *after* we had done those things, maybe I could have her again, in my bed and, more importantly, in my life. Well, maybe not, *more* importantly, but certainly equally importantly.

I nodded. She smiled and stuck her tongue out at me, and the last vestiges of fear around my heart cracked.

"I need a shower," I said.

"You do," she agreed.

"Oh, you got jokes, now? After leaving me to drown in my sorrows, a victim of drug abuse and manipulation? Now you got jokes?"

Her eyebrows flew up. "I'm so sorry, Abe! I didn't know...I couldn't..."

"I'm kidding, beautiful. Kidding," and then I did take her in my arms. Chlorine and funk be damned. Her arms sliding around my waist were like bands of heaven, and I never, ever wanted to be free again.

I rested my chin on her head and just held on, eyes closed. She held me back actively, squeezing me tight and rubbing her hands along my back. Every so often, I'd feel the warmth of her fingers playing around the hem of my t-shirt.

My body responded. Wholeheartedly. She moaned and pressed against me. Cushioning my lonely dick against the softness of her lower belly. Then she stepped back.

"Shower. You stink. And then we'll talk to Elizabeth."

"Okay." I tilted her head up. I wanted to kiss her so badly. My eyes roamed her face, her arresting eyes, that beautiful almond butter skin, and those soft lips. I remembered them. Remembered the sweetness that lay behind them. But she was right. The next time my lips met hers, I wanted the kiss to be free and clear. Pure. Reflective only of our love. Not marred by unintended fiancees and fake babies.

But because I couldn't keep my lips to myself, I dropped a soft lingering kiss on her forehead before I let her go and went to shower.

CHAPTER 38

CASSANDRA.

This was a lot. My senses were overwhelmed with Abe. I'd told him he stank but that wasn't true at all. He smelled wonderful. Like my favorite meal, my favorite candle, my favorite cologne, all wrapped into one stunning package. I wanted to lick him. Bite him. Climb onto him and absorb him into my body. I wanted to claim him as mine and tell the rest of the world to go fuck itself.

But not until we got this all cleared up. My biggest fear was that Elizabeth wouldn't believe it. That she wouldn't care. That she was somehow in on it.

But that would be ridiculous, wouldn't it? The conversation we'd overheard made it clear that she was as much a victim as Abe was.

We needed a pregnancy test. Or two. Or three. I wondered how many it would take for her to believe us. I wondered if they'd really come back negative.

I shared my worries with Abe when he emerged from the bathroom looking and smelling like a walking wet dream. I rolled my eyes at him. He had clearly done all the things: shaved, brushed his waves, put on cologne.

"Getting cute for your fiancee?" I asked, trying to tamp down the raging attraction with a little humor. Crazy that I could already inject laughter into this still not-funny equation. Knowing that Abe hadn't lied, that he hadn't strung me along, that he hadn't dipped his wick in this other woman was releasing a joy in me that I couldn't contain.

"I haven't even asked you yet, but I'm down if you are." He stopped in front of me and tilted his head, snaring me with that intense stare of his. Was he serious?

"Silly," I swatted at him. "What if she doesn't believe me?" I asked, changing the subject to one that made my heart race a little less.

"She might not," he said honestly, which I appreciated. "But I do."

"Do you think she'll take another pregnancy test? Can Vince pick one up...or a couple...when he goes to get her?"

"Yep. Already covered."

"So now what?"

"We wait," he reached for me, tugging me into the circle of his arms again. "And while we wait, we plan our future because this last month, six weeks, eternity, without you is not something I'm ever interested in experiencing again," his arms were looped loosely around my waist; his clasped hands rested on my bottom. Even those light touches had my skin singing, chirping with the need to rub against him like a cat.

"I need you, Cassandra. I love you." The world splintered into a beautiful kaleidoscope of color. He loves me.

"I love you, too," I whispered it shyly but with certainty. The grin that erupted on his face drew an equally goofy one from me.

"I love you," he repeated.

"I love you, too," I gave it back to him again.

"We're getting married," he said.

"I don't hear a question," I replied. He nodded.

"Okay," he nodded again. "That's fair. Wait on me," and he tweaked my nose with a wink.

I smiled up at him, mesmerized for a moment by the un-fettered love in his gaze. I'd waited forever to see that kind of affection and commitment. I'd thought I had it with Jeffrey, but not at all. That hadn't been love. It had been manipulation and coercion. He'd played on my insecurities and used me for my talent.

This man, this man, had let me go when he thought he'd hurt me. And instead of using me to boost himself, which was well within his rights since I was his employee, he'd stripped it all down. Gave me as much autonomy over my own talent as he could. Set me up to be successful in every way he could. And taken on what I could only assume was an irate Old Man Walker to make it happen.

This felt like love. This felt like what I wanted love to feel like.

"I will wait on you. I'll wait forever." And fuck waiting to clear this shit up with Elizabeth. I pulled him down to me until our lips met. Softly. Gently. With the promise of now and the promise of more. He didn't move to deepen the kiss. Nor did I.

Just the sweet meeting of our lips was enough. The pressure, the connected gaze. The promise.

By unspoken agreement, we separated. Came back together briefly once, and again, and again. Peppering each other with kisses until I started giggling and he scooped me up for a full body squeeze. Our eyes met, the laughter faded, and the energy shifted just as we processed the opening and closing of the front door.

Holding the intensity of our gaze, he let me slide the length of his body until my feet touched the floor again. *Later. Soon.*

Footsteps made their way toward us. The softer tread of Elizabeth's sneakers was punctuated by Vince's heavier booted stride.

As soon as Elizabeth saw us, her eyes narrowed, and her lip twisted.

"Oh, are we doing this again? Why am I here, Abe? I've already told you I don't give a fuck if you have your side shit, but for the life of me, I cannot understand why you have to keep pulling me into it. Do you understand the concept of discretion? It means *don't* tell me."

"Hey, Liz. It's not like that," Abe welcomed her in, walking to her to take her elbow and lead her into the den. I followed.

The raised eyebrow and narrowed glare she threw me told me she didn't buy it. But she allowed Abe to lead her in and seat her on the comfortable sofa.

"So what's this about? I walked away from the RHOA season finale for this bullshit. I should be resting, you know. I'm with child," she directed this last part at me.

I gave her a weak smile, and Abe said, "Yeah, about that."

"I'm not having an abortion, Abe. I know you don't want this kid, but I'm not that woman. I'm not getting rid of my kid."

"And I would never ask you to, Elizabeth. That's not why we're here."

"You said on the phone that I'm not pregnant. What was that all about?"

"Do you feel pregnant?" I leaned in to ask. A raging mistake because Elizabeth immediately turned her spit and fire my way.

"I've never been pregnant until now. I feel how I feel," here words were civil but her eyes told me what I could do with my questions.

I held my hands up. This wasn't going to go well.

"Listen. You know how badly our parents want this marriage," Abe pulled one of the armchairs closer to Liz. I took a seat at the chess table, close enough to hear but far enough away to make her comfortable focusing on Abe.

"Well, yes."

"Your mother," he paused, "and maybe my father," he looked my way, and I responded with a shrug, "but certainly your mother set us up."

"Set us up?"

Abe nodded. "Set us up. Think about that night at my office. Why were you there?"

"I came to talk to you about the pictures we'd seen in the papers from your trip to Europe with her," another spiteful glare. "I wanted to let you know...yet again...that your efforts at discretion left much to be desired."

"Did you come on your own?" I asked from the chess table. Again, I needed to shut the fuck up and let Abe handle this.

"Yes, I came on my own," she said it in a little sing-song mocking tone before turning her attention back to Abe. "Mother showed me the photos of the two of you traipsing along the Champs-Elysees. It was embarrassing. I came to talk to you about it."

"So, Juanita sent you?"

"Sent me? No. I just said I came on my own."

"Okay," Abe changed course a little bit. "What else do you remember about that night?"

"Abe, why are we doing this?"

"Humor me, please."

"Well, I arrived and Shanice was there."

"What was she doing when you got there? Was she surprised to see you?"

Elizabeth started to answer, then paused. "She was in your office. I don't really know what she was doing... straightening stuff I guess. She wasn't at her desk, though, and your door was open, so I walked in. Was she surprised to see me? I don't know. I guess she was. I didn't call on my way."

Abe nodded and glanced my way. Elizabeth tracked the exchange.

"Then what?"

"We just chatted a little bit I guess. I wasn't there long before you showed up."

"Did Shanice know you were coming to the office, Abe?" I asked. Because the piece I couldn't figure out was the timing.

"She may have. She knew I was going to see my mother that day. I hadn't been into the office and it's rare that a day passes when I don't come in at all. I usually close the night at the office if I'm not in during the day."

I nodded. It was a little risky, but what did they have to lose? If he didn't show up, they could just plan another day.

"The two of you, with your little secret glances, are starting to piss me off."

Abe returned his attention to Elizabeth. "When we were there, you started feeling hot, remember? And a little dizzy."

She nodded. "The thermostat was mis-set. You were hot, too," she said half accusingly. She really was starting to feel a little trapped. We needed to cut to the chase.

"Shanice drugged you," I spat it.

Her head whipped around to me before turning back to Abe. Incredulity was written on her face.

He nodded.

She stood up, went to gather her purse, which she'd set on the sofa next to her, "Listen, I know this isn't what you wanted, and I've already said I'll make it as easy as possible for you. But this? This is ridiculous," she muttered a few more things to herself before Abe took her arm.

"Liz. Just listen."

"I won't listen."

"You have to. Because someone has taken away your choice and your autonomy. Just listen. For old times sake. Think about who I am, Liz. I'm not a liar, and I'm not trash. You've known me a long time, and we've been friends...at least friendly...before all this."

She stopped, considering; she leveled a long look at me, trying to figure out what my presence and input might mean.

"They drugged us, Liz. We didn't have sex. You're not pregnant," Abe repeated.

Still, she hesitated.

"Take a pregnancy test. Here," I approached slowly, holding out the Duane Reade bag that Vince had left on the counter. I glanced inside. He'd been thorough. "They're brand new. All sealed," I chuckled wryly. "There are several. Take your pick. Take multiple picks."

"Try, Liz," Abe encouraged. "If they come back negative, will you listen?"

I could see the uncertainty and confusion on her face and, maybe, just a little hope.

"Okay, fine," she grabbed the bag. "I'll take the damn tests, but it's a waste of my time. Where's the bathroom?"

Abe pointed. She went.

For all my certainty about what I'd heard, the next five minutes were tortuous. What if she were pregnant? Could she be carrying someone else's child to pass off as Abe's? But Juanita and Shanice said she wasn't.

Abe reached over to pull my hand from my mouth. I replaced my fingernail with the edge of my lip and chewed away.

"Abe, what if I was wrong? What if..."

"Stop. You're not wrong. And it doesn't matter. We've started it now. There's no way I'm marrying Liz, regardless. We'll figure it out."

"You can't figure it out. If she doesn't believe it or if she actually *is* pregnant, you have to marry her. You'll lose everything if you don't."

"I'll lose everything that matters if I do," he replied, holding my gaze and rubbing the back of my hand with his thumb. "I'll walk away from it all for you. We can start from scratch. Build our own fortune."

"Abe..."

"Andi. There's no discussion here. I'm not choosing this prison over you. Godrick...Trey... wouldn't want me to, and I don't want to. It's not fair to me. It's not fair to you. And I won't do it."

"But you'll be broke. I can't let you sacrifice everything for me."

He laughed. "I'd be sacrificing everything for *me*. Not you. You're the reward," he smiled and dropped a kiss on my lips. "And, I'll be far from broke. Warwick has been diligent with my investments. I have my own money. Nothing like the Walker fortune, to be sure, but even if they cut me off completely, I am nowhere near destitute. I'll be able to take care of *you*," he chucked my chin.

"I don't need taking care of."

"True. But I want to. Will you let me?"

Elizabeth chose that moment to rejoin us. I stood putting distance between myself and Abe. If the tests were negative, and I suspected they were based on the pallor on her face, she'd need to be comfortable seeking comfort from the only person she knew in the moment.

She walked to the counter and laid them out. Six tests. All negative.

"Abe?"

"Yeah," he reached for her, but she stepped away and wrapped her arms around herself.

"Talk," she said.

So I did. Again telling the story that I'd told Abe about the steamroom.

"You couldn't see them?" She asked.

"I could not," I confirmed.

"You've only met my mother once or twice. You couldn't know her voice that well."

"That's true," I said softly. "But I do know Shanice's voice. And they called each other by name."

"But I've been to my doctor. I've heard the heartbeat. I don't understand."

That part was weird. I didn't know why her doctor wasn't telling her the truth. Unless, "Who's your doctor? Is it your doctor? Or your mother's?"

She looked up, horror written on her face. "He's my doctor. But he does know my mother. His father is her doctor." I looked at Abe. "Can you get a doctor here now? Tonight?"

He nodded and moved away from us to make phone calls.

I wasn't sure what to do. Would she want comfort from the woman who wanted the man she wanted? She took the tests from the counter and sat, just holding them and staring at them.

When I saw a tear drop to her fisted hands, I made my decision and crossed to her, knelt by her, and opened my arms. She considered, sighed, and leaned into me.

"I'm so sorry," I whispered.

"Why?" She huffed. "You're getting everything you wanted."

"I didn't want your pain. I've never wanted that." She rolled her eyes. "I'm serious. Abe told me y'all weren't actually engaged. That it was just something your parents wanted." She didn't respond.

"I've seen y'all together. Are you even feeling him like that?" I continued wondering if I was doing too much.

She glanced at me then. "No. Not really. I mean, he's cute and all," I smiled. "But no. We've never been like that. But it doesn't matter in our circles. Surely you understand that."

I nodded. "I used to. But not anymore," I said. "I love him, Liz," she looked up at that. "I really love him, and I thought I could let him go. I would have let him go if you were having his kid and if you really wanted him. But you're not, and you don't." We stared at each other. "So I'm keeping him."

Abe returned. "Doc's on her way."

"Her? I thought your family doctor was Dalton."

"It is. But I thought you'd be more comfortable with a woman. I asked him to recommend someone. He's sending a colleague, Dr. Vanessa Yvette."

Liz nodded. And we waited together.

CHAPTER 39

ABE.

We closed the door behind Liz and Dr. Yvette. They walked out head to head in deep conversation. I was glad that they had clicked, glad that it looked like Liz would have someone to help her through this.

It had been hell getting to the bottom of things. But Dr. Yvette had confirmed through a blood test that Liz wasn't pregnant. She'd also drawn blood to take to her lab to see what drug was being given to Liz to stop her periods. She suspected it was just elevated levels of estrogen, which may or may not track in the labs she would run, but at least we'd get some more information. She and Liz were going straight to her office tonight to see what else they could learn. Liz had promised to call as soon as she had anything worth sharing.

I believed she would. And I believed she would be okay. As the night had worn on, her annoyance had turned to disbelief then to horror and betrayal. By the time she'd walked out though, she was fucking furious. I hoped that fire would carry her for a while. At least through the lashing that she said she was going to give her mother.

I'd love to be a fly on the wall to see that. I'd never witnessed Juanita Brookes getting a comeuppance. It would be a good show.

"Do you think your father was involved?" Cassandra asked me.

"Probably. I certainly wouldn't be surprised. Even if he wasn't part of the execution, the idea fits him." I was fairly sure that my father was behind it or at least heavily engaged. I wouldn't tell Cassandra that, though. She had enough to worry about.

It had been a hell of a long night. It had been nearly nine when Cassandra arrived on my doorstep to change my life for the better. The rest of the night's events had pushed us well past midnight. I was ready to go to bed.

I draped an arm around Cassandra's shoulders, pulling her gently along with me toward the bedroom wing.

"Oh, you're mighty assumptive, aren't you, Mr. Walker?"

"Maybe you're the assumptive one, Ms. Williams. I'm just ready to get some rest. Where's your mind at?"

"Firmly in the gutter with yours, I suspect. And there'll be no rest until you take care of this little issue I have."

"Oh, you got issues?"

"I do. Well, more itches than issues. Itches that I need you to scratch for me."

"Gladly," I pulled her closer to my side, and we made our way to my bedroom. When I swung the door open, I said another silent prayer of gratitude for Vince. He was my dude through and through. He'd been in the room while we were dealing with all the fallout of the drugging.

The bed that I had tossed and turned in, wrestling with the sheets every night, trying to find moments of rest, had been freshly made. The sheets were crisp white and turned back. There was chilled wine and an unopened bottle of Blanton's on the low lounge table. I chuckled at the subtle reference...he knew I'd pick up on the fact that I'd be cracking the seal, no opportunity for tampering.

"Wine?"

"Sure, you can pour it. I'll probably fall immediately to sleep if I drink it, though," Cassandra said, as she slipped out of my arms toward the adjoining bathroom. I loved how comfortable she was in my space. I loved seeing her back in my space.

I chuckled and poured her a quarter glass to take into the bathroom with her. I matched it with an equally light pour of Blanton's for myself. When she emerged from the bathroom less than five minutes later, she was playing no games.

The empty wine glass dangled from her fingers. That was the only accessory she'd chosen to pair with the expanse of warm brown skin and rich brown curls. My jaw dropped. I tossed the half shot of Blanton back—I needed the fortification—and heeded her siren call.

The moment my finger touched all that warm brown, she melted into me, straining upward to catch my mouth with hers. I obliged by dipping enough to wrap my arms around her waist before lifting her to my level. So that our mouths had easy access to devour each other. I felt her legs wind themselves around my hips. My dick rose to meet her, frustrated at the confines of the compression shorts I'd thrown on under sweats after my earlier shower.

What had seemed a good idea at the time was now threatening to result in a lack of blood supply to my brain. I had to get them off. Cassandra apparently agreed because she wiggled until I let her down and immediately went to work dropping my sweats and then peeling the shorts down. The moment the pressure was removed my dick popped and bopped her her on the top of the head. She looked up. I grinned and shrugged.

"Abe!"

"What? We missed you." She couldn't help but laugh, and I joined her for the sheer joy of it.

For the sheer joy of being able to play with her again, to relax and laugh, to have giggly sex and whispered jokes.

She wrapped her fist around me, and the laughter faded. Her eyes locked on mine, and I watched, fascinated, as the desire rose in them, eclipsing everything else. Holding my gaze, she flattened my dick against my stomach and used the flat of her tongue to draw a hot wide line from root to tip before capturing as much as she could in her mouth. Then she released me and did it again.

I swayed and groaned; she wiggled and moaned. I watched through hooded eyes as she repeated the process twice more before she settled her mouth around me and sucked. I braced, spreading my legs wider to give her access to everything she wanted and to provide a broader base before I face-planted on the floor. The shit felt *so fucking good.*

She moaned again, and I tried my best to focus on her, watching her sweet mouth make love to me. I stripped off the t-shirt that was trying to impede my line of sight. Trying to get in the way of me watching myself disappear down her throat over and over again. Watching her make my dick wet and sloppy. Watching her spread her knees wider apart and slip a hand between.

That was the straw that broke me. That one right there. The one where she dipped her own fingers into her hot wetness and groaned at the sensation of filling herself up. That was the straw.

I pulled back; we both made sounds of regret when I slid out of her mouth with a wet sucking *pop!* I bent, scooped her up, and tossed her gently on the bed. God, she was so beautiful. Even more so with those mismatched eyes hot with lust, her lips swollen, skin flushed. Jesus I had to get inside her.

She agreed and scooted back on the bed, propped on her elbows, knees bent, feet apart. I paused for a moment just to take in the sight. To burn it onto my retinas with all the other images I had of her humming with need.

I contemplated. I really wanted to taste her. Really wanted to bury my head between her thighs and just eat her out for hours. But I also wanted to be balls deep inside of her, tapping her cervix with the tip of my dick, drowning in her wetness. So I stood for a moment, fisting my dick, rubbing the moisture she'd left there while I decided what to put where.

I may have taken too long because she opened her thighs further, putting the wet pink of her on display for me; then she slipped her own fingers inside, wetting them thoroughly before slipping them in her mouth to lick them clean.

"We're waiting on you, boo," she said, voice deep with hunger.

I decided and climbed over her, pressing her back into the sheets while my hips sunk against hers, sliding into her as if there was no other place I belonged. Because there wasn't.

She sighed with the feeling; I growled into her ear and began to pump. I tried for long and slow, but my dick wanted fast and deep. It wanted to brand her, punish her and myself for letting anything come between us. Between this. Between the rightness that we were.

Her hands slipped on my back, she wrapped them under my shoulders and held on for the ride, hips meeting mine thrust for thrust.

"Jesus, Andi," she was so wet, so tight, so fucking good. How had I even imagined that I could go the rest of my life without her?

"Mmmm." Her legs fell open wider, letting me sink even further into the core of her. And then we fell into a bump and grind that must have bounced against her clit perfectly because deep inside she was sucking me into oblivion. *Dear God, I'm going to die.*

I felt her mouth hot and open on my chest, the sensation sending shards of heat along my spine to pool in my nuts. I slipped my hand under her head, using her hair to drag her head back so I could score her neck with my teeth, something I knew sent her into fits. Ah, yes, there. Her hips went into overdrive, and now it was me holding on as she fought to find her pleasure on my dick.

"That's it baby; come all over me," I whispered.

She whimpered and squeezed tighter. I pumped harder, deeper, reaching as far into her as I could; she flattened her thighs on the mattress, fully butterflied for me, and I ground into her as I felt the flutters start deep inside her. I slipped my hands under her bottom, lifting and tilting her to meet my strokes.

"Oh! Oh! Yes, yes, yes...there Abe, there...like that," her moans and instructions were the sweetest sounds to my ears. I followed them, not varying intensity, speed, or depth until I felt her shudder around me, until I felt the mouth she must also have buried deep inside of her sucking the life out of me. I came. Hard and deep. Spurting stream after stream of my soul into her.

Then I collapsed. I may have passed out. I couldn't be sure.

But reality returned in the form of her soft hands stroking my back. I'd had the presence of mind to at least shift my weight, so I was only half lying on top of her. She didn't seem to mind. She was sprinkling little kisses wherever she could reach.

I wasn't sure how much time passed, but I was content to just lie there with her in my arms. I didn't want to squash her, so I shifted again, pulling her into my arms as I repositioned myself on my back. She threw a leg over mine, traced circles on my chest, making my nipples respond.

"Thank you for my company, Abe." We hadn't really talked about the transfer of ownership of the line and the commitment to underwrite her own line. It had been the least I could do. It wasn't enough for what she'd had to deal with. I would spend the rest of my life making up these months of hell.

"You're welcome. You've earned it. You deserve it. It's not a handout." I knew she took issue with charity of any sort. Which I thought was ridiculous because rich people did that shit all the time. Always wanted something for nothing; always tried to get a leg up on someone else. The fact that she was so committed to doing it on her own was noble. But I was glad I could help her and wanted her to get used to coming to me for that help.

"I know. I do deserve it. I've worked so hard."

"You have. And in a couple of weeks, everyone will know what I know. That you're the shit, and they need to get on board."

"Do you still want to transfer the line and do all this? I mean, we've learned what happened. I could just stay on at HeirLoom and ride it out."

"Nope. Neither of us is staying at HeirLoom. I meant what I said. I need to get out from under my father's thumb. I'll never be free, never able to fully chart my own course until I do."

"But what about the company? What about Godrick's dream? Your dream?"

"Our dream was to do it together. That'll never happen. And I realize that Trey wouldn't want me miserable trying to be him. He'd tell me to go make beautiful things and let him worry about the rest."

"I wish I could have met him."

"Me, too. He knew who you were, though. He approved."

She pulled back and caught my eye. "Really?"

"Really. That night I told him I thought I'd met the girl of my dreams. He said if she put that much joy on my face, then she must be special. Right before he left that night to," I hesitated, "drive home, he urged me to call you. Told me not to let happiness slip through my fingers."

I hadn't thought about that conversation in years. All my thoughts related to that night we drenched in misery. "I almost did. I almost let it slip right through."

"Well, maybe he was watching and refused to let it happen because here I am. Here we are. And I'm definitely happy."

"Me, too," I dropped a kiss on her nose and stared into those pretty eyes for a moment before I started slowly, slowly, slowly easing down her body.

"Abe?"

"Hmmm?"

"Are you okay?"

"Yep. Just hungry..." Her giggle was music in my ears, and her pussy was ambrosia on my tongue. I was indeed, happy as fuck.

CHAPTER 40

CASSANDRA.

The nerves were crawling through my gut and across my skin like ants. I tried to tell myself I shouldn't be this nervous but who was I kidding. This was it. This was the moment I'd been working toward since that first sewing kit.

I ran through my mental checklist again for the thousandth time as I snipped and tucked and brushed my way through the melee that was backstage at New York fashion week. There were half-naked bodies everywhere, and no one gave a damn. I was surrounded by a few of them as I fit the final pieces and made sure every seam was laying perfectly, every flounce flouncing, every bell bottom belling. Makeup artists and hair stylists were working nonstop stop, making our creative vision a reality. Production folks dipped and dodged through it all. It was chaos.

But it was controlled chaos. We had been through the dress rehearsal. We all knew our parts, and so far, nothing had gone wrong. Well, nothing more than the little things...missing hairpins, wrong-sized shoes. But these were the offerings to the fashion gods...give them little mishaps so there wouldn't be major mishaps.

"Cassie!"

I heard my name over all the hubub. I took a split second to try to follow the sound but couldn't pinpoint it in the mix.

"Cassie!" Shit, who was it. Was it important?

"Here!" I called out.

"There you are baby girl!" Destiny pulled me into a overly tight hug before passing me to Margeaux who did the same.

"So proud of you! It's finally happening!" Margeaux exclaimed.

Destiny followed up with a chorus of. "Aye, aye, aye!" and a hip shimmy. "You deserve all of this, and I expect all this shit to be cut down to my short size so I can wear it. Girl. This shit is dope as fuck." Destiny stared around the room where my models were almost all dressed now.

"Thanks, boo," I said, laughing but not stopping my work. "I'll see what I can do about recreating some of this in Oompa Loompa size."

"Girl, you wrong for that," she laughed. "But for real though, see what you can do."

I laughed with her. "Y'all found your seats? You can see good?"

"We are front row, ma'am. Left purses and bags to hold them. Nobody better not touch my shit either."

"They won't."

"Humph. Rich people steal, too."

"And do."

"Y'all," I was doubled over laughing now, but still getting shit done. "The seats are reserved. Nobody's gonna take your seat. But you should get back to them," I glanced at my watch. "They're probably passing champagne right about now."

"Oh, you fancy with yours, huh?"

"That's that HeirLoom long money."

"I heard that."

"You're still releasing it as your own, though, right?" Destiny asked. She was glad things had worked out between Abe and me, but her natural distrust of life in general hadn't waned.

"I am. Abe wouldn't have it any other way. Tonight, you get the first view of *Subira* by Casssandra.

"Subira? I like it. What's it mean?"

"Patience. In Swahili. I've waited so long, worked so hard, and been so patient. It's finally paid off, and I want to acknowledge that."

They both nodded solemnly. "Plus, it's a thousand and one Cassandra's out there. I'm not naming my line *Cassandra's*. That's lame."

We laughed. "Well, *Subira* it is. And I love it, too," Destiny affirmed.

"Come on, girl. The *Subira* show is about to start, and I'm not trying to miss anything. Let's go," Margeaux said. They both tossed air kisses and disappeared into the crowd.

Another five minutes, and I stepped back. All my models were lined up. The lead model was in place at the front of the line. I started at the end. All were ready to do. Fits were perfect, hair was perfect, attitude on ten.

I reached the head model and stood with her until I heard the crowd outside begin to settle down. The lights in the venue went down; a spotlight appeared on the center stage. That was my cue.

I took a deep breath, accepted the mic from Adam who, along with Tamra, was project managing the behind-the-scenes, and stepped onto the stage to introduce myself and my line.

Eighteen minutes later, I was back on stage, bringing up the rear as my models gave the public one more look at my heart and soul.

Eighteen minutes was all it had taken. Eighteen minutes saw the culmination of years of dreams, months of work, setback, heartbreaks, disappointments and deterrent. It took eighteen minutes for my models to do their thing, strutting the runway, adding a little flair, giving notes of the Fashion Fair runway from years ago. It took eighteen minutes to run through our playlist...starting with the dulcet sounds of Andre 3000's *I Really Wanted to Write a Rap Song* and wrapping with Beyonce's *Freedom.*

The applause was deafening, and the people...the people who were standing in their applause...were blurry; I couldn't see shit through my tears, but I could hear. I could hear the cheers and the whistles. And I was grinning my ass off. I'd fucking done it, and it felt like heaven.

Backstage I was hauled off my feet before the curtain swung shut behind me. My mouth was covered with Abe's. His arms squeezed the air from my lungs, and my head went dizzy from both the lack of oxygen and the speed with which he was spinning me around.

When he released my mouth, the grin splitting his face mirrored mine.

"You did it! They fucking loved you! Look!" He pulled the curtain so I could see the people still standing, milling about but talking excitedly and thumbing through the lookbook we'd given in our swag bags.

I giggled, "I can't believe it. They actually liked it!"

"They. Fucking. Loved. It!" He repeated. "You are absolutely amazing. I can't believe you're mine." He kissed me again, fast pecks that couldn't hold his excitement for me.

"We did it, Abe...this was as much you as me...your money, your support."

"No, ma'am. We ain't doin' that shit. Money ain't shit. This is you. Your dreams, your vision, your designs, your talent. Your dedication and patience. Your *subira*. I love that."

I grinned. I had no words. "And I love you." He kissed me again.

This was good. I was good. We were good.

*****

The afterparty was popping, as an afterparty should be. I'd changed clothes and was wearing yet another of my original designs. This one featured a tiny top and an oversized low-slung bottom-slash-overpiece, the material draped in such a way that it looked nearly ready to fall from my body. It gave, sari-sarong-isidwaba vibes. It was one of my favorite pieces. The wildly ethnic style was done in multiple shades and weights of denim. It was formal and casual, impractical but functional. I loved it.

I was making the rounds, Abe was back and forth by my side making it clear to everyone that I was now independent but had the full support of HeirLoom. Reactions varied, but most wanted to know when and how they could get this piece or that. It was everything I'd dreamed of.

Even the presence of Old Man Walker couldn't dampen my spirits, though he tried with the glares he threw my way. But he kept his distance. I saw him talking to Abe more than once. I saw Abe get heated more than once and stalk off. I wondered what it was about, but I would cross that bridge tomorrow. I was convinced that Abe could handle his father. And I had decided that Abe was right. Fuck his father and Juanita Brookes. If Abe was willing to walk away for me, I wasn't going to stop him. I loved him, I wanted him, and I knew we would be great together. Big words and a hard road to walk but one I would willingly walk with him.

I saw him coming back my way and smiled. His face was set, he was annoyed about something, but it settled when he saw me. A slow grin spread over his lips, and his lids dropped a little. This was one of his favorite 'fits, too. He licked his lips to let me know how he felt about all the bare skin I had on display.

"Hey, baby."

"Hey, yourself. Everything good with your dad?" I asked in spite of my earlier decision to put the topic off.

"Yeah. It is what it is. I told him we're getting married."

"Oh, you did, huh? Still haven't heard a question from you," I teased him.

"Damn. You're right. You haven't. That's on me," he smiled broadly and gave a nod and a wave to another attendee. "Come on."

"Where?"

"This way," he led me through the crowd toward the front of the room.

"Abe, what are you doing?" I couldn't stop smiling, couldn't stop laughing. The magic of the day had me floating along.

He hopped on the tiny stage at the venue, where the DJ was set up. He dapped the DJ up...this man knew everyone...and on the lean-in, whispered something. It was a short exchange, and I raised one eyebrow. He was planning something. The DJ lowered the music and passed Abe the mic.

He wouldn't...

He tapped the bulb, "Is this thing on?" Requisite laughter followed as folks realized he was taking the stage.

"I want to take this opportunity to once again thank Cassandra Williams for blessing us with the magic that her mind makes," he paused for the applause. "Cassandra, we all stand in awe of your creativity, your passion, your ability," he said to murmurs of agreement.

"Here's to *Subira*," he raised his glass to raucous cheers from the crowd. When he reached a hand toward me, I didn't hesitate. I would take this man's hand and follow him anywhere.

"Cassandra, this last year has been the most fulfilling year of my life. There's been a hole in my heart for a long time. A hole in my life, really. I thought that hole was Godrick shaped and I've been trying to fill it in ways that made sense, but it was like throwing dirt into the Grand Canyon. Little to no progress made," the crowd twittered again.

"But then you showed up...again. You made me smile...again. You reminded me that joy exists...again," now the crowd...and I...were beginning to catch on. There was no way. "You see, I'd met Cassandra before she blew the doors of HeirLoom wide open. I met her the same night I lost my brother. And I lost her the same night I lost my brother."

"Abe...," I whispered.

"So yeah, there was a Godrick-sized hole in my heart, but there was also a Cassandra-sized chasm in my soul. I didn't even know it was there. Not until you started filling it bit by bit with your laughter; piece by piece with your not-funny jokes; inch by inch with your spirit. Cassandra, my soul needs you. My soul cries for yours when you're not around. I want you to be around. Forever. For always. Let me make you happy, Cassandra. Will you be my wife?"

He passed the mic back to the DJ, and then this big man...this big, sweet, sleepy-eyed man who loved outrageous fashion and little dogs, sank to his knees, both of them.

I sank with him, because wherever he went, I would go.

"Yes," I took his face in my hands. "Yes, I will." And there, with us both kneeling on the floor, probably looking crazy as hell...he kissed me.

Cheers erupted around us, but our eyes were still locked on each other. Still wide open and locked even as our lips connected once, twice, and again to seal the promise we'd just made to each other. Then he rose, pulling me to my feet and into his arms for another kiss, more showy this time to satisfy the onlookers.

When we finally parted and turned to the crowd, I saw Margeaux and Destiny both grinning from ear to ear.

"Oh, yeah," Abe said behind me as I had already turned to walk down the couple of steps that would take us off the stage. "I have something for you." I turned back to see him holding a box that in turn, held the most beautiful ring I could have imagined.

A diamond, large and sparkling with all the fire of the rainbow, flanked by crystal clear amethysts and aquamarine. It was a dreamy fantastical concoction that spoke to my little girl dreams and set my finger on fire.

"Abe...it's..."

"Perfection, baby. It's what you deserve. It's what you are, to me, at least. I love you." A kiss on my forehead. "Now, come meet my mom." And then we did leave the stage to more applause and a crowd eager to offer their congratulations and see my new accessory.

"Your mom?" I repeated when we finally had a moment to ourselves. "She's here?"

"She is."

"Where?"

"Somewhere with my trash-ass father, I imagine," he scanned the room.

"Don't say that."

"Oh, there she is. We're in luck. She's alone," and we bee-lined our way over. I supposed not giving me enough time to get nervous was a blessing.

As it was, I only had time to take a deep breath before Abe spun me around and said, "Cassandra, this is my mom. Mom, meet Cassandra, my fiancee."

Mrs. Walker was stunningly beautiful, which was no surprise because Abe was fine as fuck, and he didn't get that shit completely from his dad.

I held out my hand to greet her, but she pulled me into a hug, "Cassandra, finally. It's a pleasure."

To Abe, she said, "I see you figured out your little mystery. I guess I was wrong; Jacob and Catherine clearly did know each other. You look just like her, honey."

EPILOGUE

Abe and I were in St. Lucia, taking a well-deserved two weeks away after the intensity of the last couple of months. I had no idea that Abe had planned this...or maybe he'd put Vince on it...but, regardless, we needed it. We needed this opportunity to relax into each other, pull apart the shit that had happened and get to a headspace where we could really start imagining what our life...together...might look like.

The night of the launch had been the roller coaster ride of my dreams, from the standing ovations in appreciation of my work to Abe dropping to his knees and making me the happiest woman in the world. I looked at the beautiful confection of lavender, teal, and icy white sparkling on my finger and smiled. It was hard to believe that we were engaged. It seemed fast, but my soul sighed in contentment, and I knew we were on the right track.

There had been a lot of not-so-happy craziness, too. Abe had apparently told his father his exact expectations and made it clear that if the board wasn't interested in his form of leadership, they could move along with their plans to vote him out in a few weeks. I didn't know how that would play out, but I suspected that Old Man Walker wasn't really all that interested in having a non-Walker at the helm. I was willing to bet dollars to donuts that he'd relent, keep Abe, and watch him elevate HeirLoom. And if not, well, Abe was brilliant and, as he made clear to me, far from broke even without access to the Walker billions. We weren't about to be out here struggling.

Not to mention the agreement I had with HeirLoom. That was ironclad. I hadn't allowed myself to sit in that dream, I hadn't had the time, but now I was set to take this running start and keep building my own. Subira was just getting started, and after pulling off this line in record time, I had zero doubts about my ability to do great things when given time to actually think and plan.

And that's what I was doing a lot of right now...thinking...because that conversation with Abe's mother had been crazy.

"I see you figured out your little mystery. I guess I was wrong; Jacob and Catherine clearly did know each other. You look just like her, honey."

I looked between her and Abe. "What mystery? I look like who?"

Abe was frozen, staring at his mother. She looked a little startled, like she'd let a secret cat out of the bag. I gave Abe a little hip-check. "Abe?"

He started and turned his attention to me, "It's a long story. But I told my mom about the photo. The one of Jacob Whyte," I nodded because what other photo could he be talking about? *"She knows him."*

"I wouldn't say I know him," Ms. Walker began.

"Okay, knows of him," Abe corrected. "And knows some of his story. I'll tell you all about it," he exchanged a meaningful look with his mom, "but later. It's a long story," he repeated.

"Yeah, you said that already," I laughed. "I hope it's not so bad that you're planning to take this back," I flashed my new jewelry, "because it's mine now."

At that, he grinned and pulled me into his side, causing the concerned look on his mother's face to melt into a smile.

"Never that, baby." He dropped a kiss on top of my head.

His mother extended a hand, "It's wonderful to finally meet you in person, Cassandra. You remind me of someone I used to care about a long time ago," she said, partially explaining her earlier comment. "She was a wonderful young woman."

When our hands connected, she tugged me into a hug. I could count on one hand the number of hugs I'd received from older Black women. I remembered each of them. They were like balm to my soul, each coming at crucial times in my life. This one was no different. Abe's mom was stronger than she looked, and despite her trim frame, I felt enveloped, protected, and most of all, welcomed. I sighed into her.

When she relaxed her embrace and stepped back, taking the faint cloud of her perfume with her, her eyes were soft. "I can't wait to get to know you better. I see the light you put back in my Abe's eyes. It's been gone a long time." She reached to pat Abe's cheek. He blushed, which made me grin.

"I look forward to it Ms. Walker," I replied honestly. "And I look forward to learning about your friend. It seems like it's going to be a fascinating story. Abe's been obsessed with this picture for a while now." I laughed about it again because whatever it was about didn't really matter to me. I had all I could possibly want tonight, right now.

"Good morning, baby," Abe's deep baritone drifted to me from the bed. I had climbed out of the plush trap earlier, careful not to disturb him but determined to watch the sunrise this morning. I'd let him sleep, though; the man had put in work the night before...he deserved his rest. I crossed my legs at both the memory of his efforts and the sound of his morning rough voice.

"Good morning, love." I shifted my attention from the commanding views of the Caribbean Sea to Abe. It wasn't a hardship to do so. I couldn't imagine ever getting tired of watching sleep-sexy Abe roll out of bed. He stretched his long, muscled body, abs, arms, and thighs flexing. My eyes dropped, as they usually did, to the V at the base of his abs; it always pointed me right where I wanted to be. This morning was no exception.

"You okay?" He asked.

"Hmm?" I murmured in response, distracted.

"Are you okay," he repeated, a little laughter in his voice because he knew my mind was on round five. I got an extra treat when he turned his back to pad into the glassed-in bathroom area. He disappeared briefly into the wood-covered water closet, emerged, tossed the towel he was using to dry his hands on the bed, and crossed the shiny adobe-tiled floor to reach me.

"We had some pretty heavy conversations yesterday," he said when we came together. I rose from the chaise I was on to wrap my arms around his chiseled waist. When he leaned against the clear glass railing, I placed my feet on top of his and gave him my weight to hold. It was a favorite position of mine. The loose clasp of his hands behind my back and the warmth of his body at my front were becoming pleasantly consistent in my life. I loved it.

"Do you mean the ones about who's moving in with whom or the ones about my being the long-lost granddaughter of Harry Brookes? Because both of them hit."

"I hope for different reasons," he quipped.

"Oh, definitely," I agreed. Then, we quieted because while moving in together was a non-issue...we just needed to decide the when, where, and how—potentially being Harry Brookes's granddaughter carried a lot more weight.

"Do you think it's true?" I asked, not for the first time. I wasn't sure how I felt about it and didn't want to get too attached to the idea. I'd never had family, never had the trappings of it. And for that matter, I wasn't sure I wanted it now at my big age. The fantasy was wonderful and could have been life-changing, es-pecially for a child who dreamed of a loving mother and father. But as an adult, I knew that families weren't always all they were cracked up to be. My chosen family...Margeaux, Destiny, and now, Abe...were more than enough for me. What good could come of being part of a world where the woman who may be my mother disappeared with no trace and the woman who might now be my step-grandmother had set her daughter up on some date-rape ish.

Yeah, I wasn't sure whether I was interested in pursuing any of it. I expressed this to Abe.

"That's fair, and I feel you. It's a lot, but we don't have to figure it out now or here. Or at all if that's what you decide. It's up to you."

Another thing I loved...the word tingled through me...*loved*...about Abe was that he let me be. I didn't know if I could be with a man who needed to express his masculinity by trying to direct my life and decisions. It wasn't a trait I'd seen in this man and that was precious to me. He was there for me in exactly the way I needed him to be.

"Thank you. There's so much to it, you know? And realistically, what good would come of it? If I were this person, what would I do, try to claim my spot at Heritage? In place of Juanita Brookes and Elizabeth? Yeah, no, it's not trouble I want."

He nodded slowly. I wasn't sure if he agreed, but I knew he'd be there to talk it out when I was ready and support me in whatever I decided.

"Would you want to know if Catherine is your mother, though, just for the knowing? My mom could tell you about her?" His arms tightened around me before he released me, took my hand, and led us to the zero-entry infiniti pool that blended seamlessly into the sitting area of our suite. The whole suite was built into the side of a mountain. As we waded into the pool, it felt like we were walking to the world's edge.

At the last step Abe tugged me forward so he bore my weight, our legs tangling in the warm water, while we moved to the edge where all we could see were mountains and sea.

"Maybe," I continued where we'd left off. "I'm curious to know what happened to her, how I ended up where I did. But as far as family is concerned, I have what I need. I have Gogo and Destiny," I said pertly, kicking away to swim to the other side of the pool.

"Oh, yeah?" He said when I resurfaced with a solid fifteen feet between us. "Gogo and Destiny, huh?"

I nodded quickly, grinning. "Oh, and your mom. She seems great." I added kicking my legs up so my toes peeked out of the water.

"Anyone else?" He asked, stalking through the water in slow, strong strides. It would have been less nerve-wracking if he'd just swam. The power it took to move through the fairly deep water without it looking like any effort at all had me wet as, well...water.

"Your dad?" I put a finger to my chin in thought, and bounced in the water a little. "I mean, I'm sure he'll come around. I'm a loveable sort," I added as he took another couple of steps, muscles shifting in his arms and chest, water sluicing out of the way on his approach.

"Mmhmm," he growled. "Anyone else?" He was maybe three steps away now. My eyes widened, I bobbed in the water, excited nerves making it hard to keep still.

"Killmonger?" I squeaked just as his hands closed around my waist to haul me against him. The water was warm, as were the big hands he set to roaming over my body, tugging at the strings of the tiny bikini I'd stepped into as soon as I woke up.

"Killmonger, huh? Woman, if you don't stop playing with me," he palmed my now bare ass, fingers coming together in the most delicious way between my cheeks.

"Okay, okay," I breathed it, delighted with the little booty massage I was getting. I squirmed, trying to shift his fingers just a little bit. "You, baby. You are my family," I wrapped my legs and arms around him, caught his gaze.

I watched as his eyes danced from left to right, taking in the mismatch in color. I watched the love and affection that swam in the depths of his gaze as he focused on me and blessed me with that lazy-ass smile. I counted my lucky stars and said silent, grateful prayers that life had led me back to this man. That the fates had seen fit to spin the block and put us back in each other's orbit. We could have so easily missed each other, missed this.

"Yes," he said, "I am. Forever and ever. In every iteration of life."

A NOTE FROM TAMALA

Thank you for reading Abe and Cassandra's story.

Their chemistry was unmistakable.

Their connection was unfinished—until now.

Writing their journey was a joy, not just because of the heat and heartbreak, but because I had the chance to create a dynamic, complicated woman making grown-woman decisions about the kind of life—and love—she wanted. I love that even in their happiness, life is still happening around them. Challenges don't disappear. Questions don't vanish. That's real life, isn't it?

So if you closed this book with lingering questions—about legacies, family secrets, and the woman who nearly unraveled it all—you're not alone. Abe and Andi have questions too.

Which brings us to Liz.

She wasn't easy to love.

But she was never the villain—just a woman trapped in the wrong story.

In *Coming Around*, she finally gets to write her own. It's a standalone romance with its own heat, heartbreak, and hard-won redemption—but it's also the second half of this duet. Because the past is still unraveling. And some truths refuse to stay buried.

Coming Around brings the story full circle—with forbidden longing, sharp dialogue, legacy drama, and a slow burn that just might surprise you.

If you're ready to see where the Walker legacy leads next, I hope you'll turn the page and follow Liz on her journey.

Thank you for reading, for feeling, and for allowing these characters into your heart.

With love and gratitude,

Tamala

About the Author

Tamala C. Jones is a Southern girl through and through—born, raised, and educated in North Carolina by a high school English teacher and a U.S. Army Master Sergeant who jumped out of planes with the 82nd Airborne.

She started her first romance novel at twelve, already hooked on Harlequin paperbacks and sweeping historical love stories. Even then, she wanted to see herself reflected in the pages she devoured. She paused the dream long enough to earn a doctorate and build a career in academia—but she never stopped craving stories where smart, complex Black women took center stage.

Now, she writes contemporary romance for grown folks: stories full of heat, heart, emotional tension, and characters navigating real-life stakes. Her books are intentionally crafted—rich in story, sharp in dialogue, and unapologetically sexy. Because Black women deserve love stories that make you think, make you feel, and occasionally make you need a cold shower.

These days, Tamala lives her own love story with the man who swept her off her feet over Colt 45 and homemade spaghetti. Together, they're raising three beautiful kids, two cats, and a dog. When she's not writing love stories, she's reading them—or doing the work that (for now) still pays the bills.

ALSO BY:

COMING AROUND: A Love, Legacy & Second Chances Novel
(Contemporary Romance)

THE BILLIONAIRE'S ACCIDENTAL HEIR
(A Sexy, Fast-Paced Standalone Romance)

THE LOVE, LEGACY & SECOND CHANCES DUET
What Goes Around
Coming Around

Excerpt: Coming Around

"**D**on't embarrass me while we're here," my mother said from the front passenger seat of the Escalade my father drove. She was turned toward the backseat, her left hand braced against Dad's headrest. It was a familiar position from which she'd been issuing warnings to me and my sister for twenty-odd years. It gave her a clear line of sight to pin Maggie and me with the stinkeye.

"Mom, we're adults–" Maggie began.

"One of us is," I muttered.

"One of us is," she immediately mimicked in a ridiculously lowered voice.

"Agreed," she said louder to our mother, and stuck her tongue out at me, "Mom, *I'm* an adult," she continued. "You don't have to warn your twenty-plus daughter about her behavior at a social function."

"Twenty plus what?" I said to Maggie, then to Mom: "I really am twenty-plus-several years and I'll keep an eye on my baby sister," a kick aimed at my shins barely missed, "so you can relax. As long as Uncle G doesn't start spouting off about how dad should've never left the family business and getting slick disrespectful."

My father chuckled as he made a slow right turn in Manhattan traffic; Mom sent him a slicing side-eye.

"If your Uncle Godrick has words to say to or about your father, your father can more than handle it." She rubbed her hand along the back of his head, smoothing his deep waves. "You two," she said, turning the full force of her maternal warning eyes on us again, "will behave."

I gave her an 'of course' look. I wouldn't dream of doing anything to ruin my boy's night. Trey had been featured on Forbes Magazine's Thirty Under Thirty list. It was a huge accomplishment. And as much as we didn't fuck with this side of the family, we all loved Trey. He was as opposite his father as any child could get...other than the driving need to conquer the world.

"Is he seeing anyone?" Maggie interrupted my thoughts.

"Actually, yeah. Says she's 'the one' but it's early days still."

"She'll be here tonight," I said. "I think she's about your age. The two of you can play together."

"Again, full grown over here," she replied, skimming a hand down her front to draw attention to the fact that puberty hadn't missed her.

"Still a baby over there," I corrected, "and I'll be watching to make sure none of these soft clowns forget it."

The few minutes it took to reach the venue, pass the keys to the valet, and ride the elevator to the rooftop was passed with Maggie taking her revenge for my teasing. It would, apparently come in the form of match-making tonight."

"You relax, big brother. I'll have you all set up in no time," she said as she and my mother scanned the room from the entryway. There was a sea of Black excellence in the room, one of the smaller ballrooms at the Drake Hotel.

Satisfied that the room held plenty of opportunities to get into trouble, Maggie and my mother wandered off toward one of the appetizer stations where a small group of women who looked vaguely familiar were gathered. Maggie tossed a nefarious eyebrow wiggle at me as she trailed off behind Mom.

"You set yourself up for that one, son," my dad clapped a big hand on my shoulder, as we began a slow stroll around the room, navigating the light crowd of people. I expected we'd end up at one of the nicely stocked bars I'd spotted.

"I did, didn't I?"

"She's not completely wrong you know," Dad followed up as he nodded at folks who nodded at him. "I'm not about to arrange a marriage for you like my brother is doing for Trey, but I wouldn't be mad at another daughter and some grandbabies. I wouldn't be made at all."

"Arrange?" I asked because Trey had not mentioned this.

He shrugged. "Arrange may be a strong word. But I know they've had a young lady in mind for him for several years. I understand she's who he's dating."

That was new information.

"I see you'll be following up on that," he chucked. "But back to you, don't wait so long that your mother starts taking pages from that book."

I laughed, not feeling pressured in the least. "I hear you, Dad. I'll see what I can do."

"I'm sure your mother would appreciate it. And I'll deny it til the end of my days if you tell her I said that."

"Noted. But you realize it's easier said than done."

He nodded. "Believe me. I realize. I'm not rushing you. Just providing direction," he chuckled again, clearly amused at himself.

"Well, well...Warwick Walker...my eyes must be playing tricks." The exuberant greeting had both my dad and I turning...we were both named Warwick, after all. After the requisite re-introductions and expositions about my size at the time of our last meeting, I excused myself to let my father and his acquaintance catch up.

Moving solo now, I cut a far more direct path to the closest bar. The turnout was good. I was glad to see so many folks showing up for Trey. He deserved it in every way. But it wasn't so crowded that I felt like I might crush people. I knew, objectively, that I had learned to manage my size long ago. Time spent on the basketball court and, at my mother's urging, in dance classes, had given me tight control over my body but I was still, simply put, a big man. Crowds weren't my favorite; even in light ones like this, I had to be careful not to step on some tiny person.

Like now. The woman standing in line in front of me had spun around, each hand occupied by a glass of wine, and proceeded to almost plow right into me. I easily sidestepped to avoid the collision. But she overcorrected and began to teeter on the stilettos that adorned her feet. I plucked one of the glasses from her and took that now free hand to offer stability. Which was easy because again...I'm a big man, not easily moved.

"Oh, thank you," she breathed, annoyance and relief fighting for dominance in her voice.

"Of course," I waited, holding the flute of champagne I'd taken from her, while she righted herself. She wasn't tall, but neither was she short. I was an easy six-four and I could've dropped a kiss on the top of her head without much effort. I guessed five-eight without the heels.

I watched as she moved this way and that, verifying that no stray drops of the wine had marred her dress—a long quietly golden affair that hung in a slim, body-skimming line from the thin straps that crisscrossed her bare shimmery shoulders. The gold of the dress and the sparkling brown of her skin were a stunning combination. She hadn't yet let go of my hand, and while I wasn't exactly holding it...more acting as a convenient wall while she leaned her weight on me, that weight was oddly perfect. The place where her skin touched mine, the wiggle of her fingers resting on my hand, the absolute trust she was placing in me to hold steady while she teetered and balanced, all had me waiting patiently for her to finish and look up. The need to know what she looked like behind the waterfall of long dark hair was growing exponentially.

Satisfied that she'd escaped unsplattered, she huffed a little breath and slid her hand from mine. My fingers clasped, reflexively, around hers at the last moment and finally, finally, her gaze collided with mine when she glanced up in surprise.

Brown. But not brown like I've ever seen it. Her eyes were a rich, bottomless brown, like molten cocoa. Dark, enigmatic, hypnotic. And, maybe, interested? *Nice. I'd like more of that, please.*

She tugged her fingers again and I released them. I watched as she wiggled them a bit. Was she trying to dispel the same tingle I'd felt as she slid her hand away?

"All good?"

"I am. Thank you again. I didn't realize you were there when I turned. I should have been paying closer attention."

"It's okay. I take up a lot of room. I should have given you more space." I let my eyes skim her face cataloguing the warm shimmer-dusted toffee brown of her skin, the pink that rode high on her cheeks, the full spread of her glossed lips. Lips that were currently turned in a rueful twist.

"Well, yes, there does seem to be a lot of you," she reached for the wine glass I still held. "I suppose you spend a lot of time apologizing for being in the way."

I laughed because clearly, she had no concerns about hurting my feelings.

"Not anymore. High school, though? That was a different story."

She grinned and my heart stuttered. Those full, glossy lips parted and the sun may as well have shone its light directly on me. I could feel my face freeze, knew I was staring stupidly but *Jesus* she was beautiful. And I knew what I'd seen when she first turned my way.

"I'm sure it was," she laughed softly and that sound matched the warm beauty of her eyes, low and melodic.

"I'd be happy to tell you about it. Regale you with tales of my trampling small children and pets," I joked, hoping to hear that velvet-wrapped chuckle again. She didn't disappoint.

"That would be quite interesting I'm sure," she said with another smile, "but I have to decline."

Fuck.

"Why?" I asked and mentally slapped a hand against my forehead.

She let one eyebrow ride up.

"Am I required to offer an explanation?"

I felt the grin spread across my face. She took no shit. "Not at all. I fully respect your decision. I'm just curious as to what they should put on my tombstone when they find me dead of a broken heart in the alley outside."

She rolled her eyes and the smile on my face spread further. *Yeah, this woman was made for me.*

"Silly."

I laid a hand on my chest, clutching my pearls. "Silly? Never that. But I am curious. You can, of course, tell me to fuck off. But what is it that's keeping us from taking the first step in the rest of our lives together?" I waggled my eyebrows at her to make that statement a little less corny.

Another eye roll. "Perhaps my boyfriend? The one I'm happily committed to and waiting for to arrive."

Fuck, again.

I'd never been one to roll up on another man's woman. That shit was low. But I know dudes who moved by the mantra 'If you leave the door open, I'll invite myself in." I wondered if her man had left his door cracked.

"Lucky man," I commented while I tried to formulate a reply that would firmly express my interest and willingness to steal her from whatever punk-ass relationship she currently thought she was in without sounding like a total asshole.

"I'm the lucky one," she said; a little smile tilted her lips. I felt an answering twist somewhere in the center of my chest. "I'm actually meeting his best friend tonight. Well, technically, his cousin."

Fuuuuuck. Please, Lord. No.

"Duece!" I heard from somewhere behind me. It was Trey. I turned to see him and Abe striding my way.

Well, shit. I turned to the woman I was trying to close to see her focused on Trey, face lit, smile bright. Whatever passing interest I may have seen flit across her face was nothing compared to this.

Trey shot me a grin, dropped a quick pound against my raised fist, and walked right past me to pull the woman into a respectful-of-her-finery hug and drop the kiss I'd been thinking about on top of her sleek head.

"You two would find each other. Liz, this is Warwick. Deuce, this is Elizabeth, my fiancee."

"Fiancee?" I felt my world tilt again, my stomach swooped before righting itself, a hard hot knot settling low in that organ.

I watched emotions play across Elizabeth's face. She was nervous, wary.

"It's an aspirational title," Trey said before coming back to me for the slap and hug of our greeting. We held the hug for a moment...it had, after all, been over a year since we'd been physically in the same room.

"It's good to see you, guy."

"You, too. You, too. We have to do better." The words were low, heartfelt.

"Agreed," I held a moment longer, another thump on the back and release. Then, to the woman who'd caused my whole future to flash before my eyes, I said, "It's good to meet you–officially–Liz."

Trey resumed his position beside her, pulling her into him. It was a position she willingly took and leaned into. I slid my hands into my pockets, contemplating. I decided to air it all out. It felt like the quickest way to dispel the faint worry that I thought I saw in Elizabeth.

Oh, you know all her moods and secret thoughts now, I guess.

I chuckled at myself before speaking again. My words were directed at Trey. My gaze was on Elizabeth. "You showed up just in time, my guy. I was just in the process of asking your girl out."

Trey laughed, unbothered. "It's your impeccable taste that has let our friendship last this long. I'd've worried about my own decision-making if you hadn't." He let his hand slide from Elizabeth's waist to take one of the glasses she still held. He sipped and took her free hand in his to hold it by his side. She leaned further into him.

"And how'd that go for you?" Abe asked, turning from the bar where he was placing his order. I signaled him to order for me, too, before responding.

"She shot me down immediately. Some shit about a wack ass boyfriend," I joked, comfortable in the knowledge that Trey knew beyond a shadow of a doubt that I would never move on his girl. Because I wouldn't. Not knowingly, at least. Lizzie–I wondered if people called her that—was now my sister for all practical purposes.

"Her taste is also impeccable." Trey quipped, his full attention on his beautiful girl.

I took a stiff swallow of the bourbon Abe passed my way. "Well, welcome to the family, Lizzie. You chose the best of us."

ELIZABETH

"Welcome to the family, Lizzie. You chose the best of us." I let a sigh of relief relax my shoulders and focused, not on the 'Lizzie' crooned in a baritone so deep I could barely hear it, but on the second half of the statement, *'You chose the best of us.'*

Godrick had told me about Warwick, of course. He'd painted him damn near a saint—certainly the best version of a friend a man could want. He'd been so excited for us to meet tonight. I should have known when I took in the man's sheer size that this was Warwick, best friend and cousin extraordinaire but I'd been admittedly a bit overwhelmed. I'd not been prepared for him to be so...much. Handsome, funny, clever. And magnetic in a way that would be far more interesting—and less unsettling—were my heart not already accounted for. I'd once asked Godrick whether he was closer to Warwick than to his brother, Abe. He'd looked at me in utter confusion and, now that I thought about it, had never actually answered.

"Thank you," I said to Warwick, before turning more fully to Godrick to whisper, "And I'll thank *you* to have a conversation with me before you go tossing around your 'aspirational titles'." It was a soft rebuke, jokingly made, because truthfully I would wear the title of fiancee—and wife—proudly for him. He was a wonderful man, kind and honest, thoughtful and generous with a dry sense of humor that matched mine. Plus, he could cook and didn't mind doing so.

"Oh, I have every intention of having a conversation with you. Sooner than you might think," Trey whispered in my ear.

I grinned into his brown eyes, all thoughts of the earlier interactions gone, and tightened the hold on the hand that held mine. "We've only been dating a few months. It's far too early to have 'conversations'," I whispered back to him. "Don't tease."

"Is it?" He pondered, turning the full force of his beautiful smile on me. He was gorgeous; my heart rate ticked up. "I've been called a lot of things. Tease is rarely one of them." He considered me for a long moment before sending a look to Warwick and tugging me a few steps away.

"It has only been a few months," Trey agreed as he guided me toward a small nook that held a portrait of some pillar of New York's Black history and a small fichus. My stomach began to flutter. "And I'm not asking,"–*Okayyy*–he took the champagne from my hand and set both our glasses on the small table with the plant. "Not yet." The flutter returned. "But it's something we should talk about," he realigned our fingers, danced his along my forearms and back to clasp my hands in his much larger, much warmer ones. "It's something I would like to talk about."

I felt the color crawl up my face and tried to control the grin that took possession of my lips. "I'd like that, too."

He glanced around the room, judging the sets of watching eyes. Then he shifted slightly, blocking me from view with his wide shoulders, and dipped his head to lay a soft kiss on my lips. I eagerly accepted it, just as eagerly returned it, letting my lips cling to his and my eyes flutter closed. We both sighed into the kiss. This thing between us was easy and natural. Comfortable.

When he raised his head, his eyes were slightly darker, and, not for the first time, I wondered what it would be like to be wrapped in his arms, the recipient of all his attention. We hadn't taken that next step. I, personally, had *never* taken said step and I wondered, now that we would be having *conversations* what we would decide. The romantic in me adored the idea of waiting until marriage; the woman in me, less so.

Trey tugged my hand again, bringing me back to reality.

"Come on," he said and slipped his arm around my waist. "Let's dance. I want my arms around you and that's the only way I can make that happen in this crowd."

TWO YEARS LATER: ELIZABETH

The rain was such a fucking cliche. But it matched the muddled grey swirl of despair that now resided in my brain, throughout my body. At least the fresh air, waterlogged at it was, was better than the too-close cloying feel of the sanctuary. The sanctuary I'd just sat in for over an hour listening to Trey being eulogized.

The tears rose and overflowed again, streaking unchecked down my cheeks to dampen the high-necked, long-sleeved black crepe dress I wore. I was too hot, too sad, too angry, too bereft. Too everything.

I felt Mother's hand on mine. Surprised at the small comfort, I clasped it and leaned toward her.

"You're ruining your dress," she pressed a silk handkerchief into my hand. "Try to manage yourself."

I let her hand go and tried to turn my attention to the words being spoken for the interment. But my mind stuttered and rebelled, refusing to stay centered on the fact that my beloved was about to be lowered into the ground where his body would return 'to that from whence it had come. Ashes to ashes. Dust to dust.' I just couldn't. So I didn't.

I knew I would pay for it. Knew I'd hear Mother's voice incessantly about how I'd disgraced the family, shown no respect for tradition, and embarrassed her with my uncontrolled show of emotion. So be it.

I began to slip out of the row I was seated on, the row that gave me a fully unrestricted view of the obscenely ornate coffin where it sat primed for lowering. The whole show was another excessive nod to the extreme wealth Trey's family possessed. A full 50 x 50 tented structure had been erected over the grave and interment site. It was fully decorated, nearly as well-appointed as the church had been. The sides were lowered to block prying eyes but the front was open and, beyond the morbid sight in front of me, I could see out across the rest of the memorial park. Rolling green hills dotted with tiny acknowledgments of loved ones lost. I couldn't take it anymore.

I slipped past the disapproving eyes, past his parents and Abe. I could hear the chastising change in the tenor of the preacher's voice as I excused myself. But I wouldn't worry about that now. I'd add it to the bucket of things I'd concern myself with once I got this cinderblock off my chest. I pushed the heavy cotton swag of the tent aside and stepped fully into the weeping, overcast day.

I made my way toward a stone bench. It was as far as my numb legs and mind could take me. And it was far enough. I'd only needed to get out of the tent. Away from everything that was so Not Trey. I wanted to rage and scream and curse every foul spirit for the drunk driver who had slammed into Trey's car the same night he accepted the reins as CEO of HeirLoom Textiles, his family's conglomerate. It was all he'd wanted. All we'd waited for. Our lives were supposed to be beginning now. We were supposed to start planning the wedding. We were supposed to start making babies. We'd picked out a condo. And now we were here. Doing *this*. I couldn't understand it.

The drone of the preacher's voice broke through. His volume had increased. I could see the tent clearly from where I was but couldn't see inside. I wondered if they'd started lowering the coffin and tears stung again. God, I needed Trey. He was–had been–my escape. We'd been that for each other, really. Pinpoints of sanity in the insanity that was our world. I could already feel myself spinning. Unsteady, ungrounded, unmoored.

"You're going to make yourself sick," the deep baritone sounded behind me. My heart thumped, startled and I turned to find that Warwick, red-eyed, and seeming a little less gargantuan than usual, had approached along the path behind me. He flipped open the umbrella he carried, took a seat on the bench beside me, and shielded me from the rain.

"The bench is wet," I said, unconcerned that he'd already sat. It had taken all my reserves to muster the energy to speak at all.

"You're still sitting on it," he observed.

I shrugged and turned back to the tent, watching as if I could see the goings on inside. I couldn't.

"Are you going back in?" He asked.

"No."

"You can't just sit here in the rain."

I turned to him, contemplated. He had kind eyes. Like Trey. Trey had the kindest, gentlest eyes. Except when we made love. Then they were fierce and intense. "Yes. I can," I said and turned back to the tent and rolling hills. I was glad we'd decided not to wait. I was glad I had memories of being in his arms, of being that close to him. I wished I were pregnant. I was not.

"Come," he said and reached toward me, "let me take you inside the church where it's warm and dry. We can wait there until it's...over."

I shook my head, still watching the tent. I didn't want to be out there, where that still, lifeless version of Trey was. But I also didn't want to leave until it was done. Until he was resting peacefully and undisturbed.

"Then I'll wait with you," he settled more fully on the bench.

"No," I said. And that sounded harsh and hateful even to my grief-dulled ears. "I want to be alone." No, that wasn't quite right either. "I need—I need to be alone." I heard my voice crack. I was so tired of crying. So awfully tired of the hot achy eyes and stuffy nose, but mostly of the aching, gaping hole that the tears did nothing to fill. "Please leave me alone," I whispered.

Thankfully, blessedly he rose. "Okay, Lizzie." *There.* A little thump of response. A tiny, infinitesimal betrayal. Anger bloomed.

"I said, leave me alone. And don't call me Lizzie."

He obliged; but left the umbrella.